CW00766458

Kuchenga is a writer, journalist and speaker with work on many media platforms including Stylist, British Vogue and Netflix. She has contributed short stories and essays to several anthologies, most notably *It's Not OK to Feel Blue (And Other Lies)*, *Who's Loving You* and *Loud Black Girls*.

Owing to a lifelong obsession with books and the written word, Kuchenga studied Creative Writing at The Open University. Her work is focused on the perils of loving, being loved and women living out loud throughout the ages. Her first novel, *The Library Thief*, is the ultimate marriage of her passions for history, mystery and rebels.

She currently resides in Manchester where she is determined to continue living a life worth writing about.

THE
LIBRARY
THIEF

KUCHENGA
SHENJÉ

SPHERE

SPHERE

First published in Great Britain in 2024 by Sphere
This paperback edition published in 2025 by Sphere

1 3 5 7 9 10 8 6 4 2

Copyright © Kuchenga Shenjé 2024

The moral right of the author has been asserted.

*All characters and events in this publication, other than those
clearly in the public domain, are fictitious and any resemblance
to real persons, living or dead, is purely coincidental.*

All rights reserved.
No part of this publication may be reproduced, stored in a
retrieval system, or transmitted, in any form, or by any means, without
the prior permission in writing of the publisher, nor be otherwise circulated
in any form of binding or cover other than that in which it is published
and without a similar condition including this condition being
imposed on the subsequent purchaser.

A CIP catalogue record for this book is available from the British Library.

ISBN 978-1-4087-2683-9

Extract on p vii from *The Mothers* by Brit Bennett
(New York: Riverhead, 2016)
Extract on page 387 from *The Long Song* by Andrea Levy
(London: Tinder Press, 2011)

Typeset in Berling by M Rules
Printed and bound in Great Britain by Clays Ltd, Elcograf S.p.A.

Papers used by Sphere are from well-managed forests
and other responsible sources.

Sphere
An imprint of
Little, Brown Book Group
Carmelite House
50 Victoria Embankment
London EC4Y 0DZ

The authorised representative
in the EEA is
Hachette Ireland
8 Castlecourt Centre
Dublin 15, D15 XTP3, Ireland
(email: info@hbgi.ie)

An Hachette UK Company
www.hachette.co.uk

www.littlebrown.co.uk

In memory of
Castella O. Shenje (née Ricketts)
1953–2020
a.k.a.
Mummy

Maybe she'd never really known her mother at all.
And if you couldn't know the person whose body was your first home,
then who could you ever know?

The Mothers, Brit Bennett

Prologue

The story starts with a scandal that I thought would end my life. Fortunately, *my* scandal didn't kill anyone. In fact, it pales in comparison with what I went on to discover at Rose Hall.

Thus far, the way I see it, in any good life you need to die several times to really lead a life worth living. There are little deaths and there are big deaths. My tale has both – and the real tragedy would be if this story were to die with me.

I was lying when I swore I would take this secret to my grave. I had no right to promise that.

Granger's Bookbinders,
143 Long Millgate,
Manchester

Rose Hall,
Lancashire,
20ᵗʰ November, 1896

Dear Mr Granger,

I trust this note finds you in good health and
that business is as steady as when last we met some
years ago.

I write to you with an unusual commission. I will
not trouble you here with the details of my current
circumstances. Since the untimely death of my
beloved wife, Lady Persephone, it seems the fates are
in conspiracy against me. Suffice it to say that I find
myself now in need of your excellent services and on a
far grander scale than before.

The library at Rose Hall is, as you are aware,
extensive. I am proud of the rarity and quality of
the books it now houses, a collection that I have
painstakingly curated over many years. I now find
myself in the unhappy position of seeking a buyer for
my collection. Many of the books, due to their age
and mishandling by less cautious owners, are badly
in need of restoration. There are perhaps some two
hundred such artifacts. The nature of my circumstances
make it necessary that this work be carried out to the
highest quality and with the greatest rapidity. Since
no bookbinder in the North West possesses skills equal
to yours, I thought of you at once.

Please inform me as soon as you are able whether it is within your means to accept such a commission.
Your obliged and affectionate friend,
Lord F. Belfield

Chapter One

I fell in love with the feel of the cotton before I fell in love with the books. Leather felt too masculine and reptilian. Cloth was so much warmer and didn't slip out of my hands as easily. As a child I played underneath the tables and made toy families from the scraps that fell at my father's boots.

He would never talk to me about where the cloth we used came from, nor the contents of the books we worked on. There were a lot of things my father wouldn't tell me, and rather than keeping me ignorant, his silence made me more curious. And fortunately, I was surrounded by the means to nourish that curiosity.

Most of the time we spent together as I grew up was in silence, folding, bevelling and smoothing. I sometimes wished my fingers could be as thick as his; he didn't grimace when schooling leather and cloth into precise lines under his digital tutelage. I tried to be like my father, but all the books he left lying around gave me opinions.

I arrived at the front door of Rose Hall looking more ragged than I would have liked. My breath was far from fresh, and the hair pins and clips I had used to imprison the frizzier strands had been loosened by the bumps of the rickety carriage. I had been dropped at the top of a tree-lined drive that was at least a quarter mile long, if not more. The December mists obscured my vision, and I could only just make out the shape of a grand house, the likes of which I had only really seen on biscuit tins in the windows of Manchester's new department store, though I had imagined them as I read Brontë, Austen and Radcliffe. Even with the curls of mist in the air, I could tell this was a very English dwelling. As I approached it my feet slipped and shifted on the gravel, unused to navigating such terrain after only walking on cobbled streets and across wooden floors.

Lord Francis Belfield of Rose Hall had been my father's long-standing customer. He was the only man I'd ever seen look luxurious without any air of pomposity. The men of Manchester were not known for wearing velvet, so the sheen of his jackets always marked him out as distinguished. It felt completely fitting that Rose Hall was an ode to symmetry and a more tasteful example of the grandiosity of the mid-eighteenth century. It was an early Georgian home of Lancashire sandstone. Even though my father hadn't mentioned it, the period of the building's erection and the mercantile success of Lord Francis Belfield were all I needed to know to deduce that the building and its grounds had been purchased with plantation wealth.

I knocked on the forest-green door and left my suitcases on the ground, hoping that looked more elegant than being strained down by the weight of my clothes, books and binding tools. In my pocket, my fingers found the folds of Lord Belfield's letter. I inhaled, recalling once more the story I had so carefully rehearsed.

The door opened and a pair of prominent blue eyes glared at me through the crack. 'Well?'

'Miss Florence Granger for Lord Francis Belfield, please.'

I took in the lines, too many for the face of someone who was still clearly a young man. The hand holding the door open was rough and calloused.

'He is expecting me,' I added.

'No 'e is not.'

I blinked, having not expected resistance this soon.

'I assure you I arrive here at the request of Lord Belfield himself. I am from Granger's of Manchester.'

The door widened and there stood a long-limbed boy of no more than twenty. His movements were almost feline. The way he handled the door without effort despite its apparent heaviness was quite a marvel.

'We are bookbinders. I've been sent to care for your master's collection.' I retrieved the letter from the pocket of my coat and held it out.

He made no move to take it, but instead chewed his bottom lip, realising there was truth to my words but clearly unconvinced by me. A female tradesperson at the door to Rose Hall was probably not a common occurrence.

'Young man, I excuse you of your impertinence, but I have

7

been travelling for some hours and would like to rest,' I told him, trying a sterner approach. 'Please fetch your master.'

''E don't rise before midday most days anymore. You can wait in the kitchens, if you like.'

Now it was my turn to falter. I had no way of assessing how appropriate this was. Should I be seated in the parlour? If I allowed myself to be taken to the kitchens, was I aligning myself with the downstairs staff? I was an artisan, not a servant. But a sharp ripple through my stomach made the decision for me.

'Very well, so long as your offer comes with a cup of tea.' I sighed and crouched down to pick up my suitcases.

'No, m'lady. I'll tek those.'

He ushered me into the reception hall, lifting my bags up to his sides as if they weighed nothing at all. The door chuffed itself closed behind us with a low groan. The darkness of the perimeter indicated that there was no draught coming through, nor a single sliver of light. A curtain hung to the right of it and the man gave it a sharp tug. It concealed the entrance entirely once pulled across, an odd choice. It gave the sense of being sealed into the house somehow – not being able to see where one could escape.

Stepping into the hall, I was compelled to look up. It was a huge atrium, with dark green textured walls and candles placed at regular intervals which gave the illusion of a warm, close space. He led me over a black-tiled floor, underneath a vast yet delicate brass chandelier aglow with coppery bulbs. At the back of the hall, under the bifurcated staircase, he opened a hidden door which led down to the kitchen. Before I had reached the bottom the herbaceous and deeply woody smells of the kitchen came wafting up to greet me. It was divine. But when we reached the flagstoned room I saw there was nothing on the stove; I could only imagine that months of cooking in a room with such small windows had baked the scent into the walls.

I was seated at a wooden table facing an array of copper pans and white jugs with the high windows behind me. It was clearly a kitchen intended for many staff, but there was none of the expected bustle. Where was everyone? I shifted uncomfortably as I cast about for something to say, before realising that I didn't know the young man's name.

'What is your name?'

'Wesley.'

'Wesley what?'

He gave me a strange look. 'Bacchus. Wesley Bacchus. I'm the footman.'

He was telling me that as a footman, his surname did not matter. Of course there was no reason that I, as a craftswoman, should know the intricacies of these hierarchies, but I sat in silence, not wanting to betray myself further by speaking again.

I was grateful when the cook came in some minutes later – from a pantry, I imagined – but she barely looked in my direction, merely banging a pan of water onto the stove. My stomach growled something fierce when she entered, almost as if my belly knew that I was meeting the person in charge of feeding the house.

I waited for her to acknowledge me, while Wesley continued to look on with a smile playing about his lips. But she only retrieved a mug and a caddy, before placing a steaming tea in front of me with a snort. My shoulders slumped. I hadn't expected to be treated as a lady, but had hoped for at least some respect. Would my father have received such a poor greeting? I sipped the tea, grateful for its sweetness and warmth as the cook clattered about with her back to me. As I finished, she returned to the table with a thick slice of ham sandwiched between two slices of bread. There was also a large apple on the plate and in her other hand was a pewter cup of water. She'd clearly heard my stomach. But her face showed no compassion as she laid the blessed offering on the table.

With one last assessing glance at me, Wesley left, and the cook returned to the stove, making it clear she had no intention of speaking to me. I decided I could forget my manners just as she had hers, and devoured the most delicious meal I'd had in weeks. Salty ham on pillowy bread, with a delightfully sour apple and water that tasted like it came from the purest spring to cleanse my palate. After greedily wiping the crumbs off the plate with one of my fingers, I took out *A Christmas Carol* from my coat pocket and started reading until the words on the page began to blur. The beast of a carriage I had travelled in overnight had creaked with the strain of being drawn up even the slightest incline. Combined with the cold that jolted me from slumber, I had only been able to sleep in fits and bursts.

I awoke, suddenly, with my head on my crossed arms in front of me and my wrist soaking wet from my dribble. The plate and pewter cup had been taken away and Wesley was standing above me, a mocking smile about his thickish lips.

'I'm sorry to wake you, Miss. Lord Belfield says he'll see you now.'

Wesley led me back upstairs, and down a corridor. As we passed a tall, gilded mirror, I stopped, horrified by my reflection. My hair, after only days left to its own devices, was now once again completely untamed. My eyes were bloodshot with fatigue and my skin was pale, making my freckles stand out. Hastily, I tried to force my frizzed hair back beneath its pins as Wesley stopped too. He watched me with amusement until I had done the best I could, and we continued on our way.

I thought back to the last time I had seen Lord Francis Belfield. His best features were his long fingers, which were always encased in tight kid gloves that he never took off. Oh, and the smell of him! Rich pepper with a botanical soapy undertone, which always impressed me. Not in a way that would make me swoon. He's not the kind of man a girl like me is meant to fall in love with. No, what I felt was awe. A man of his fortune had surely seen more of the world than most. He'd have tales of St Petersburg, Constantinople and Siam. If only I could ask him. The need to convince him of my employability made doing so inappropriate.

The door opened onto the parlour, and immediately I could see that the man I remembered from our shop was very different from the man who sat in front of me. He was wearing a turmeric-coloured silk waistcoat embroidered with indigo plants, paired with dark trousers. He had clearly dressed hastily, and a thread towards the bottom of his trousers was loose and trailing on the floor by his feet. I inhaled deeply but could not catch the spiced vegetal scent that usually accompanied his presence. He was much thinner than when I had last seen him, and his eyes drooped as if he had suffered many a sleepless night. He stood up from his seat to shake my

11

hand but returned to it quickly as if he couldn't bear to hold himself up for too long.

'My name is Florence Granger, sir,' I began, but he waved a hand.

'Yes, yes, I remember you. But why has your father sent you all this way without an escort? It must have been a frightful journey.'

'Oh, no, Lord Belfield. The journey was fine.' I cleared my throat to make space for the bigger lie. 'My father sent me to complete the work on your collection that you requested.'

He looked at me aggrieved. Offended, even. The way his forehead crumpled made me more aware of the thinning hair at his temples. Even dishevelled, he was no less handsome. However, I pondered whether he might feel a sense of loss for the way he used to look. On my previous viewings of him, he looked like someone who was used to being seen and spoken of as a very handsome 'young' man. Although he wasn't superbly weathered, he now had the face of a man who had endured. A sad wisdom brought the tops of his eyelids a little lower. His jawline was a bit less tenderly set because his teeth were more used to being gritted together from stress. I supposed it was grief. He had lost his wife less than a year before, after all, leaving him with only his son.

'Why on earth would he do that? This hasn't even been discussed. Had he accepted the commission, I would have had the books sent to Manchester.'

Ah. This I had not considered. I remembered the words on the letter. I was sure that it was an invitation to stay and restore the library. My mouth was dry as I prepared my next lie.

'Lord Belfield, you are one of our best customers. We would like to come to you as it will save you the transportation of the works back and forth. If I have any need for extra materials, they can be quickly sent here without any trouble.'

His brow furrowed and he clenched and unclenched his right fist.

'Miss Granger. It's inappropriate for a young woman to be sent to work in the house of a recently widowed gentleman. It just won't do, I'm afraid. It's ... I must decline. I'm sorry for your having been sent all this way but I will of course arrange for your transportation back to Manchester.'

I was stunned that he stood up to shake my hand. Considering he was rejecting me and, unbeknownst to him, casting me back into sure-fire destitution, I would have expected more of a gruff dismissal than this tender farewell. Before I had time to choke them back, tears began freely flowing down my face. If I could have stopped myself from crying, I would have.

'My dear. Honestly, what's the matter? It's not more than a day's travel to get back to Manchester, surely. Please do not be so distressed. I will send the books on after you. Here, take a seat. I'll have more tea sent up.'

I shook my head as I sat in the chair beside his, declining his offer of tea I feared I could not keep down.

'What? You must tell me, what troubles you so?'

I hadn't prepared for this. I thought he might resist a woman working to restore his collection alone, and request my father come and join me. I never expected a refusal to even entertain the notion of my staying.

'Lord Belfield, I came here because my father was too proud

to ask you for this arrangement himself. His eyesight is failing him, and he knows not how long he can continue working.'

I was still able to tell the story I had prepared, albeit a more rambled version, and emotion brought my accent out more strongly.

'Sending more than two hundred books back and forth could take up to a year. We were hoping that if I came and worked up here the task could be completed more efficiently.' My voice broke, but his gaze on me had softened so I continued.

'Please, Lord Belfield. I beseech you to reconsider. I will work for a reduced fee, and in half the time if you let me stay.' This line was delivered with a very slow blink, knowing it would emphasise the tears that still clung to my lashes. He leaned back in his chair and reached for his pipe on the side table.

'I have the utmost respect for your father, but how do I know you would be as capable a binder?' He inhaled his pipe deeply, considering me. I wasn't afraid of being appraised carnally, but I realised that was not what he was doing. He was assessing my skill. Looking to see whether I had inherited my father's thick, leather-accustomed fingers or if I would be too dainty to wield the tools necessary to restore an entire collection to a condition worthy of sale.

'The usual place for a book to break is along the joint – the working part of the book. When this happens, the book needs re-backing.' I spotted a book on a side table and strode over to it, berating myself for my boldness but knowing this was the last attempt I could make to secure my place here. 'May I?'

His eyes narrowed but he made no moves to stop me, so I

lifted the book into the air and continued. 'This is in desperate need of attention. You see how the book components are at risk of separation? For this I would recommend lifting the old cloth of the spine and rebinding the back of the book in a matching material.'

'It is a very old book, and well thumbed. But the spine has an inscription, a priceless one, and I would not want it replaced.'

'Of course, I would trim the original spine to fit the new one in a way that none of the information is lost.' I reached into my pocket. 'I did a similar restoration on this book, for my father's mother before she passed. It was only a copy of *A Christmas Carol*, but she loved it so and couldn't bear to lose it after it fell in a bucket of water as she mopped the floors. It is important that the new spine be created from non-perishable materials for the sake of preservation, and though I have carried it with me since her death, the spine is no more worn.'

He took the book from me and examined it. I could barely draw breath as he opened the first page, then the last, and turned a few pages with excruciating gradualness.

'How long will the restoration take you?'

'No more than six months Lord Belfield,' I said meekly.

'Make it three.'

Three months was scarcely enough time to get back on my feet, let alone complete what was sure to be the biggest task I had undertaken on my own. I took in his demeanour, his steeled look and set jaw, and I knew that this was it; he would not be negotiated with. The offer was a three-month stay or a carriage back to destitution tonight. I nodded.

'I will pay you half the rate I originally offered, but you will have board and food while you complete the task at hand. Wesley will arrange you a room in the attic, with the other servants.'

'That's perfectly appropriate.'

He gave me a small smile and stood, indicating I was being dismissed. 'I will personally let you into the library every morning barring Sunday. You'll be wanting to go to the parish church?'

'Yes, my lord. Of course. Thank you.'

'Wesley will take you tomorrow. I've not attended since my wife passed.'

So grief was the reason for the change in him. I had never met Lady Persephone, but I had wondered about her after meeting Lord Belfield. Was she as beautiful as the woman of the Greek myth, who found herself caught between two worlds? What would it have been like to be married to a man with the whole world at his feet? Did she read the contents of his grand collection, and did they discuss the books together as my father would never deign to with me? And how did she die? I was curious about her, but all I said was:

'I'm sorry for your loss, my lord.'

He waved away my sympathy as he pulled a cord beside the door.

'Monday morning. Seven a.m. sharp.'

Wesley glided in, regarding me with narrowed eyes before gesturing that he would be escorting me to my room. I couldn't tell if this expression meant he was displeased or intrigued at my success.

As we mounted the staircase I noticed how tall and slight

Wesley was. His jacket was pulled taut with the strain of carrying my bags, revealing the tiniest hole at the shoulder seam. The butlers in the novels I read were always sticklers for such things as having one's uniform pressed and immediately mended when necessary. If there were a butler in the house, then I was sure Wesley would have been admonished for the tear.

By the middle of the staircase I was beginning to lose my composure and get a bit breathless. As I got to the top step, I was lagging behind by quite a few paces and I paused to take in the majesty of the entryway from above. As it was daytime, with light sources coming from different directions, the dark colours of the walls and carpets were far from gloomy. Such a large space, but so little echo because of the padding that came from the green carpets and heavy dark curtains. Textures upon textures, so that the atrium had the real feeling of welcoming you into a cosseted space of snug homeliness, even though this was one of the hugest private spaces I had ever been in. Moments later we had left that behind for the labyrinthine custard-coloured corridors that led to my bedroom on the upper levels.

Wesley was still expressionless as we entered my dim sanctuary. After everything I had endured recently, the last thing I needed was a new enemy; so I smiled widely at him, thanking him profusely as he set my things down and left me in the small attic room. The space was quite bare, with low-hanging wooden beams, but it was clean, dry, and for now, mine.

Chapter Two

The wind whistled through the nave of the church as we entered the next morning, whipping away any feelings of relief I had managed to hold on to from the night before. As the icy air made its way through my thin sleeves and raised the hair on my forearms, a memory of the hot burn of pleasure in my body, a mere two Fridays before, surfaced.

Breathing deeply, I tried not to think about Everett's umber eyes fixed on mine, or the rhythm of his breathing which now punctuated my thoughts. The stained-glass saints above the altar peered down at me with placid incredulity. My first time in a church since it happened, and these were the thoughts in my head. Shame sent heat rising up my neck and rushing to my face as Wesley directed me towards the seventh pew on the left.

Even the judgements I imagined raining down on me from the saints above would not have been enough to distract me from the glances and cupped whispers that our entrance elicited from the congregation. Before I had time to form a thought, my hand crept to my hair, fingers checking the strands still lay flat and contained under my hat. Though she was long dead, I could hear my grandmother lamenting how pretty I could be as the metal comb lay heating on the stove with the blue flames dancing around it.

It was around my seventh birthday that she came back from the Bon Marche department store in Liverpool with that comb, and with the full support of my father insisted on using it right away. My hair was wild, she'd said, and it had to be unsavaged.

Under his watchful eye she would take the hot metal comb and run it through the lamb's wool I was born with – nothing like my father's own downy hair – until it became more acceptably pliable. I had to hold my ears down away from the comb and use my hands to cover the skin on my face and at the nape of my neck. She still singed me to pieces. With each flinch I noted my father getting some sort of satisfaction from the smoke that rose from my temples. He very much deemed the practice worth my discomfort. Five days later, my hair had fully reverted back to being all coily. Wild as it was, I loved seeing myself again. It became routine on Saturday and eventually I learned the benefit of not flinching. The following morning we'd go to Sunday mass, where I would receive a sharp rap on the knuckles and a scolding if any of it escaped its bonnet. I always thought it was because she hated to see her hard work go to waste, but as I grew older, I realised it was because she couldn't stand to hear the ladies whispering about us.

There was never any resemblance between me and the rest of my family. I supposed I must look like my mother, but I had no proof of this as she had died when I was too young to make any memories.

Like the church I attended with my grandmother, the social standing of the attendees was apparent from the way they were dressed. In the first five pews sat the landed gentry with wives in black or navy satins and velvets, the most ostentatious in deep sapphires, emeralds and violets. All the husbands in the same uniform of morning suit with their hats laid next to them beside their well-trained children praying piously or with their eyes fixed ahead. I knew enough to avoid wearing anything made from loud rustling material, but I felt plain and shabby in my grey dress and threadbare shawl. We sat among the staff. Governesses, footmen, maids and gardeners; all clearly sat in order of importance within the small village, and then their own households. With our position in a pew so far back, I could discern that the standing of our household in the local area was middling. I was shocked by this, considering the impression Lord Belfield had made on me in Manchester. I wondered if his position in his village had diminished since his wife died, or if he had never sat in the front rows with the satins and velvets. However it came to be, it was dispiriting. The notable reaction to our entering the church went beyond the other serving staff, and families in the rows in front of us were barely disguising their glances and hushed comments. It was impossible to mistake the nudging elbows and widened eyes as we took our seats. I fixed my gaze on a candle in the pulpit, holding my head high to indicate that I had no shame in my appearance, ignoring the stabbing in my stomach which said otherwise.

'They just need something new to talk about,' Wesley muttered. 'No one has seen the master in weeks, so they need some sort of scandal to make sense of it.'

So my presence at Rose Hall had been taken as continued proof of some sort of scandal. I knew that a young woman visiting alone would be cause enough for the whisperings. I had thought my pairing with Wesley would quell any social rumblings in that regard. Much as I did not long to be classed with Rose Hall's downstairs, would they not just see us as two members of staff dutifully attending church on the Sabbath? If I were such a Jezebel, wouldn't I eschew church because my true job of seduction would require me to remain in the house alone with Lord Belfield? Perhaps if there were children to teach and I were a governess, eyebrows might not be raised. As it stood, I had no innocence left to bolster me from the suspicions that swirled around me.

I looked at Wesley then, and reflected that unlike Lord Belfield he was too wispy, too youthful, for anyone to see him as my lover. His angular frame, lank hair and large blue eyes gave him an effeminate profile. He would make a superb waiter at the Savoy from the drawings I had seen in magazines. More marionette than debonair. His lips were as full as mine and together, I suppose we looked like brother and sister.

An altar boy lit the candles, signalling the service was about to begin. I raised my nose to catch the smells of old wood, paraffin and wax which were incenses that pervaded through our shop in Manchester. When darkness descended and my father's eyes began to strain, I would light the wicks that illuminated our evenings and allowed us to continue working. So much of my life had required constant worrying and minding. If my father hadn't been so dead set on tossing me into the street, I'd have worried for his welfare.

The vicar took his place at the pulpit, and Wesley nudged me to stand. He continued to do so throughout the service for the hymns and gestured for me to sit before the reading of the lesson. I could see him noticing my finger trailing along the words in our shared hymn book and then mumbling the correct responses to the prayers in time with everyone else. I pondered whether he could read well, or at all. Both of us would have left school at a similarly young age, but I had not had to stop learning.

When it came to his sermon, the vicar droned on for an inordinate amount of time and I found my thoughts drifting to what my grandmother might have thought of my inauspicious return to the house of the Lord. Would she be proud of how industrious I had proved myself to be? Likely she would be thankful that I was pious enough to find myself in communion with a new congregation.

She loved me. I've no doubt about that. She never let me doubt that. From the way she told it, my father had just arrived at her doorstep with me on his return from Jamaica, where he'd gone to make a fortune. He'd married my mother days before they sailed to Montego Bay and returned to Manchester a penniless widower with a child.

My thoughts drift further, to my father, and the disappointment in his eyes last time he looked at me. Would he be relieved I was finding my way back on to the right path? I doubt this would even be deemed the right path, considering all the deceit it had taken to get here. I shuddered to imagine Lord Belfield discovering that I had been cast out by my father – and the reason why.

As we stood for the next hymn, I shook off my former sins. I had nothing to answer for if people were suspicious of Lord Belfield's intentions towards me. The true source of my shame would set sail across the Atlantic and if I behaved well enough, my tainted reputation would be cleansed by the distance I had put between myself and my former life.

I felt lighter on the walk back to the house with Wesley. The undulating road had been rather frosted on our walk towards church, but on the way back the occasional flashes of sunlight had taken the threat of a slip off the road. My feet were already becoming accustomed to the gravel.

While we had barely spoken on the way to the church, now as we made our way back, and having seen me trail all the written words throughout the service, Wesley had questions about my trade.

'How many books have you read?'

'I really couldn't tell you,' I replied.

It was as if Wesley's character had been behind a taciturn veil up until now. His inquisition wasn't new; I just hadn't been privy to the person who was demandingly curious by nature. Even if the questions would be seen as a bit silly by others, his interest in me made me feel that his distrust was melting.

'Hundreds?' he asked.

'I imagine so.'

'Thousands?' he asked.

'Quite possibly.' I wanted the chance to collect my thoughts before re-entering the house. Tomorrow I would begin work on the library and I needed to be rid of any feelings of inadequacy before doing so. My father always worked unthinkingly and hated when I was too inquisitive. I was only just beginning to appreciate how much I must have annoyed him with my incessant questions when he was simply trying to get on with the task at hand.

'What's your favourite book?'

'That's an impossible question!' I exclaimed.

'Why?' he asked, with such sincerity he made my teeth ache.

'Well ...' I wanted to give him an answer that felt as truth-filled as he did. 'When you've spent that much time mending and caring for all kinds of books from different ages, it's really quite difficult to not see them all as your children.'

He nodded and stuck his bottom lip out and looked pensively towards the trees on the crown of the hill up to the left of us.

'I'd love to read one, some day.' His tone was wistful, and as a tradesman's daughter, this could have very well been my destiny. I felt a sudden rush of gratitude for my upbringing. For the books and the words that swirled around my brain once I had read them, telling me that even I had rights that were worth fighting for.

'Did Lady Persephone read as much as Lord Belfield does?' I asked.

Wesley looked surprised at this. 'More, even,' he responded. 'If she wasn't reading, she was writing.'

I cleaved to the notion of her as a ravenous book eater. I

had up until then only met a few women with my particular affliction, and though I had heard of many more, of course, I had not been fortunate enough to gain any as companions. Lady Persephone sounded like someone I could have bartered novels with secretly.

I had become used to having to consume books in secret. I often had to read books my father had bound on commission by candlelight once he slept. Knowledge that was so particularly precious, only available to me for as long as the clock might allow. His illicit trade in erotic novels from the continent notwithstanding. The more esteemed the gentleman procuring it, the smuttier the content, it seemed. But there were also the more morbid books, which taught me so much about the body and our organs. I depended on the erotic for intimate knowledge of sensual arousal. I depended on the doctors' treatises for knowledge of my body's inner workings and how to avoid conception and deal with all sorts of aches and pains. Occasionally to muse on what might cause life to leave the body.

'How did she die?' I asked Wesley.

'At night.'

Why would he tell me the time she died, rather than *how* she had died?

'Yes, but what happened?'

He paused and looked at my face as if trying to deduce whether I was indeed trustworthy. We were alone, but nevertheless he whispered: 'They found her in the river on the first warm day of March just gone. They think she fell in upstream and drowned.'

I put my hand to my mouth because ... Well, I'm not sure why. To stop myself from saying something silly.

We walked in silence for a bit. Then Wesley explained further.

'It weren't 'cos of you that they're all a bit frosty towards us in the village, y'know. They turned when she passed because ... Well, we're tainted by their suspicions, aren't we? There were always whispers about what happened up at Rose Hall and now with him being so withdrawn they think it's probably guilt, because of all the things the family did in the Indias. Bringing back all the witchcraft and stuff.' He paused. 'They'd ask me, you know? If the Belfields did native stuff like dance round Bengali fires in the garden or make potions from plants from Jamaica or whatnot. It's 'cos he talks too much about his travels and seeing all these delights. Makes them suspicious when an Englishman enjoys life abroad too much, probably. But they've no right suspecting him of wrongdoing. Lord Belfield ran to the river as if she'd still be there when they came to tell him they'd found her. It took three men from the village to bring him back home. He might still be there if it weren't for them. It was frightful the way he took the news.'

'Well, of course.'

'I put so much effort into making him perfect gin and tonics, because it's his favourite drink. But he rarely asks me these days. Just drinks straight gin out of the bottle. He gets so confused about everything but no one could give him the answers he was looking for ... She must have tripped or summat.'

'But why was she out at night-time, walking alone?'

Wesley sighed resignedly. 'No one knows.'

Silence returned and I knew not how to lift the mood again. Wesley being so inquisitive was what shifted us from sombre conversation back to talkative brightness.

Next came a flood of questions about Africa and the Orient that I did my best to answer as fully as possible. Being asked all these questions made me feel like I could go inside myself to all these worlds that books had given me, which I would normally reside in alone. My father always seemed beleaguered by my questions. As if my mind fatigued him. I felt sad he never seemed excited to have a child as precocious as me, though this might have been different if I had been a son. Having Wesley plunder my brain in this way made me feel swollen with untapped knowledge and ever so ... alive.

'You can ask me anything, Wesley,' I said as a sunlit Rose Hall came into view after a bend in the road that descended into our home valley.

'Oh, I promise you I will,' he said, smiling at me. I returned his smile, pleased to have at least one friend here. The speed of the platonic intimacy might have surprised someone else. When I look back now, I wonder if it was merely the lithe effeminacy that made all his movements so unthreatening. I do believe it was more than that, however. There was such a sprightly energy about him. I felt like we were two deer in the forest and I had merely been born one spring before. We both had so much to teach the other, but because of my age I knew just that little bit more of the world that lay beyond the forest we called home.

Chapter Three

The cook, I had soon learned, was called Baxter. The three of us ate in silence that night. I could see Wesley was itching to talk to me, but he wouldn't dare while Baxter was sat between us at the head of the table. I hated the silence, so took to reciting moments from Wilde's *Salomé* over and over in my head. The words created a gentle reverie in my mind, an oasis of calm and noise which I couldn't seem to function without. I had always found such comfort in this method in the constant quiet of my father's presence.

A beautiful princess, you want to watch her, but remember terrible things may happen if you stare.

I snatched glances at the way Wesley held his spoon with such precision that he avoided making the chinking sound as the metal hit the sides of his bowl, by scooping it upwards at the last moment. Over the course of the past night and day I had come to admire his beauty, and I had found myself wondering if one of the many rooms in the house contained a painting of him like Wilde's Dorian Gray. Though I did not see him as an aesthete. He had a curious mind, but still not much appreciation for art and beauty. Looking at his facial features as he chewed on our roast dinner, I was right to see him as feline, but not in the way of a house cat. He was far more similar to a semi-tamed leopard. Moving through the world with a placid, masked elegance, but ready to pounce on our new friendship with zeal.

I, on the other hand, looked far from elegant. My hair was bigger for one, and this morning even my desperate pinning had barely contained it. I pulled self-consciously on a tuft, worried that Baxter would think me unkempt. Others had often seemed to take my wild hair as proof of my wild nature.

Wesley watched Baxter rise from the table to fetch the suet pudding and custard from the stove. He leaned across the table to me conspiratorially.

'If you'll let me, I can comb your hair tonight.'

I gave him a right queer look, by way of response.

'I used to see Sibyl – Lady Persephone's lady's maid – comb her hair. It were a lot like yours, thick, frizzy and just so much of it.'

'Wesley, you don't have to,' I replied, but my heart quickened at the thought of it. I had not had my hair combed by someone else since my grandmother passed, and I knew already that Wesley's hand would be far gentler. 'That is far beyond your duties, I cannot possibly ask that of you.'

The impropriety of it made me wince. Imagine if we were to be discovered. As fey as Wesley was, to be found so intimately engaged when we were not quite the same sex was to risk losing our positions.

His eyes widened and he exclaimed, 'But I want to!'

Something about the warmth in his eyes caused me to relent slightly, and my hand drifted to the top of my head, teasing the tangled strands apart with my fingers.

Baxter looked back at us briefly from the stove, eyes narrowed as if she'd heard an irritating fly buzz. Wesley leaned in closer to me, his breath now tickling my earlobe.

'It's easy. You just start from the ends after you've put a little bit of the oil on to smoothen it all. I'll come after the lights are out when the house is quiet.'

I knew there was nothing sordid in the suggestion, but still my breath caught in my throat, and I lost the ability to speak.

He leaned back slightly, locking eyes with me, and brought the three middle fingers of his left hand up, using the right to point at them in turn. 'Olive oil. Lavender oil. Rosemary oil. There are loads of each left. Don't worry, I checked before dinner,' Wesley said.

Baxter walked back with the three small bowls. After she set them down and we both thanked her, silence returned and so did the careful rhythm of Salomé.

Looking for the princess, commenting on the strange look of the moon, slipping in blood.

We all finished eating our last mouthfuls within moments of each other. Baxter leaned back and rubbed her stomach with both hands.

'That was really somethin' special, Mrs Baxter. Thank you.' Wesley exhaled appreciatively.

She merely sighed and nodded at him in lieu of giving an answer.

'Yes. Brilliant, Baxter, thank you.'

'Well I don't need to scrimp on portions with there being so few of us now,' Baxter deflected.

'How many staff were there? Before, I mean,' I said.

'Five more. Butler, footman, two housemaids and a scullery maid too,' Wesley answered.

'And we struggled to get things done with them too, house this size. Now look at us. Run ragged.' Baxter grumbled.

'Oh, we do all right. It were a lot of fuss and bother before. It's just the cleaning now and I manage all right, don't I?' Wesley offered.

Baxter gave him a sceptical look. 'If you say so.'

'I don't know what Baxter is complaining for. She's the one with no extras to do. She cooked then and she cooks now,' Wesley ribbed.

'You cheeky sod.' Baxter flicked her tea towel in his direction.

Wesley picked up his bowl and went round to collect Baxter's at the head of the table. I would learn later how unusual this was. In the heyday of Rose Hall, the butler would have occupied Baxter's seat and officially dismissed us once the meal was over. But Baxter was so naturally dominant, she only needed a few words to be uttered to direct and delegate down here. At the time, I truly just thought this was the natural order of things. It was only later that I realised the topsy-turvy nature of the service dynamic. What went unsaid was how much safer Wesley was in a smaller staff. I'm sure the masculine energy of a butler and another footman would have made his swishy ways all the more glaring in comparison. I watched Wesley glide out of the room to take the bowls to the sinks in the scullery and when I looked back at Baxter, a smirk hovered about her lips.

'You're barking up the wrong tree if you confuse his attention for affection Miss Granger. He's not like other boys, y'know.'

Heat rose in my cheeks as I wrapped my head around the idea of Baxter thinking I was smitten with Wesley, of all people. Not wanting her to think of me as silly I said:

'Well, I'm not like other girls, Mrs Baxter, nor am I smitten, so I do think Wesley and I will get along swimmingly.'

She suppressed the smile spreading across her face and rose from her chair, which I took as a cue to vacate mine.

I was so used to my grandmother's rough and frustrated hands tugging at my hair from the root, that Wesley coaxing my hair gently through the brush was a shock at first. Before he started, Wesley explained that the wisdom of controlling hair as thick as mine was to arrange it into smaller plaits in neat rows, rather than the two plaits that was the custom for much straighter hair. I was nervous to have Wesley in my room, in case anyone were to hear us, but I didn't tell him that. I had so few belongings with me there was little to prepare or clean away before his arrival either. I sat in a chair and Wesley stood behind me. Our necks were both elongated by the task at hand and looking at us in a mirror I remembered a drawing of girls in a Turkish harem in a book that my father kept in the cupboard of his bedside table. When Wesley was on the third braid by the nape of my neck, I asked him to tell me more about the late lady of the house.

'Oh, Lady Persephone? She took a long time to warm to me,' he said.

'How? With your charm and sharp wit, I'd have thought you'd win her over in an instant.' My tone was playful, bordering on mocking.

'I didn't see much of her.' If he caught my tone, he ignored it and continued weaving strands of my hair round themselves. 'Unless her sister-in-law were visiting, Lady Persephone mainly kept herself to the morning room and parlour on the ground floor, and Lord Belfield mainly resided in his bedroom and the library.'

'It doesn't sound like they spent very much time together.'

'Well he couldn't really pry her and Sibyl apart, to be honest.'

'Oh, so when you say kept to herself—'

'Well, a lady spending all her days with her lady's maid *is* keeping to herself, int' it?'

Of course I did know this from reading constantly about the upper classes. One's butler or lady's maid was an extension of oneself. So if I were to ask if Lady Persephone had been alone, then Wesley or Baxter might say 'yes', even if Miss Sibyl had been sitting two feet away from her doing embroidery or mending a hole in a glove.

'She didn't like to be looked at for too long by anyone else,' he said distantly, his eyes fixed on a small crack in the wooden beam above us.

'What do you mean?' I asked, turning to look up at him. 'For too long?'

'Oh, well.' He paused as he waited for me to turn back, then dipped his fingers into the mixed oils on the vanity table before starting on the fourth braid. 'She were just skittish. Like a small dog that runs from thunder in a storm.'

'Why?'

'Well, I don't rightly know, Miss Granger,' he replied in a rather remarkable imitation of my voice.

'Where did you learn to do that?'

'Oh, my mother used to love my imitations. I'd have her in stitches all the time – copying people.'

A softness came into his eyes when he spoke of her. All I knew of her was that she worked in a factory in Manchester.

'You are close to her,' I said.

'Oh yes. A mother's love always makes up for a father's disappointment. At least it did for me,' he said sadly. He eased strands of my hair apart, separating each one with such careful, delicate movements.

'What does your father do for work?' I asked.

'He works on the docks near Salford,' he said, smoothing more oil into my scalp.

'Ah . . . I see.' I sighed.

'What do you see?' Wesley asked, and a sharpness to his tone suggested he thought I was patronising him. His fingers, poised to coax more of my hair through the bristles of the brush, paused.

'Well, I'd assume he's the sort of man who would only be impressed with his son if he worked a job where a man was in danger of losing his fingers every day.'

'You're right there.' The brushing resumed.

We continued like that for a good half hour, Wesley telling me about his family, who all inhabited much more desperate lives than those on my street on the other side of Manchester. We weren't that far from home really, but it felt like it. In fact, in that room, with Wesley brushing my hair by candlelight, it felt like everything was an ocean away. His pace slowed as we got towards the front of my hair, as if he didn't want to stop. I didn't want him to either, but his fingers were working their way down the last plait.

'Right, so when you wake up in the morning, just unravel them all and comb it through with your fingers.' He wiped his hands lightly over my crown to remove the remaining oil from his palms. 'It won't be straight, but it will be smooth. Then you can more easily arrange a nice coiffure.'

'Oh, Wesley, I wouldn't know how.' I laughed.

'It's easy. When you go in the library tomorrow, you'll see all the ladies' magazines that Sibyl would read. Lord Belfield would bring them back with him from Liverpool you see. That's where she learned how to do it all.'

'All right, if you say so.'

'I'd come and help you more myself, but I can't come across to here too often. If Mrs Baxter finds out, she'll start thinking we're paramours or something.'

The giggle inside of me tickled my tonsils. I swallowed it to save his pride.

'Yes. No, of course. I completely understand.'

'I'll come back in a couple nights' time though, promise. I've really enjoyed myself.'

'Wesley, I—'

I was cut off by him bowing down to kiss me on both cheeks. I was taken by complete surprise and lost the ability to speak for a moment.

35

He stood up straight and nodded down at me while touching my shoulder.

'That's how they do it in Paris.'

He left without another word, and I sat for a while with conflicting emotions, my cheeks tingled with the spots he had touched with his lips, and wondered how a footman in the Lake District knew anything about Paris. Eventually I stood and dressed myself for bed, blowing out the candles on the table and leaving the paraffin lamp by my bed that made the filigree pattern dance around the walls.

I felt overwhelmed by my luck. I had managed to fashion a new career for myself out of just a well-timed interception of a letter and a few strategic stories. I had a new friend who adored me. I was in a clean bed with a herbaceous smelling head of neatly plaited hair. I had so much to be thankful for. A sensible girl would have just laid there, given thanks and gone to sleep to get as much rest as possible before starting work the very next morning.

The problem is, I've never been known to be sensible.

You see, I couldn't get what Wesley had said about Lady Persephone out of my head. That she *didn't like to be looked at for too long.* As if there had been something one could uncover just by staring at her. I was gripped by a desire to know what she looked like and I knew sleep would elude me because all of my new thoughts and questions were blustering around in my mind. There must be a portrait of her somewhere in one of Rose Hall's many rooms, I thought, and I wanted to see it.

I eased my door open and slipped out, pulling it to without allowing the latch to click. There were three empty bedrooms between mine and Baxter's room at the end of the corridor, which had a carpeted step down to the stairs to the first floor. There was light coming from beneath her door and I heard some soft yelping and rustling as if she had an impassioned terrier struggling under the covers with her. Had there been another man besides Wesley on staff, then I might have guessed that she wasn't alone. But I knew she was.

Down the stairs to the first floor wasn't a problem. I had been informed by Wesley that Lord Belfield was drinking a lot more since his wife's passing, which was hardly a surprise. A heavy drinker wasn't likely to hear me padding about on the floor that held his bedroom, Lady Persephone's bedroom and their son's bedroom. Their son was away at school, I'd learned from Wesley. Still, I took great care to tread lightly as I headed down to the ground floor. That a married couple of the upper classes lived such separate lives wasn't what piqued my curiosity. It was the gaps in what had been conveyed to me. All tragedy and no romance. No marriage was that pure. If the circumstances of Lady Persephone's passing were honourable then the details surrounding her death would be more forthcoming. Where was her lady's maid now? I smelled the whiff of scandal, and I just had to know what it was.

As I crept into the morning room, my foot caught on the large Persian rug and almost sent me crashing into the coffee table. I managed to twist my body to avoid it, but I still landed on the floor with an audible thud. I sat there with the breath momentarily knocked from my body, heart pounding, waiting to be discovered. Minutes passed before my breathing regulated. I thought I heard movement for a moment, but realised it was the light draught of the only half-drawn flapping curtain covering the front door. I stood. It was warmer down here than upstairs, but I shivered as the chills and the fear of being caught left my body. I took in the morning room, with its pale-yellow walls and pink velvet seats. It was pretty. I could imagine the lady of the house spending her time here. A bureau in the top corner of the room lay open, displaying letter-writing materials. I had only taken two steps towards it when I saw the glinting grey eyes of a beast in the doorway.

The creature emitted a low growl, and the threat of it stopped my heart. One bark from this beer-bellied gargantuan hound and my new, safe, and all too temporary haven would be ripped away from me. I was a complete stranger to the mastiff, and I knew that I couldn't do a nice whinnying voice and encourage playful engagement, nor could I just ignore it and hope to rifle through paperwork in the bureau. We stood, eyes locked, both waiting for the other to make the first move. He – for surely all mastiffs are male – lifted his nose to the air, catching my scent. His sole role here was to defend his family's territory. He would smell that I did not belong, that I was an intruder, an imposter, and alert the entire house to my presence. My eyes darted round, looking for any possible exit or hiding place, but there was none. The only exit would be back past the growling mastiff.

He lowered his head and stalked towards me. My chest began to strain, and I realised that I had not drawn breath since locking eyes with the hound. He padded closer to me before coming to my legs and sniffing my exposed skin. I let out a whimper as he raised up on his hind legs, placed his forepaws against my chest and began to sniff at my hair. Some of the oiled strands had already freed themselves from the plaits and I felt the dog's warm breath brushing past them.

He dropped again to the floor and rubbed himself against my legs, seeming to decide I was not a threat. The relief flooded from my mouth in a long shaky breath, and I sank down to my knees. The mastiff dragged the length of his body against my slumped frame, and I reached out to stroke him behind his ears. So much for a guard dog. A terrier would be more appropriate at alerting the house to a braided woman in a white nightgown conducting a night-time investigation. Thankfully, he was quick to accept me as a wandering insomniac member of the family. He took his leave and plopped himself by the fireplace with his head facing away from me, now utterly disinterested in my presence. Freed from fear, I went and sat down at the bureau.

A black address book. Lists of flowers and plants in the garden that needed attention. A bundle of letters from an Arabella Sey of Liverpool, and on the flat top of the bureau, two framed photos of incriminating weirdness.

The first was a family photo of Lord Belfield, Lady Persephone and their son. Lady Persephone. How had Wesley not mentioned how strikingly ethereal she was? A seated woodland nymph if I had ever seen one. She was a small woman with such blonde hair it looked practically snowy white in the photograph. And her features were just beyond description. There was something incongruous about her beauty. Nothing British about her at all, but a mix of what I had come to compartmentalise as features of particular parts of Europe. Nordic colouring with a nose that was close to Roman, but a fullness in her other features that suggested ancestry at least as far south as the Mediterranean. Full lips and high pillowy cheeks. She had the aquiline eyes of an eagle. A sharp gaze that always betrayed her curiosity. Who was this woman? Where was she from? To be named Persephone, of all things. Here she was, The Destroyer. With the features of an angel, but the fearsome look of someone the gods have done more wrong than anyone here on earth could.

The second photograph was even more puzzling. A coloured woman in a riding habit, wearing a jauntily placed top hat, a neat wool jacket and a long skirt, holding her riding crop. Self-assured and brimming with joy from a life of ease. Could this be Persephone's lady's maid? That she was black was a shock. I thought back to the way Wesley whispered about her in a mysterious way, without mentioning she was coloured. Where would she have even learned to ride? And would it not be more fitting for the lady of the house to be fond of horse riding?

Forgive me, for my thoughts were, and still are, being fuelled by my prejudices, but I could not understand why I was looking at a black lady's maid with all of the imperious regality of Sara Forbes Bonetta. I opened the back of the frame for clues, but all that was there, in cursive, were the words:

Darling Sibyl, 1892

Was this Lady Persephone's hand? Had Sibyl not wanted to take this picture of herself with her when she left? Surely she had been the one to gift it to Lady Persephone. Where was she now?

A passing sneeze from the mastiff by the fireplace raised the hair on my arms and reminded me of how late it was. I placed the photographs back into their corners and backed out of the room facing the mastiff to make sure he wasn't interested in following me.

My ascent back upstairs was hushed for the most part, although I could hear the swish of my nightgown between my thighs. On the third step from the top of the stairs on the second floor my foot caused a creaking that was positively orchestral. How had I not elicited this on my way down? Once the sound came to an end, I stood there, frozen. No lights came on. No one came rushing through. I was safe.

Walking back to my bedroom at the end of our corridor I felt valiant. I have always had a nose for a good story and from all my observations I could deduce that there was a scandalously pungent one here. Something was afoot and had been for a long time. Looking back now, I can see I was on the hunt for new scandals in the hope that the revelations would distance me from memories of my own.

I opened my bedroom door, and as I stepped into my room, I heard the click of a latch from down the corridor. But there was no light coming from Baxter's door when I had walked past it, I had been sure. Nevertheless – had she seen me?

Chapter Four

For breakfast the next morning we ate kedgeree. A rich and complex dish consisting of cooked, flaked fish, boiled rice, parsley, hard-boiled eggs, curry powder and cream. My father would have balked at eating something so highly flavoured for a breakfast meal, but I rather liked it. It was a fun turn to have such different savoury flavours for breakfast really. It would also be my first day of work at Rose Hall, and I would finally be allowed to enter the library.

'It's been a long time since he's requested kedgeree, or anything quite so decadent for breakfast, so it looks like someone's picked his spirits up for him,' Baxter said, glancing at me as she set it down. 'You won't have long to eat it, mind you. Expect that bell to be dinging any second now.'

'He has asked me to meet him at the library door at 7 a.m.,' I said with a crisp smile.

Baxter frowned slightly in return, recognising my reminder

that I occupied a different space in the home than she and Wesley did.

'This meal is just fabulous, Baxter,' I relented, trying to smooth things back over.

'His ayah taught me to make it.'

'His what, sorry?' I asked.

'His ayah,' Wesley chimed in. 'I thought you woulda known that word with all your reading. It's what you call a nanny, but only if they're native.'

I did know the word, but I had only ever seen it written down. It sounded different coming from their mouths. Like they were saying 'higher' but without the letter h at the beginning.

'He were born in Bombay or something, weren't he, Baxter?' Wesley said.

'No, Calcutta. The family went up to the mountains when it got too hot,' Baxter muttered without looking up at either of us.

The customary silence settled over the table as we began to eat. I thought about those who lived their life in service and how they fascinated me, even then. Besides the skills of their trade, they also came to learn of the lives, experiences and travels of those they served. It wouldn't surprise me to learn that Baxter had never left the North West of England, but here she was with an intimate knowledge of the cuisine enjoyed by the British Raj, merely to recreate the dishes Lord Belfield had come to know in his sweltering childhood.

It also helped to explain why Wesley was so proud of being able to serve the perfect gin and tonic. In the days when they had a full staff and a teeming household with visiting guests, it must have been the way to distinguish himself and be called for when there were people to entertain. Perhaps that which was served at the dinner table also educated everyone about the culinary spoils of the Empire. Was this not all on full display at the world fairs of London?

With ten minutes to spare, I brushed a couple of yellow rice grains from my skirt and stood up, picking up the tool bag next to me. My father's dictum throughout life was that 'if you want to be on time, you need to be early'. He would say it to me gruffly as he hurried me along streets to appointments, or as we worked late in the night to finish a commission which was not due to be collected for another day yet. For all his faults, I still felt an ache for him as I squeezed the leather strap of my bag tighter.

'Good luck with it all,' Wesley said with more excitement in his voice than I felt.

I smiled gratefully at him, and he beamed at me from his seat. I could count the rice grains caught between his teeth.

'Lunch is at twelve,' Baxter said pointedly. 'Not a moment later.'

I nodded at her and scurried out of the kitchen, up the stairs to the ground floor and stood by the library doors, waiting. At 7 a.m. precisely, the gong in the grandfather clock sounded, and from around the corner came a mildly disheveled but still rather dashing Lord Belfield.

'Ah, Miss Granger. I do appreciate punctuality,' he said warmly before I had the chance to greet him.

'Why of course,' I said, angry at myself for sounding so breathless.

We stood in the hallway facing each other and I thought he

was appraising me or waiting to say something grave. I took in his ensemble. It was wildly mismatched and crumpled, as though he had dressed in a rush. He was wearing a white shirt beneath a waistcoat with yellow piping, grey tweed trousers and moccasin loafers. The whole outfit gave him the impression of being a younger rebel. I wondered if that was intentional, or simply the result of not having enough staff to assist with his dressing and styling.

'You're in the way, Miss Granger,' he said, motioning to the door I was standing in front of.

'Oh goodness. I'm sorry.' I twisted out of my position, knocking my bag hard against the window in the process.

He mercifully ignored my awkwardness as he stepped forward to grip the brass doorknob and inserted a chunky iron key into the keyhole. He pushed the door slowly, so that a great whoosh of the most delicious smelling air came out to beckon us.

I was enticed to the point of intoxication by the wafting aroma. I stepped into the room as if in a trance, inhaling the scent and deciphering the bark undertones, sweeping sandalwood and fragrant top notes of bright orange and rose. The north-facing chamber was perfect; no sunlight ever reached this side of the house, so the large windows in front of us did not allow any bleaching rays to damage the floor-to-ceiling shelves of books upon books upon books. To see so many shades of brown was reassuring; it indicated leather to me, and that at least I knew how to handle. I ran my eyes along a shelf adorned with cobweb ropes, examining the leather-bound books with spines the colour of a deep gravy, some with gold lettering embossed on the spine but most blank except for some clean raised ridging. The oldest books were closest to the door to the right of us, and a sliding wooden ladder went on for sixty feet or so. At the end of the room, perpendicular to the wall of books, stood a proud cherry oak table with green leather on top, lion legs and stacks upon stacks of papers on top of it.

'Of course, I had not expected work to take place in here,' Lord Belfield said, following my gaze. 'Though I should have asked Wesley to clear a space for you to work when it was apparent you would be staying.'

I was so enraptured by my new workspace that I couldn't respond. My eyes greedily drank in every detail. Someone more used to riches might have viewed me as being silly to be so speechless. The room was modest in comparison to grander libraries of country houses, and there were sheets of dust covering most surfaces. The grandiosity of Chetham's Library in Manchester with its medieval history and sable wood was a reverential sanctum. This library was so much lighter in feel. Far more welcoming and homely, because of the honeyed wood, than imposing and macabre. Lord Belfield strode over to the table and began clearing it. Next to the table was a black, square wire cage, no higher or broader than the table, around three feet square, with many books stacked on top of each other somewhat precariously. From where I stood, I could see that this was his ornate collection. The covers all looked somewhat decorative and distinct from each other, and I couldn't wait to get closer to see all the intricacies of the spines.

I had never been in a room with such a pleasing, cool air, peopled with books that looked so warm to the touch. My father's workroom had occasional whiffs of niceness from books, but the prevailing smells were more metallic in nature. Grease and linseed and turpentine. This was a place entirely for leisure, so no working smells had permeated it, leaving only the aroma of knowledge making. Wisdom so ancient as to be made elegant. To have a room such as this dedicated to a collection of literary treasures. What luxury!

I had acclimatised enough now to take a few steps into the room, and I noticed that as the shelves went further back, more coloured spines popped out. Crimsons and roses and russets; sages, chalks and ochres. There was a blue rug which covered the majority of the wooden floor, but it left a large expanse of polished floor exposed, and my footsteps made a noticeable clicking sound as I walked, peering at the layers and layers of books around me.

Lord Belfield, facing away from me, busied himself with the task of paper clearing and a gaping hole in the seam of his waistcoat dragged my attention away from the room. I felt sad looking at him. His visits to my father were those of another person entirely. Someone who had the exacting standards of a dandy, an immaculate wardrobe and an elegant and very much alive wife.

I recalled him mentioning to my father that he had met Lady Persephone in Paris. I had always assumed her to be *une femme Parisienne*: a well-born French lady who would only have considered marrying an Englishman of the upper classes and genuinely good breeding.

'Lord Belfield, if I may, you could get that rip in your waistcoat darned. I would offer to do it for you, but I am not handy with a needle and thread.'

He turned around, quite flustered.

'Oh, I dare not entrust it to anyone. Far too much sentimental value. It's from my days in Oxford.' He looked out to the grass beneath the window. 'It feels like that was a lifetime ago.'

'How long ago was it?' I asked.

'Just twelve years,' he said. 'But here I am a father and a widower. I'd never have thought it possible.'

I wished I had something meaningful to say, but what comfort would any words I had be to him? I knew nothing of the pain he'd gone through – yet.

I walked towards him and placed my bag in the space he had created.

'What's in this cage?' I asked.

'Oh. Yes. It's the exotic collection. Japanese. Sanskrit. Even some African, would you believe? You've heard of the library of Timbuktu?'

'Yes,' I lied. I was astounded to learn that Timbuktu was an actual place. Such a name. I thought it had just been created for my children's stories. It sounded highly fictional. In the way Lilliput was the perfect name for a land of short people. Or Atlantis as a naturally vast place in the middle of an ocean.

'There's a Koran here with sand in the crevices. I've even got a lectionary with an ivory covering of St Martin which I think has a splodge of blood on the back. Although perhaps I was swindled by a Catholic who put some juice from a tomato on it and left it in the sun.' He chuckled.

It was not funny, but I had to laugh too. My laugh was too high pitched and sudden to be natural, but it would have been far more awkward had I not, and I needed to remain on good terms with him. I had such a good bargain here, and I wish I had treasured it more at the time. To be working with exotic books in a beautiful library and my only requirement was to laugh at the jokes of a father who missed his wife and child. Rather than appreciate that, I was preoccupied with trying to work out what kind of a man made jokes about blood on ivory-covered books. Was he truly broken, or had he been the one to break everything open? I had no understanding of how this home had come into being and fallen into such a state, or how a man who had not yet kissed forty years of age could find himself in such a desperate and dishevelled state of being. My sympathy for him would be tested, though.

After the awkward chuckles I had sent back to him, we settled into silence, and he looked over a few of his shelves and wiped away some dust with the sleeve of his jumper.

I began to assess the books before me that needed immediate attention, and just as I was feeling along the split spine of one, I heard Lord Belfield say, 'Well, I'll leave you to get on and come to see how you're doing just before lunch.'

'Yes, Lord Belfield. Thank you.'

With that he left the room, closed the door behind him and I heard the clicks of the key turning in the lock. He had locked me in.

Chapter Five

I was startled to find myself locked into the library so uncer-
emoniously. Was I supposed to be at the mercy of Lord
Belfield's memory? What if there was a fire and no one
remembered me until my escape way was snatched in flames?
But moreover, why lock me in at all? Did he think I might run
away with the most valuable tomes wedged into my armpit,
for the three-and-a-half-mile run to the village? A village
where everyone knew him and would march me back with
the stolen texts, only marred by a bit of mud splatter from
my failed escapade? Or did he just like the idea of having a
nineteen-year-old girl locked away in his library, like a doll
trapped inside a house who could do nothing but wait to fall
victim to the grubby playtime fingers of their owners?

I felt owned. But there was nothing to do but get to work.

After what must have been almost two hours, there was

a thunderous knock at Rose Hall's front door. I remember how faint I felt, as every drop of blood in my body turned to lead and sank to my toes, so sure was I that my father was on the other side of the door. I was convinced that he had somehow discovered my dishonesty and travelled here to end the ruse, and drag me back to be disciplined in Manchester. The pounding at the door echoed its way through the house like earth-shaking thunder. I clenched my lips together as my eyes began to sting with tears of disappointment. My nostrils were already filled with the sulphurous cloud that often hung about my father because he made so little effort to wash more than once a fortnight.

I listened to the front door creaking open.

'Good morning, Sir Chester,' came Wesley's meekly greeting. The fear left me immediately, my blood began flowing through me again and I breathed a sweet, shaky sigh of relief. Not my father. I could hold on to the illusion of safety, for a while longer at least. Curiosity consumed me as I heard the unmistakeable smack, smack, smacking of sweaty leather gloves against a still clammy palm.

'Good grief, there's no need for you to stand around here salivating over me. He knows I'm coming. You can go and get back on with your flower arranging now.'

I was surprised I could hear so much from this spot behind the library door. All had gone quiet. I slinked back to my desk, fearing Lord Belfield was on his way. Was Wesley just standing there with the guest, or had he gone to fetch the master?

My question was answered as a chuff of air whooshed into the room, and Wesley appeared in the open doorway. The key had obviously been left in the lock. He motioned for me to come towards him and I held my skirts up so as not to catch on anything as I scuttered over to him. It was amusing to see Wesley in his cleaning attire. Black trousers and an oversized white shirt with an apron on and a scarf around his head, holding a duster with a mucky cloth tucked into his waistband. He looked like a French maid. Men's clothing, but still with an air of the androgyne because of the softness of his face. I noticed his cheeks were quite flushed now that I was close to him.

We stayed close to the wall and watched the two men walking across the hall from our peering point – the crack in the open door that concealed us. Lord Belfield had his pipe and a stream of smoke swooped behind him. We followed the trail emitted by the meagre genie, guiding his guest into his opium den. The billiard room was just beyond the dining room, which was where I assumed Lord Belfield was taking this guest. Wesley ushered me quietly through the open morning room door, then through into the dining room.

'Who on earth is that?'

'It's his brother. Sir Chester.'

I nodded, but Wesley put his finger to his lips before I could speak again. I threw him a questioning look and he put his other hand onto the brass doorknob by way of reply. He twisted it slowly before the door opened into a sour, windowless room that had wine bottles lining the walls and a corkscrew on a dining table covered in an impossibly pristine white cloth. Wesley pointed at the doors of what looked like a cupboard in the middle of the wall. We leaned towards it and heard a blustering conversation on the other side. The sound of the men talking was crystal clear. I realised that it was an interior glassless window between this wine room and the billiards room, which probably served as a sort of bar when entertaining.

'It's like my wife has died.'

'Rather inconsiderate of you to say, considering I am actually widowed,' Lord Belfield replied.

'I had to get the locks taken off Violet's bedroom door because she wouldn't even let the maids in. She refused to let them open the curtains, so I had those taken down as well. The cook found her in the cellar this morning. Asleep on the floor with the cat beside her. "Just give me the dark," she said as I dragged her upstairs. *Give me the dark*. What on earth is that supposed to mean?' A heavy sigh. 'I'd have her put away if it weren't for the cost. If it weren't for the whores in Manchester, I'd be going insane myself.'

'Your vulgarity knows no bounds, Chester.' Lord Belfield sounded disgusted.

'At least your wife gave you a son. Born as he was seven months after the marriage, I'd wager you'd know more about vulgarity than you let on.'

'I take it this conversation is nearing its end? Shall I have Wesley fetch your coat?'

'Why in God's name did you keep that pansy on staff, out of all the staff you let go? Why didn't you keep the tall one? Philip?'

I looked to Wesley to see if his jaw was tightening and was shocked to find he was smirking. Happy to be discussed? No, not in this way. More likely that he was glad to be under Sir Chester's skin. But why?

Lord Belfield's voice drew my attention back to the wall.

'We've discussed this before. Philip was ageing out of the role in a way that was unseemly to all concerned. Wesley was a much better man for the job.'

'A man who smells like powdered sugar is no man.'

At this Wesley cocked his eyebrow and rolled his eyes to heavens. It was true that Wesley was oddly sweet smelling. However, it was completely incorrect to liken his scent to sugar. There was something gourmand about him, but it wasn't just sugar. It was creamier. A caramel smell with a floral edge that also had an oriental and green depth to it – cardamon, perhaps. I found myself edging closer to him, trying to catch his scent like a hound. Wanting to see if I could sniff out what it was about him that attracted Sir Chester's disdain.

There was a deep, heavy sigh.

'So what do you suggest we do now?' Lord Belfield's words were clipped.

'Well I'm going to keep seeding her quince until a bloody sprog pops out. There's nothing I haven't tried. Once she is truly too old, then I'll find a way to get rid of her.'

I hoped the silence that followed was filled with the disapproving look of an appalled Lord Belfield. I wasn't scandalised by the brutality of Sir Chester's words. I knew worse barbarians than the callous brother of Lord Belfield. Or I should say, considering what followed, so I thought at the time. However, what I was concerned with in that moment was the moral reaction of my employer. If Lord Belfield had as low an opinion of women as Sir Chester appeared to, it wouldn't bode well for me.

'That is truly repulsive, but I was not speaking of Violet,'

Lord Belfield said. 'Well, not exclusively, anyway. I mean what will we do with our investments.'

'Sell this house once and for all, firstly.'

An audible gasp escaped me and Wesley gave me his first ever look of annoyance, but the men on the other side of the wall were too enraged with each other to notice.

'I'm not selling Rose Hall, Chester.'

'Bloody hell, Francis, you've got to see sense. Our houses were built for families. Violet refuses to give me one and yours was decimated just as it was getting started. We can't afford these places any longer, and we need to move down to London.'

I put my hand to my chest as if to calm my heart down.

'It's expensive and a stinking sink of a place.'

'Not in places like Richmond or Hampstead. They're as green as here,' Chester said.

'But it's really not comparable, Chester. I'd never be any-where near as fond of a home in London as I am of Rose Hall. Finding a place large enough for a decent library would be close to impossible.'

'But you're selling the library,' Chester objected. 'That's what we agreed.'

'I'm selling the most valuable items,' Lord Belfield cor-rected him. 'The money from the sale will be enough to cover most of Rose Hall's costs for some time. I've someone dependable working on them right now.'

'Would you stop clinging to Rose Hall! Maybe I should burn that bloody library to the ground.' Chester's volume boxed its way into the room and made both Wesley and me clench our fists and raise them to our mouths.

'Compose yourself,' Lord Belfield said, his tone even, as though he hadn't heard a word of Chester's outburst.

'Dear brother, you're insufferable. No one bloody cares about books. Do come along – we're businessmen, not librarians. Besides, my anger at you is understandable, tethered as I am to your financial decisions. You may be my elder, but there was no need for you to be left in charge of the entire estate. I deserved more than a measly pay out. If I were in charge, I would have generated more capital than you have.'

'I disagree,' Lord Belfield said impetuously. It sounded like he was trying to assert himself as the older brother. He wasn't enjoying being challenged. To even have his decisions questioned suggested a diminishment of power. His authority was very much assailable.

'Yes, well. The point I came to make is that regardless, we must shift our investments and use our government connections to protect said investments. Father lost everything because of sugar and those goddamned abolitionists. If we'd not been rightfully compensated for the Africans lost, we'd have been paupers tin-panning on the streets.'

'You exaggerate.'

'I. Do. Not!'

'We still have the land, and the coolies are less hot headed by all accounts. More expensive for sure, but there's more money coming in now. It's steadying.'

'No, Francis. It is not. Sugar is and has always been volatile. Better we do the sensible thing and invest in things, instead of people, now. Like rubber in Indonesia and copper in Rhodesia and diamonds in South Africa. The question of the Boers will be dealt with soon enough. The most golden days of the Empire lie ahead of us, not in the past, I assure you. The plantations gave us the capital. Rose Hall is the biggest asset of course, but there's still more. All the lands we own? We haven't lost everything at all. Now we can use that to invest in the spoils of the future. I demand that you come down south with me and see for yourself. A few drinks with the right sort down in Mayfair will have you seeing my side of the coin. I will convince you.'

I could hear the thud of Chester's fist against something solid. I felt that he would make a good politician. I disliked almost everything that came out of his mouth, but nevertheless found myself riveted by his rhetoric.

'I'll be leaving now. But think of what I am saying. We must act fast, dear brother. Particularly in Africa. Half of Europe has pitched up with determination for as expansive a claim as Zeus might dare. France is sure to make a mess of it. Cool-headed Britain is needed there to really keep the natives in order. We've always been better at that. They were in charge of Haiti, were they not? Jamaica could have gone the same way. Imagine if they were running South Africa. Washing diamonds in champagne. They'd be fighting the Zulus for not making enough cheese!' Chester bellowed.

We heard Lord Belfield's footsteps creak the floorboards furthest away from us.

'It's difficult to take you seriously a lot of the time when you're so lazy with your supposedly comedic commentary, Chester,' he said, pulling the door towards him.

With this, Wesley hurriedly pointed at the door, frantically motioning for me to return to the library. I dashed back through the drawing room and slipped through the hall. I gingerly closed the library door behind me just as I heard the brothers step into the hall, and forced deep breaths into myself. I was relieved not to have been seen.

Bread from the oven was laid before us at lunch, and Baxter grumpily instructed us to hold our horses for it to cool down a touch.

'Oh, Baxter, honestly, I can't wait another second,' Wesley moaned, practically salivating.

But she gave him such a scowl that he made no moves towards the food. Slowly and quietly, I took my smallest finger and dipped it into the piccalilli I'd already ladled onto my plate. The sour-sweetness of it was too much to handle. I moaned as saliva filled my mouth, which earned me a sharp look from Baxter.

When we were finally allowed two slices each, the steamy vapours rose off the bread. Baxter slid a generous lick of butter across it, which melted givingly on spreading, and the taste of the ham, cheese, tomato and lettuce with piccalilli was nothing short of heavenly. I complimented Baxter after my first mouthful, to no response from her whatsoever. Her stoicism was almost growing endearing. Almost. I could always trust in her steely waters. Wesley and I spoke nothing of the billiard room conversation we had overheard. I am sure he refrained from gossiping to stop Baxter from learning that even though she was one of the few who had been kept on, none of their futures were certain.

The day sped past in a flash after that. I started binding the most decrepit but simple novels. I was onto my second by the day's end, using the list of almost two hundred books that Lord Belfield had provided. As the clock struck five in the hallway, I left everything as it was on the table, desperate to begin my nightly routine as soon as I was released from the library.

I barely remember what we ate for dinner, or how I passed the time between then and the stillness of the night. My memory resumes when Wesley rapped his nails on my door twice. I put a cushion at the end of my bed and sat between his legs again, happy to now have a ritual with the sweetest-smelling friend of my life thus far. I had arrived at Rose Hall only days ago, but I felt a kinship with Wesley that could have been forged over many months rather than weeks.

'What's a coolie?' he asked as he scratched my scalp for me and I leaned back into him further.

'Hmmm?'

'What's a coolie?'

'Oh ...' He'd evidently not understood that part of the discussion. 'An Indian worker. Not West Indian. I mean ... not an African in the West Indies.' I hoped the gesticulating I was doing that felt senseless to me was making sense to Wesley somehow. 'As in someone from India who's gone to the Caribbean to work.'

'You would have thought we'd have given them less confusing names by now.' I was sure he was shaking his head. 'Why would you give two places so far away from each other the same name?'

His innocence endeared him to me. I felt like I was discussing places that had never known famine or slavery.

'Well, the Indians are used to the heat and are comparatively rather civilised, actually. They're doing well in Kenya,

South Africa, Trinidad. The heat doesn't bother them, so whether they're in fields or working at an office desk they won't faint or get scorched skin like we tend to. Less prone to disease too, obviously.'

'Oh. Well, that's good.'

It was my turn for questions.

'What's made Sir Chester's wife so ill, do you think?'

He paused. 'Lady Violet?'

'Yes,' I said.

Wesley sighed before gathering three strands to start braiding.

'She's in mourning for Lady Persephone still, isn't she. They were ever so close.'

'Oh, they were?'

'Hmmm,' Wesley said. 'They were ever so fond of each other.'

Chapter Six

From all that I had gleaned in the weeks following my arrival, this Christmas at Rose Hall was set to be quiet. Not only was the pallor of mourning draped over the house because of the absence of Lady Persephone and the savagely reduced staff, but Daniel, the lord and lady's son who was boarding at a school near the Scottish Borders, had chosen to remain there for Christmas.

Lord Belfield departed for Sir Chester's two days before Christmas Eve with the mastiff in a carriage.

I came down to the library on the morning of the 22nd December to find the library door locked, the key nowhere to be seen. Lord Belfield was obviously protective of his collection; although he hadn't locked me in again since my first day, he habitually secured the door. But he had made no mention of how I was to continue my work in his absence. I would have loved to have it open for my personal perusal and hide away in there with a book of my choosing, one that I wasn't tasked to work on. Still, I supposed, if the work took longer due to circumstances outside my control, that might buy me more time in the shelter of Rose Hall. I had nowhere to go next.

With no master to feed, Baxter all but disappeared during the days and this left Wesley and me with the house to ourselves, and less to do than the Vestal Virgins. Lying around talking, Wesley was filled with questions about all of my Christmases past. I told him it had just been me and my father since my grandmother's passing, and it was left to me to fix the Christmas meal. I wasn't that good at cooking, but my father had never complained. And one Christmas he had been soft enough to bring me a crate of womanly reading to swoon over. Sweet novels with happy endings of marriage and contentment.

Wesley told me about his family, who were poor by anyone's standards, but he grew up with more laughter than I would know how to handle. I didn't ask him why he wouldn't return home for visits, although I could have a good guess.

Christmas Eve arrived, and I read the opening of *A Christmas Carol* to Wesley by the fire in the drawing room. He lay his head in my lap like a puppy. Anyone looking at us might have thought we were lovers. I was growing to love him in the way Plato loved Aristotle. That is to say, there was something high minded about my feelings for him. I felt his innocence merited protection. Unmonitored as we were, nothing but purity was brewing between us. We went to midnight mass and were afforded a ride back from our neighbours – I suppose the Christmas cheer in the air swept away any whiff of scandal related to my presence.

On Christmas Day, Baxter wished me a Happy Christmas first. She was no more talkative than usual but there was a levity in her step. Lord Belfield had left us a joint of roast beef and Baxter spiced it up nicely and served it with roast potatoes, parsnips, carrots and Brussels sprouts. We ate in silence, and she went to bed soon after, leaving Wesley and me to sit by the fire again. He had swindled some brandy from the cellar, which was so strong that it turned our minds woozy in just a few sips. Wesley danced for me, which caused me to laugh so much I got the hiccups, and that only encouraged him to move his limbs more widely and accidentally knock over an antique jug. I was devastated, but you'd never know that from how much I was still laughing. In our drunkenness, he told me that it would not be that big a calamity.

Boxing Day fell on a Sunday that year. After midnight mass on the Friday evening, Wesley and I didn't feel like going on the Sunday because we were a little 'churched out'. It wasn't a joyous thing to do. Even though it was Christmas and it was sweet to see the local children holding their candles and such, there was still such a solemnity about the proceedings. I have always felt there should be a celebratory air around Christmas. Being with Wesley and rambling over the hills made that feeling come to the fore between us. We were work free and giggly.

That afternoon we trundled into the village to have another look at the nativity scene at the front of the church. It was quite gaudy really, but the convivial scene was enough to inspire a litany of questions about Bethlehem which knocked into questions about Palestine which knocked into me telling him about Father Christmas being a Turk and ravishing him with all I knew of the Ottomans. Wesley's deference towards me was sweet and mewing. Though he was taller than me, there was no doubt that I was the big sister who knew so much about the world. Just as I was telling him that it was Rome and Constantinople that had spread Christianity far and wide, we came over a hill and Rose Hall came back into view, accompanied by a wailing. He gasped and I stretched my neck further out of my scarf. We quickened our pace and as we came closer to Rose Hall the wailing got louder and louder.

Lord Belfield sat on the stone steps in front of the open door with his face in his hands. A striking man – who could only be Sir Chester - was marching up and down the gravel with a woman's shoe in his hand. So forceful was the bluster of his personality that as we were approaching I remembered that this was the first time I had laid eyes on him. The man I had imagined as I skulked behind a cupboard door with Wesley some weeks ago was not anything like the figure who now paced around the carriage ahead of me. A good six inches taller than Lord Belfield, he had a very slim but athletic frame with broad shoulders and a tiny waist which made his top half seem quite triangular. His perfectly combed light brown hair had been pomaded to within an inch of its life. He spun around at the sound of our crunching footsteps and his face lost its contortions at the sight of us. He had the impossibly clean look of the upper classes. Devilishly smooth-shaven and peachy mark-free skin with a high forehead and angular cheekbones. Only his green eyes, narrowed at the sight of me, betrayed the wickedness beneath. He undressed me from toe to head and his lip curled when his eyes rested on my bosom.

'Good golly!'

At this exclamation, Lord Belfield looked from Sir Chester to Wesley and me and then his eyes caught mine. His sheepish expression looked almost apologetic but I wasn't sure if it was because of the lascivious way his brother was assessing my form, or the calamity of the scene before us.

'She won't get out of the carriage,' he said. Then, catching himself because he remembered that I had never met his family before formally, he rephrased, as he stood and brushed himself. 'Do forgive us, Miss Granger. I'm afraid Lady Violet has found herself ... You see, this is the first time she has been here since my wife's passing. I'm afraid she is somewhat ... overwrought.'

I focused my gaze on the shoe dangling from Sir Chester's hand and Lord Belfield went on to explain.

'Ah yes ... Well you see—'

Sir Chester abruptly interrupted him. 'Her shoe came off when I was trying to help her out,' he said, before placing the pipe back between his lips. The smell of the tobacco was rather sour, like oolong tea that had been steeped in apple vinegar.

'Chester, this is Miss Granger, the young woman restoring my book collection.'

'Yes, yes. I guessed that dear boy.' He only nodded at me.

All through this introduction the wailing had descended into whimpering. I dared not address Sir Chester yet. His air was threatening, somehow. And yet I couldn't bear the sounds of such clear distress without trying to help.

'May I meet Lady Violet too please?' I asked Lord Belfield.

He looked at me with surprise. As if my self-possession had startled him and he was embarrassed by it. I felt like Matron turning up in the boys' bedrooms, demanding to see the drawer where he kept his underwear.

'Why ... Yes. That's ... I'm not sure if ... But, yes, come round here perhaps and ...'

It occurred to me that when he was in the library talking with Chester, he was the older brother denying financial access to a future he was trying to avoid. He could speak to Chester sternly because of their familiarity, but also because he was defending everything he cared for. I wondered if his current fluster was because he was being compelled to air out the sodden family laundry.

I followed him around to the side of the carriage to see a tall blonde woman in the furthest corner of the carriage, looking truly bedraggled in a black crepe dress, with a blotchy reddened face and a wet stockinged foot next to her still neatly booted one.

She stared at me, with some curiosity, her breathing rapid.

'Perhaps the gentlemen could leave me with my lady for a brief while,' I said, turning boldly to Lord Belfield. Looking relieved but still flustered, Lord Belfield accepted. 'Yes. Ummm. Thank you. That probably is best. Chester, let's go and get a drink inside, shall we?'

He exhaled with relief. He had been longing to scuttle away. The embarrassment of so much emotion being on display, I imagined. The scene much more fitting for a melodrama set in a Mediterranean country. The Capulets and Montagues would have been more cool-headed if they had hailed from Cumbria rather than Verona.

'Excellent idea.' As if he had just finished a good game of cricket. You wouldn't think his petrified wife had just wet herself.

'May I?' I said, pointing at the shoe dangling from his hand.

He walked towards me holding it before himself. I gingerly grabbed it by the shoestrings, careful that our hands wouldn't touch.

Sir Chester and Lord Belfield turned and entered the house. Wesley, who had been standing there staring at the ground the whole time, only looked up at me once they had gone. Wordlessly, he nodded at me and rubbed my forearm before going back inside himself.

I sat in the doorway to the carriage as the horse whinnied and scratched the ground with its front hoof.

We sat in silence for some minutes, and I only looked up at Lady Violet a few times as her breathing calmed down.

She was the one to speak first. 'Well, this is quite the introduction.'

I chuckled. 'These are not normal circumstances, I take it?'

'No.' She sneered at me. 'Obviously not.'

It was as if being found dishevelled by someone as beneath her as I was, meant she had to reassert which of us had the right to ask questions. Who even had the right to feel sorry for whom? She had detected my pity and needed to refuse it in order to regain her composure.

'I'm sorry.'

She seemed to unbend a little. 'I told him I was not ready to come, and I was practically bursting for the loo, but he refused to ask the driver to stop and now ...'

'Oh, it's all right. It's just water really, isn't it?'

She looked at me strangely. As if my dismissal was evidence of my own weirdness.

'So, you bind books for a living, do you?'

'Yes,' I responded.

'I didn't even know that was an option for women, frankly,' she scoffed.

'Lord Belfield doesn't feel it should be.'

'Well, most men wouldn't, would they? Look what happened to Mary Wollstonecraft.' She adjusted her undergarment. 'Punished in the worst ways for daring to think freely.'

'Yes, but aren't we both better off for her having tried?' I said.

I smiled at her. She smiled back.

Having formed at least a little bit of familiarity I decided to venture: 'Why won't you come inside, Lady Violet?'

She wasn't offended by the question. 'It's not the whole house. I don't want to go in any of the rooms she lived in. I don't know why ... but I just can't. And Chester forces me to do things he knows I don't want to do. He's insufferable.'

'I see,' I said.

She deflated somewhat having said it.

'This isn't how she would want you to feel after everything that's happened,' I offered.

'How do you know what she would have wanted? You never even met her.'

'Well, no, but—' I felt hot.

'I assume people have been gossiping about the two of us, have they?'

'Most definitely not. I assure you Lady Violet. I spoke out

68

of turn.' I could see that she was nettled, and I was eager to change the subject.

'What if we only went in the rooms she didn't use? You could come in round the back. Wash yourself downstairs. I could bring you another dress and we can go straight to your bedroom. Maybe you can talk to your husband there.'

'Chester and I don't share a bedroom,' Violet protested. I'd forgotten that people of their class wouldn't.

'Well . . . that makes it easier, then,' I countered.

'I don't want to see him,' Violet said.

'Neither do I.'

I knew that I was stepping out of line, but at this she laughed. She got up of her own volition and came out of the carriage. She put her unbooted foot on the ground and winced from the chill. I took her hand, and we hobbled around Rose Hall and down some stone steps to the kitchen. As we entered, Baxter kept her back to us as she stirred a pot on the stove. I knew she could sense Violet's presence but was choosing not to embarrass her by acknowledging the strangeness of the scene.

I felt valiant for having gained Lady Violet's trust so quickly. With her hand in mine, I was emboldened. My sensitivity could fill the cracks in the house that felt like it was crumbling around me. I was silly enough to think my coming here could save them all. In my naivety I did not realise that Sir Chester's presence would imperil me in a way I never had been imperilled before. This man who had ripped the shoe off his wife's foot rather than give her the comfort I just had.

Chapter Seven

A few weeks into January, the warmth and spice of Christmas seeming far behind us, Lord Belfield asked me a question while we were both working in the library which shattered the illusion of serenity that I'd festooned myself in. With the new year, he had begun to join me each day. For what purpose, he made no effort to explain.

During Violet and Chester's stay, only the brothers dined together. Violet ate all her meals in her room. Every other day or so she would go for a walk in the gardens, and I could see her from the library window as I worked. She was quite green fingered. Pulling up a root or a weed that had been strong enough to sprout in spite of the cold. Pruning a few trees or shrubs. Even planting some of the herbaceous borders in preparation for the warmer weather. It all looked a bit spartan even after she had done what she had, but I knew the planting of seeds and shearing of bushes and such only gave out in glorious abundance many months after the initial work had been put in.

Being a child of the city, I had many questions I would have asked her if I'd felt bold enough, or if she'd given any indication that she wanted to continue our initial intimacy. But perhaps our introduction had been too embarrassing, for she barely acknowledged me. Not even Lord Belfield and I had discussed it, in spite of working close enough together in the library on some days. Again, he would have to be the one to broach the subject of Lady Violet and Sir Chester's evidently volatile and mostly estranged relationship from each other. Did they not spend much time in each other's company because when they did, their conflicts engulfed them? Had they once been passionate, and had the absence of any children cooled their ardour to the point where only pain and resentment resided in the bed where they had first sown the seeds of their affection? These were the questions I pondered.

But the first question out of Lord Belfield's mouth on that day in January had nothing to do with his brother and his wife, as I had hoped. It was still early, long before one might hear Chester blustering his way down the corridor or see Violet in the garden muttering to herself as she picked at the leaves of a bush. Lord Belfield asked his question as if we were in the flow of an ongoing conversation.

'Some women are going to university for their own edification, even though they shan't be awarded a full degree on completion. Does that interest you?'

A bold and unexpected bolt to be lanced at me out of the January blue. The way he asked gave me the impression he had been thinking about putting it to me for a while. Almost as if he had conversations with me in his mind when I wasn't around. Or maybe that's what I hoped was the case.

'It's not something I've ever considered before, honestly, Lord Belfield,' I responded unblinkingly.

'What? Speak up fair lady, you're as far away from me as Juliet was from Romeo on the balcony.'

On New Year's Day, Lord Belfield and Sir Chester had moved another table into the library at the opposite end to where I was working. Lord Belfield and I faced each other from our stations, but he rarely spoke to me, and I dared not look at him. I felt happy to have a silent companion while I worked. Lord Belfield was nothing like my father, but one similarity was that we were comfortable working soundlessly together in the same space. Furthermore, he seemed so much less curmudgeonly than I had first thought, especially compared to his coldly callous and calculating brother. The stone regard with which Chester looked at me made me feel that I would be slashed in two if he stared at me in anger for too long. Such evil power in his gaze, like a male Medusa.

Perhaps I should have suspected that Lord Belfield would not forever leave me to follow his instructions without supervision. Although my father's silent presence had at times caused me disquiet as we worked, to once again have stoic male company absorbed opposite me was rather reassuring. I watched Lord Belfield working a lot, snatching glances whenever I could. Hoping to see something revealing – to no avail. His face was too often expressionless, and I worked better because of it. Every few days or so, Lord Belfield started our sessions with more instructions on which books needed rebinding and how and with what. Apart from that, we focused on what lay beneath our hands, and never each other, from 7 a.m. until 5 p.m. daily, with an hour for lunch at midday. The first time he spoke more than monosyllabically to me in three weeks, other than to give an instruction, was to repeat his question about my future. I exaggerate. Perhaps it was just two weeks. January does have the tendency to drag on.

'Don't you think you would do well by yourself to remain in education?'

'I said I have never considered it, Lord Belfield.'

'Well, why ever not?' he asked briskly, cleaning the nib of his fountain pen on a square of navy cloth. 'It's either that or become a governess really, isn't it?'

How to say that I had never considered that profession because no one had ever considered me for it? To have been sent to school at all felt a luxury on the street we lived on, where most girls began working just after losing their first set of teeth. At sixteen my teachers felt me modern for having the profession of bookbinding so readily available to me because of my father's tutelage. As did I. I recognised the fortune I had afforded to me by birth, and I never questioned it. Until I had to, but by then it was too late. Even with no home and no family to speak of, it was bookbinding that I trusted to keep me afloat.

'I know more of the needs of books than the needs of children, Lord Belfield,' I said, my voice cracking.

'Yes, well be that as it may, this profession is hardly respectable for a woman. My brother's outburst before Christmas, for instance. Hardly talk a woman should be privy to.'

How did he know we had been listening?

'There's a crack in the adjoining room window,' he explained, as if he read my thoughts. 'Even if I hadn't heard you clattering about in the window, I could quite clearly see two bodies pressed against the wood like an amateur Sherlock and Watson at a variety show.'

Such a blithely delivered revelation. I steeled myself for my sure-to-follow termination.

'Lord Belfield, I am truly sorry. Please believe I have never experienced such shame.'

'I doubt that. For is it not shame that delivered you here?'

I brought my hands up to my mouth to stifle the sob that spluttered out of me.

'Miss Granger, please. The dramatics aren't necessary. I am a well-travelled man. Many experiences are laid at the feet of a young man of means while on his grand tour, and most of Europe's maidens were in much more vulnerable positions than the one you find yourself in. I assumed you had done something that others would consider irreproachably sinful. However, I don't feel you deserve to be punished for what I might guess were some brief moments of passion.'

'Well ... Thank you,' I said, wiping away the tears and staring at him with equal amounts relief and disbelief.

'I can see you are somewhat surprised by my leniency. But did you honestly not think I would piece it together eventually?'

'Piece what together?' My heart was thumping in my chest. I had no idea how much he knew. Had he spoken to my father?

'You arrive with a hefty bag of not very much and a

74

concocted story with more holes in it than a wheel of cheese from Emmental.'

He looked at me pityingly, as if it were something he'd known as soon as I had knocked on his front door. As if he knew my fate before I did.

'Not only did you not ask me if you could return to see your father at Christmas, but you've not even sent him a letter since your arrival.'

Now that was a glaring mistake on my part. Lord Belfield would have expected me to keep my father abreast of my progress.

'Well, you're a lucky one in some respects. You're young enough to not see when you've left yourself without much to protect your future. However, Miss Granger, I do believe you to be intelligent. You are a conniving young lady. I should know, because I married one and on discovery of her manipulations, I chose to be impressed rather than humiliated and married her rather quickly.'

Lady Persephone. My breath caught in my throat. It was the first time he had mentioned her since our first meeting.

'But you see, you're a vixen whose foot has just escaped a snapping trap. Forgive me, but you need to be more sentient than primal if you are to survive. Such short-term thinking will not save you from destitution in the future. A position as a governess would be most suitable for someone of your learning.'

He was such an odd fish. I could not fathom why he would want to steer my life in whatever direction. I was neither a family member nor his ward. But his treatment suggested a duty of care that was unexpected. Furthermore, I resented that my bookbinding skills were being so summarily dismissed. Why should I throw my many years of training to the side on the whim of this lowly aristocrat who had suddenly decided to shuffle me from room to room as if I were a figurine in a niece's dollhouse?

'I thank you Lord Belfield, but I do already have my trade.'

He waved a hand as if to dismiss my words. 'No one will employ a female bookbinder, so put that thought out of your head at once. You'll end up on the streets selling the only thing you have readily available to you. There is no way for a girl as intelligent as yourself to succeed without losing your honour. This is not Italy, where a courtesan receives a pension as long as she is industrious enough.'

I blinked at him, unable to speak. Is this how he truly saw me? I felt chastised, because I had believed bookbinding to be a trade of respectability that would be far more accepting of me as a woman than so many others. My eyes stung, and I was unable to stop the tears from flowing freely down my face.

'You came here without a plan. Now you have one. You will leave here with a reference to at least get a start in some house with children who will hopefully adore you as much as Wesley does.'

Of course, I knew how Wesley felt about me, but to hear it from the mouth of someone I didn't believe paid attention to him, me, or us as friends made my heart glow despite his bleak assessment of my circumstances.

'I trust you enough to leave you among the possessions I value the most. It goes against my instincts to leave this door unlocked when I am not inside.'

The library door was open and at that moment, in walked

Lady Violet silently, carrying books. If my head had been down focusing on work, as usual, I would not have heard her entering.

'Good morning, m'lady,' I said, which caused Lord Belfield to turn his head towards his sister-in-law in the doorway.

'Good morning, Miss Granger.' She nodded at me.

'An impromptu visit from an earnest reader!' Lord Belfield exclaimed.

'Well, I might visit more if it weren't locked outside of shop hours.' She glanced in my direction briefly and then walked towards Lord Belfield's table and set down the three volumes in her hands. 'I forgot I had these.'

'These are—' Lord Belfield started.

'The Greek books Persephone was trying to convert me with,' Lady Violet finished.

Lord Belfield picked them up one by one. 'Now let's see what she gave you. *The Trojan Women . . . The Iliad.*'

'And *Jason and the Golden Fleece*. I mean, it is all quite swashbuckling stuff. They're all marvellous but I really seek something a bit more . . . pastoral.'

'Restrained,' Lord Belfield suggested.

'If you say so. But reading about these impassioned, intrepid Europeans in impossibly fatal situations always leaves me feeling dehydrated.' Lady Violet tittered.

'I suppose Jason is left feeling quite spent by the end.'

Lord Belfield inhaled sharply.

'Yes, precisely.'

He sneezed.

'Bless you,' Lady Violet and I said in unison. My exclamation brought me back into her attention. She looked at me again and I realised that during their interaction she had forgotten I was there. The way they spoke to each other was platonic and warm and convivial. Brother-in-law and sister-in-law who had known each other for years. He had lost a wife and she had lost a close friend. Now here they were, bonding over books. It lit me up inside to witness.

'Might you try reading *Tess of the d'Urbervilles* or *Far from the Madding Crowd*, m'lady?' I asked.

'Hardy,' Lord Belfield said.

'Thomas Hardy,' Lady Violet said, quickly asserting that his offering was not necessary, because she knew who I was talking about.

'He does tend towards the maudlin after a while, does our Mr Hardy,' Lord Belfield suggested.

'As do I,' Lady Violet replied, taking a seat in the bay window.

Lord Belfield nodded, meeting her gaze directly. I got the sense that she knew him better than he knew her.

'Regardless, Miss Granger, Francis doesn't consider anything as contemporary as Thomas Hardy for this hallowed chamber,' she teased.

'Yes, well. A library is surely for books that have proved the test of time. These books are precious mostly because of their age, of course.'

'That one isn't,' I said, scratching my cheek. To think, only moments before Lady Violet turned up I had been so thoroughly upset.

'Which one?' Lord Belfield asked.

He had to know the one I was talking about. His hand was on it.

'The bright green one at the top of the stack there. The rest are old, but that one isn't. Look how fresh the leather is!'

I had never noticed it. It only caught my eye now because of how clearly it gleamed itself out as 'new' among the other aged tomes it sat on top of.

'It's my wife's diary. I've been working my way up to read it.'

He shooed his hand off it, which suggested he didn't want me to ask any more questions. Why keep it here, away from her letters? I longed to read it. My mouth was wet at the prospect of getting to know the daily musings of the fair-skinned blonde lady of the photographs I had seen. Lord Belfield probably kept it locked away in a desk. Or the cage with the exotic bound books. The ones from Timbuktu and Persia and Japan.

'I can lend you my Hardys, Lady Violet. I have both the aforementioned in my room.'

'How kind,' Lady Violet said.

'You're very welcome to them. There are also a few of Lord Belfield's oldies that might meet your taste in spite of their age.'

'Honestly!' said Lord Belfield, feigning offence.

'I will have to discuss my literary needs with you further,' Lady Violet told me.

I shivered with delight at the thought. I wasn't so naive as to think that being as well read as I was could put me into the same class as Lord Belfield and Lady Violet, but in spite of my recently aired faux pas, I felt this conversation was proof that I was at least on their level in an intellectual sense.

'Lady Violet,' Lord Belfield said, reaching for the pipe in his pocket. 'Do you have an opinion on Miss Granger's professional intentions? Bookbinder, university student or governess?'

Her eyes narrowed into not quite a sneer as she looked at him, then her gaze relaxed as she turned to consider me.

'What would you like to do, Miss Granger?' she asked slowly. Not patronising, but her tone suggested I should take time to cogitate before responding.

I looked at Lord Belfield, expecting that he might be watching me with intent, but instead he was poking the tobacco into his pipe. I turned back to Lady Violet, who was patiently waiting with her lips only slightly pursed. Was I taking too long?

'I . . . I have to say that I am not yet sure. I think they all may prove to be fulfilling to me for different reasons. I think if my ability to support myself weren't of issue then I would immediately choose university, because that would offer my mind the most chance to breathe and expand and learn.' I felt like I was standing at the front of the class reciting a poem or speech I had stayed up late to learn by heart.

'Interestingly, finding a husband at university would be the wisest of choices. Good conversation and someone who you're assured has the ability to truly look after you,' he said before going in for his first puff. I stared at him. Was he deluded? A woman in my position would never be accepted at such an institution – and even if I were, what gentleman would set aside my status? Lady Violet looked at Lord Belfield with what appeared to be a hint of disdain.

'Now, Miss Granger, wash your face before you go down for lunch.'

I rose from the table fatigued. I felt as though I had just

been beaten within an inch of my life, equal parts valiant for having endured the brutality of Lord Belfield's truth-telling, and battered from his statements landing like sharp slaps. Then for Lady Violet to turn up and transform the library into a sort of pre-revolutionary Parisian salon before chewing over my future. It was all quite dizzying.

'Thank you, Lord Belfield,' I whispered as I walked past him, his head back down to his papers. His air of superiority irked me. The way he saw it, I was merely a piece to be shuffled from square to square as he saw fit. I knew that I should have felt gratitude, but in truth, my main feeling was one of annoyance.

Just as I came to the door he said, 'Oh, and Miss Granger?'

'Yes?' I spun around.

'Don't think for a second that you can eavesdrop without consequence,' he said, his voice suddenly flinty. 'And if there is any brandy-drinking to be done in this house, it will be done by me. If I catch you straying outside the bounds of your employment again, I won't hesitate to send you back to your father.'

It was as if a viper had been circling my feet without my knowledge, and now it had struck. I had got too comfortable, and he had reminded me in no uncertain terms. He was not merely an employer. He was my master, and he was frighteningly omnipresent.

I gave a disconcerted nod before spinning back round to escape and leave him and Lady Violet to discuss God knew what. I was embarrassed that my admonition had come in front of her, when I'd hoped we might become friends of a kind. But she was looking at neither of us, her attention directed out of the window towards the hills.

Lord Belfield blew a smoke ring, then turned his head away from me, dismissing me. I had underestimated him so completely. He had watched me for weeks, giving not one clue he was assessing me so thoroughly. I wondered if his wife had feared him as much as I now did.

Chapter Eight

One might have thought that, having been so thoroughly unearthed by Lord Belfield, I might have become less mischievous or at least reduced my audacity. I had clearly underestimated his intelligence, and my reprimand had left me shedding a secret tear, though I would never have admitted it to Wesley. I could not afford to lose this commission and my place at Rose Hall. As it was, I only had a matter of months before I would need to find another place to go, and Lord Belfield had made it clear he didn't believe I could pursue a trade as a bookbinder. My future looked dire indeed, unless he would help me when the work was finished.

I reflected on what I knew of my mercurial employer. Lord Belfield clearly had a temper when he was pushed, and perhaps I'd be a fool to trust him, but in other moments I had seen his generosity. Our Christmas presents had been in the kitchen on Boxing Day evening. Bolts of cloth for sewing: a dark blue tartan for Wesley, grey-green felt for Baxter and a damask-pink cloth with a print of indigo and red currants for me. I'd never worn anything that bright and delicate. I felt like a debutante who'd been promised the chance to finally 'come out' in the spring on the horizon. There was also a box of oranges and dates. The sheer consideration of it all had overwhelmed me. No one had silently specified my desires since my grandmother's passing.

Many nights Baxter mended things on the kitchen table after dinner. There was a hum throughout the house before people's lights went out. When I first arrived I had enjoyed having so much uninterrupted reading time. I would take a book or two from the library to paw through that evening. Soon this became too repetitive and lonesome. I was just waiting until it was quiet enough for Wesley to join me in my room. So, instead, I tried to spend time with Baxter. I wished I could trust her enough to ask the questions I had about everything. It wasn't to be. She spurned any effort I made to bond with her somehow.

Being so used to being ignored by my father made it a bit less unbearable, I suppose. Whole stretches of days would go by without him ever making the effort to speak to me.

I had little idea what I was doing with cloth as expensive as the stuff Lord Belfield had gifted us. Baxter had a few paper patterns that were kept in a cupboard and I just copied her. A skirt was less difficult than I had imagined. The notes on the pattern were in French, so I told her what some of them meant. She remained grumpy and too taciturn for friendly conversation. So we just sat there, sewing in silence. At least I wasn't alone. But still ...

I wanted to know more about Lady Persephone's death. Ever since I had arrived at Rose Hall, it felt as if there was something unsaid about the tragedy, a thread that if unpicked would unravel everything. I was not afraid of a little disruption, though. Drowning in a river at night struck me as an unlikely accident, and if Lady Persephone had been intentionally killed then my last encounter with Lord Belfield at least made me wonder what he was capable of.

I resolved to start by finding out who knew Lady Persephone best. I was deeply curious about the story behind her horse-riding lady's maid, with a skin colour that originated in deepest Africa.

My father had printed leaflets and other literature for Quakers, who were known to be a community founded on goodwill and humility. However, from the discussions I once heard my father having with a Quaker minister, I suspected them of being rather arrogant in their stoicism. I would not have had the temerity to speak up from my position in the kitchen, eavesdropping on the conversation next door in the workshop. However, it sounded misguided to revel in bringing about the end of a subjugation of African peoples that our ancestors were the ones to have enslaved in the first place.

The minister spoke of Africans like children. Something I could not agree with, because since freedom their ascent had been so rapid. How could a whole sector of humanity once viewed as animals now be writing books and teaching in universities and the like? We had been lied to. The picture of Lady Persephone's lady's maid proved this to me. She wasn't performing haughtiness or playing dress-up.

Her sophistication looked as natural as the soft gentility of her smile. She looked like she was born for the life she was living.

Two days after Lord Belfield upended my world, I left church in an orderly queue of parishioners. The priest stood by the church doors to shake hands and exchange a few kindly words before his congregation exited into the January cold.

'Nice to see you settling in, young lady,' he said, clasping me in a clammy grip. In my experience, men of the cloth were quite learned folk, but something about him irked me. The smell of him, first of all, was somewhere between offal and the dank emissions from the corners of a pond that got no light. For him to be a man of God was astonishing, smelling like that and speaking of Africans having an inherent inferiority. It appalled me to reflect on the inferiority of Africans being one of the favourite themes of the clergy, but moreover I'd never met one that smelled as bad as him. Nevertheless, it made the gulps of the crisp outside air all the sweeter.

The women from the village had become used to me by now, and they felt confident enough to engage me in a bit of tittle-tattle outside.

'You can see Baxter's been feeding you well. You won't fit in that dress for much longer if you're not careful.'

'Oh, leave her alone. She's a growing girl.'

'I didn't mean anything by it. I were just saying.'

It was thoroughly entertaining to have one's body and personhood being discussed so ardently. I should have known their names, and I'm sure I had been told them, but by this point I had to pretend.

'We saw the master of the house going past on his horse with his brother. He's looking a lot better, poor chap.'

'Grief takes time,' Wesley piped up beside me. This shocked them. To be interrupted firstly, but secondly because Wesley was offering wisdom they felt more qualified to possess.

'It's awful all the same. She were ever such a beauty. We both said so. Didn't we? She were very pale, but not sickly looking. Elegant.'

'Wesley said that the accident shook you all,' I said. 'No one saw Lady Persephone go down to the river on the night in question?'

The women pushed away from the church door, as if shielding Jesus on the cross above them from the dastardly details of Lady Persephone's passing.

'*The night in question.* Would you hear her? The right poshest of sorts, you are.'

'No one saw her, but we know she fell in because Pawsey, the delivery boy, he brought a snatch of her skirt fabric in from the bridge the day after, didn't he? The police weren't even involved until then. We thought she had just run away when Lord Belfield came round the village the next day asking if anyone had seen her. He went crazy when he was handed that fabric. Understandable really. But still, to see a grown man howl like a baby like that ... Heartbreaking.'

'So the police did get involved?' I asked.

The two ladies nodded. 'We sent Pawsey to get Sir Chester, but he were halfway to London already. Had left the night she went missing, apparently. Had to turn right back around once he got there and received the telegram Lord Belfield sent him at the post office.'

'We could hear the howling of Lady Violet and Lord Belfield from here. Carried on the wind, that did.'

We fell into silence as if we were listening to see if their cries persisted.

I could breathe in the suspicion that Sir Chester wasn't quite in the clear. Even if he had left that night, he could still have done something criminal on his way to London. Attacking his brother's wife and making a run for it, for example. Also, any alibi he had conjured up from someone he could comfortably pay off was no real alibi at all. I couldn't brazenly pinpoint him as a suspect yet, but I could clear up who else was on the list.

'So, it was just Lord Belfield, Lady Violet and Miss Sibyl at the house until Sir Chester got back, was it?' I pushed.

'Precisely,' they told me. 'I wouldn't put it past the nigger girl she had to push her in, either. She were probably jealous or summat.'

And with that utterance, all chances of closeness with those women was cut off for me. They didn't say the word with any malice. It was just descriptive. But regardless, their lax accusation of Sibyl was clearly based on nothing but suspicion because of her colour.

'Unlikely she'd push her employer into a river in the dead of night and rob herself of a job and potential freedom,' I retorted. 'We know how much her people value their freedom, all things considered, don't we?'

They both cocked their heads to the side and nodded with downturned mouths. It was something they'd never thought to consider.

'God bless you both,' Wesley said to smooth our departure. 'Wrap up warm, you two. The wind coming over the dale heading back up to Rose Hall will slice you in two, I promise yer.'

That night I asked Wesley:

'What did you think of Lady Persephone's lady's maid?'

'Sibyl? She was all right, mostly.'

Two days before I had vowed, once I'd patted my face dry, not to tell Wesley of Lord Belfield's discovery of our misdeeds. I was scared that if he was frightened of us being more closely monitored than he had imagined, he would stop coming to my room.

'How do you mean? Did you not like her?'

'No, I thought she were lovely. But she weren't very open. I don't even know where she were from, really. I don't think she were born in Africa or the islands or wherever. She grew up in Liverpool. I mean you can't mistake what they sound like, can ya?'

'She was from Liverpool?'

'Yeah. She told me that before she cooled off on me, 'cos of something I said.'

'What did you say?' I asked.

'Well, I didn't mean to offend her.' He was stalling.

'What did you say?' I wouldn't allow it to go unsaid.

'I asked her if she had a tail.'

I pulled myself away from the grip of his hands on my hair. The heat generated from sitting between his legs evaporated immediately and my back felt colder than before.

'Why would you ask her that?' I said, looking up at him.

His hands were in mid-air, the right hand holding the comb as if it had been frozen when I moved away.

'I had no idea it was that bad, I promise,' he said, lowering his hands at the same time as his head. 'I just ...'

The cold had descended into my bowels, and I shivered as it began to spread.

'Miss Granger, don't look at me like that ... please ...'

It struck me that I was on the precipice of losing something precious between us. I did love him at this point. Until Wesley said what he did, there had been something incredibly childlike about the budding friendship between us. There was nothing childlike about us now. Now I could see that in order for our bond to continue deepening I had to see him as a man who had made a grave mistake, then forgive him. It also wasn't lost on me that many a person would see my indignation as an overreaction. Wesley's misguided statement just reflected how most Englishmen viewed their darker brethren. Even someone as supposedly radical and kind-hearted as William Blake had been unable to divorce jungle motifs from his poetry and art concerning Africans. Why would I expect Wesley to be any more enlightened than the average passer-by? Although I had access to books only normally made available to the elite, I could understand where Wesley's thoughts came from. We had all supped from the ladle that stirred a cauldron of collected myths and misunderstandings.

'OK ... all right.'

'I'm sorry honestly. I'm really sorry I said it.'

For some reason I felt the need to say something less declarative than 'thank you' and less appeasing than 'apology accepted'. It wasn't my place. So I said nothing.

'Will you let me finish your hair?'

I swivelled back round and settled back between his legs.

'It was my brother who said it first,' he continued. My silence was obviously an invitation for him to keep going.

'When we were kids, we'd play in the barn and we'd be having a laugh and making up worlds and going on adventures. Well, my brother would pretend to be Dr Livingstone and we'd be the Africans and we'd dance around and make noises and have such a laugh and everything and he'd tell us to shake our tails and we'd do it and just be laughing and everything. I just thought that's what made them different from us. 'Cos otherwise, it's just the colour, isn't it?'

'They don't have tails, Wesley,' I said quietly.

'Yeah, well I know that now, don't I!' he said, nudging my shoulder.

He finished combing my hair and I had no idea what to say to make it better. What he'd said had made me sad to my core.

'What was she like?' I finally asked. 'Sibyl?'

'Baxter didn't like her. Said she thought too much of herself for a negresse. Oh, and the other staff were put off by her putting on airs.' He considered for a moment. 'She read as many books as you did. She said it was because Lady Persephone wanted her to read them before she did to make sure they were worth her time and such. But I doubt that were true because Lady Persephone didn't really enjoy reading as much as her embroidery. Sibyl were always cajoling her to finish. Or maybe I'm just saying that because Sibyl read faster than what she did. They were both proper readers. Always talking about books and mining the library and whatnot. They loved to sing, too. Sibyl is a soprano and Lady P were a contralto. Is that it? They were always going back and forth about it whose voice was what. All the qualities

91

and whatnot. I don't know what them Italian words mean really, but they sounded lovely.'

'What did they sing?'

'Oh, like churchy songs I suppose. Not ones that we know. Not the ones from our church, I mean. They were different. A bit more lively than ours. Far more emotional. Lady Persephone would be doing her embroidery and Sibyl would be cleaning up around her and they'd just be singing. It were really beautiful actually. But it angered the staff.'

'What? Why?'

'Hmmmmm.' It was fascinating to me, the things that Wesley didn't spend time thinking about. I knew that if I had been privy to the interaction of a lady's maid and the lady of the house that I would not only be thoroughly observant, but also if their actions angered people, I'd be obsessed with the reasons why.

'Well, they were too close, really,' he mused. 'There needs to be a separation between upstairs and downstairs, don't there? And with them it just wasn't like that at all. Lady Persephone treated Sibyl like she were family. The staff thought it dangerous. They hated that Lady Persephone let Sibyl ride her horse.'

'Isn't that Lady Persephone's right? Didn't she need her mail delivered or some such?'

'Well yeah, that's the reason she gave. But I'm sure Sibyl went out without any correspondence on her person most times. I didn't tell anyone, but I knew. The butler at the time said Sibyl should have asked him to arrange sending her post. Besides, it's just not done. A lady's maid just isn't supposed to be riding a horse at all, let alone that of the lady of the house. It were highly unusual. And with her skin colour it just looked more unseemly. She never came into trouble though, fortunately.'

'Well, that is something we can be happy about.'

Normally, our evenings rattled on to bedtime with so many things left unexplored because we excited each other so much with our conversations. Wesley made me feel like a kaleidoscope at the amusements by the Blackpool Beach, twisting and twisting with colourful impossibilities of feeling weaving themselves into each other inside of me.

He leaned down to kiss the top of my head as he usually would, but I moved just beyond the reach of his lips. Then Wesley got up and walked towards my door. Just before he opened it he gave me a side smile that looked somewhere between relief and defeat.

Minutes later, I had two pairs of woollen socks on and had swaddled myself in a dressing gown over my night gown and had a scarf round my neck. I needed to read Lady Persephone's letters and nothing would have stopped me. Even if the library had ever been left unlocked, I wouldn't have been brave enough to enter and root around for the diary in the dark. The letters, however, were out in the open. Their contents were obviously innocuous in comparison with what I imagined would have been in her diary, but there would still be stacks of clues about who she really was as her own woman, rather than Lord Belfield's wife.

I also needed to leave behind the puffy, noxious tension that my interaction with Wesley had generated. The warmth of my room was no longer inviting. I wanted to get to the coolness of Lady Persephone's morning room with her letters and begin getting to know her. I padded my way down the stairs, avoiding all the creaks and thumps I had made on my earlier journey down to the drawing room. This time, the mastiff didn't even rise from the chaise longue. I ruffled its neck as I moved towards the desk. Still unlocked. I opened the drawers and took out the first letter. Now I needed light to read it, but to have brought a lamp would have been too silly an endeavour and I dared not whisk the letters up to my room. I swished over to the window and said a prayer of thanks for the moonlight just unveiled by a passing cloud. The letter began:

My Dearest Percy,

Every letter I receive, I wait to hear that you have settled things with Sibyl. You have no reason to be sour with her, given what she has sacrificed for you. You are miserable because your son is far away from you in school. It's hard. You think I don't know? Orion, my only son, gone because he chose to pass over away from us. Yes, it is sad. But we can confide in each other. We must depend on each other.

You two cannot afford to drift apart after all you've been through. She knows your husband well. You know this. You must listen to her. Protect the marriage, my dear. You must work on the marriage. For all our sakes . . .

Chapter Nine

I had skimmed through two more letters and returned to mulling over the strange wording: '*he chose to pass over away from us*' when the mastiff noticed the sound. It wouldn't have registered as anything to pay attention to without his head switching up and left, towards the gentle creaking of wood coming from where I feared Lord Belfield's bedroom might be two rooms over above us. I waited by the curtain, my ears straining to catch another sound. I felt confident that I had done enough to descend the stairs quietly. It wasn't my first time, after all. I considered that anyone discovering me there, holding the personal correspondence of the lady of the house, would balk at my audacity but be a firm defender of my lunacy for ever more.

The creaking ceased, and so a few seconds later I crept silently back to Lady Persephone's desk and placed the letter back on top of the others. I intended to read them in reverse chronology. That way I need not mess up the order of them.

I left the morning room and ascended the staircase as soundlessly as I could. Just as I reached Lord Belfield's floor and turned towards the final staircase up to the servants' bedrooms, I heard a rustle behind me and turned to see a womanly ghost running away from me. I stopped in shock. She wore a pink dress with a translucent bow at the waist and white lace at the neckline, soft curls cascading beneath. I'd seen her before. Impossible as it was, it was unmistakably Lady Persephone. I recognised the dress from the picture I'd seen.

The tall, elegant woman rounded the corner, vanishing from sight. I tried to fathom what my eyes had just witnessed – surely not a ghost. I didn't believe in such things. I felt a creeping suspicion. If I was right, then the woman had every right to be scared. But why should I be? She was running away from me, after all. She meant no harm. A sweet but artificial scent of violets followed her down the hallway.

I clutched my India rubber hot water bottle tighter to me and smiled with the assurance that my cotton sheets would snuggle me back that night. All could be well, as long as I played my cards correctly. I returned to my bed as quietly as possible and slept somewhat peacefully considering the acid on my chest choked up by the strife of the day.

The following morning Baxter served us creamy porridge with tart strawberry preserves. I had stopped the effusive commentary on her meals, but I still had to thank her cordially. She ignored me, as was her way. Baxter and my father should have married, based on their temperament alone. Wesley smiled at me sheepishly. I smiled back, but there was too much on my mind to chatter in the way we had got used to.

Persephone's mother was Miss Arabella Sey, I had discovered from the trove of letters. Her mother being unmarried fascinated me. Was Persephone illegitimate? I knew her maiden name to be Nostos, which I guessed to be Greek. I had just assumed her mother would have the same name. Why wouldn't I?

After a tantalising opening, the rest of the next few letters had been unremarkable. Miss Arabella shared information about the neighbours she lived among in Liverpool. Other than that, she asked incisive questions about Persephone's home life and how her grandson was faring at boarding school. The hints of discord between Sibyl and Persephone left me feeling quite flummoxed. Why on earth would Persephone's maid 'know her husband well'? There was something improper about the relationship that I could not quite put my finger on. And as much as I had despised the women of the village for suspecting Sibyl, I couldn't help but wonder if she might have a scandalous reason to want to dispose of Persephone. One that they had no idea of. As much as I liked Sibyl, this woman whom I had never met, I couldn't deny the smell of an unmistakeable aroma. A motive.

And then there was the 'ghost' I had encountered upstairs ...

The loud clinking of Wesley's spoon on his bowl brought me out of my reverie. I looked at him as he pushed his chair back in a huff. The back leg scraping the floor told me that he was feeling frustrated. He always lifted his chair a touch for he liked his movements to be maidenly. Perhaps he thought that my being quiet had something to do with our conversation last night. I did not think less of him for being resentful. Or for trying to withdraw from me emotionally because he believed I had deserted him. I just would not indulge him.

When he returned from the scullery, Baxter and I had both finished and though I tried to catch his eye as he collected our bowls, he avoided contact. Just as he reached the door, I chose to say something.

'Oh, Wesley, you left something on the table.'

He looked at the table blankly before looking up at me.

'What? No, I didn't.'

'Yes, you did . . . your lovely smile.'

Wesley grinned. I hadn't done anything wrong and I could have remained attached to that, but instead I chose to let him know that I had forgiven him completely. Having had to endure Wesley's sullenness that morning, I was truly put off perpetuating our feud.

Lord Belfield calling me a vixen days previously had felt like a sharpened sickle cutting me down to size. An hour into working with him that morning, I decided to match the candour with which he spoke to me before, in the hope of easing the tensions between us.

'Lord Belfield, might I be so bold as to ask you a question, please?'

He regarded me softly before putting his pen down.

'Yes, of course. Do go ahead.'

I gave him an assessing look.

'I was just wondering if your brother, Sir Chester, is as well read as you are?'

He took his glasses off and rubbed them with a handkerchief. He was cooling off.

'Why do you ask?'

'Well, it's just that in our overhearing of him,' I skipped over this quickly, hoping it didn't arouse any further anger, 'he seemed to imply the restored books may not fetch as much as you might have hoped. I wondered if his assessment was based on any knowledge he's gleaned from contemporary sales in London. Or perhaps he just can't appreciate the value of your collection for some other reason? My father told me the best stores are on Charing Cross Road and I wondered if they are places that Sir Chester frequents regularly, if at all.'

He placed the glasses back onto his nose and said brightly, 'No, Miss Granger. My brother is neither a good reader nor is he particularly well informed as to the true value of my collection.'

He pursed his lips and narrowed his eyes at me. As if he were considering whether it was worth putting his family business into the space between us for examination. He exhaled and leaned back in his chair, looking at the ceiling before he turned his head towards the window and began speaking as if to himself. I had to hide a smile – somehow, I had hit upon a confidence that Lord Belfield wanted to share.

'We were born in the wrong order. He has all the ambition of a first-born prince. Now, he is boxing at the atmosphere because he feels his inheritance to be too paltry considering the strength of his talents.' He gave a wry smile. 'You would think he were the elder, because he is both taller and broader than I am. Perhaps others don't consider his size to be an indicator of his greatness, but I always did. He snapped at my heels every step of the way of our childhood. Ruled the rugby field when he came into my school, while I was always middling at the sport of cricket, which I loved. We both got into Oxford. I hated that he followed me there,' he admitted, looking vaguely guilty. 'I didn't think he was quite smart enough, if I'm honest. Alas, there he was. A blight on my independence. His view on how I was failing to forge ahead properly was constantly offered. And it's all based on his roughshod opinions cooked up while drinking his pint of lager in the bath. So no, Miss Granger, my brother is not as well read as I, but it's hardly ever seemed to matter.'

I felt like Pandora opening the box. I had invited the confidences, but his vulnerability felt noxious – there was too much of it. No man had ever been this honest with me, I suspected. Fortunately, I was not speechless.

'I do believe you have the wisdom of an older brother, Lord Belfield. Perhaps you were born in the right order for the protection of all that does matter.'

He sat up in his chair at that and clenched his hands together before him.

'Perhaps you're right, Miss Granger. Perhaps you're right ...'

I put my head back down to work, considering the bridge between us at least partially reconstructed.

But apparently, Lord Belfield was not finished with me. 'Did you ever wish for siblings?' He surveyed me intently, as if there was a correct response to give.

'Why, yes of course. I had a selection of dolls whom I ruled over domestically in the fiefdom that was my bedroom. I enjoyed them all the more because they couldn't challenge me in the way a girl is forced to get used to.'

He laughed raucously. Smacked the table, even. The sharp sound was all the more shocking because the library was normally silent.

'Was it just working with your father that turned you into a reader? Or was it the loneliness of being an only child? Your sensitivity suggests the latter!'

I was stunned to find him probing me so, but decided to reward his vulnerability with some of my own.

'*Black Beauty,*' I said.

'Excuse me?' His eyebrows danced.

'*Black Beauty* by Anna Sewell,' I clarified, resting my chin on my interlocked hands.

'Ah! I see.'

'You see, my first love was a much-maligned horse: '*Do you know why this world is as bad as it is? . . . It is because people think only about their own business, and won't trouble themselves to stand up for the oppressed, nor bring the wrong-doer to light . . . My doctrine is this, that if we see cruelty or wrong that we have the power to stop, and do nothing, we make ourselves sharers in the guilt.*'

'I dare say a simple children's story made a liberal out of you.'

'My father would agree with you. He forbade me from reading it eventually. I refused everything else, you see. I'd finish it and just go back to the beginning. Eventually he wrenched it from my grip under my bed blankets. Smacked

Dickens into my hands to wash out my eyes with. Hated it at the time, but of course I'm glad for it now.' I smiled.

'Would your father be impressed by the work you've done for me thus far?'

Having up until recently assumed that bookbinding would be my whole future, I had not given thought to the fact that by leaving the trade behind I would be severing the last link between my father and me. We would have so little in common – if we were to meet again. I looked at the table in front of me. The leather scraps lying beside a perfectly bound book with brand new debossed lettering on the spine.

'Well ... if he was, he definitely wouldn't praise me for it.' I scratched my neck which felt suddenly taut. 'He sees very little point in praise. In fact, he felt too many compliments would spoil me as a child and thus never gave me any, just in case someone else would be foolish enough to do so.'

The look coming at me from Lord Belfield was pitying but not cheap. He did know how it felt.

'But yes, his standard is so exacting, I don't think he'd allow anyone to know he was the one to train me up to this standard, if he were not happy with the level of work I can do now.'

'Well, that's something at least. So few women get to enjoy what you are currently.'

I felt nauseated by the last statement. Firstly, because I had not been privy to a man choosing to consider the plight of women, excluding the man who was the cause of my own downfall – and he'd had decided anarchist beliefs. Yet Lord Belfield's statement also nauseated me because I was almost certain I did not agree. All the women on the street on which I lived worked. If they weren't in the factories, then they were doing laundry or raising a brood of children. Only in the houses of the upper classes like this one had I ever heard of a marriage producing only one or two children and that being considered the woman's only job. Furthermore, Lord Belfield spoke as if I had hiked myself up to a mountain of independence. But I was not safe. I had little security outside of the temporary benevolence he was seeing fit to bestow upon me. We had such a good rapport that morning that I dared not disturb our rapprochement with anything like my real thoughts on the matter.

'Yes. Thank you, Lord Belfield.'

Without any further instruction I got back to work on the green leather beneath my fingers, smoothing my steel ruler over the cover to create a crease at the edge of the spine. The silence that returned between us was far less oppressive. I couldn't call it a camaraderie, but our conversations about our respective childhoods had reassured me that Lord Belfield didn't view me as entirely disposable. The winds in my sails were a little gentler, but my direction was nevertheless far truer. I would never be his equal and there was no sense of teamwork fostered between us; he had his work and I had mine. Nevertheless, I now suspected he had been too shy to suggest us working in the same room at first, because in doing so he would have risked exposing his loneliness.

When lunchtime came, I rose with the midday gong and nodded as I walked towards his table to reach the door.

'Miss Granger, before you go, might I ask if you know how to ride a horse?'

Now, this winded me. He had seen the conditions in which I had grown up. He spoke to me as if I were Tess of the d'Urbervilles – merely one marriage proposal away from joining him in his upper-class status. Perhaps the loss of so much of his fortune had made him feel closer to my financial status and he mistakenly thought I had ever had any of the pastimes and pursuits that he thought it natural to grow up with.

'I must admit, Lord Belfield, that I do not. *Black Beauty* is the closest I ever came to a horse, apart from the ones that pulled our trams.'

'Right, I thought you didn't . . . Would you like to learn?'

Chapter Ten

For me to become a woman who rode would be just too sweet
for words. It was almost thwarted by Lord Belfield suggesting
that I would learn to ride side saddle. Perhaps most people
would consider me obstinate and ungrateful for informing my
employer that if I did not learn how to ride astride the horse,
then I would not learn at all, but I had been dependent on
horses to pull carts and stagecoaches, and I knew their power.
The last thing I wanted to feel while on a steed was dainty
and unstable.

'Besides,' I told him, 'both Marie Antoinette and Catherine
the Great rode astride their horses.'

'That's hardly encouraging,' he said.

I had not met a man like Lord Belfield before. His desire for
me to be left better off for having met him was not subtle, but
neither was it self-promoting. He delighted in my improve-
ments as a person. I did not trust him fully since I had seen

the other side to him, but I saw no need to not indulge myself in everything he was offering me. Although I was losing out on having time to myself to read. Lord Belfield took my Saturday mornings away in trying to make a rider out of me.

The walk to Hurrel Farm was a muddy one. Wesley was tasked with taking me and even walking on the grass banks by the road the ground sucked at my boots, threatening to pull me under. I don't think Wesley minded giving up his Saturday morning to take me, because he never turned down an opportunity for us to spend more time together.

Our calves strained as we turned into the field that took us to the thatched cottage with a smoking chimney. We walked past the open door, and I suspected I smelled bread baking, but my nostrils were robbed of the joy by the assault that came next. Manure. It was so strong and foul-smelling it caused my eyes to sting. The thing I found most fascinating was the sheer beauty of our environment, despite the smell. Hurrel Farm was a dwelling that Constable would have found charming enough to immortalise in paint. We were in a vale of sorts. Hills on either side of us were craggy with moss, and the rocks and trees had withstood more history than I had yet read about. I longed to stand still in this spot and see the seasons change; have spring rung in around me with the appearance of pale greens and yellows, advancing into the dark iron-greens of a summer in the full swing of life, with birds bustling until the hills turned copper and russet, breathing out the last of its flames to rest into the glacial beauty of winter. The magnificence of the place rushed through me, to the point I was sure I would start to giggle with happiness.

By the time we reached the paddock, the smell had got

stronger, but my feelings towards it had changed. The offal of the earth, I told myself. The smell of life itself. And there at the entryway to the stables, beyond the paddock, stood my instructor.

'Good morning, Joseph,' Wesley trilled.

'Good morning, Wesley.' Joseph turned to me. 'How do you do m'lady?'

'Oh, I'm not a lady,' I corrected him. 'I'm a binder, here working on Lord Belfield's books.' I leapt forward with my hand outstretched. 'Florence. Florence Granger.'

He gripped my hand. 'Joseph. Joseph Hurrel.'

I couldn't tell whether he was mocking me. I was so nervous. Perhaps it was his height? Six foot two, I guessed. But no, though his frame was one of strength, he was the sort of man who looked like he was as soft hearted as he was hard featured. A bear of a man, with thick furry forearms and a barrelled torso. I had been reading of men knocked out by drink at the docks and awaking at sea to find themselves stolen, to work on ships for the rest of their lives. I could imagine such a fate befalling Joseph. His eyes were too trusting – a light blue I remember seeing once in a rockpool. His top lip was thin as that of the one on my favourite childhood doll, but his bottom lip made up for it by being more than twice the fullness.

'Lord Belfield said I should come to collect her at 2.30 p.m.,' Wesley muttered, giving Hurrel a hard stare.

'As you wish,' Joseph replied simply.

'Thank you, Wesley,' I said, watching him turn to trudge back alone.

We walked deeper into the stable and I met the mare

who would soon become the love of my life. Miss Mabel. Chestnut brown and flirtatious as anything, she nuzzled my hand with her nose when I approached her. Joseph handed me half of a brown apple and I fed it to her, adoring the chomp chomping sound that affirmed her satisfaction. I went to nuzzle her neck.

'Careful,' Joseph said. I looked towards him, not sure if I had made a mistake. 'Don't get too comfortable with your new friend. You won't be riding her for a while yet.'

I must have looked crestfallen, because Joseph doubled over and slapped his thigh.

'Don't worry, it won't be that long. It's just that you've got a lot to learn about how to take care of her first. As you said, you're not a lady, and I don't intend to be treating you like one.'

He started walking back towards the entrance, where two grimy shovels stood against the doorframe. I was sure one would have my name on it.

Lunch couldn't have come quickly enough. Splattered with manure and mud, but not able to tell the difference between them, I washed myself down with a bucket of water and a green bar of soap in an outdoor sink. I knew my skin would tighten irreparably once I began to dry.

Joseph had been nowhere near as chatty as Wesley, but he occasionally imparted short pieces of wisdom about nature and animals, and farms and markets. He was of the land in a way I would never be, no matter how much hay I would be forced to wade through in the weeks to come. All this toil before I'd even learned how to get onto a horse, let alone ride one. I couldn't imagine an agricultural life with me in it. So punishing, with only a few moments a year when one was rewarded with a yield worth smiling at. And that was only if everything went well!

Just as I was patting myself dry, out came a rotund, red-cheeked woman wearing a lightly stained cook's apron. This was Joseph's mother.

'Well, hello there, my love!'

'Oh! Oh, I'm sorry. I'm almost done, ma'am.'

'Oh, don't you worry my love, you take your time. Your tea is waiting inside. You can just call me Mrs Hurrel if you like.'

'Thank you. I'm Florence.'

'Oh, I know who you are, my love.'

Mrs Hurrel was as portly as Baxter, but far more vibrant in her ways. She hustled and bustled about the kitchen like a whirling dervish. Both she and Joseph had warm brown hair with a ginger tinge, and she had a few white strands peeking through at her temples and around her crown.

'How is your master up there in the house, all on his lonesome? A terrible business, weren't it?'

I was desperate to tear into the Lancashire hot pot steaming before me, but I didn't know how I could do so courteously without answering her questions. I had no idea even how to begin to answer, while maintaining my diplomacy. But I hoped that Mrs Hurrel's conversational gambit would give me an opening to ask more about the late lady of the house.

'Mother! Would you let the girl breathe.'

'Oh, you quiet yourself, lad. She should know! She's been up there at least a couple month now, haven't you love?'

109

I picked up my spoon. 'Yes. I arrived a little before Christmas,' I said, fingering my spoon. 'Early December.'

'Tuck in, don't let it get cold.'

And so I did. I devoured the meat first and scooped up the sauce, so rich was it, glossy on its surface with butter and orange flecks of carrot. Delightful, and I told her so.

'Oh.' She blushed. 'You're welcome, my love. But now you've had a few mouthfuls, you're surely restored enough to tell me how he's doing.'

She poured me some milk in a pewter cup.

'Lord Belfield . . . He's been very good to me. We work very well together.'

'But it's you doing all the work though, int' it? He's not binding any books. He's not got the skills that you have, does he?'

I felt my cheeks get hot. I ought to have been glad my professional purpose at Rose Hall was known around the village. They hadn't branded me a harlot.

'I'm just glad that horse will be getting a good run-around. She's been ever so restless since the lady's maid went back to Liverpool.'

I seized my opportunity. 'When did she leave?' I asked.

'She hung about quite a while after Lady Persephone died last March. I think Lord Belfield was a bit *too* fond of her, if you catch my drift.'

'Mother!' Joseph objected, with a full mouth. He was almost finished.

'Well, it needs to be said. What's a lady's maid doing hanging about once the lady of the house has died? It weren't proper.'

'Well, taking care of a house that size is a lot of work,' I offered, though I thought back to Arabella's assertion that Sibyl knew Lord Belfield well, and the signs there had been trouble between Lady Persephone and her maid . . .

'She were doing a lot more than taking care of the house,' Mrs Hurrel asserted. 'She left after she had put on a lot of weight, and she stopped horse riding, which is always a sure sign that something inside her shouldn't be jolted about . . .'

My stomach dropped. Was it Lord Belfield's child, then?

'Mother, if you don't stop . . .!'

'I'm just saying,' Mrs Hurrel ploughed on without remorse, 'she was a very sophisticated woman in many respects, but she still had the spirit of her people, didn't she? Her behaviour was something that should be paid attention to.'

'You are spouting nonsense now,' Joseph said, scraping his bowl. 'Don't listen to her,' he instructed me.

'She'd do well to listen to me,' Mrs Hurrel protested.

I agreed. I wanted to know more.

'How do you mean?' I poked. 'Should I be concerned?'

'Well . . . I know it's been a long time ago now, but when Lord Belfield's father was on their plantations in Jamaica or Trinidadia and wherever, it's said he was intoxicated by 'em. They've got all sorts of tricks and witchcraft, don't they. All I'm saying is, what if the maid did something to knock off Lady Persephone? You don't just stumble into a river at night, do ya?' I felt a humming through my body. Mrs Hurrel was voicing the very suspicion I'd been toying with. Perhaps Lord Belfield hadn't been the only person at Rose Hall with a temper. 'And then who knows what herbs and spices the maid could have used to lure Lord Belfield upstairs,' Mrs Hurrel continued, oblivious. 'Who knows? All I'm saying is she was obviously well educated to reach that station in life and riding a horse and all that, but what if at night-time her natural natures took over? She always struck me as quite a seductress, is all I'm saying.'

'Mother, that's enough!'

'Oh, please Joseph, it's fine,' I stepped in. 'It wouldn't be the first time a man of a grand house took a mistress from among his staff, would it? Perhaps Sibyl didn't have much of a say. I'm more interested in why Lady Persephone would find herself by the river at night, honestly.'

Joseph glared at me and then his gaze softened, as if he realised his consternation was showing and he had to put his wall back up. He scratched above his ear and feigned disinterest.

'But now I think of it,' Mrs Hurrel mused, 'I can't accuse Sibyl of pushing her missus into the river. They were thick as thieves for the most part. And I don't see the other posh ladies treating their lady's maid like she did. Probably *too* friendly. She'd never have killed her, if she had any sense. No. She liked the job. She liked her missus and she was hardly going to marry Lord Belfield when the lady of the house was out of the way. It probably weren't her.'

If Sibyl really was pregnant when she left Rose Hall, I didn't think we could discard her as a suspect so easily – not with everything else I'd learned. I left that to one side for now, though.

'But you *do* think someone killed her?' I leaned forward and placed my chin on my fist, rolling my elbow into the table.

112

'I do,' Mrs Hurrel said. 'She wasn't given to night-time walks, so I hear, so the whole thing smells very fishy.'

'But who else might have resented Lady Persephone enough to do her harm?' I asked.

'You see, that's the thing. She were well liked,' Mrs Hurrel mused.

'But Sibyl can't be the only one with a reason to want her out of the way?' I probed.

Mrs Hurrel smirked at me. She'd been waiting for someone like me, I could see. Joseph refused to give her questions a decent reception. Finally she could share her theories.

'Well, you'd think it might have been Lord Belfield first, wouldn't yuh? I can't think of what she might have done to anger him enough to do all of that. He's not really known for his temper.'

'That would be Sir Chester,' I prompted, though I quietly rejected Mrs Hurrel's generous assessment of Lord Belfield.

'That would be him. And he's got it in him,' Mrs Hurrel agreed with malice and glee. 'He were a right tyrant when he were a boy. Killed a cat for no reason. Punched a tethered cow in the nose as well. He were always right strange. And if I'd had a daughter I wouldn't have left her round him unsupervised, if you know what I mean. Far from gentlemanly, that one.'

'But on the night she died he was halfway to London, wasn't he?'

'Thass not quite right. He was halfway to London by the time we knew she was gone the next day, but that doesn't mean he didn't kill her before he set off. I'd still put him in the frame, actually.'

I was thoroughly enjoying Mrs Hurrel's investigative insights. I felt as if I'd stumbled into a Wilkie Collins mystery. To cover up my delight I asked a neutralising question.

'Is there anyone else?' I asked.

'No one brave enough to rob themselves of a place in heaven,' Mrs Hurrel grumbled.

We'd gone over the members of the household that the ladies of the church had mentioned, but that couldn't be all. 'Where were the other staff? The butler, the other footman besides Wesley, and the scullery maids?'

'Well, it were Easter Sunday. They were all with their families except Wesley and Baxter, who stayed behind to take care of things. I would have said, otherwise. I don't forget nowt, me,' she responded, a bit offended.

'That's too true, that is,' Joseph added, before belching into his fist.

'So who was around that night?' I asked, realising that Mrs Hurrel's musings had hardly been complete if they overlooked Wesley and Baxter.

'Lord Belfield. Lady Violet. Sir Chester. Wesley. Sibyl. Baxter.' She opened her eyes after saying it and her ice blue eyes twinkled with mirth, though I thought Joseph looked freshly annoyed.

I was scared of Lord Belfield, obviously, but to think of him as a suspect in the death of his wife? Did he have the capacity? Hadn't he been generous to me, even though I had taken many a liberty? How far could he be pushed before his rage ranneth over? He had a temper, and nothing could anger a man more than his own wife, of that I was sure. But being nagged, running off to the pub and returning determined to

114

knock one's wife about a bit was a working-class phenomenon. Ladies weren't even beaten, let alone murdered. My
thoughts scandalised me.

'So those are our suspects?' I confirmed.

The peal of a crow squawked through the air at that most
morbidly convenient moment.

'Don't know why any of them would, but that's who
were about.' She clapped her hands to her belly and leaned
back a bit.

In mere minutes I'd received more information than I could
have in a whole week of snooping. And although Mrs Hurrel
hadn't included herself and Joseph on her list, I added them
to my own. You never knew. They were hardly very far away
and in fact Lady Persephone had died closer to the farm than
Rose Hall, having been found in the river which was only
minutes' walk away from where we sat.

I wiped my mouth contentedly.

'Good afternoon, all,' Wesley broke the silence between us,
without knocking to announce his arrival. How much had he
heard? I wondered.

Had he been here the whole time?

Chapter Eleven

I need not have worried too greatly. I had forgotten that Wesley had been prepared for a life of service in ways I had not, and thus discovering me gossiping probably wasn't the criminal act I felt I had been committing when he first walked in the room. I didn't at first notice the handful of winter heather and honeysuckle he had bunched in his right hand. Where had he found those on the walk back here? I hadn't seen anything floral. Wesley handed them to Mrs Hurrel, who was very enamoured with him, and Joseph looked on his mother fawning over Wesley warmly. After pleasantries were exchanged and Wesley had drunk a glass of milk, it was time for us both to go. Mrs Hurrel hugged me goodbye, smelling of toast with dripping.

Our brief embrace nourished me no end. I was so hungry for affection and only newly aware of how little I had grown up with. I knew of the seven forms of love the Greeks had spoken of, but had always attempted to diminish the importance of *storge*, unconditional familial love. I wasn't an orphan, but my father's cold demeanour had made me feel like one on occasion. Yet here I was being embraced by a savoury-smelling fat woman who made me feel cosseted in her presence.

I walked out of the cottage feeling warm and full bellied, even as my mind buzzed with possibilities, thinking about Lady Persephone's fate. The wind snatched me back into preparedness for the long muddy walk back to Rose Hall. Just as I pulled my hood up to save my ears from aching in the icy gales, Joseph came running out of the cottage as if he had been chastened and pushed out to save us.

"Old up, you two. You can't be walking back there with this wind whipping ya and the mud and all that. I'll grab the horse and you two can sit on her and I'll lead you back along the road.'

Wesley and I looked at each other questioningly. Would it not be more polite to decline? But then I looked behind Joseph and saw Mrs Hurrel with crossed arms in the doorway and I knew it would cause Joseph more trouble if we were to trudge back without his assistance. Besides, I was eager to mount the horse even if it was to be led along, so I was the first to say, 'Why, thank you, Joseph.'

We must have looked a right sight that day. I got on Mabel first because, despite his gangly limbs, I was taller and more buxom than Wesley. It felt more natural to have his slight arms clinging around me. He rested his cheek and, I imagined, closed his eyes once we got going. Joseph was happy to lead us both and walked on the grassy strips along the side of the road where he could, although I heard the mud sucking at his galoshes.

When we came over the crest of the hill, the wonder of

the landscape made my heart swell once again. The wintry celestial landscape looked so dangerously beautiful, and my gaze was drawn to the river that snaked through Rose Hall's grounds. Had Lady Persephone gone for a night-time walk, alone, and simply stumbled? Or had she had company that night? However she had ended up in the waters, to be caught in the cold and wet without a warm, homely destination nearby was to court death at that time of year.

Just as I was musing on the inhospitable, wintry land, a V-formation of Canada geese swooped into my view from just above my head and filled me with courage. These were not just birds toughing it out through winter – they had come here because, cold as it was, it was warmer than their home. A cynic would take it as a sign that things could always be worse. But the loving affections of Wesley, snoring gently on my arm, the helpful, barrel-chested Joseph, and the rotund Mrs Hurrel that had birthed him, filled me instead with optimism. No matter how harsh the circumstances, one could always hope for love and warmth somewhere, as long as you were willing to take flight to find it.

However, as we descended the hill into the valley where Rose Hall lay waiting, the sight of a carriage broke the snugness of my reverie.

'Wesley, wake up.' I pinched his arm and made him jolt up. 'Is that not Sir Chester's carriage?' I said, pointing at the front door of Rose Hall a few hundred yards away.

'You've got the eyesight of a marksman, you 'ave. Joseph, hold up here.'

'Thank you so much, Joseph,' I added. 'We'll walk from here.'

Sir Chester might be safely inside the house already, but we both knew it wouldn't do to have me on a horse with a dozy Wesley clinging around me. As natural a position as it was, if Sir Chester were to see me encouraging Wesley's effeminacy, the consequences were sure to be quite dire.

'So, I'll be seeing you next Saturday then.'

Wesley had taken Joseph's helping hand to dismount but he stumbled into him anyway. Joseph was so strong he was able to stay rooted, then offer me his hand in turn.

I gripped his forearm instead of clinging to his hand. Wesley might have enjoyed feeling like a damsel, but I definitely did not.

All the snoozy feelings that came from our familial morning disappeared on our final stretch of the journey. As we trudged the last few hundred yards towards Rose Hall, I caught Wesley looking at Joseph's retreating back a couple of times, as if he wanted to escape the chilly foreboding scene ahead of us by running back to him. I was certain that we were walking back into a house with at least two suspects in Lady Persephone's death, and I was determined to dig to the bottom of it.

Chapter Twelve

As the next day was Sunday, Wesley and I trotted out to church at our usual hour, with full bellies of Baxter's delectable kippers and potatoes. The warm salty butter had prepared our throats for hymn singing and I felt lubricated enough to reach for the soprano notes.

We kept our gloved hands in our pockets as usual for the season, but I noticed myself scanning for any early signs of spring nevertheless. Perhaps the hint of a bump of an emerging bud on the younger twigs. My father had taught me to listen out for the trills of the mistle thrush, but I heard none that day.

As we took our seats on our regular pew, I was reminded of Mrs Hurrel's indiscretions the day previous by the entry of a midnight-blue-suited Sir Chester, along with Lady Violet in a navy gown with a surprisingly lively purple hat. They nodded at parishioners before heading towards one of the front pews, as was their privilege. A hush had fallen over the congregation on their entry. They were definitely the most winsome couple of the day by far, and the glamour they emitted corralled the gazes of all to snatch a look at the sight of them. Tall and elegant and refined. Such envy they inspired. Sir Chester obviously had more disposable income than Lord Belfield in order to afford such delectable fashions. Nevertheless, I felt my own sense of power swell, knowing that on their last visit I had found myself sneaking away Lady Violet's sopping wet stockings for immediate washing. I hadn't told anyone of the mottled, blotchy skin of her ankle on that visit, because of how her husband – now sitting with his head bowed – had wrestled her tight boot off her ankle with such force. To think that behind this couple, the very vision of bourgeois serenity that day, was a story of pain and enduring dissatisfaction. Anyone besides me in the church must have been looking on them both with excitement for the beauty of their offspring. Only Wesley and I knew of the cacophony and melancholy any child of theirs would be born into. I felt unjustifiably smug for knowing what so many others did not.

That evening Baxter was busier than ever. With Lord Belfield, Lady Violet and Sir Chester to serve dinner to, I insisted on helping prepare the vegetables for her at least. Wesley took up the roast chicken, potato dauphinoise and green beans with carrots with a light gravy. While he served, I read my novel in the kitchen and Baxter washed up around me.

The priest had given a sermon about Jesus, Mary and Joseph's wilderness years in Egypt, which had galvanised Wesley into pummelling me with questions about Egypt on the walk home from church. During our dinner, the conversation moved on to Napoleon's campaign in Egypt and how Admiral Nelson had thrashed him with his deft naval manoeuvres on the Mediterranean.

After dinner, Wesley and I ascended to my room as usual, hearing the brothers drinking and smoking in the billiard room. I found I had no desire to eavesdrop on them this time – Lord Belfield's warning had not deterred me from sticking my nose into his wife's death, but I was not so foolish as to repeat the same misdemeanour twice.

As Wesley and I settled into my room, I reflected that my respect for him had grown beyond where I had anticipated. Every so often he would use words like 'natives' and 'savages' that revealed he still saw Europeans as more supreme beings than the 'dusky hordes' he questioned me about. No questions were as feral as what he had asked Sibyl, and his inquisitive nature meant he would not long be held hostage by the stereotypes spread about those we had colonised. I was determined that he would drink in the truth that they were our equals.

So obsessed with thoughts of faraway places was Wesley that I read him a good thirty-five pages of *One Thousand and One Nights* when I would usually cap him at twenty, maximum. It was so late when I sent him back to his room, that having tip-toed my way down the corridors to ensure the brothers had ceased their Scotch drinking and cigar smoking in the billiard room, I felt confident visiting the morning room that night. I snuggled up with the mastiff on the chaise longue to read Lady Persephone's letters once more. I was planning to work my way through as many as I could. I was now incredibly impressed by and fond of Lady Persephone's mother. She was a stalwart of her community, as I saw it. Doing her very best to uplift the fortunes of the negro community of Liverpool, almost to the point where she saw herself as one of them. I admired the dedication for its selflessness, and how she did not patronise or infantilise them at all.

Still, she was a mother, and her anxieties over Lady Persephone's wellbeing were very much connected to her bearing a healthy son. It struck me how the spirit and values of Jane Austen's era had persisted. That a woman's security was still determined by her ability to provide her husband with an heir, and Miss Arabella had for the first months of the marriage constantly reminded her daughter that she had been accepted as a wife because she was viewed as a good investment. With news of their son's birth reaching her a little under nine months after the wedding, the tone of the letters became a lot more sprightly, with Lady Persephone's future now secured.

'I knew it!' I heard a hiss from behind me.

My head spun round and caught the horrifically illuminated sight of Sir Chester, his face lit from below by his paraffin lamp. The mastiff's head didn't raise at all. I felt betrayed by his continued slumber and that he had not alerted me to Sir Chester creeping up on me. But of course, why would he? Sir Chester's presence was even more familiar to him than my own.

'Look at you, snuggled up with our Old Archibald there. Like a little field mouse or rather a frightened little shreeew,' he purred as he got closer.

I felt frozen, but I couldn't possibly remain in such a

relaxed position when my lungs couldn't get enough air into them. I swung my legs down off the chaise longue.

'No, no, my dear. Please stay seated. We must talk about all this. Because I have been wondering how you've got the trust of my brother Francis and that pansy he calls a footman. You two have been burrowed away playing Ring a Ring o' Roses somewhere, no doubt? You like men with squeaky little voices like his, do you?'

If I had been an actress, I would have made more of an effort to be expressionless. I failed in this attempt. I had been discovered being a brazen investigator, rather than the surreptitious sleuth I had believed myself to be.

'I must say, you're prettier than I would have thought you'd be when I first heard about you. A bookbinder's daughter. One expects some dumpy, pie-faced, teapot debutante returning home unbetrothed at the end of yet another season.' He pinched his nose and sniffed. 'Yet, here you are, the jammiest bit of jam, even if you are more exotic than my usual tastes.'

Finding myself prey to this newly arrived predator, I couldn't help myself from pursing my lips a touch and squinting my brow in consternation. I would have snarled if I could.

'Francis tells me you were born in Jamaica. One of the white creoles, I assume? Francis can forgive a bit of mud in the bloodline as long as it's well covered up,' he snickered.

I should have been more outraged, perhaps. I had been born in Jamaica, but both of my parents being white should have kept me from feeling so slighted. 'There's no mud in my bloodline, sir.'

It was none of his affair – I only chose to put him right

because I did not want him to know that my maternal bloodline was obscured to me and therefore feel he had one over on me.

'Right, right. No, of course not. You wouldn't be able to read so well otherwise, would you. No, no, your intelligence alone proves you as one of us, my dear. Probably some randy Sicilian or Maltese sort snuck his way into a grandmother's knickers at a carnival.' He laughed loudly at this.

'Sir Chester, I must retire, for I have work in the morning.'

'Sit down and stay where I tell you!' The force of his words felt like a curse, even though he hadn't sworn. 'Strumpet.'

He paused for a moment to observe me, and licked his bottom lip. 'We both know I could have you sacked for rifling through my brother's dead wife's correspondence. He tolerates more impertinence than I would, but even dear Francis has his limits.'

He sat, before taking his pipe out and starting to stuff it, looking up at me, studying my face for reactions. I stifled panic by setting my jaw.

'I was merely—'

'You are in danger of being taken as a new recruit to the whorehouse I frequent, if you don't infuse your tone with some feminine humility.'

I fell silent as he struck a match and puffed smoke out of his nose like a dragon.

'Having read all of those letters immediately after Persephone's death myself, I can assure you they reveal nothing of why she killed herself in the way she did.'

I looked sideways at him. He spoke with such assurance. Did he truly believe she had killed herself, or was he covering his own tracks?

125

'Was she not upset in the weeks prior?' I asked, as meekly as possible. He seemed happy to grandstand. I gladly allowed it, as it diverted his attention away from my misdemeanour.

'She didn't seem so.' He spread his legs even wider to accommodate himself, leaning forward and placing his elbows on his knees. I could tell he was happy I had asked him. He was able to show himself off as the smart one. The man who *really* knew what was going on, even if he came by that knowledge through villainy.

'The times she spent with Violet made her more chipper. They laughed like larks in the weeks before her death. I had hoped they were both with child. I'd tried to get Francis to seed her again, at the same time as I was trying with Violet. We could have celebrated a double pregnancy that way.'

I couldn't help myself from recoiling. 'How romantic.'

'Romance isn't a male concern,' he dismissed me. 'Hasn't Darwin confirmed that we're all just animals really? That's why romance is your main concern as a woman, and power is my main concern as a man. It's just our nature. The problem of letting women get an education to your level is you want silly things like the right to vote when you've no idea what to do with it, and would just get distracted by the politician who's the most dashing. Which of course would mean if I were a candidate, then you would vote for me.' He laughed again. It was hollow. A laugh that was not meant to be joined in with. A laugh that heralded the amusement of one.

'Wouldn't I vote for a woman, given that chance?' I thought of the only man who had ever debated me on this subject, and what he would think if he could see me now.

He coughed at that.

'So it's not only the vote you want, but an influx of women into Parliament. What's next? A wet nurse as Speaker of the House? Embroidery hours at the House of Lords?'

Fatigue from his pontificating was slumping my shoulders forwards.

'Please, Sir Chester. I really must get to bed.'

He regarded me with suspicion. I knew I was not exhibiting enough awe for his liking. The truth was his immaturity lessened his power on other people. He loved the sound of his own voice and he knew too well that his features marked him out as handsome. There was nothing naturally held or elegant about the power he had. His privileges as the brother of the lord of the house were so thoroughly undeserved. I couldn't respect him, even when he held my fate in his hands.

After a long, torturous pause, he smirked. 'Fine, I will let you get to your bed.' He put up one finger to stop me from leaping to my feet. 'However, I expect something in return for my silence about your duplicity. I called you a mouse, rather than a snake, because you're so unwitting. You may be conniving but your poverty makes you too desperate. A morsel here. A morsel there. Skitting about at night when you think no one can see you. But I am the snake. And one day soon I am going to let my python out of its cage.'

I hadn't noticed him leaning back in the chair. He had his pipe puffing away in his left hand and his right hand was now rubbing the fly and thick band of his trouser. I stopped breathing, because I finally gathered what he was threatening me with.

'Perhaps you didn't know that snakes feed on mice?'

Against all my power, my rage made me cry a single tear.

I didn't notice the drip until it was cooling the underside of my chin.

'Now run along, my little mousey. I'm not hungry for your furry bits tonight. But I assure you I soon will be.'

I rose and backed away from him, catching sight of him beginning to stroke himself as I left the room. I had refused to give him a view of my posterior, but when I reached the door I turned and practically ran to my room.

The brush with Sir Chester kept me awake for a long time. The way he had spoken to me made me feel like I would never be safe from his intentions ever again. I felt the consequences of Sir Chester holding power over me could save me from becoming wretched in a way only another woman could understand. With only Baxter and Lady Violet in any kind of close quarters, I really didn't have anyone I could confide in. It felt like I was the easiest prey he had ever laid his eyes on.

By the end of that week I had only begun rebinding the pages of one of Lord Belfield's most valuable books: the first collected edition of Chaucer. It was nowhere near complete, but the leather was one of the thickest I had ever dealt with. I was used to doing two or three books a day before that week, but this one was delicate and I was held back by my shaken confidence. So it was that by the time I walked with Wesley to my horse-riding lesson on Saturday, I was sombre from this lack of progress, as well as severely chastened by Sir Chester's warning.

This time, instead of Wesley walking back alone, Mrs Hurrel called him into the cottage. I had found myself scratching my eye with my little finger because a stye had developed the previous morning. I knew touching it was inadvisable because it would just be irritated further, but I had to itch it somehow. A light rubbing meant I could forget it for at least a minute or two afterwards. Until the tingle returned again.

'You'll sit here and keep me company while I boil my son's shirts, won't you, my lovely!'

Mrs Hurrel's intonation was not that of a question. Wesley smiled at the sight of Joseph and me preparing to leave the cottage. I hadn't wondered if there might be some envy about Lord Belfield elevating my station with horse-riding lessons. Perhaps that was why I caught him looking at Joseph's retreating back with an expression on his face that seemed almost hopeful. And once I smelled the manure, my spirits began to rise too.

'It was good that mi mother made me take you and Wesley back last weekend,' Joseph told me. 'I was going to take another week or two before I let you on her. It's best to let yous get to know her a bit first beforehand and everything, but you'll be all right to ride her properly next week.'

I flushed with pride. How funny to be proud that a horse liked me. I had thought the only person it was essential I impress was Lord Belfield. As I entered the stable and heard Miss Mabel bustling about, my chest filled to bursting with excitement. I was just so happy to have made her feel safe with me already. I came up on her stable door.

'Well hello there, my girl. Good morning, my Mabel.'

She popped her head out over the door and I rubbed her face up and down. When I was by her nose, she raised her head to my fingers and gave them a nibble, which made me giggle.

'Give 'er some of this.'

Joseph handed me half a browned apple from his pocket. So thick was his trouser leg, I'd not even noticed anything making the pockets bulge. The practicality of men's clothing always provoked so much jealousy in me. It would be so much easier for me as a bookbinder not to have full skirts catching on things all the time.

Mucking out the stables took us all morning. My eye was itching me a lot by the end. The other three horses in the stables, Paddy, Bilitis and Langston, were a bit more mopey than Mabel. Lord Belfield had told me about his love affair with Langston over the years, but I didn't know who rode Paddy or Bilitis. I could have asked Joseph, but he was so evidently impressed by my ability to work beside him quietly, I did not want to disturb the peace. With the stables all swept out and lovely looking, he led Langston, Bilitis and Paddy out to the paddock for exercise and I waited by Mabel's door for him to come back and get her out too. I stood there rubbing her head and longed to tell Everett about how I was now feeling.

Everett, my anarchist firebrand. The one who had put thoughts of freedom and revolution into my mind as things that could exist outside of stories about uprisings and bloody battles in foreign lands. When he spoke to me, England seemed like a sleeping giant with bloody teeth. He made me feel that once we woke up from our working slumber and devoured the rich and the royal, we would live in a world ruled by no one but our own desires. I had rubbed his neck in our after-moments, too. Touched the parts of him that smelled animal. I missed him so much. In spite of his betrayal.

Joseph came back in, opened the stable door, placed Mabel's harness on her and then led her out by the long rein to the paddock as I walked behind. By the gate, he took all of that off and released Mabel into the field where she got off to a right gallop and circled Langston, Bilitis and Paddy. They were like children playing in the streets.

'You aren't to listen to my mother about Sibyl, you know,' Joseph interrupted my musing. 'She deserves a whole lot more than this world will be willing to give her, that's for sure.'

How funny that he should be taking up the cause of Lady Persephone's lady's maid. Perhaps they were involved, I thought. Could Joseph be the father of her child? It seemed too incredible.

'Were you good friends?'

He turned to look at my face for insinuations and I gave him nothing to find.

'No, I wouldn't say that. But she were very intelligent. Very intelligent,' he repeated. His sincerity took me by surprise.

'And you won't love Miss Mabel any better than she did.' Was this now a defence of her? A challenge?

'We can leave these lot out here while we go and have lunch.'

We trotted back and at the outdoor sink I washed myself up as best I could, but my eyelid was feeling almost heated now. I dared not touch it because I was sure it would make whatever it was worse. We stepped into the kitchen and found Wesley wiping out jugs while Mrs Hurrel was rolling out pastry.

'What's that on your eye you?' she said, looking at me.

'Come 'ere.' Wiping her floury hands on her apron, she came over and pulled at my eyebrow to look under my lid. 'You've got a nice stye there, my love. 'Old up. Sit here, will ya!' Plopping me on a chair at the table, she went into the pantry and came out with a chunk of salted pork belly. 'Close your eye and put your head back,' she said, slapping the pork onto my eye. Wesley laughed and so did I.

'Yer laughing now, but you'd be crying before bedtime if it weren't for me. The salt will draw it out, I promise yer. It'll be gone by Monday.'

The nattering that followed had little import but such flow. One might have thought Wesley and I were as much her children as Joseph was. Mrs Hurrel was proud to tell us that Joseph had caught our lunch the day before. Brown trout from the river that ran through Rose Hall's grounds. We had it with boiled potatoes and pickled fennel with orange, and a delectable crusty loaf with butter. I never thought I'd eat something as exotic tasting on a farm. Good humoured as I was, I couldn't have imagined the spell being broken.

Two heavy knocks on the door sounded out, and then there stood Lord Belfield and Sir Chester. We all stood up and brushed ourselves off.

'No, no, I'm so sorry for interrupting. Stay seated, please.' We all sat back down, excluding Joseph, who walked towards the men. 'Yes, Joseph, dear boy. I've come to get Langston to ride into town and ... Chester here will be watching over things while I'm gone. When I'm back he'll take Paddy and Bilitis home with him. I told him what a good job you've done looking after them. Thanks for all of that, but if you wouldn't mind saddling Langston up now, I'd be grateful.'

'Yes m'lord.'

With that, Joseph rushed out and the two men followed behind him. I had been watching Sir Chester's face the whole time. I was wondering if he intended to leer at me surreptitiously from now on. Nothing of the sort. He looked a bit bored if anything; said nothing and refused to look at me at all. He nodded at Mrs Hurrel when leaving, and that was it. We stood at the window and watched Joseph wrangle the two stallions and the two mares back into the stables one by one.

Lord Belfield suddenly pointed at the sky and swung back, mumbling something. Mrs Hurrel went to the sink and started scrubbing. I brushed at the crumbs on the counter with a tea cloth, trying to seem occupied and as if we hadn't been watching them all from the window.

Lord Belfield knocked and stuck his head into the kitchen. 'Miss Granger.'

Wordlessly, I placed the tea towel down and went out to meet him.

He reached into his breast pocket and took out a brass key with a red strip of silk on it: the key to the library, which I had never before been allowed to handle.

'I would like to entrust you with the key once and for all now, my dear. You've been here long enough, and as I am away for a short while, you can continue with your work alone.'

I reverently took it from his outstretched palm and slid it into my skirt pocket.

'What do you say?' Lord Belfield looked at me quizzically.

'Oh. I'm sorry. Umm, thank you m'lord,' I said.

He nodded.

'Have a safe journey,' I added. With that, he swivelled

around and ambled off to the stables to join Sir Chester and Joseph. I went back inside to join Mrs Hurrel at our station by the kitchen window.

A few minutes later, they were saddled up and riding off into the intermittently sunny day. Joseph's shoulders were notably slacker by the time he got back into the kitchen. Mrs Hurrel patted his back when he sat down and put a bowl of rice pudding with strawberry jam in it before him. We all ate a bit slower than he did. She got up to give him another bowl as soon as he'd finished, without him even having to ask.

'I'll walk you two back now, won't I?' Joseph asked. We bid our goodbyes and Mrs Hurrel hugged both Wesley and me, and I felt newly devastated in her embrace. Last weekend when we had left, this farm kitchen had been an oasis. We could speculate on the lives of those at the big house, untouched by them. With Lord Belfield coming down here I was newly aware of how precarious all our lives were, dependent as they were on the moods of a quick-thinking aristocrat. And to leave Sir Chester at Rose Hall while he was gone. Well, why wouldn't he? I only hoped that Sir Chester's visit would be short, and that he would be gone before he could make good on his threats to me.

On top of Mabel walking back, the sun did come out properly and made the valley glow green in a different way. Was the grass on the hills looking a little more verdant, or was that wishful thinking on my part? I couldn't be sure.

'I'm sorry you're losing Paddy and Bilitis to Sir Chester, Joseph.'

'They ain't mine to lose, Florence. It's all Lord Belfield's,

134

to do with as he pleases. This land, the horses, the farm, the cottage. It's all his.'

I had assumed wrongly that the Hurrels' home was theirs. It hadn't occurred to me that they might also be in a position of dependence. None of us owned anything of substance like Lord Belfield and Sir Chester did. Looking down the road, Joseph sighed, scratched his beard and grunted. I had nothing to say in response. I had been silly to think that I might create my own future. It was now clear that it would most likely be decided for me.

Chapter Thirteen

Wesley took Lady Violet's meals up to her room and at first, my only contact with her was to fulfil her book requests. She would send me a note with something like *'tragic love'* and I would place *A Tale of Two Cities* or *Wuthering Heights* by her door. I'd wait around the corner to see the door snatch open and her pale hand reach down for them. Her latest note had read *'exotic adventure'*. If I were less selfish I might have given her the copy of *One Thousand and One Nights* I was reading to Wesley, but interpreting the request a bit more loosely meant I could give her *The Wonderful Adventures of Mrs Seacole in Many Lands* and *The Jungle Book*. For the first two days of Lord Belfield's trip I never actually saw Sir Chester, either. I would just hear him behind closed doors, blustering away. And the smell of him: Scotch, cigars and juniper berries. That last aroma was his cologne. His facial hair was so neatly kept, one could guess he was very good with a razor.

*

I had done most of the smaller and less damaged books by this point in early February. I had chosen to start with them because they were easiest, and seeing them stacked together was most illustrative of my progress, even if there was so much more to do. I focused on the leather cover repairs. Very few needed a whole front or back board replacement. It was mostly corner deterioration and head bands being worn down that needed the most attention. I could use wax and find close-enough paints to disguise my alterations. The trick was obviously not to make them look as good as new. Far from it – what was necessary was to make the books look as if they had been much better taken care of. A book's ageing is part of its charm, after all. I was ensuring the books' conservation. Restoring them to the standard to which they should have always been kept. Once each book's external appearance had been taken care of, then I would work my way through page by page and look for rips and tears that I could fix with Japanese *washi* paper. A sliver here and a sliver there would cover up the small rips and minor missing chinks of a page. The pastes I used were translucent enough to ensure the look of the repair wasn't too homely. Invisibility is what one aimed for, even though my father had showed me over the years that it couldn't ever be fully achieved. A competent bookbinder could always find the spots in a book that were new. The too-smooth bevelled edge of a board, the too-neat cut of a new leather turn-in, or the very minor, but nevertheless notable to our eyes, colour difference between old paper and new.

The stacks of books I had amassed were an accomplishment for sure. Yet I knew that the harder work lay ahead, and my time was running short.

In the days after Sir Chester had threatened me with the rubbing of his groin, Lady Violet seemed suddenly more present, occasionally drifting along as though keen to engage me in conversation, though she never did. I thought back to when I had hoped we could connect over books, and wondered if she had merely viewed me as a curiosity, just as Lord Belfield appeared to. And perhaps now she had identified her husband's interest in me, and was seeking to guard what was hers. The upstairs of Rose Hall struck me as a poisonous place.

When I could escape her in the library, I leaped on the opportunity for more of a challenge in order to distract myself. In moving to the collection of larger, older books, I had to work on a greater level of deterioration. Coming up with creative solutions would take up more space in my mind than the thought of this man of shallow ambitions, who was eager to expose himself to me as his first punitive action, and his untrustworthy wife.

I needed hot water. Baxter lent me one of her copper kettles and a large rectangular enamelled tin dish normally used for roasting. I placed the copper kettle in the library's fireplace, warming the water until it was hot to the touch but not boiling. I poured the water into the tin and then placed in the stuck-together pages of mouldy books; ones that had truly fallen apart at this point. For each book, I would then take my pliers to delicately prise apart the delicate sodden pages. Once a single page was freed from the glued stack, I could use my horsehair toothbrush with its ivoried handle to rub off the adhesive at the edge, very gently. And I would then take each page out of the water using tweezers to grasp it along the same edge, before placing it on a clothes-drying rack, which I kept far enough from the fire to keep the pages from being scorched, but close enough to dry them out from the hot air.

My movements had more range. Instead of staying sat at the desk with my metal rulers and scalpels and leather hide, my back ached less from the different stages this new work took. From desk, to kettle, to fire, to water bath, to gently craning overhead, to tip-toeing to the clothes rack with translucent liberated pages of text. Once dry, they could be rebound into the original order, looking as if the pages hadn't been much fingered.

I hoped that on Lord Belfield's return, I would have proven my worth to him with the perceptibly crackpot idea of using nothing but hot water to restore a book that hadn't been opened in perhaps a hundred years. I could only complete one book that day; the pace was painstakingly slow. I was proud of what I had done, but I was still nowhere near confident I would finish in a month – the schedule we hadn't discussed in some time.

The silence of Rose Hall at night, after long days alone in the library, always made my loneliness more complete. Growing up in Deansgate had meant growing up with noise. The clip-clop sounds of horses drawing carts, and the distant, sooty, steaming belches of trains pulling in. Even the splashes of the canals at night-time.

I'd only thought about the cacophony I was used to once I had heard the solitary, muffled sounds of Rose Hall at rest. Trees might whoosh and rustle, rattling the panes of the windows. An owl might telegraph its feelings over the night air and rattle me with its interruption. My spirits submitted to each whistling gale. In my night-time reveries, just before bed, I would read out loud in a voice I hoped would summon my mother back to me; that the wind would whip her ghost in through a crack in the window, and her cool hand could stroke the top of my head as I lay there. I had always hoped for a haunting. And not of the kind that I had witnessed in the hallways of Rose Hall.

But that night, the second after Lord Belfield's departure, my reverie was broken by the sound of broken glass.

A symphony of shards splintering and then raining down, like ice picks being rattled on a wooden floor. I shot up in my bed.

It didn't take me too long to get myself together, because my lamp was still lit. My head scarf had slipped off, though. I went over to the small table I kept by the window, to use the oval mirror that reflected back my blanched face and dark eyes. As I tied my head scarf back on, my eye was caught by the movement of a figure below, racing down through the grounds towards the river and its bridge. The intruder! I guessed male, because of the height and breadth of him. He was only in sight for a few seconds before the gloom swallowed him, but long enough to confirm I wasn't imagining it.

I hurried to my door, socks on, paraffin lamp in hand. I creaked it open and saw Baxter at her door in the same position. Wordlessly, we walked into the hallway and saw Wesley ahead of us on the staircase below. How he had got himself out of bed that quickly, I did not yet know.

We caught up with him. Descending the stairs together, they were both focused on the front door, but I felt a draught from down the corridor as we reached the ground floor. Looking down the hall to the library door, I could see it was wide open. My heart jolted. Had I not left it locked? Impossible to think otherwise. After Lord Belfield's dressing-down after Christmas, I had been especially worried about keeping his trust. To go from being locked in, to being left the key when he was away, was an indication of his growing trust in me. For my own peace of mind I had determined it was locked before every departure by twisting the knob and giving it a push. When I was working, I kept the key in the door, and when it was locked, it was in my skirt pocket. Two locations determined by the actions of my day. The best pickpockets of Swan Street would have struggled to whistle the key away without me noticing. I was sure that no precious books could be stolen by an intruder under my watch.

I tapped Wesley on the shoulder and pointed my lamp down the corridor, illuminating the open library door down the way. We three of us crept towards it and the air got colder and colder as we approached. We stepped inside to see that the library's bay window had lost a pane – cleanly. Nothing jagged remained, but there were three rivulets of blood dripping down the pane below, and as I drew closer I saw that they were on the inside. The size of the intruder was immediately brought back to my mind. He couldn't possibly have pulled himself through that opening. A child would have been able to – even a tall twelve-year-old, say. But no one of bulk. And definitely not the full-grown man I saw running away.

'Mind your feet there, Floss,' Baxter said. She'd never called me that before. To hear it in another circumstance would have made me feel almost giddy. But it was not enough to quell the rising panic in me. What had been taken? The exotics were my first thought. The ivory covers of the lectionary were almost priceless. The Bibles? Even the Greek books were of considerable value.

My first layer of worry was that this breach would lead to my dismissal, because Lord Belfield had left me with a key and entrusted me with the collection's protection. It wasn't my fault – or at least I didn't think it was – but would that matter when Lord Belfield found out? The man was the richest I had ever met, but had I not heard it alluded to countless times that he was beleaguered with money troubles? Would I not be punished for what could be a devastating financial blow?

The second, and admittedly thicker layer of worry, was that the intruder had stolen something that I had laboured over for hours. I had done all sorts by this point. Gold embossing that was as intricate as it was beautiful. Expertly prised apart centuries-old pages that were stuck together. I had worked so hard. To have hours and hours of my work stolen out from underneath me – the thought made me want to howl.

I went to my list on my desk. The books I had worked on were ticked off. There were still more books unticked than ticked, but nevertheless, cross-referencing what was on the list with what had been taken from the library was my first priority. I intended to locate each one individually, which would require a whole lot of back and forthing, climbing the ladders that allowed me access to the higher reaches of the library shelves. However, I knew the collection so well that if something significant were missing, I should notice it quickly. I was in this room every day. I knew the collection intimately. Nothing looked out of place, and I could see no gaping holes in the ranks of Lord Belfield's books. Nevertheless, I kept my eyes scanning and skimming.

My frantic search was interrupted by the meek voice of Lady Violet in the doorway behind us.

'Has there been a break-in?'

Lady Violet's groggy appearance at the door was just another bizarre happening that night. That Sir Chester had not risen too was apparently not suspect, I discovered later. He was a big drinker and so it followed that he was a heavy sleeper, and had remained in his bedchamber. The mastiff mainly slept at Lady Violet's feet when she came to stay and so Archibald's distraction from guard duties also had an explanation of sorts.

'I'll have to ...' I gulped. 'I will ... write to Lord Belfield, in the morning.'

'Yes, of course. You must,' she said.

'I won't sweep up the glass while Sir Chester is sleeping,' Wesley said.

'Oh, don't worry, he'd sleep through an elephant race.'

'It's better when the sun comes up, for the light and everything, though.'

'Yes. Very well, then.'

Even though I had taken it upon myself to write and inform Lord Belfield of the break-in, it wasn't lost on me that Lady Violet's reportage would hold the most authority. I knew it was incumbent on me to convey to her that I was searching thoroughly. Even though none of the valuable books were at the other end of the room nearer the window, I would make sure to have her see me checking the shelves there too, so she would report my care for the library. She wasn't directing us, or interrogating us. But Lady Violet was the only one present who wasn't an employee. That this had occurred while Lord Belfield was away put all of our positions in danger. She was the only one with nothing to worry about.

'Can you see if anything valuable was taken, Miss Granger?' she asked me.

'Not as far as I can tell. All the exotics are still in the right place in their cage. The big pricey tomes, as well. They didn't take the lectionary, and that's worth more than I can say.'

With Lady Violet's lamp too, there was now enough light in the room to illuminate things rather well. As she strode off to speak to Wesley and Baxter at the other end of the room, a red ribbon caught my eye, bright where it lay beside the white covers of the ivory lectionary. The key itself was not a glinting brass, but dull and darkened with usage. The key to the library – *my* key – was on my desk.

My throat constricted to the point I could hear my breath becoming raspy. I was fortunate that the others were deep in conversation, so I was able to snatch it up and into my right hand. My night gown had no pocket in which to deposit it. Fortunately, it was small enough to pinch into my palm with my bottom three fingers, concealing it from view. My thumb and index finger were stiff enough to bear the weight of my lamp.

I made my way to the other end of the room so that I could search the shelves near where Violet was standing, unnecessarily.

'No, nothing is out of place, that I can see.'

She was watching me intently, but not staring at my hand where the key was concealed, at least. Her attention made me feel guilty. How had the key ended up on my desk, in the night? I would never leave it there. It went only from my skirt pocket into the door and then back again. I'd been certain of its location. If anyone else were to have seen the key, maybe they would have suggested I left the room unlocked, and thus was responsible for the intruder getting in. But this was impossible. I hoped it to be impossible. I struggled to think of what to say, so I just said what I believed to be truthful.

'I don't understand why someone would risk getting caught breaking in, and leave without taking anything.'

Chapter Fourteen

The following morning I walked into the kitchen to the salty smell of kippers being boiled on the range.

'You haven't slept,' Baxter accused as I walked in. 'Look at her eyes, Wesley. You look like you're grinning at the daisy roots, you do.'

'Well, I couldn't very well sleep with all last night's goings on, could I?' I was still flummoxed by the intruder, and the strangely untouched state of the library. I chomped and huffed down on the salty kippers and buttered bread.

'Slow down or you'll choke,' Baxter told me.

I drank some tea to appease her. 'Thank you,' I said, sighing with appreciation.

I had not slept because I had been trying to reconcile the man I'd seen running from Rose Hall, the broken library window, the key on my desk – and the thief who had taken nothing.

If someone had broken into the library to steal from Lord Belfield's collection, why wouldn't they have at least seized the priceless book from my desk before escaping into the night?

I couldn't shake the uncomfortable suspicion that signs pointed to someone in the household. Someone who would know if I left the library unlocked out of carelessness – though I could hardly believe it of myself.

Now, I couldn't help contemplating the possible motives of Baxter and Wesley, feeling a prickling unease as I remembered Wesley had been out of bed in a suspiciously short span of time. But why wouldn't they be loyal to Lord Belfield? He wasn't just their employer. He had become a protector of sorts, guarding them both from the outside world. An old cook who would struggle to find a place in another home. An effete footman who smelled of sugar and violets and had a delicate constitution. They had more freedom in this house than I'd heard of for anyone else who worked in service. They had the freedom to dictate their days, with no butler to command them now. I only saw them when they were in the midst of doing something frightfully useful, but as soon as we weren't in each other's view I was sure they did as I did and lay around doing the things that brought them joy. I couldn't be the only one who found somewhere dark, warm and discreet to go and touch myself sometimes, imagining I was being touched by someone else. Everett the anarchist, mostly.

And it was hard to suspect Lady Violet of performing a ruse – even if she were less weak and meek than she had made herself out to be. If she wanted to take one of Lord Belfield's books without his permission, why would she break the window? And who had I seen running away from the house?

Joseph? He definitely could have smashed a window in, perhaps to steal something I hadn't yet identified as missing ... What he would steal, and why, I couldn't fathom. But he had the ability.

Just before midday, a knock came on the library door as I sat checking through my list of Lord Belfield's books, still puzzling over the mystery. A thief caught breaking into a house like this would run the risk of corporal punishment, as well as a life-altering prison term. I couldn't imagine why someone would take that chance unless they were desperate to steal something to sell – though perhaps they had panicked?

Lady Violet rustled in, and who should be behind her but Joseph, with a pane of glass and a crate of tools.

'Miss Granger. I do hope you don't mind, but I thought it best to be a busybody and hurry down to the farm to get Hurrel here to fix the window for us. You must be utterly freezing.'

He nodded at me. Such a big brute of a man, but always being led and instructed to do things for others. He'd have made a fantastic soldier or gladiator in Ancient Rome. A formidable size, with shoulders that wouldn't buckle under an axe.

How well did she know Joseph? He'd never mentioned her, and he had no reason to be up at the big house. Horses? All ladies rode horses, obviously. Was Bilitis hers? I was surprised Sir Chester could even afford to keep two horses, with his constant grabbing for money, but then again Lord Belfield had clearly been keeping them for him for some time.

'Oh no, it's fine. I wore an extra cardigan and I've got an India rubber hot water bottle on my lap here,' I said.

'My, my. How industrious you are at making yourself toasty!' She paused and then cleared her throat. 'But anyway, my dear, I'm sure you deserve a break. You are looking so tired.' However, hers were the eyes that looked a little reddened at the inside corners, I noticed.

'I was up all night,' I said.

'I'm sure you were.'

A silence mushroomed up between us that made me suck my teeth distractedly, extracting a flake of kipper from a back molar. Lady Violet drifted over to Lord Belfield's desk but didn't touch anything.

'I hope you managed some sleep last night, Joseph,' I said.

I had startled him. His neck snapped towards me and he brought his hand up to salute me like a soldier reporting to a general.

'Thank you, Miss Granger.' He smiled awkwardly. A side smile, as if he were embarrassed to be acknowledged by me, almost. Our conversation when we were alone was amiable, so I took his withdrawn demeanour to be a response to Lady Violet's presence.

'If we're all in here, I'll put the fire on,' I said. 'Lord Belfield likes it warm, but I'm fine without, honestly.' I hadn't planned to use my kettle today, which I'd returned to Baxter the previous afternoon. My nerves were too brittle to do such delicate work that morning.

I shook off my blanket as I rose.

'My father has the constitution of a Scandinavian. I'm sure we're descended from some sort of Viking marau—' I paused.

I had reached the mantelpiece where the matches were laid. Wesley always left the fires ready to be lit. Lord Belfield preferred wood to coal. Less soot. Less effort in some respects. I expected the logs to be there, whole and ready for kindling. I knew that's how he had left things yesterday, after he swept out the grate when I was done with the kettle and tidying up the last dried-out pages of the book I was working on. I had walked us both out afterwards. But even though the fire was out, I could see that it had been lit – more than that, it had been roaring. The tell-tale ashes. The pleasingly black logs were totally flamed through. Some time between leaving the library yesterday late afternoon and this morning, when I had believed the room to be locked, someone had lit a fire.

'Miss Granger?' I heard from somewhere behind me.

I hadn't realised that I had frozen into stone. The Medusa in question lay among the logs. Flecks of green from the leather covering were still visible in patches. I knew what lay in the fire without having to reach down for it.

'What is it? Are you quite all right, Miss Granger?' Lady Violet was by my side now. She brought her hand up to my shoulder.

I pointed towards the charred diary. The diary I'd had every intention of searching for and reading during Lord Belfield's absence.

She didn't follow my finger. She just looked at me unblinkingly. 'It's her diary,' I whispered. Joseph didn't turn to look at us.

It was only on my utterance that Lady Violet looked into the fireplace. She crouched down, as did I. From her skirt pocket out came a large handkerchief in paisley, purple and green. Someone had tossed the diary onto the logs. Had it been in the heart of the fire, then there was no doubt it would have been fully consumed. Lady Violet lifted it out of the grate and placed it in the handkerchief. The entire back of the diary was gone.

I gasped.

This caught Joseph's attention, and he turned to look at us. But catching my eye, he turned back to the window as if he hadn't heard a thing.

I felt such loss. The pages of a dead woman's diary had been almost completely burned away. I felt grief for what could never be regained. Her thoughts. Gone.

I knew how important it was that the diary was kept in the right conditions from now on, if we were to have any hope of preserving it. What singed pages were left were framed by ashes, waiting to be blown away. I stayed Lady Violet's hands as she reached for the handkerchief, and I took over, bringing each corner of the handkerchief over the front page so that I might tie the ends together and create a cloth basket underneath. Her unceasing stare let me know that we were now conspiring. I hung it on the fireside companion toolset, minimising the friction and pressure on the pages by keeping it suspended. In the absence of a padded box, this was the best I could do for now.

When I was done, we rose together.

'You'll keep that safe, won't you?'

I nodded.

She retreated to go back to Joseph. I was shaken by the discovery. For now I had a bit more of an explanation as to what had happened last night. Someone – presumably the intruder

I had seen escaping into the trees – had broken into the library in order to burn Lady Persephone's diary. They had been only partially successful. Had they been disturbed by a sound and raced out with the job half completed? The fire was not roaring when we entered, of that I was sure. I would have noticed the smell. We all would have. Had they been in the library for some time, the fire already gone out, and they hadn't noticed before leaving that the diary wasn't fully burned? What had made them run away in such haste, then? It seemed unlikely. A whole new set of questions was arising.

Joseph had now fixed the window into place with Lady Violet by his side, and was smoothing the putty around the frame. I was sure fingers as thick as his would leave an indent, but when I went past later, whatever technique he'd used made it seem like he had smoothed it with a tool used for icing cakes.

Neither of them bid me goodbye once the job was done. I was just left alone to contemplate the discovery. Joseph had definitely heard everything. And Lady Violet was sure to tell me what I should do later. The three of us were the only ones who knew the diary was the reason for the break-in. And as far as I knew, Lord Belfield was the only other person who had knowledge of the book. I had no idea whether he had finally mustered up the courage to read it.

I kept Lady Persephone's diary in the safest place I could. Bound up in its cloth on one of the hooks in my bedroom closet, where it wouldn't be bashed by any movement. I could hardly wait to read it, but it would require time and patience to piece it together, and I could no longer keep my eyes open . . .

*

152

After lunch the following day, Lady Violet sidled up to me in the entrance hall as I was coming up from the stairs to the kitchen. I barely noticed the hand at my back. She didn't ask me to go outside with her. I just followed, as if entranced. She only spoke when we were in the garden.

'The other night must have left you shaken?'

'Yes, yes . . . I suppose it did.'

'So many valuable things in there, and Francis always so quick to talk about his library's worth. I think it was only a matter of time before a thief tried their luck.'

'But nothing was taken,' I protested. My bones told me that the diary was the true reason for the burglary.

'As far as you know,' she said.

'As far as I know.'

She pulled me down onto a bench facing the southern hills. I wished I'd brought a scarf. My exposed neck felt the wind tickling.

'Miss Granger. I no longer think we should tell Lord Belfield about the intruder.'

I snapped my face towards her. I had stumbled over my attempts to write the letter yesterday morning, and after we had discovered the diary, I had left it aside. But not to tell him was unthinkable.

'I can go and telegraph him at the post office myself.'

'No, no. It's not the logistics of it, my dear. It's your welfare that concerns me.'

'I'm fine,' I said, though my gut was churning at the thought of his reaction.

'You are now, but you won't be if you're dismissed for carelessness,' Lady Violet pointed out, giving voice to my fears. 'We both know you weren't the one that placed Lord Belfield's collection in jeopardy, but I've seen so many staff dismissed for things outside of their control. He might over-react if he receives a letter like that and isn't able to see for himself that no harm was done to his precious books.' She seemed genuinely concerned.

She was right. I had that fear already and now she was stok-ing it, without meaning to increase my anxiety, I suspected. It was just truth.

'Sir Chester is fully unaware of there even being a burglary. And our darling giant Joseph won't tell anyone. He's incred-ibly discreet, I assure you.'

'But ... what about when Lord Belfield returns?'

'Well, if as you say, nothing of value was taken, then he will be much calmer to see that for himself.'

'Well, he is going to notice that the diary's burned almost to ashes,' I countered.

'Imagine placing the charred pages of her diary into his hands. It's ... too frightful for either of us to contemplate doing to him,' she said. 'Better not to mention it – why bring his attention to something he might not even discern is miss-ing? He has been avoiding that book for a year. There's no reason he should think of it now, and his desk is a mess so he'll hardly notice its absence easily. And if he does for some reason, we just have to hope he doesn't become too angry with you as the library's keeper.'

I shook away the shiver that had just swum up my spine.

'We're talking about your future here,' Lady Violet said firmly. 'I know your background only a little, but I'm assum-ing you ran away from Manchester because you couldn't deal with your life there. I'm assuming you also can't return? Let's let sleeping dogs lie.' She took her hands off mine and clapped them to show we were done. She was back in charge. I couldn't protest.

Chapter Fifteen

Lady Violet and Sir Chester left without much fanfare. I liked Lady Violet a little more for keeping the break-in a secret from him. There was no way Sir Chester wouldn't use it to put my position in jeopardy, so I was glad to see them go. Another advantage of them leaving was that I could now do my best to salvage the diary and read what was left.

I did all the delicate work in my bedroom after Wesley left for the night. The person who had burned the diary was of a callous mind, I was sure. The first few barely singed pages were the only ones I could easily read. A delightful recollection of a trip to London in 1895 where Lady Persephone waxed rhapsodical about the joy and beauty of the inaugural First Night of the Proms at the Queen's Hall, where she deified the new works most of all: *Monsieur Chopin* and *Monsieur Bizet*. I longed to hear what she had heard. Lord Belfield was pleased, but nowhere near as excited as Sibyl, apparently. It surprised me that she would have gone along with them. Was that the done thing? The proms were meant for the general public to have more access to good music, I supposed.

What followed were descriptions of the landscape around Rose Hall that would have made William Wordsworth swoon. She loved being in nature and rambling over the hills, evidently. Her descriptions of the river felt particularly poignant, given her fate. But Rose Hall itself, and what she thought of its inhabitants? I couldn't tell, because that's where the papers started to become far more damaged. Two thirds of a page at first. And then half. Snatches of sentences became more foreboding:

'... *how could I not be scared of him* ...' at the top of one page.

In the middle of another: '... *in the corridor he grabbed me by the* ...'

The worst: '... *at night he comes in unannounced* ...'

Like me, she found herself being chanced upon in the dark. Would the man she feared be one who would harm me, too? Did I face the same dangers she faced?

The week of work that followed was unremarkable, in stark contrast to the melee in my mind, until Thursday morning. I awoke with a far-too-familiar deep, continuous ache in my lower abdomen. I groaned with the knowledge that the next few days would be a slog. Our porridge breakfast tasted like it had whale oil in it for some reason. I've never had whale oil of course, but it's what I imagined it would taste like: irony, fatty and sea tinged. I kept it down.

I worked that day on the gentle dust-scraping and grime-wiping of some Greek books I couldn't decipher at all. I could stay seated and rub my belly under the table.

Lunch was a distraction – the usual ham, cheese and pickle on crusty bread with an apple for dessert. It wasn't something I could get bored of eating. The textures and flavours of the ham and cheese, in particular, varied so widely. I remember that day was apple-smoked ham and Wensleydale cheese and the yellow mustard tasted a bit hotter than usual. I wanted to be back with the burnt diary. Anytime I wasn't reading it felt wasteful. There was so much to piece together from the gaps.

Was the man she was afraid of the same one who had tried to destroy the diary? Was that the man I had seen running off during the night? If he thought the diary was wholly destroyed, that meant I was in less danger perhaps, because he wouldn't think I could find and read anything that might incriminate him. But the man I was most fearful of was Lord Belfield. Smart as he was, surely he would note the diary's absence eventually. I was the one who had the most reason to fear the repercussions of its destruction.

Mounting the stairs after lunch, I felt the twinge that promised a rocking of my world was to come over the next hours. A separation of myself was necessary. I could still take part in conversations if called upon, and any sighs or yawns I emitted over the course of a sleepy afternoon were no more strained than usual. But I had to pretend that my insides weren't taut with a growing agony. Inside me, the girl behind the placid mask mewled without restraint.

In other countries, I hoped there were different customs where women didn't have to pretend, and could be afforded a day or two of respite without too much explanation. Perhaps somewhere in the South Pacific there was an island where women could spend their few days a month resting together in the shade, and bathing in the sea at sunset.

After dinner that night, the pain had intensified to the degree I felt that I had a band of demons inside me dancing Ring a Ring o' Roses and giggling out spurts of fire. I was sweating to the point that my underclothes were dampened when I stepped out of them in my room. I was desperate for sleep, for at least in a loss of consciousness I would not feel. However, the battle for slumber was lost, because a team of demons was dedicated to my pain.

I lay in bed twitching and turning, clutching my abdomen while doing my best to breathe into it as my grandmother had told me to. I tried to ride the pain, as it were. I longed for her presence at so many times, but particularly at times like these. It wouldn't do to discuss such matters with anyone besides a close female family member. With no mother or sisters, she was all I had. Perhaps she had suspected her early demise, because a lot of the girls at school were clueless when their monthlies had arrived. In her own brusque, matter of fact delivery, I had been shown where and how to place my towelette, and the specific undergarment to wear to ensure it wouldn't be dislodged throughout the day. She had taught me how to make towelettes from discarded clothing one afternoon after church, and then instructed me on how to wash them and where to dry them so that my father would never come across them. I couldn't imagine how I would handle it all when I gained a husband and children, though. The whole process of subterfuge was such a rigmarole. The only way I was currently keeping the household unaware of my monthlies was because I had such nice long stretches of time alone.

Rising from my bed, I gave myself a quick rinsing and replaced the towelette with a newer one. I was gasping for a peppermint tea. I descended the stairs with much more confidence than I did when conducting my night investigations into Lady Persephone's belongings. After Sir Chester found me reading her letters, I had contemplated ceasing my snooping and just going to bed at the right time like a normal person. Then I decided against it. I kept up my night-time visits to the morning room to read the letters. I felt that by continuing to do so, I was accomplishing two things. I was fulfilling my mission to understand what had happened over the course of her life, in the hope that it might help me understand why she had died in such an unexpected way. Furthermore, I was defying Sir Chester. I was not some girl he could scare and harass back into timid behaviour. I was not weak. But when I got to the bottom step before heading down to the kitchens, I admit I did feel weakened.

I held onto the banister as my breath whistled sharply through my teeth, and I bent over, staring at the mottled carpet pattern as the pain spreading to my kidneys twanged its way throughout my lower back. This was a rough one. I wanted to cry ... So I did. Just happy to be alone with the injustice of it all. One cheeky bite of an apple, and millennia later, here we all are, cursed by her actions. I sobbed silently coming down the kitchen steps until I noticed a flickering light coming from the kitchen. Baxter must have left one burning absent-mindedly. I heard a sound as I moved towards the range and I swung round. To my horror, there she sat. Baxter, staring right back at me from our table, enshrouded in a shawl I'd not seen before with a mug in her hands and a candle in front of her. I just stood in the doorway, not knowing what to say.

'Well, we were bound to start overlapping at some point soon, weren't we lass. It's been more than a few months.'

I must have looked confused, because she went on to explain: 'Oh of course, your mother weren't around to tell yer, Wesley told me. You don't know then. Don't stand there gawping, come sit down, you silly mare.'

I crept towards her with hunched shoulders. She stood up and went to the range, and from a saucepan she poured into another stone mug and came back to place the steaming brew before me. She sat down and wrapped her shawl back around her shoulders.

'You're cold, are ya?' she asked. I shook my head. Her crystal blue eyes assessed me for expressions of contradiction.

'It's normally the two of you nattering on, with me listening to your oriental tales and jungle adventures, but here you are quiet as a church mouse. There's nowt to be ashamed of. It's every woman's cross to bear.'

'I'm not ashamed,' I whispered.

'Well good. There's peppermint, ginger root and yarrow in that cup there. Should take the edge off your pains.'

'Does yours hurt?' I asked.

'Not as much as yours, I don't think. I saw you trying to soldier through at dinner, but it's not the sort of thing Wesley would notice, is it? He didn't come to your room tonight 'cos I told him to leave yous alone.'

Horrified, I looked up at her from my cup.

'There's very few secrets in this house, young lady. Besides, the way you clatter about at night, you might as well have them ring the church bells before you go gallivanting room to room. You're lucky Lord Belfield drinks that much. He'd have caught you at it in the old days.'

'How long have you been here, all in all?' I asked.

'Twenty-eight years. I came here when I was thirteen. I were raised over in Bolton.'

'You're forty-one?' I exclaimed.

'Well, thank you very much for sounding so surprised. I'd love to see how you'll look after a life of service!'

'No, it's just that ...' I was scrambling. I had no ready defence. To see her as I saw her now, her age made sense. Hair in two plaits either side of her ears and the eyes focused on me with a liquid intensity I had not yet experienced. The fact she seemed so aged to me during the day was because of her own reticence, although I dared not say anything like that to her. Grumpiness aged people. When I first read Scrooge in *A Christmas Carol* and saw the long, sharp-nosed drawing with him doddling about in oily rags, I had comfortably assumed him to be one hundred and one.

'I came here as a scullery maid, didn't I? It were only a few years, but it took my youth from me. Once there was the opportunity to work solely in the kitchens I leaped at the chance to have my work between just two rooms instead of every room in the house. I'm not posh like you, so there were no chance of becoming a lady's maid or housekeeper. I come from common folk and my miserable face suits me just fine. All that smiling and scraping and bowing you two have to do upstairs, wouldn't suit me.' She sighed.

'I'm not posh,' I countered.

'You're posh enough to become a governess.'

I think I might have scowled at her, but she merely smirked. I wasn't angry at her as such. It was more that I had assumed a house of this size would afford privacy to everyone within it. I had gathered such scant information on everyone, excluding Persephone and Wesley. Yet, Baxter, Sir Chester and Lord Belfield were all blessed with information about me that I had no say in them knowing.

'I don't know if I even want to become a governess.'

'What you want and what you need are two different matters, my girl. Don't kick a gift horse in the mouth!'

It was her turn to speak with anger now. I raised my eyebrow at her, wondering at the source of it.

'You seem to be doing all right?'

'Oh, do I?' she scoffed.

The silence that fell between us was clammy with her regret and resentment and my fear and confusion.

'Now look here, you. All your books and your reading has got you in the door, but your books and your reading won't save you from being alone in your old age. You're too smart for the likes of all the men I know and you'll be older than me before you blink a few times. At least if you're a governess you can save some wages, or become a teacher or whatever else. You're not demure, but many, including myself, have had that work in our favour. You take him up on his offer and you'll thank me for it.'

The tone she was speaking to me in was one that I would reserve for insulting a man who was daring to overcharge me down the market. But I felt warm for her consideration of me, even though it meant I was obviously much more visibly adrift than I had thought myself to be.

'What will happen to you after here, do you think?'

Her eyes took on a maudlin quality at that. Not tearful as such. More mournful. Even though she had told me more about herself tonight than on any other night, there was still a whole orchard of fruits left for me to pick at, in order to learn about how Baxter had journeyed from girl to womanhood.

'Who knows, my love. But some day soon, I won't be sitting here plugging back tea and hoping for a pain-free night with you.'

'Baxter ...' I reached across the table and touched her hand. 'Are you ill?'

'What?' She screwed her face up at me. 'No. No! You're far too sentimental you are. I just told you, I'm forty-one. My monthlies won't be with me for much longer.'

I cocked my head to the side in shock. 'They ... stop?'

'Didn't no one ever tell you?' Baxter said, on the edge of laughter.

No. My grandmother had left that bit out of our serious chats. It hadn't occurred to me that there would be an end to the monthly pain. I started grinning. What joy! The comfort with which old women carried themselves made such glorious sense to me now. How light one must feel as a woman in her later years. The end of one's lower organs wringing themselves in contortions. A cramp-free life?

'You'll be going through a change and on the other side of that, it's easier. After a while at least ...'

The cramps I had been feeling had dulled over the course of this talk. My mug was now empty but I upturned it anyway, to sup at the last drips.

'There's a full kettle for your 'ot water bottle on the range there. Take one of them cloths and carry it up to bed with yous. Mind ya don't knock the cork out when you're in bed. You'll be wetter than animals left off Noah's ark if you do.'

I was stunned at the relief Baxter had bestowed upon me. The prospect of becoming an old woman had never felt so bright. I wouldn't be an old lonely crone. I would be a well-rested reader with many memories of inquisitive children biting for the knowledge of my own mind.

Because what distinguished me from Baxter was the education I had given myself. Her warnings were based on the way her life had turned out. The always vaguely miserable woman who was buxom in a way that was definitively not maternal. She was close to no one. No mention of her in Lady Persephone's letters. No jokes about her recounted to me by Lord Belfield or Wesley. She wasn't feared. She wasn't ridiculed. But worst of all for her, she wasn't considered. She was on my list of suspects in Lady Persephone's death because she was always in Rose Hall. Occasionally going to the village for certain things, but no real social connections to speak of. Her life was practically hermetical. Thus, I couldn't cook up a motive for her being involved in the drowning. She could so easily be outrun, portly as she was. The crime itself was not how she would likely choose to hurt someone she wanted gone. Maybe it was just having supped from a herbal concoction she had brewed, but the only way I could see her harming somebody was through the act of poison. Arsenic sprinkled into the cream layer of a Victoria sponge maybe. But no, not really. So maudlin was she in her isolation, the verve it would take to commit homicide had seeped out of her in one exhausted sigh decades ago.

My pity for her forced me up from the table. I needed to get away from her before her sadness could infect me too.

I held the hot water bottle in my hands at the door and turned back to see Baxter smiling at the table.

'God bless you, Baxter ... Sleep well.'

I ascended the stairs feeling like I'd flown a good deal lower than Icarus had. Thus, I comfortably glided down the landing all flushed from the warmth of the wind.

Chapter Sixteen

I did not know when Lord Belfield might return, and despite my fear of his fury at the loss of the diary, I reduced my work to half speed while taking even greater care over each tome. I needed to extend my stay here at Rose Hall as far into the future as possible. Speaking with Baxter had made me more aware that whatever income I might have secured in the short term, my future as an unmarried woman was still horrifically uncertain unless I had some reference to become a governess.

Another girl in my situation might have thrown all her efforts behind making herself as decent a prospective wife as possible. One could argue that most girls would. However, I felt marked. I knew too much about a man's carnal desires for a woman who had never shared a bed with a man before. Even if one were to come along who did not suspect that I had given away the purity that girls were taught to guard and treasure, he need only ask a few questions for my true nature to be unveiled. I was a girl forced into ripeness by forbidden lust. In spite of my age, I no longer saw myself as youthful. I knew too much.

The last thing my father had called me on the night he threw me out had confirmed me to be a harlot in my own mind. Thank goodness for his books on anatomy that had taught me how to avoid anything that might lead to pregnancy. I resisted that act, in spite of being asked constantly to perform it with the man who had ended up running away and leaving me heartbroken.

The pains in my abdomen and lower back rolled through me in waves while I worked and turned the problem of the diary over and over in my mind. The work of piecing together its charred pages was delicate, and I was in no state to continue just yet – but I had enough evidence to consider in the meantime.

The first mutterings I had heard about Lady Persephone's death all splattered Lord Belfield with the spit of suspicion. I got chills around him because of how he could slip from charming benevolent to all-seeing punisher in the space of one conversation. He enjoyed the power of his position as Lord of Rose Hall, but he wasn't barbaric. As for motive, just being married to someone for long enough would provide a litany of reasons why someone's rage for their spouse could spill over into wanting them dead. However, things weren't lining up to see him as a suspect truly.

The diary was the rub. He was not in Rose Hall for the diary's destruction. There would be no reason for him to break in to do that, even. The intruder and the murderer were the same person. Even though Lord Belfield would ordinarily be suspect number one, everything I had discovered thus far seemed to be ruling him out.

So what of the women? Sibyl and Violet. Sibyl could have travelled up from Liverpool and broken into the house she knew so well. Her relationship with Lady Persephone was indeed strange. For a lady's maid (and a coloured one at that), she had so many privileges that seemed untoward: horse riding, singing with her lady and attending the proms. It all seemed to suggest she had something over Lady Persephone that was garnering her such preferential treatment. Also, the way Miss Arabella would mention her to Lady Persephone in her letters was odd. Mysterious as she was, I could definitely see her employing some kind of black magick to whistle the key out of my pocket somehow. Was she some kind of trickster? It pained me to think of her as a murderer when I had defended her from so many prejudicial assessments. I didn't want it to be her – but it could be. For a jealous maid to want the lady of the house out of the picture was an oft-told story, after all.

Lady Violet I could attribute less motive to. No motive at all, in fact. She was thus far merely a kindly sister-in-law who borrowed books Lady Persephone suggested. However, being childless was a reason. If she were barren, as Sir Chester said, maybe her jealousy of Lady Persephone's fecundity might have propelled her into a murderous rage?

It felt far more likely that Lady Violet would murder her *own* husband. She said he was sleeping in a drunken stupor on the night of the break-in. Was she protecting him? His alibis for the nights of Persephone's death and the library break-in were both tenuous. I knew him to be nasty enough to grab anyone by the throat whom he felt stood between him and the life he wanted. I could see him bribing butlers and footmen to keep their mouths shut about his true whereabouts. I could also see him being the man running to the river on the night of the break-in. For the person I saw from the window was definitely a man. The way he ran was ... heavy. Like his footprints would have been cleanly visible if he were running across mud instead of grass. Unless there had been more than one intruder? A duo?

Baxter pretended as if the night before had not happened at breakfast, lunch and dinner. I deduced she didn't think it decent to mention women's business in front of Wesley. I felt no shame about it, surprisingly, but of course it wasn't the done thing. Wesley certainly knew less about our bodies than the average male, and would be utterly disgusted if he were to learn the details of what we were currently enduring.

I had hoped to continue our conspiratorial meetings in the kitchen over the next few nights, before I returned to my candle-lit reading of the burnt diary. There was no chance of that happening, of course. I descended the stairs to the kitchen the following night, hoping to see Baxter sat in front of a cup of the tea concoction she had served me. Instead, I found a kettle of warm water on the range and a strainer with the herbs inside for me to pour the water over myself.

To suspect those I was closer to as the intruder made me feel even more grubby. Wesley? He could have dashed back up to his room in time to meet Baxter and me in the corridor. He wasn't just awake at the time. He was sprightly. The sound of the glass breaking hadn't been the reason he was awake,

I knew that. Remembering the image of him that night, something struck me. Pink lips and cheeks. He had looked so flushed; one might have accused him of having been wearing rouge on stage for a music-hall performance.

And motive? He was always probing me for stories and fascinated by the secrets I shared with him. Yet there was no talk from Wesley of whom he might be creeping out at night to go and see. If he was 'that way', then there had to be someone close by for him to be 'that way' with. It wasn't a stretch for Lady Persephone to have become privy to his escapades and been murdered because she threatened to have him dismissed, or some such. I prayed that this was not what had happened. But against my deepest hopes, I had to admit, it wasn't an impossible scenario. He was also just about lithe enough to fit through the window. But to do that, run across the grass and be back in the corridor with Baxter and me in good time? Had it been a number of seconds, or minutes, between seeing the figure running across the grass and coming into the upstairs corridor?

Joseph was also a good fit for the intruder in some respects. He was too bulky to fit through the broken window, but his tools being so readily available to fix a broken glass pane was rather convenient. Or maybe he was the type to just be around to fix anything. A shelf, a door hinge, a rickety gate. This was what threw me off about him, too. My gentle giant Joseph. Why on earth would he murder as delicate a flower as Lady Persephone? They had so little cause to speak to each other, but more than that, he was the sort of man one would feel immediately safe around. The type to nurse a bird with a broken wing back to health. A murderer? I just couldn't fathom it.

I knew that being with Baxter again would have felt consoling. The one person I was sure was not a suspect. Not the man whom Lady Persephone was so scared of in her diary. Not the man I saw running across the grass. Not the intruder who had burned the diary. Still, she had left me alone once again. There was nothing convivial about our relationship to go along with her innocence.

Sipping the lukewarm, barely infused tea was still nice, but I couldn't fathom why Baxter would allow my loneliness to return and flourish when she knew how little female company I had growing up as a girl. The flashes of compassion she showed me were always so fleeting and reminded me of the truth of my situation. That there is no replacement for a mother. You only get one, and mine had died before I'd ever been given the chance to know her. Mere fantasies existed where memories of our time together should have been. Without motherly instruction, was I not bound to make the mistakes that led me to that stone kitchen, sweating my pain into a cup that no longer had any steam.

Before the colour of daffodils and bluebells arrived, a fragrant sweetness came on the air. It was a promise that soon the folly of nascent growth would interrupt the soil with shoots of audacity. Where once the earth was solid with ice, the soil now looked wet and ready to host growth.

I came out to the garden this day because Baxter had returned to her stoic silent treatment of me. I was aware that my longing for better treatment from her was because of a lifelong hunger for motherly attention. My lack of a mother, however, could not compel her to fulfil that role. At the time

I thought it was because I was just not interesting enough. I would later suspect she sensed that something about me was not quite right, not quite the same as she was. Or perhaps, she was just so naturally terse that our arid relations could bear no fruits of affection.

Feeling pathetic, I had come out to the garden to see about her vegetable patch. Over breakfast Wesley had asked Baxter about the chard, carrots and parsnips that she had been tending to and I decided to come and have a look for myself. Her patch was a large section of garden on the north-western flank of the house. It got no more than two hours of sunlight in the morning and maybe four or so hours as the sun raced towards setting.

I was out here during the day only because Lord Belfield was still away, his return still filling me with dreadful anticipation. As the cat was away, this mouse wanted to play, because the less work I did in his absence, the longer I would be able to stay. Assuming he didn't dismiss me in anger over the library break-in, my emerging strategy was to promise I could have the work done over the next few months, but do my very best to extend my labour until the end of the summer at the very least. Of course, I was aware that Lord Belfield's financial situation was dire, but it couldn't be so bad that he would struggle to pay me for work that was understandably overdue. And I hoped that he was desperate enough to prepare the collection for sale that he would not want to dismiss me and engage another, more costly bookbinder to do the rest of the work.

Looking over Baxter's vegetable patch made me feel miserable. The colours were, as of yet, unremarkable, and my disappointment in this fact was not so much because I had hoped to find something here that might dazzle the eye. It was more a whimpering realisation that I had come here to find things about the growing vegetables to compliment Baxter on: 'Those carrots are coming along nicely aren't they?' Or some such commentary. I couldn't make anything up because that would have only marked me out as inauthentic and confirmed the unbridgeable distance between us. When I learned that we now had a monthly cycle that neatly overlapped with each other, I was initially hopeful that our bond would deepen naturally. However, to find that I was all alone making the herbal tea on the second night meant the pain I was feeling shifted from my abdomen and lower back to my chest and tightened my diaphragm with an increased aching. Baxter obviously did not relate to my feelings that independence and solitude could produce a loneliness that one feared was possibly unbearable, So I turned away from the vegetable patch feeling despondent and walked down to the bridge where Lady Persephone had met her end. The postboy found me marvelling at the snowdrops that bloomed along the banks. The letter from Liverpool told me Lord Belfield would return two days later, on a Thursday afternoon.

As the door to Lord Belfield's carriage opened, I waited on the doorstep like a housekeeper. In a way, that was beginning to be the case. I knew every inch of this house, having been here for several months. Wesley fetched his luggage and even though we did not speak at great length, I could tell that Lord Belfield was quite happy as a result of this trip. I hoped his good mood would be to my benefit. He had new bolts of cloth, joints of ham and beef, a sack of basmati rice, oranges, lemons and limes and some new books and magazines that had come in from Boston, Massachusetts. The day was chilly, but he looked flushed and rosy. He smelled of soot and bananas and olive oil. The soot made sense because he'd been near the docks and steam trains, I imagined. But the bananas baffled me. I had only smelled them once before. A crate of them had been lifted from a barge and caused a great furore from the young ladies from school surrounding me in Manchester. We had read about them in our novels, but to see the green things turn yellow in the shop windows, ripening until they were ready to eat, felt truly salacious. We tittered at their phallic shape and made jokes about them bursting in our mouths. One girl made the mistake of joking about it in front of her mother and received a slap that could be heard three doors down.

Once he had changed out of his travelling wear, he came into the library to see the work I had done in his absence. Back in his beloved yellow-piped waistcoat, we sat next to each other on my working desk and together examined all the books I had completed in his absence. His grin was ecstatic.

'Miss Granger. You have outdone yourself.'

I believe I did start blushing at this statement.

I turned my head to look at him while he fingered the spine of yet another Bible. His moustache had grown but had been clipped neatly. His skin also looked plumper somehow, less fatigued. He then decided to spoil the moment.

'Oh, I should let you know that Chester will be visiting us for the weekend.'

I inhaled and coughed with surprise, a globule of phlegm spattering my top teeth.

'Will Lady Violet be with him, sir?'

'No, no. I think not.'

That put me more in danger. He was less likely to do anything too dastardly if his wife were under the same roof, I had hoped. Although Lady Violet had behaved oddly after the last time he threatened me, whatever her reasons, I hoped that the library incident had brought us onto new footing. I hoped she might be an ally. If he was here alone, with the intention of devouring me in the way he had insinuated, the only thing that stood in his way was the lock on my bedroom door.

'It's truly a marvel that someone as young as yourself could restore so many works,' Lord Belfield said.

He smelled one of the Bibles I had just finished. There had been sand in the spine and whole sections stuck together. It was now renewed without compromising its aged integrity. I had made it look like it had been well cared for, instead of abandoned in a damp attic corner to be consumed by mould, as it had been by a prior owner.

'Your work is not speedy by any means, but like all good things, quality takes time.'

My strategy had worked.

'We almost lost it all,' I blurted out.

Lord Belfield looked at me quizzically. I hadn't meant to slice the truth open like that. In my head I had thought it best to begin with a softer lead in. But while he had been speaking, I felt myself waiting for the merry-go-round to pause long enough for me to jump on, and so when the gap came, I took it.

'I mean ... Something happened – while you were away,' I stumbled.

'What happened while I was away?' His voice rose.

There was no way to back away from what I had started. I kept my voice low and looked at the floor.

'There was an intruder, we think. We all heard the window breaking in the night and came down to investigate,' I said.

'When?!' he boomed.

'A little over two weeks ago,' I told him.

I looked up from the floor and saw his hair had fallen out of place. A curl danced on his forehead, tickling his brow. His chest rose and fell, and I could hear the breath coming out of his nostrils. He stood up and went to his desk and unlocked the top drawer. This was where he kept his col- lectible fountain pens. I'd not thought of them. He ran his fingers over them all. I'd only ever seen one or two, and I wasn't sure how many were there. Perhaps they were all investments he didn't care to tell me about. One of them had a Japanese porcelain casing, I knew that much. White with periwinkle lettering. He picked it up and rolled it between his fingers. He finally breathed out of his mouth and his shoulders slumped a bit. This must have been his favourite. It struck me for a moment that, for a man who paraded his library so proudly, Lord Belfield's first concern had not been for the books.

He looked up at me. I bit my top lip and braced for what was to come. I'd never met his gaze long enough to discern whether his eyes were grey or blue. Now they were locked on me in such a way, I could see that they were a penetrating crystal blue.

'You could easily have telegrammed me from the post office,' he said, seething.

'I didn't want to ... I couldn't ...' I stammered.

'You were scared.'

I nodded.

His face hadn't softened. He scratched his neck, looked away from me to sigh, and then turned back to me again.

'What did they take?' he asked.

'Nothing,' I said, my heart hammering.

He considered me briefly. Walked over to the bookshelves.

'The lectionary is still here?' he asked.

'Yes m'lord.'

'And the other exotics?' he asked, scanning the cage.

'I can promise you everything is accounted for. I checked your collection against my lists thrice over. Nothing was taken. I think they were scared off before they could locate what they had been looking for.' I would start crying soon. That always helped. In fairness, I was quite overcome.

He sat down at his desk again, finally, and he gestured for me to be seated at mine. I'd been standing like a child in a dunce cap, waiting for one's proper chastisement.

'I can understand why you would think I might punish you for such a thing. I can.' He took his pipe out and started stuffing it with tobacco from a new tin that had a ship on it. 'The thing is, I gave you a key to show I trusted you. Now here you are, not trusting me.'

I couldn't say anything.

'Perhaps if something had been taken, I might feel differently, but I doubt it, Miss Granger.' He lit the tobacco. 'I really do doubt it.'

'Forgive me,' I said, looking back at him. He wasn't sneering, but he was considering me. The flash of anger was passing, but what replaced it was having a deeper effect on me. Looking at the fatigue on his face made me feel down-hearted. I was looking at a forlorn man who felt constantly assailed. Lady Violet had been right. His grief was such that hearing that his wife's diary had been committed to the flames would have been the last straw. If it were merely his anger I had had to deal with, I would have felt compelled to push through and confess that to him, even if it did place my living in jeopardy. But why pull out the heart of a man when it was already broken? Whatever else Lord Belfield was, I did believe he was a grieving widower.

'Go and have some lunch, won't you.'

He flicked his pipe out into the ashtray.

'Thank you, Lord Belfield. I'm sorry.'

He nodded his head, but wouldn't look up at me.

I didn't feel like I had quite got away with everything. At any moment he could ask where his wife's diary was, though my eyes fell on the mess of his desk and I felt reassured that he had not attempted to sift through it with any urgency. But should he ever choose to, his current compassion would surely make his eventual wrath all the more harmful.

And with Sir Chester's visit impending, I had another danger to contend with. He was the wolf waiting to attack at the height of the harvest. If I was a chicken, I had never been plumper.

Chapter Seventeen

I must be forgiven for only being able to recount what happened before and immediately after he attacked me. What took place in between will always be too overwhelming. Some of my recollection is patchy, but there are images, sounds and smells that are forever imprinted on my mind's eye.

After dinner on Saturday, I left the table and raced to my room. I'd told Wesley not to bother coming that night, because my hair was still smooth enough for church tomorrow. He would be on call for a few hours yet anyway, as Lord Belfield and Sir Chester would be drinking and playing chess.

Sometimes nerves keep one awake, but that night my slumber was quick to arrive. I much preferred to be asleep than awake with Sir Chester in the house.

When I awoke, the moon was full and pouring its light into my room. What sound had roused me, I couldn't tell you. The sound of Sir Chester sitting on a chair and smoking, wasn't enough to have done so. Silhouetted in silver, his nudity was almost ghoulish. He had found a way to unlock my door and had then undressed himself entirely, and I in a trice felt myself drowning. I was terrified. His clothes lay at the bottom of my bed, and I felt the weight of them on my feet. I shuffled up the bed, removed my pillow from behind me, and crunched up into a ball with my back to the headboard.

He licked his fingers and then asked, 'How have you been?'

The absurdity of the question was almost comical. I refused to answer.

'Young lady, I could have come at any time before now,' he told me, casting aside the gingerbread package. 'Come along, you've had time to prepare yourself for the inevitable. You might as well try and make this a pleasant experience for us both.'

I could not agree to surrender to his dominance over me.

'How did you get in here, when the door was locked?' I whispered.

'I went to boarding school from the age of seven, dear girl. If a locked door ever stopped me from entering a room, then every single day of my time there would have been quite horrible.'

'You're horrible,' I said.

'Yes. I am. I am also quite possibly the most powerful man you will ever meet, and only set to become more so. Having you as my mistress is going to be incredibly useful. But you must be broken in. That's why I'm here. It's the sort of thing that will definitely happen to you as a governess as well, and so you'd better get used to it.'

'I won't.'

He put his hands between his thighs. 'Say that again.'

'I will not,' I repeated.

This excited him. He stood up and in one pace he was by my bed. I don't think I screamed, but something caused him to hit me. With that I was almost out. Frightfully dizzied, at least. I couldn't tell up from down. Except I knew he was on top of me. There was a searing pain from down below but with his hands round my neck, the impossibility of breathing was my main concern. I couldn't hear anything either. Was the bed sheet around my head? I couldn't breathe, so I was sure I was set to die. And what a way to go. With all my dignity taken, and when I would awaken I was sure it was hell that I'd be delivered to.

But then another man's voice sliced into the cloud of confusion I was entangled in.

'Good Lord, man. Get off her!'

And somehow, I was on the floor now. Ripped nightdress. A nosebleed giving me the taste of blood at the back of my throat. A goose feather in my ear? I gulped at the air. Great balls of it. I was alive. I couldn't tell if I was fortunate or not yet.

'She begged me to come here,' Sir Chester chuckled. He brushed his hair out of his face, looking bashful. As if he was more amused than embarrassed.

'Please Chester,' Lord Belfield said. 'Not again.'

Sir Chester bent down and got his trousers on, then his shirt. His modesty was back rather quickly, all things considered. Meanwhile, I lay there clutching my ripped nightdress down the front but feeling too shaken to check that it was covering everything.

Lord Belfield turned to the doorway. 'Baxter, please.'

I hadn't noticed her and Wesley standing there. Like frightened mice. Had they been the ones to hear everything? Certainly, Lord Belfield's room was too far away. Why hadn't they tried to fight him off me? It need not have lasted this long.

Baxter came back from her room with a nightdress of her own. Wesley had a bowl of water and a towel. The whole scene was so improper. But it was Sir Chester that had made it so. I think that was why everyone busied around me with a 'needs must' energy about them.

'Don't you dare look at me like that, Francis. You're hardly a man of good reputation anymore.'

The roar that came from Lord Belfield rattled the windows. 'I'VE NEVER DONE ANYTHING LIKE THIS, YOU GREAT SWINE!'

'No, but you married a nigger and passed her off as one of your own though.'

They all froze. The slingshot of gossip was obviously one never delivered to their ears before. It brought me back into the room in a way nothing else could.

'Lady Persephone was an albino,' I said. I thought of the photograph, of her impossibly pale skin and plump lips.

'Well, you're the smartest whore I've ever met, that's for sure.' Sir Chester was determined to cause even more devastation than he already had.

Only then did he start buttoning up his open shirt. He was revelling in the moment. Some part of me had left my person and watched what had happened to me from the furthest corner in my room. I was still watching myself now.

Shivering, but amazed that I was still able to piece together the weird off-kilter thing that now seemed so obvious. Even though it hadn't been, really. Chester was continuing to smack us around the face with context.

'You haven't guessed that the negro lady's maid was actually her sister yet though, have you, Detective?' He turned from me and cast Lord Belfield a dismissive look, reaching his top buttons. 'She's been snooping through your dead wife's things by the way, Francis.'

The heads of Baxter and Wesley poked forward unnaturally, like cuckoos out of a clock. So stunned that their necks craned away from their bodies.

Lord Belfield slumped on the bed. Head in his hands.

'There's very little chance of secrecy if my brother is around, obviously. However, if this news leaves this room, then you'll all be without work. I refuse to have anyone disloyal work for me.'

With both Sir Chester and I newly clothed, there was nothing more to keep anyone in my bedroom. Baxter led me into her room, and I slept in her bed that night. She wasn't cuddling me when I fell asleep, but she was when the sun came up.

Sir Chester left that morning and all four of us went to church together for the first time, as if to cleanse ourselves of the sins of the men of the household.

Chapter Eighteen

The incident with Sir Chester took place on the night of Saturday 27th February, 1897. It took some years for the day to pass without me remembering its significance. Alas, those first few months I was in a distracted reverie of sorts. I busied myself as best as I could. The first Monday after the attack, after a solid day's work – for there was no discussion as to whether I was ready to work again or not – I moved my belongings from that bedroom to one further down the hall, next to Baxter's.

By the Tuesday morning, when I settled down again to work on a new batch of Greek books, I was sure that Lord Belfield intended never to discuss the weekend's events with me, and I would continue my vow to myself to be as silent on the subject as Harpocrates. However, when he entered the library some time after I had, I noticed that his eyes were both brighter and larger than usual, and that he had a laconic air about him. The new egg-yolk stain and toast crumbs on his shirt suggested that he had dropped a piece of his dipped toast on himself during breakfast. He sat facing me on the edge of his table, at the other end of the room. His left arm hugged his stomach and his right hand stroked his chin. Before he exhaled into the space, I thought I heard a quiet groan.

'I cannot apologise enough for Chester's behaviour.'

He was talking as if his brother had merely said a naughty word or two while inebriated at dinner. I couldn't respond to such a tentative recognition of what he'd done to me.

Lord Belfield didn't quite hang his head, but he stopped staring. As if he was too ashamed by my silence to keep looking at me. He stared instead at the centrepiece of the blue, pink and cream rug design between us.

'I mean, he wasn't always like this, you know. That is to say ... he was always a bit rambunctious, but – well. Not violent in that sense. Just a bit of horseplay. And our father liked him for it.' He scratched his chin. 'No, it was more our bloody school.'

At this, he took the pipe and tobacco tin from his trouser pocket. Stuffed a wodge into the top hole with his thumb and reached into his other pocket for the matches.

'By the time he got to Oxford he had been broken into something different.'

He lit the match and puffed his cheeks on the pipe, with the flame getting larger and the smoke coming out like a pot-bellied genie might spirit up into the atmosphere. What would I have wished for?

My mind drifting was punctured by him saying:

'He was probably buggered senseless.'

Lord Belfield shrugged and looked out of the window on the very cloudy day. It was impossible to think of Sir Chester enduring a night attack akin to the one he had put me through. And why had Lord Belfield said 'probably'? Shouldn't he have known, having gone to the same school only a few years before? But moreover, why was Lord Belfield's tone so ... indifferent?

I had said nothing up until now. I felt that Lord Belfield had steered our vehicle into a cul-de-sac.

'Was everything Sir Chester said true?' I finally mewed.

He contemplated me for a few seconds and then came to sit on the window seat closest to my table. It was the spot I would choose to sit in when I was alone and a book I was about to work on proved itself to be worthy of a moment's reading.

'Yes, Miss Granger. My wife was a negro. It was hard to think of her as one at first. Such exquisite features ...' He paused. 'But in time, things revealed themselves in her character that were ...' he opened the window, upturned his pipe and emptied out its contents with the burnt match. Then he restuffed it.

'Now, you must understand, this isn't a question of refinement. There was nothing uncouth or savage about her. About either of them. Both Sibyl and Persephone had quite marvellous educations, considering their backgrounds. Those books you're currently working on belonged to her father, in fact. A wedding gift from him to me. I resolved to marry her, in spite of her origins. She proved herself deserving and I am a man of my word, you see. I had no idea Persephone and Sibyl were sisters and discovered my wife's blackness only after I had proposed. By that time – well – things were underway. Our son was . . . Anyway, the details don't matter. The point is, it became a minor concern that was very easily concealed. Sibyl and Persephone made quite the impenetrable dyad, but no one in Paris knew of Persephone's true ethnicity . . .'

He stopped suddenly, realising that he had been talking to himself. If memories were hot air balloons, then this one was in danger of floating too far up into the atmosphere. I decided to bring him down to land.

'Well, Lord Belfield. Your family's secrets need not leave my lips in any church gossip; I assure you. But there are things I must ask for that I do believe I am now worthy of being indulged in.'

'No surprises there. Discretion is more assuredly achieved when paid for than gifted. Please proceed, Miss Granger.'

'I need more time to finish the library. I've done my best to do so in haste. However, I can't fudge any more corners in the pursuit of an arbitrary deadline. I do believe I will be in need of another four months to finish this work here.'

Lord Belfield met my gaze.

'At the very least.' I leaned my head to the side before clasping my hands and rubbing my thumbs together. The work wouldn't take this long at all. However, I deserved the money, I felt. Reparations are more likely to be mischievously taken than happily given. After what I had just been through, a number of weeks' pay for doing not much was a step towards some sort of justice.

He bit his lip and nodded, and I exhaled quietly through pursed lips. I would not have to plan my next steps too soon, and my reprieve might allow time for a path to reveal itself

to me. He blew a puff of smoke out, shook his head and per-
formatively rolled his eyes.

'I take it you're not quite done, Shylock.'

I stifled a giggle with a soft clearing of the throat.

'Your brother informed you that I have been reading the
letters Miss Arabella sent to Lady Persephone,' I said.

'I do hope you do not intend to gloat.' He lifted his chin.

'Goodness, no,' I protested. 'It's just they've had – or I
should say – *she's* had an impact on me.'

'In what way?' He tapped his fingers on his pipe.

'Her intellect. Her warmth . . .'

He scratched his beard.

'Go on.'

'It's just that I am eager to enquire about Arabella and
Sibyl's current welfare,' I said.

His eyes narrowed at me slightly.

'I make sure they are well taken care of.'

'Oh . . . well. I was also wondering . . . I have no family ties
to you. No one to take care of me after I leave here.'

'You're asking for more money?' His cheeks puffed out and
his jaw set in a new way.

'No. My request isn't financial at all.'

'That's a relief, at least.' He took a drag on his pipe
and exhaled.

'I want to write to Miss Sibyl Nostos.'

His discomfort caused his torso to twist towards me, away
from the window.

'Pray tell, why on earth would you want to do that?'

'Well . . . to be frank, Lord Belfield, I've never had someone
I have felt so practically connected to. We are not too far apart

in age, and I am riding the horse she rode. Knowing that she is the sister of Lady Persephone is surprisingly comforting. Now I know why her mother mentioned Sibyl so much in the letters.'

'Hmmmmmm.'

'Like I said, I have no desire to gossip. However, it would appear we share a great many interests. There's no other girl of my age and standing nearby who I might ever call a friend in that way.'

'And her being a coloured woman does not disturb you?'

Why would he think that? Had I not proven myself more enlightened than all of that already?

'No, of course not. Why would it?'

'I see . . .'

He came over to my table, took up my pen and wrote her address down. I read it and noticed immediately that – of course – it was the same as her mother's.

'So, is that everything?' he asked, puffing on the last dregs of his weakened pipe.

'Yes, I think so.'

'Good, good.'

Lord Belfield made to leave the room. Just before he reached the door he turned and said 'Ah, Miss Granger,' as if he were just walking in for the first time.

'Yes,' I answered.

'With Chester, I think it best . . . You see, it's not practical to have you go anywhere else when he comes again. But I can promise you will never be left alone again when he's in the house. Perhaps you could ask Baxter if you could share with her again on the nights that he comes to visit.'

'Yes, Lord Belfield.'

I didn't expect any grand gestures where he was concerned. This was his brother, and I was a mere employee after all. Yet, the shock singed its way through me regardless. What had happened to me was unfortunate, but it would never be treated as criminal. I knew that from then on everyone would consider it to be a mere overflow of male passions – if it were to be spoken of at all.

As spring came rolling across the hills, the sweet fresh smell of Wordsworth's daffodils ushered in a blurring of memory that I responded to kindly. The acuity of my memories in those first weeks had been close to paralysing. I worked a great deal to keep my mind off that night. Though it played itself over and over incessantly. Flashes that came back time and again, but never in the same sequence. My mind preferred the chaos to chronology, which in time I was glad for.

When I couldn't think, I wrote. Letter upon letter, pages long, to Miss Sibyl Nestos of Hope Street, Liverpool. Her replies were shorter than mine, but her warmth smudged the indigo ink lettering on the pages and her vocabulary was so precise, that I clutched each letter in my hands, hoping her eloquence would wind its way into me.

Finally, after many letters back and forth, I invited myself to visit in summer. I pretended I had a bookbinder's and library to visit in Liverpool. She felt compelled to explain the family set up I would find on arrival. Herself, her twin boys – still only a few months old – and her mother, Arabella Sey. What must her neighbours think of her? I thought when she described it all to me.

From what tids and bits Sibyl had told me, her mother was a widow, the daughter of Jacob Wilson Sey – the famed businessman of the Gold Coast who sent his children to be educated in England. Her father was a descendant of a Black Loyalist soldier from the American revolutionary wars, who had sailed to Liverpool after winning his freedom fighting in the name of King George.

I read almost all of her letters through once again on the train journey from Kendall to Crewe, Joseph having taken me to the station in Lord Belfield's carriage. I sent Lord Belfield's mail before boarding the train, and waved Joseph off on the platform as if he were my paramour.

Thankfully, the train journey allowed me to bypass Manchester entirely, though I could still see the belching soot from the citadel on the horizon as the train whizzed by. Changing at Crewe, I boarded the train to Liverpool and took out a book of poetry by Emily Dickinson. I swooned over the words like no other poet I had read thus. So seditious did I believe the poems to be, that I expected a policeman to arrest me as the train pulled into the station. After the whizzing green of the country came the red brick of the city. And there, on the platform in the steam, in a cream calico skirt and blouse, with her hair piled up into a regal chignon, stood the best girl-friend I would ever make in life. Sibyl.

Chapter Nineteen

I could tell Sibyl wasn't particularly impressed by me, because she pursed her lips in amusement as I clambered onto the platform from the train. I had sweated my hair out on the carriage ride and two trains to Liverpool, so that when I stood before her my hair had frazzled out to quite the bouffant underneath my straw boater. She was wearing a boater too, but it was leaning a little forward over her brow which cast her face in shadow, and made her bright brown eyes twinkle all the more from the dusk under her brim. I had hoped for an embrace – we had shared poetry, after all – but instead Sibyl put forth her hand for a very committed handshake.

We turned to walk out of the station and, as glorious as the architecture was, I couldn't help but notice all the soot blackening the walls. My throat tickled and what I hoped would be a mild throat-clearing grunt turned into a full spluttering fit of coughing that I was sure was making my eyes bulge out rather unattractively. Sibyl thrust a white handkerchief into my hand and rubbed my back. No one around us was looking, but the shame I felt was quite total. She reassured me.

'Oh, you poor thing. It's all that country air you're used to having. Your lungs have been made too tender for the city.'

I felt the need to protest, '. . . but I grew up not too far from the station in Manchester, I assure you I was once quite used to the air being like this.'

'Yes, yes of course. Let's hurry. Once we're past Parliament Street the air gets a bit clearer.'

She was right. The roads rose away from the docks and afforded the breeze I needed. I gulped down air that was free of the carbon granules and miscellaneous vapours that moments before had caused such eye-watering bronchial destruction. But meeting Sibyl's mother Arabella would knock the wind out of me even further.

'You see, the fierce face of a Coromantee woman. I know these people, my dear. Yes! Come here, my dear.'

Before I knew it, I was bustled into the embrace of a diminutive dark-skinned black woman who was only two thirds my height, but twice my strength. Her fragrance was deep and buttery. I had never smelled shea butter until that moment, and its sweet savoury smell of caramel tallow spoke to me of elsewhere. Nothing that grew in England could smell like that.

'It's such a delight to meet you, Miss Sey.'

'My dear, I am not in a courthouse. You can call me Miss Arabella!'

'Oh. Oh yes. Thank you, Miss Arabella. Thank you.'

I was flustered because I could not think of a way to work back to asking what a 'Coromantee woman' was. It sounded like a rather fierce description. Sibyl's smile became devilish, watching me get caught up in Miss Arabella's greetings. The more I fumbled around her, the more it seemed she was enjoying herself.

'This house is really quite lovely.' And it was. A small terraced Georgian home with a wide-enough hallway, two bedrooms – one rectangular, one square – upstairs and two square rooms downstairs – one a living room and the other a kitchen. I suspected the outhouse would be in the yard beyond the kitchen, though I couldn't see it from any window, which was nicely discreet.

'Come through for some tea, won't you,' Sibyl said, ushering me into the kitchen. The walls were painted claret red and cast-iron pots blackened to a high shine hung on rough hooks equally spaced on the walls. I took my seat at the kitchen's round table. A moment later Miss Arabella was before me with an enamel bowl of sudsy green water. I looked up at her, aghast by my own ignorance. Did she want me to clean?

'You can wash your hands here, my dear.'

'Oh, oh. Yes. Why, thank you.'

I bathed my hands and rubbed my palms together. I did want ever so much for her to be impressed by my washing. I felt like I was back with my grandmother, when she would inspect my nails to ensure that I was more ladylike than grubby child. Then I heard water splashes that were not my own. Over in the kitchen sink sat the loveliest terracotta cherubs I had ever seen. Big-eyed and glistening, the boys blinked at me in fascination. I took the clean tea towel from Miss Arabella's arm and dried my hands off.

'Such beautiful baby boys you have,' I said.

Sibyl looked over at them with pride and then back to me.

'Apollo and Artemis. I would have given them African names, but I know my father would have wanted them to be Greek named, as we all were.'

Lord Belfield was the father of these giggling slippery boys. How did I know? Their jutting foreheads were smooth where his was wrinkled. The slope of their jawlines was his, as well as the angularity of their cheeks. They weren't the dead stamp of their father, with their caramel skin and tufting textured hair on their temples, but they were unmistakeably his in spite of those differences. He was their father. I covered up my shock by exclaiming quickly:

'Sorry. Yes, your letter said that your father was very much interested in the classics.'

'Far more than interested. Obsessed, at the very least. The Greeks more than the Romans. His benefactor was part of the expedition that brought back the Elgin marbles.' She rose when saying this and walked over to the sink where Miss Arabella now stood too.

I did not see Sibyl as a harlot. She was clearly well-educated, and whatever had transpired was not necessarily as sordid as others might have imagined. I could give her that grace. However, meeting the evidence in her twin boys' faces was rather confronting. I had to keep from staring, so that my scandalised thoughts did not appear. I wanted to further examine what felt to me quite unmistakeable. Sibyl had been pregnant with Lord Belfield's children while Lady Persephone was still alive. They couldn't have been conceived when Lord Belfield was crying on her shoulder. The boys were too big.

No need to support their heads anymore. Big, bouncing, beautiful babies who made noises and expressed themselves and turned, often in unison, to look at whatever had caught their eye. Her sister's death had occurred when the boys were gestating in her belly.

Sibyl washed her hands in the same bowl I had just been given and reached for one of the boys at the same time as Miss Arabella reached for the other. Wordlessly they towelled them both dry and laid them side by side on a wooden bench, then reached for a pot of shea butter, rubbing the stuff between their palms until it became a slick creamy paste before they rubbed the babies down head to limb. The gurgles and giggles made me feel ever so zestful myself. I had never seen babies be handled like this. Rubbed down and cared for so briskly and yet smoothly. The boys obviously loved it, and the massaging must be so good for the circulation, I thought. Encouraging the growth of healthy robust limbs.

I knew Miss Arabella had been born in the Gold Coast. Her bombastic, lilting tones confirmed this. However, Sibyl was clearly living a life different from any I had read about. She really was of a different culture entirely, even though her clipped pronunciation revealed she was definitely from the same country as me.

Clothes were popped on both the boys in a jiffy and we were then faced with giggling, smiling little tykes who were just so joyously happy with themselves.

'Here here! You hold one and I can make you the tea.'

Miss Arabella handed me the boy and I took him into my lap and cradled him. He pawed at my bosom and it made me feel quite queer. There was a part of me that longed to know what it felt like, to have a child suckle at my teat and feel a sweet feeding be sucked out of me. However, I also felt my ribs constricting, because I was scared. He sat perched so comfortably now, but at any moment, I might mindlessly shift myself and drop him. How many books had I dropped accidentally? How many cups and glasses had I broken? Now, here I was with a babe with a soft head who could be damaged for life if I were to do the same. Yet I was sure to. One day I would not be looking and there would be his hand on the stove, or slammed in the hinge of a door. I held him closer and his clamouring for my breast continued.

'You see. You see dat boy dere. All-ways wanting more milk, eh.' Arabella came over and tickled his neck and eased out more giggles. 'You like breast too much. Haey!' She pinched his cheek. 'You like breast too much.'

She was tickling his neck but looking into my face. Assessing me for evidence that I might make a good mother one day, maybe? She looked quizzical. As if she thought that there was something funny about me? But it wasn't untrusting. My nervousness amused her? Or she liked me? Eventually, she moved off to make the tea.

What followed was a love story. It was the tale of Christopher Nostos, a descendant of a former slave, Neville Nostos, who had fought on the side of the British in the American War of Independence. He had won his freedom in so doing and then come with his former master and now employer to Liverpool, of all places. Raised in a home where the story of his grandfather became legend, Christopher kept in contact with the family who had brought his grandfather to England, and it was they who had paid for his education.

The Nostos family were self-named. Neville chose the name Nostos on the boat to England because of the stories the sailors told, and with no idea what his African name might be, a name that spoke of a homecoming seemed to make some sense. It did appear a painfully ironic name to choose. Ripped from Africa, then ejected from America for fighting on the wrong side and ending up in England as a new home country. This was not a journey in any way similar to that of Jason and the Argonauts. The Argonauts truly did get to go home, and had no need for new names, having never lost their own.

Miss Arabella Sey explained that Christopher had told her this story when they were courting, and she had found it as enthralling as I now did. Arabella's father was an industrialist who had become rich on trade in the Gold Coast and sent his daughter to England for an education. Not knowing anyone here, it only made sense that an enigmatic Christopher had swooped in to romance her with discussions of books that they had both read. They married, but Arabella chose not to tell her father of the marriage until she could return to the Gold Coast to tell him herself. Legally, she was Arabella Nostos now of course, but she kept using the name Miss Arabella Sey in her correspondence to maintain the ruse. Other husbands might have objected but Christopher, being an educated man of reason, could write it off as a trifling matter. He was not easily emasculated.

Sibyl was born first. Persephone came second and a son, Orion, followed her. Both Persephone and Orion were albino. The bullying had been relentless. Schooled at home by their parents, they were only somewhat protected from the judgements of the community.

The circus became the family pastime. Lights and animals and tricks galore. Eventually, hanging around afterwards, they caught the attention of the circus owner. With much persuasion, the children were taken under the wing of an Italian impresario. Taught all sorts of stunts and skills, and horse riding, too. With two albinos and a dark-skinned African girl now part of his retinue, the programme had its exotic billing.

Travel around Europe was a life-changing, eye-opening, whistle-stop tour of cities from Warsaw to Barcelona and, of course, Paris. Here, Sibyl had caught the eye of Lord Belfield as she played The Riding Negresse. Dressed up as a lady of high society who had the beating heart of an African warrior princess.

However, the freedom of Paris at the beginning of la belle époque couldn't extend very far. Although he loved Sibyl, marrying a woman of her hue was out of the question. Persephone and Orion could pass as white when out on their own. Thus, Persephone was the one it made more sense to court. Lord Belfield proposed to her out of the blue and thought Sibyl would be elated that he had found the most peculiar solution. Marry the sister, and allow them both to live in his country house as lady and lady's maid.

Of course Lord Belfield had told me otherwise – that he had not known Lady Persephone was albino, nor that they were sisters. I was sure he had not wanted to admit to me that he had been more calculated in his choices. Sibyl as the jilted, dark-skinned sister, forced to accept the role of mistress as compensation, had less reason to be vague with the truth.

Sibyl promised me she had scratched him to pieces for his hubris. Smashed plates and cups aroused the neighbours in their posh Paris dwelling, but thankfully not the police. Once the dust had settled, and Lord Belfield had made certain financial promises to them both, his plan made more sense than the rage both sisters felt inside, and therefore made it irrefutable.

Orion, with the discovery that a life passing as white was within his reach, waved goodbye to his mother and sisters and they had not heard of or from him since.

The sisters had returned to Rose Hall, where both Persephone and Sibyl had to become used to domestic life after the glittering ways of travelling exotic entertainers. Their father passed away before the birth of his first grandson. Persephone's pregnancy and birth consumed them both. Sibyl stopped her intimate moments with Lord Belfield thereafter.

It wasn't until Persephone's death that their passion was rekindled, and this had now resulted in the birth of the boys. Sibyl was an expert storyteller, and if I didn't have contradictory evidence, I would surely have been convinced. This being our first time meeting, she had no reason to think I would forgive her for conducting an affair with her sister's husband right under her nose. Or even if Lady Persephone had been fully aware, such an arrangement would be sinful in the minds of many people – although not my own. I knew how things could become so complicated. Once one convention is thrown out of the window, others tend to follow, thus, Lord Francis Belfield had sired three sons from both the Nostos girls. One wife dead and a living, breathing mistress who must someday explain this tawdry tale of confusion to her nephew Daniel, who whiled his childhood away in a boarding school and had no explanation for why he tanned so deeply in summertime. It came as a shock to me that Daniel was not albino too. But apparently, it was not a sure-fire thing that would always be passed on. He had no idea that Sibyl was his aunt, nor that he was a light-skinned mulatto.

This tumbling out of the Nostos family secrets had not been given freely. Two cups of tea and a coddling of a baby were not the reasons Sibyl had told me all of this today. I had earned it. Writing to Sibyl in the aftermath of what Sir Chester had done to me, I shared everything that I couldn't discuss with Baxter and wouldn't discuss with Mrs Hurrel. I had to tell someone. I didn't use any words that were too vulgar, but by her response I knew I had conveyed the full extent of the assault with my language of allusions. I think it was after the fourth or fifth letter that it became apparent to me that I was writing to both of them. Their handwriting was mighty similar, but Miss Arabella Sey's tone had something jollier about it and Sibyl's hand had an ever-so-perceptible slant to it. I wasn't offended; I was glad for the attention.

I had poured out my suspicions about Sir Chester's viciousness, my thoughts on Lord Belfield's grief and shiftiness, and Lady Violet's like-minded intellect and only slightly concealed mistrust of me. The loneliness of Rose Hall had been dispelled by this new connection I had forged. Sibyl had begun to send me pamphlets about women's suffrage and with that I knew I had found a proper friend, before we even met.

'You see. You run around with these white girls, and you will get yourself in trouble,' Miss Sey said.

'It's just a meeting,' Sibyl replied, rolling her eyes.

'You want take your babies to House of Commons?'

'I have much bigger ambitions for them than that.' Sibyl smiled.

The jocularity between them was so well-grooved, it made me think of a carpenter bevelling the edges of wood, and the peels of wood curling up, making smooth laughing sounds along the way. They jostled and poked each other with the jokes that only they could make.

Christopher, the father of the house, gone. The middle daughter, Persephone, I thought likely murdered, without anyone held accountable. The youngest son, Orion, living as a white man, with no contact with his former family at all. Arabella and Sibyl were the only ones left from the family that once burst against the walls of their home. Now, these giggling and gurgling boys were their future. The offspring of scandal but with the innocent faces of chubby cherubs.

'Don't be too long,' Miss Arabella said, hugging me before she turned away from us both with a kiss of her teeth. 'These girls.'

There was a light drizzle in the streets. We walked towards the docks in a comfortable silence. I wished Sibyl would walk closer to me, but she kept a respectable distance. We weren't yet sisters. Although I knew so much about her, and I longed to ask inappropriate questions about Lord Belfield. If he was nice to her in the main, or blew hot and cold like he did with me? He wasn't her husband, but I wondered if it felt like he was when he came to visit now. She knew him so well.

Instead, I settled on a mundane question.

'Was your father quite tall?' I asked.

'You're asking because my mother is small.' She turned to me, amused.

'I suppose so.' I shrugged and smiled it off.

'Yes. Yes, he was tall. My mother thought he might be Hausa, but of course we'll never know that for sure. Percy and I both took after him in looks and height. Orion has the same round cheeks as my mother. Only a few inches taller than her, as well.'

Walking along with her, every negro man we passed tipped his hat towards her and she nodded back. I started doing it too. It was lovely to feel some sort of kinship with the blacks of the area, when until Sibyl I had never considered any black person I had met as potential kin. Why would I? I didn't know there were this many in Liverpool. When we got to the dock she shouted out at one lifting a box.

'Agoo!'

The man grinned a gleaming smile and shouted back something unintelligible to me, but so full of mirth, it made me smile too. I looked back and forth between them shouting at each other and felt so lucky to be with her, this multilingual mother taking me to a women's meeting. I waved back at him as we walked away and Sibyl seemed amused, so I felt comfortable to ask her.

'Why did your mother call me a Coromantee woman?'

'Oh. I'm sorry. I keep telling her you wouldn't know where your family are from.'

'Oh,' I said, surprised. 'But I do, generally. My dad's family are all from Lancashire. I never met my mother's family, but I think they were from the North West too. That's what my dad's mother said anyway. They both met soon before they went to Jamaica and had me.' I wittered on.

'And what about the African side?' Sibyl asked.

'African side of what?' I stopped in the street. What was Sibyl talking about?

'Your family. My mother thought you were Coromantee because they were known as quite fierce. The slaves that always caused trouble. She meant it as a compliment.'

I was thrown. She thought I was ... So, I laughed. A good belly tickling laugh. Deep and funny to the point of queasiness. Sibyl looked at me with scrunched eyebrows.

Then it hit me. There was pity on her face. She thought I was in denial.

My laughter subsided and all that lay between us was a sooty train that belched out the truth having passed right between us.

'You think my mother was ... a negresse,' I whispered.

'A mulatto or quadroon at least,' she said, far too loudly.

Could it be? Was this even possible? I was quite flummoxed by what she was proposing.

'Have you seriously not looked in the mirror and wondered? Florence, do come along.'

'What do you mean?' I had stood up for Sibyl to the women of the village, but it had never entered my head that I might be like her. I was too light to be ...

'Florence! Look at your nose. Look at your bloody hair, for Christ's sake. Your skin may be light, but those are not European features. Did you seriously not know?'

I hadn't known. Here I had been listening to a family story of black people with albinism having the opportunity to pass as white, not once having considered that I might have African ancestry too.

But it made some kind of sense, somehow. It had never been said so clearly before, but perhaps ... The kids in my area used to call me Blackie but I never took them seriously. I just thought it was because they found out we lived in Jamaica when I was a baby.

I would never know where I came from, I realised. My father was a ghost to me now. Had he dwindled away? Was he feeding himself? He had never needed to. My grandmother cooked his every meal until he left for Jamaica and long after his return, until I could take over from her. I think I was seven. How could he not have told me that my mother wasn't entirely white? Or perhaps he didn't know? I hated him. But I missed him.

Sibyl's annoyance was making me angry, though. Why was she annoyed? *I* was the one who'd been lied to. She was annoyed by my ignorance. I was angry at her dismissal of my innocence.

I could see the reasons why life might have left her smarting. An obviously intelligent coloured woman who was pretty and had marvellous proportions. Kept from living any respectable life, and she had run off to the circus. Fallen in love with an aristocrat who wouldn't marry her because she was so dark, but instead married her albino sister, who ended up dead some time after. It all had a whiff of the Boleyn sisters.

Regardless, Sibyl had things that I never would. She knew where she came from, as I now realised I perhaps did not, and she spoke a language that evidently fortified her sense of self. She had a natural mothering instinct with her boys, and I suspected I never would feel that a baby latching at my breast was anything but a parasite. Maybe if I still had my mother like she had hers, it might feel more natural to desire children. I would have been taught how to hold them and how to wash them and care for them. I had dragged my doll around with me in such a forceful way as a child that, to my dismay, one day her head just fell clean off.

I wondered what my mother had looked like. And then I found that I could not continue down that path, in that moment.

'There are questions I daren't ask you, about your sister and what happened to her,' I said to Sibyl with some timidity. I felt the need to change the subject, and in my mind, the diary still loomed large. Sibyl would have seen her sister writing in it, surely? She must know who Persephone was afraid of at least? But I couldn't volunteer information on the break-in or the diary for fear that it would break her heart anew to know that it had been practically destroyed.

Sibyl's sigh was long. She blew it out like she was cooling down food she was about to feed the boys.

I looked out to the docks to give her a moment to collect herself. After a half minute of silence, she was ready to start saying what she felt comfortable saying.

'Never once did I consider the chance that I would grow old without my sister.' It was somewhere between a whisper and a croak. If there were a glass of water in front of her, she would have had to take it. Instead, she just coughed into her fist. And then she pointed her finger at me.

'I wasn't jealous of her!' she said emphatically. 'I loved my sister more than anyone can know. I defy anyone who would say otherwise.'

'I am sorry for your loss,' I said. I hadn't meant her to feel accused.

She shook her head and shoulders as if she'd got a shiver. 'We were not together the night she died. I mean – I didn't know she wasn't in her room.'

'I believe you,' I said, looking at her with as earnest an expression as I could muster. 'I understand.'

She couldn't bring herself to say she had been with Francis that night, but to have my reassurance melted her stiffness somewhat. Her eyes were wet.

'How could you possibly understand?' She squinted at me.

The air around us was thicker and wetter than when we had first ventured out. I could smell the stone of the pavement. The moss between the bricks.

'He loved you first. It's not so grand a leap to see why you might turn to each other in grief.'

Sibyl searched my face for signs of disingenuity. Not seeing anything untoward, she shrugged. I'd only got at some of the truth. Not all.

'At any rate, I did not steal her husband away from her. *She* would not resent me for the choices I made,' she said firmly.

'Does your mother?' I asked.

Sibyl scratched her neck.

'My mother is not very Christian in her outlook. We're alike in that way. Although she's far more joyful about life than I, we've always seen eye to eye. My mother is exceedingly ... practical.'

It was my turn to nod.

'We don't talk about Percy with each other. It's not that we pretend she didn't exist. We just don't ... mope about her together. Occasionally we'll reminisce on a happy memory. When we were all together. My father alive. Orion still with us. But she's never cried in front of us. I've never seen my mother cry. So, I offer her the same courtesy,' she said.

I felt the sky spittle something onto my nose, as if by accident.

'How did she find out about Lady Persephone?' I asked.

'I sent a telegram from the post office,' she said.

'Oh,' was all I could think to say.

'The post office was full of people. No one could bring themselves to be ... Oh, I don't know. I practically ran out of there afterwards. The hate they had towards me was ...' She shook her head.

'I'm sorry,' I said.

I was apologising for them, more than saying I was sorry she went through it. Although, that too, of course.

'I know she loved me.'

She looked out to the docks again and wiped a tear away and then quickened her step. Rain rolled in from the docks and its droplets made Sibyl's blouse darker. She was walking ahead of me by a pace, and I didn't want to catch up to be in tandem with her. As it came down a bit heavier and started hitting my face, I felt it was finally appropriate for me to cry too. I felt like I was crying for her, at first. She'd clearly wanted to swim in the misery of her grief but had decided to rise back to the surface and carry on trying not to feel.

By manipulating her into discussing Lady Persephone I had hoped to confirm my suspicions that whatever white lies I had picked up on were a result of shame rather than malice. But she was better at recovering from the quicksand of sadness than me. Always swimming away from the vortex at the centre. Her memories gave her strength. I surrendered to its pull, saddened at not knowing anything about my mother at all. Grieving for someone I had never known. Did she look like me, I wondered again? Or was she darker? She must have been – at least a little. Her hair was like mine though, surely! Her nose? Growing up in Jamaica, she wouldn't have needed to deny her blackness, perhaps. If she were lighter than so many others around her, that may have conferred whiteness upon her regardless, though? It was the not knowing, and never being able to know, that made my own tears flow now. The rain was making them invisible, I hoped.

Chapter Twenty

We arrived at the church hall. Around the back we could see lights, but we stood in the gothic arches of the main church to arrange ourselves before making our way there. Sibyl used her handkerchief to pat the droplets out of my hair, which I'm sure had swollen in size in the shower.

Her hair was still quite tightly arranged, the pinned chignon just under her boater. I think I noticed something glistening by her edges. Some sort of pomade perhaps, to keep it in place? She really was more than pretty. Her eyebrows were so sweetly tended to – swanning out in a flat line until a sweet rise to a soft curl at the end. A proud nose of excellent proportions above sharp lips that rested in a smile. Full cheeks and a chin with the softest ever trace of a cleft. She had the face of someone who could be quite serious if required, but never lost sight of the need for wit and mischief. Her body wasn't as athletic as I remembered it in

Persephone's picture. A bigger bosom and a thicker waist, but obviously men would still go crazy for her. Whereas I just felt pudgy and pasty and now damp next to her. Having patted me dry, she noticed my tears.

'Oh dear, are you all right? I haven't upset you, have I?'

'What? No. No, don't be silly. I'm fine.'

I whipped away from her, and we dashed to the church hall ten steps or so away across the gravel.

In the room, all eyes turned to her. Well, us, I suppose in a way. But her, really. Her blackness drew all eyes towards her. But they couldn't see mine. No surprise, because I hadn't seen mine either. But now I acknowledged that my nose was as proud as hers. My hair frizzier than hers – in a different way, obviously. But she was a negro through and through, and I was . . . I didn't know what I was.

'Ladies! Ladies! Welcome. Welcome.' A pigeon-shaped woman descended upon us and introduced herself as Mrs Slocombe. We were hustled up to the front of the room.

The class stratification of the space was quite clear. The educated wives sat up front. Buxom women with neat blouses and smelling of rose water and talcum powder. Not much speaking here at all. Tight smiles and the faintest nod as we sat down among them. Behind us were two to three rows of working women in drabber clothing. Dark brown wools and mustard green cardigans on top of a beige apron or two. From them came the smell of sweat and dripping. The sour smell of their toil and meals. A year ago, I would have been sat among them. At the back of the room were the poverty-stricken. They were too far away to smell from here, but I could see what they would smell like. The great unwashed huddle of mothers with not enough to feed their children, being tended to by volunteers bringing them a sandwich and a lukewarm cup of weak tea. The rest were drinking dandelion and burdock from metal cups. We gladly accepted them. But just as I was raising the cup to my mouth, Sibyl put her hand in the crook of my elbow and only ever so gently shook her head. I followed her lead and placed the cup beneath my seat.

What followed was a round of lectures. The first was a spectacled doctor describing the evils of alcohol and how a temperance movement would benefit society. The curdling cries of crashes and wallops from returning husbands from pubs and football games was such a part of our childhoods, and I don't recall this ever being discussed. Yet my father never hit me when he was drunk, which had made me think of him as a cut above the other men in the area. He'd wobble on his feet and grunt and bash into things. But he always left me alone. The applause at the end was rather tame, and only came from up front really.

The second lecture came from a headmistress from a local girls' school about the need for public education for girls to be made a national law. At this, Sibyl took out her small notepad and scribbled down I don't know what, but she was very much engaged. Her note-taking drew eyes back towards us again. I was sure that her colour was part of the reason we had been placed here, as well as our clean clothing. Younger than the ladies sitting around us by miles, it was clear that we were single ladies of some sort of means. But her colour too was some proof for the organisers of the absence of prejudice. It looked good for them to have a coloured lady among their midst. The applause for girls' education was more solid and came from the whole room. Although, again, it was loudest up front.

The last lecture was the most rousing. A Mrs Millicent Fawcett, who spoke passionately of the need for women's suffrage, animated us all. From the middle section came utterances of agreement throughout her talk.

'Yes m'lady!'

'Quite right she is.'

It was no surprise to me that the workers were primed for more political involvement. The strength of the local unions had been made apparent to me by Everett. He had spoken of how it was only because of them that little children were no longer losing fingers, limbs and lives in whirring factory machines. And now here we were, reaching for grander heights. For women to receive the vote and one day become part of parliamentary activity. Even though it was the women from the middle and back who deserved it the most, surely we all knew it would be the women up front who would gain their share first? I did, anyway.

After the rousing applause for the last lecture, there was some milling around, but no one came to talk to us. Sibyl seemed unbothered by this and after we went to the loo, we bid farewell to Mrs Slocombe before we made our way home.

On the way back to Sibyl's house we spoke about what it would take for England to give women the vote, and it energised me that in spite of the clipped words of Mrs Fawcett, we both saw much violence ahead and neither of us were put off by the thought of being involved in lighting the necessary fires.

*

The Nostos household was a proud one. The Georgian architecture was portly and the light from inside drew us towards it from the bottom of the street. Rose Hall was so gothic and intimidating, but this was a home for a loving family, and it was delightful to return to after our women's meeting.

We knew Miss Sey was not impressed, because she refused to ask us about it. Curious, because one would think a widow who had never socially carried her husband's name would be more of a firebrand than she actually was. It was a surprise to me that Christopher Nostos would have even allowed it. But we were in a new age, after all. A time where Mrs Millicent Fawcett could travel up and down the country recruiting women to a suffragette cause that would quite certainly mark us out as hysterical agitators in need of being impregnated more regularly.

That night, my mouth felt new sensations. The orange curry placed before me was as brightly coloured as the lava from Vesuvius. And the rice! I had never ever tasted anything quite like it. The grains were all separate, for starters. Even Baxter didn't know how to cook rice without it forming clumps of stodge. But Miss Arabella's was so fluffy and light that I was sure if I threw a handful into the air, the rice would take flight like a flock flittering home across the ocean to South Carolina. The curry was so highly spiced, I was surprised the boys liked it. Baxter would have said it would make them colicky. But wolf it down they did, with little resistance, apart from their giggles allowing them to spit some down their fronts.

Before bedtime, more washing. Lavender soap and talcum powder for under the arms afterwards. It was lovely to be this clean. Then we shared a cream they had made, of rose water, glycerine and olive oil. Its emollient texture made my skin feel plump and I was sure it would be restorative. Catching a glimpse of myself in the mirror I looked comically greasy, but with no men around to know the secrets to our endeavours to remain youthful, who cared? I had not looked at a man in that way since Everett and the scandal we had brought down on my head, in any case.

Miss Arabella told me I would sleep with her, and Sibyl would sleep in the larger master bedroom next door with the boys. I'm sure when the boys grew older they would have this room and the master would be the domain of Sibyl and Arabella. Mother and daughter sleeping together every night. What joy! Not only to have a mother, but to be able to be that close to her every day. The only mystery for me was what happened when Lord Belfield came to stay. I knew he stayed here with them too, but would Sibyl hand the boys over to her mother for the nights when they sought to be alone with each other?

Miss Arabella and I read by lamplight for an hour or so. Half an hour in we heard one baby cry, and then the other joined in for good measure.

'It's fine, Mother. Don't come,' reached us as Miss Arabella was putting her second slipper on. So she got back in the bed and opened up her book again. We heard the boys settle. Was she suckling them both? One on each breast? I must ask her what it felt like. Was she comfortable being drained two at a time?

My eyes started drooping first. I wished Miss Arabella good night and turned away from the lamp to face the wall.

Some minutes later, the lamp was turned down and I felt Miss Arabella curl up into a ball facing away from me. I was happy that I could still feel her heat in spite of the gap between us in the sheets.

Horror came the following morning. After a dream of black faeries dancing round a fire and purple rain falling down that did nothing to stop them from their revelry, I rose into the horrendous realisation that in the night I had turned over and cuddled Miss Arabella. I was so appalled that I gasped and woke her.

'I'm so sorry. I don't know what came o—'

'Good morning my dear. Please, please.' She laughed.

Shouldn't I be embarrassed? She was ready to start the day as if it were the most natural thing in the world that she had been cuddled in the middle of the night by a woman she had only met in the flesh yesterday. Maybe it was? Apart from my grandmother, which I could scarcely remember – and one night in Baxter's room when I could not sleep in any case, so spent most of it sitting by her window shuddering with the aftershock of what had happened – I had never shared a bed with anyone before. The smell of Miss Arabella was more enticing and I obviously couldn't help myself from doing what I had always dreamed of. Curling into a woman I had every reason to trust.

That morning was a busy affair. Changing the babies' nappies and the cooking of breakfast. Clanging around and gurgles and crying moments followed by more giggles. Tea with bread and lemon curd and eggs with onions in them. Everything about them spoke of other places. I felt like I had spent the night in a home with an African family who had travelled as much as Phileas Fogg.

Miss Arabella hugged me so tightly, I got tearful. 'You will come back soon!' she demanded.

I didn't have the words to explain the confusion I felt. I had arrived as a wounded girl-child and now I felt lost in a new way. I really did want to know where I was from. Was I Coromantee in the way she had suspected? I really wanted to be Coromantee, I realised, though I didn't even know what that would mean. If I was descended from slaves, I'd be a mix of different tribes, wouldn't I? These questions couldn't find their way out.

Miss Arabella, seeing that I was struggling, kissed her teeth and said with smiling eyes:

'My dear, whether you are from Brazil, America, Jamaica or England; once you are black, you are all African to me.'

I was so astounded by her generosity that all I could do was nod and stutter.

'I promise. I'll come back.'

The sun was back out as we walked to the station, and my 11.37 train had already pulled in to the platform when we arrived. Sibyl was bursting with chat of poetry and politics and history. I got the sense that even though she didn't know me well yet, that she was glad for my company. Was she lonely? Did she miss her sister? Quite definitely we were two women who loved to read, and being close enough in age, we could understand the winds of change that were on the way, and wanted to get swept up in them together.

At the platform, she grabbed me by the shoulders and looked me dead in the eyes.

'I very much want us to be good friends.'

'So do I, Sibyl. So do I.'

She was ever so intense. I had been so worried she wouldn't like me when I had first written to her. And last night, when she found I hadn't guessed that I might not be all white, I feared I had failed. That not knowing my mother was some sort of . . . I don't know. If she had been fully negro, surely I'd have known. But now I wanted to know, and because Sibyl and Miss Arabella had seen it so clearly, I wanted them to help me know too.

Sibyl kissed me on each cheek like a Parisian. I giggled at that and then climbed onto the train.

'I'll write to you. I promise,' I said.

I waved at her out of the window as the train pulled out.

To say I trusted Sibyl is probably too much. I trusted that she had not murdered her sister. She had lied about the time the boys were conceived. I could afford her that lie. I knew it was more out of embarrassment than malice. I had considered the possibility that Lord Belfield and Sibyl had never stopped being intimate. They had all met in Paris, and their licentious behaviour was as stereotypically French as one would expect. There was no lid on the bottle of impassioned carnality they all seemed to swig from, far too indulgently.

It was quite clear to me that Lord Belfield's marriage to Lady Persephone had been one of convenience. Even if her sister had lived, Sibyl would have had to be sent away. It would have been reprehensible to reveal the *ménage à trois* arrangement that had caused both sisters to have sons who were both cousins and half-brothers. They were worse than the nobility of Versailles in that respect. Sibyl's choices, specifically, were immoral in the eyes of many, but this did not qualify her as a murderess. She loved her sister – I knew that much now. Furthermore, she wouldn't have been able to rip herself away from the boys to be the elusive intruder that had broken into the library at Rose Hall. Lady Persephone had not named Sibyl as the one she was scared of before she died. He was still very much at large.

Crewe came so quickly that I wasn't by the door when it was time to change, so I huffed and puffed my way to it and tripped a bit as I stepped onto the platform. By the time my train to Oxenhope arrived ninety minutes later, I was calm and deep into the new novel Sibyl had given me. The only thing that pulled me out of it on the train back to the lakes was an unbelievable sensation in my abdomen.

I was quite sure that I felt something inside me kick.

Chapter Twenty-One

My grandmother was the only one I knew who had called them 'monthlies'. It had occurred to me as I grew older that this was a rather curious euphemism, but to use any language that might be more accurate or related to anatomy would be seen as vulgar, so I never thought to say anything different. After the night with Sir Chester, it hadn't come, and because I was then on the same cycle as Baxter, she was the one to notice. Or rather, at the allotted times in March and April, I got scared and shuddered at the fear that the worst had happened and then she brought it up when we were alone and had seen I had no need for her teas.

'It's the shock,' she told me brusquely. 'They'll come back and cause you pain.'

Because I wanted it to be true, I just got on with things. When May came I got some spotting and a twinge. Nothing heavy, but it was at the right time, so it counted. That's what

I had hoped. June, nothing. But because of the spotting . . . I'd convinced myself there was nothing to worry about.

By the time I got off the train at Oxenhope, it had happened twice. The first movement caused my heart to sink underground. This was it. My ending. No future whatsoever. Unmarried and pregnant with the child of a man who had spurted his hate inside me. At the second movement, I was enraged. How could he? I wanted to flush it out with vinegar. I couldn't bind books. Lord Belfield would have to get rid of me with no reference to help me find a position as a governess.

The oxblood red of the station sign and platform lamps taunted me. Did girls who got violated get let into heaven? I wasn't as bad as the others. It wasn't fornication if he had taken me by force. Now, I'd have to raise his baby. I thought about throwing myself under the next train that pulled in. But that wouldn't be fair, would it? Imagine the impact on the station master who found me. And all for what? A woman who hadn't taken enough care to do what was sensible, wedge a chair under the door knob as an extra precaution, and not antagonise a nasty piece of work?

No . . . What I needed to do was finish the library before I became noticeable, and run off with the money and a reference from Lord Belfield. I would find a place where I could give birth quietly and hand the baby off to someone deserving. I could turn this all around with the right planning. Yes, I had saved myself before when my father ejected me for being brazen enough to enjoy the touch of a man I had fallen in love with.

I found a carriage man at the station entrance and paid him

to take me to Rose Hall. The breeze off the moors was lovely but I was still hot. Panting came naturally to me.

I'd taken such care to only let Everett do the things to me that wouldn't result in this situation. I'd tested it out. When we'd play families as children, I would take a boy or two away from the rest and we'd find a quiet place. I never let them put anything inside me down there except maybe a finger or two, or I'd put them in my mouth.

By the time Everett came along I was more experienced than any girl he'd met before me. The boys I grew up with would whisper about what we got up to, but not too loudly, because they were scared it would stop. Nevertheless, the girls could guess why I would go off with them on my own, and soon enough I lost their companionship. Because most of them didn't read, I didn't see it as any great loss. Books filled up the space that loneliness created. I preferred the girls in my stories anyway. Plucky and industrious sorts who had big adventures.

I found the boys' jokes silly and shallow. But I loved their excitement. They learned my rules. If they hadn't washed it, I wouldn't touch them, and no dirt under the fingernails which also had to be nicely cut. No hang nails. I'd inspect them before I let them touch me. I made them bring me gifts. Toffee and bonbons and soap and little trinkets. Sometimes, I'd have to tell them off for bringing me something that belonged to their mother or their sister. I knew they didn't have much. However, around Christmas I might even get a doll or a clockwork toy. Having seen my father wander off with a prostitute, when he didn't know I could see him, I was sure that what I was doing was different. No money changed hands.

He'd left me alone to go down the pub when I was, say,

twelve or thirteen. I shouldn't have been out but, anyway, I was. He wasn't stumbling drunk, but I was transfixed by seeing him swaying, hands in pockets, smiling impishly at this red-lipped, ringlet-haired woman. She was quite obviously a mulatto, though this wasn't of interest to me at the time. We all knew where the ladies of the night worked – so-called even though they worked during the day as well. I wasn't piqued to ask how she got where she did, or where she might have come from. All I knew was I wanted to be nothing like her, but still hold the power that she did. To make my father be excited to see me. I was set for more, I told myself. The fun I had with the local boys was all a bit of practice to tantalise my future husband with. I might understand the male body as other girls did not, but technically I was still a virgin. I was saving it. I only liked them touching the outside, anyway. Now look at what Sir Chester had done. The first time a man had forced himself in, and I had been left with the worst possible outcome. To become an unwed whore who would be left holding the baby.

The rose bushes at the front of Rose Hall had finally bloomed in my absence. From a distance, one might mistake them for a classic red. But as I closed in on the front entrance, they revealed themselves to be the brightest of pinks. Damask. Far more vibrant than I might have guessed. The effect was not delicate. It was almost threatening to see the bursts of them in the bushes. It hurt to look at them for too long.

Lord Belfield was the one to open his own front door when I arrived back at Rose Hall. Rather unbecoming, but he had his reasons, I was sure. Goodness knew where Wesley was.

Walking up the stairs, he carried my small case and asked me hurriedly, 'So how is she?'

'Who?' I pretended not to know.

'Sibyl,' he hissed at me. 'She's all right now, isn't she? When I was last there, we argued.'

I shouldn't know all of this, I thought. There were no rules of propriety he wasn't willing to break. It was infuriating.

'Quite fine, Lord Belfield. We had very pleasant days together,' I said.

'Good, good. She took you to one of those women's meetings then?'

'Yes, we did hear a few lectures,' I said, a little surprised that he knew about this side of Sibyl.

'Good, good, good,' he said. We were by my door now. I took my case from him and went into my room. I couldn't talk to him, or even look at him.

'You know, I introduced her to a bit of that sort of thing myself, Miss Granger,' he said.

'I'm sorry?' I couldn't bear it.

'Mary Wollstonecraft. I mean, I know you know of her. But she didn't. I gave her *A Vindication of the Rights of Woman*.'

'Oh right. Well ... that's nice,' I said, sitting on the chair by my window.

'I think in time women should have the vote,' he said.

What did he mean by 'in time'?

'Yes, Lord Belfield. All things happen in good time.'

'Yes, precisely, Miss Granger,' he said, scratching my floor with his foot before asking, 'Miss Granger?'

'Yes, Lord Belfield.'

'Are you sure you're quite well? Ever since the ...'

So, he still felt guilty. Good. He should do. I had no plans to tell him of the baby. I had no plans to tell anyone. I had to think of a plan first. And soon.

'Yes, I am very happy I got to see Liverpool. The boys were a real treat. And Miss Arabella was really so welcome. She really made me feel at home,' I said, purposefully not answering his question.

He wagged his finger at me. 'She is a smart girl that Arabella, I tell you. A credit to her people. The intellect in that family is really quite something.'

I clenched my pelvic floor and a bead of sweat rolled from the heat of my hairline to land on my dress. It would not have surprised me if the droplet congealed like wax, going from the incandescent heat of me to the chill of the cold outside. How could he speak of a fifty-three-year-old woman so patronisingly? Why wouldn't she be smart? The intellect of both Miss Arabella and Sibyl wasn't news to me. We'd all read far more books than he had, for all his pride in his precious library. He took my silence for an agreement.

'Now, I must tell you, I'm heading down there myself tomorrow.'

'Oh, really.' Thank goodness. I couldn't bear to be around him much longer. Of Persephone and Sibyl both, he was so undeserving, in spite of his financial fortune. How could Miss Arabella bear him as her son-in-law and guest?

'Yes. Probably a fortnight. But don't worry. You won't be alone. On Sunday Lady Violet will arrive. Without Chester. You and she will be fine together.'

'Yes, Lord Belfield.'

'You're being ever so formal with me.'

'Am I?'

'Yes, you are.'

I refused to appease him.

'Look, I know what happened was awful. But I've given you a home of sorts, and I'm determined to give you a new living. I've asked Lady Violet to train you a little in the art of being a governess, seeing as she had one herself as a young woman. The library's almost done with. What have you got left? A few weeks at most before you'll need to find a new position. What has it been? Well over six months? Well, that's double the time you agreed to when you first arrived.' His expression had been cool, but now he leaned into his more genial persona. 'And I'll give you a reference, if Violet approves too. Let's not be too sour with each other now, all right? Things always work out well in the end. Miss Granger?'

He had made a few points, and reminded me that I could ill afford to dismiss him.

'Forgive me, Lord Belfield. It's been a long journey. Yes, I agree with you. I'm ever so grateful. I'm sorry I was surly. It's the fatigue, and the heat ...'

'Yes, Miss Granger, yes of course. Listen ... I have grown very fond of you. I was a shell of a man when you first arrived. Now ... things aren't so bad. You can even go horse riding with Lady Violet if you like? Joseph has been tending to her horse again while you were away.'

A good three acres lay between Rose Hall and the forest. In the first acre or so were bushes: a collection of evergreens, holly and hemlocks and boxwoods. They'd not been trimmed in a long while and thus intruded on the pathways, with one or two of them having kissing branches that met above. Beyond them was a more intentionally designed space where lawns were bordered with bushes that were decidedly more twiggy. Surely, these were the parts where children would have found more opportunity to play. There were stone walls and boxes on the edges of expanses of lawn that would be the perfect spots for picnics and summer parties. No one had mentioned such events occurring, but a house of this size and status was built to impress and entertain.

However, there was no wall that looked inviting enough to sit on as the light drew in that late evening. The moss looked sodden and as if it would soak through my skirts so as to make dinner distinctly uncomfortable. I hugged my cardigan a little closer to me. I had counted seven minutes since I had been outside, not very long, but I knew a shiver might enter me if I stayed out here too much longer.

If by some leap of the imagination the stain of this experience could be washed out, then might I end up in the gardens of some other country house as a governess, with children trailing behind me as we chose flowers that we could press? The Latin I remembered best was always related to the natural world in some way. It tickled me to think of myself in a studious capacity, teaching children of the ancient world, through plants and stories. Is that what a governess would do? And was that path now closed off to me, as bookbinding had been?

I brushed my hands on a conifer bush and its softness surprised me. Then I noticed something at the base of the bush. A flash of lilies of the Nile, shimmering voltaic white and lilac, in the border bushes' shadow. Now that I had caught sight of them, my eyes became alert to their presence in clumps underneath all of the bushes. As I spun around the lawn to peer underneath, it was almost like the street lamps being turned on as Manchester settled into evening. Standing on the top floor of the Prudential Assurance building where a friend of my father's worked, I saw how the lights came on in stages. Street by street illuminated as if the electricity was itself infectious.

Melancholy enshrouded me like baby's breath in a bride's bouquet. Except I wasn't betrothed to anyone, and the likelihood that I never would be had just increased. I always knew my time at Rose Hall wouldn't last for ever, but before Sir Chester, things hadn't been so desperate. To have saved myself from ending up on the streets had left me relieved. Surrounded by wood and books, I was buffeted away from the existence my father had threatened of dank moss and wet stone. Scraps of discarded dinner picked out from bins. Now, because of the baby's heart beating away inside me, that was again on the cards. I couldn't see my way through or a way out.

Then in that moment of stillness, I heard a clang. Its source? The shed around fifty yards from where I stood, only partially visible through the twigginess of the bushes. I could have ignored it. But I stared at the shed as if it might come alive. Something had fallen. A spade? A rake? Perhaps a fox or rabbit had trapped itself into a corner from which it couldn't escape? I walked towards the shed, hoping I would open the door and become an animal saviour.

Instead I got the biggest shock of my life thus far.

Joseph was leaning against a work table, head thrown back to the ceiling, with his eyes closed and mouth open. Steam was pouring out of him. Kneeling before him was a woman wearing the blue dress with pink blossoms, the one I had seen dashing down the corridor only weeks into my time at Rose Hall. Lady Persephone's ghost was there, pleasuring Joseph with her mouth, his hands either side of her head, covering her ears. Grunting and thrusting.

Was this what I had looked like doing it? How could I escape what I was seeing, without disturbing them both? What was Joseph doing here at this time of day? Who was this woman who looked like Lady Persephone?

Just as I thought I could quietly close the door without being noticed, Joseph looked down on the woman who he was thrusting into with such yearning ferocity and, seeing the new light that illuminated her, looked back towards the door. His eyes met mine and – mid thrust – his body froze. The woman's head struggled from his hands and kept bobbing, the only thing that moved in the scene, until she too froze. We were figures trapped in time and dust at Pompeii. A tableau that, if reproduced, would have been hidden in the British Museum's basement, for what it depicted was too salacious for the eyes of ladies.

Slowly she turned her face towards the door. I looked down to meet the eyes of the closest friend I had yet known. There, ensconced in Lady Persephone's dress, with rouged cheeks and a honey-blonde wig, was an impossibly stunned Wesley.

I stumbled away from the door. Not daring to run away, just desperate for our gazes to be broken. But I had left the door open, and this was undoubtedly impolite. I took two steps towards it to veil the scene of the man and the cross-dresser.

'I'm ever so sorry,' I said, closing the door on them both. I turned to run but found I couldn't. One step in front of the other was all I could manage. Then I felt a jolt at my shoulder, and the next thing I knew I was on the ground. I was yanked up and found myself confronted by the still-sweating face of Joseph, maniacally glaring at me while gripping my arm.

'If you tell anyone, I'll chop your head off,' he promised. I was outraged. Not at the sexual act I had witnessed, but this manhandling and the threat of violence was a step too far.

'Oh, good lord, Joseph. Please stop. She won't tell anyone. Tell 'im, Miss Granger. You won't, will ya?'

How had I not taken note of the effeminacy of Wesley's voice before? It simpered in a range that was above mine. Far more syrupy than any man I had known before. Higher than mine.

'Considering what I just saw, you aren't man enough to handle me, good sir.' I yanked my arm away. Joseph stood there, huffing at me like a bull. I instantly regretted saying it. I was just reaching for whatever immediately came to mind, even though I was obviously no longer in danger.

'I won't tell anyone,' I said, smoothing my skirts. 'I've done what she was doing to you, too.'

I felt dizzy. Wesley was before me, but it felt improper to refer to him as thus. She was different. To say 'he' felt thoroughly rude.

'It is so reckless to do this with Lord Belfield not away.'

The bravery of standing there in Lady Persephone's dress required an explanation, but not one I needed right then.

'I've got work to do.' I looked past Joseph and directed at her, 'And so do you, missy.'

I spun around and walked as quickly as possible into the house. Once inside, I closed the door and what fizzed up in me were the most explosive giggles I think I've ever experienced. Now that I was alone, I put my hand over my mouth and chuckled into my palms until they were clammy.

I couldn't believe it. Wesley and Joseph's act was the same one that had caused me to become practically destitute. Now I had to keep their secret, so that they wouldn't meet a fate worse than my own.

That night over a dinner of corned beef hash, broccoli and gravy, I struggled to maintain a sense of normalcy between the thoughts of the baby, the unsolved mystery of the diary and what I had seen between Joseph and Wesley only that evening. Baxter was no more sullen than usual. The thought of her discerning that there had been a scandal in the garden filled me with dread. I had deduced that she was not a religious woman, and for sure she knew Wesley to be sensitive in a way that was not manly. However, we were still in danger of facing some sort of retribution for being the sodomite and the harlot. Perhaps one would call me presumptive for naming Wesley thus, when I had only seen the oral act. However, from the literature I had found underneath my own father's mattress I could infer that where there was fellatio, sodomy was surely to follow – if it hadn't occurred already.

That night I thought it a good idea to cleanse the air with a Bible story. I spoke of Jesus forgiving Mary Magdalene for her sins as a wayward woman. Her own tears she used to wash Jesus's feet. How fundamental she was to our knowledge of

Jesus having risen, being the first to witness his resurrection. So disinterested was Baxter that I only noticed that she had fallen asleep with her first snore ripping through the kitchen, at the same time as Wesley scooped up his last spoonful. Three apples, a plate of shortbread biscuits and a glass of milk were already in the middle of the table. Wesley looked up at me sheepishly as I reached for my first biscuit.

'Did Jesus only forgive her because she stopped fornicating?' he asked.

'No. Even with what she was known for, she had more honour and goodness in her than those who considered themselves more respectable than she. There's nothing criminal about the things we choose to do when we love someone.'

I think I saw Wesley's eyes get wet when I said that. He reached for an apple and chomped into it. This roused Baxter back awake, and we pretended as if she hadn't dropped asleep at all. I made things more normal by waxing rhapsodical about the beauty of the lilies of the Nile bordering the conifer bushes, and Wesley said summer would truly have arrived when the path was cleared to the churning white waterfall. He promised to take me to see it.

'You go up and I'll clean up,' he said after we had finished our dessert. I knew he would come into my room to do my hair a short while after.

I had hoped that telling the story of Mary Magdalene would grease the wheels between Wesley and me, and demonstrate that what I had seen in the garden was not going to disrupt our friendship. Nevertheless, he combed my hair in silence, just stroking and parting it over and over, without his usual intention. It was like he was stuck in the preliminary actions, scared of what our usual intimacy might bring up tonight. As if he were fearful of combing up my disapproval. So I just jumped right into the question that would break the seal open:

'Have you worn women's clothes for a long time?'

I felt him pause. And then he started on the first braid at the back of my head. He was doing it much smaller than normal tonight. I usually disliked him doing them this small because it took longer to undo them in the morning. But I knew that in allowing him to go ahead, I was giving us more time to talk.

'My mother found it funny. Apparently, I started when I were young and when mi father weren't there, we'd play dress-up in her room. It were all rather innocent to begin with.'

'Oh, I see.'

'But I have to say, it wasn't her fault that I like boys. I just do. I don't know why. I just do.'

'Yes, Wesley. I know. There's nothing wrong with you.'

There was a tightness to his voice, as if the words he was speaking might snap his neck and have him faint over me.

'The love that dare not speak its name,' I said. It pained me greatly to think of someone as talented as Mr Wilde wilting away in Reading gaol. The frothy folly of *The Importance of Being Earnest* was a delight for me to read over and over. It was impossible for me to think that a man who could produce such levity and delight could ever be seen as someone evil or improper. I could imagine Wesley would play Gwendolen Fairfax quite brilliantly, having seen him play Lady Persephone so well.

'I always played the wife with the boys in my area. I wouldn't let the girls take my role, either.' He laughed for the first time.

'Then as we got older ... they asked me to start doing other things to them. They weren't forcing me or nowt. I wanted to. Sometimes, they'd bring me something to wear of their mother's or their sister's or whoever. And I'd ... just be a girl for them. I know it's sinful, but ... it's just what they like. And I like it too. So that's all really.'

The strain had left his voice. From my position, between his knees I could feel him relaxing for having told me. Somehow, I knew that this was the first time he had told anybody.

'I get them to call me Anne. But it always ends up being Annie.'

'Why that name?'

'Oh, 'cos of Anne Boleyn. I love playing the temptress, you see. I think that's why Joseph said he was gonna chop your head off when you found us.'

I spluttered into my lap and the howling that came from me was that of an animal. Perhaps it was because we knew Lord Belfield was soon to be away that I had such heightened disregard for boisterous mirth. Baxter had been half asleep at the dinner table. We didn't mind our noise at all that night. I got hiccups and started slapping the bed frame, I was that giddy. I had to hold my breath in ten-second bursts until they subsided. My hair was done now, anyway. I stood up and sat on the bed beside Wesley and took his hands into mine. I looked into his violet blue eyes and felt such adoration for the child looking back at me.

'I can't judge you, Wesley. I've done what you've done and that's why I'm here.'

'How'd you mean?'

'Well . . . my father threw me out because he walked in and found me like you. On my knees.'

'I didn't think girls did it too. I thought you didn't have to because he could just—' Wesley pointed at my crotch. 'Y'know.'

'Well, we don't want to get pregnant out of wedlock, do we? But besides all that, from what I read in my father's naughty books, it seems like on the continent women are doing it all the time.'

'Well, if they're French, that's hardly a surprise. I bet the Italians do it a lot too, don't they?'

'Yes. I should think they do.'

We chortled and then silence returned.

'What were his name?'

'Everett,' I responded. 'He was an anarchist.'

'What's that mean?'

'Well . . . he basically saw us as being on the cusp of creating a new world. No more lords or ladies or governments. All the workers of the world uniting to have a freer kind of life. No rulers as such.'

'Wouldn't that be chaos?'

'Not necessarily. It's probably more like the way things used to be before we had money and owning land and stuff.'

Wesley nodded, but I wasn't sure he understood.

'I loved him.'

Wesley rose from the bed to go and look out of the window. It was almost as if he couldn't bear to look at my face as he told me, 'I love him too.'

*

The days after raced by. I cared not for my work, which had become more dutiful. This did not diminish my efforts or lead to a reduction in quality. I just felt less precious about the books I was working on. I had often assumed it was ironic that my father appeared to love books less than I did, when binding them was the profession he had dedicated his life to. But I could understand him more now. What lay between our fingers were books. As a reader, what lies between one's fingers is a whole new world. The practical overrides the mystical when it's what puts food on the table.

Although my belly was full from another one of Baxter's breakfasts and I still had a room of my own at Rose Hall, I didn't feel any kind of security. I could be out on my ear in a mere number of weeks, my teeth-grinding reminded me.

The sun shone brightly as I walked with Wesley to the farm that weekend, after a week's work where my mind was elsewhere the whole time. I thought about couples in love and why they featured so much in the books I chose to read so often. I would never have considered myself a romantic, but it's what pulled me into any story I picked up, if I was being truthful. I doubted Joseph was literate. But literacy of letters isn't required for love, is it?

'I think a girl loved me once,' I told Wesley.

His eyes found mine and we slowed our pace to a dawdle. It would have been too intense to keep looking at each other, so we kept our gaze on the path ahead.

'Nothing too much happened,' I said. 'Only one time.'

This wasn't quite true. It was a few times. And it was quite lovely. Kissing, mainly.

'Who started it?' he asked me.

'I think she let me know and then ... I kissed her,' I said.

Wesley picked at the skin around his left thumb nail.

'But you're not like me though, are yuh? You don't love women. I can only love men. I'll never learn to be normal. Not like you.'

I could offer nothing to contradict his assertion. It was true. I didn't love women in that way.

'You said you loved Joseph. Would you do anything for him?'

Wesley nodded.

'Would you lie for him?' I said.

Wesley kept walking, but I stopped. Only a few paces ahead, he turned to look at me.

'Were you in the library that night?' I asked.

Wesley stared at me. Not on the verge of tears. It was the wind that had moistened his crystal blue irises. I had him, though.

'I had a key,' Wesley whispered.

'You took mine,' I said.

Confused, he shook his head. 'No. I have my own. I found it in one of Lady P's skirts almost two years ago.'

'Oh, I see.' But I didn't. Who had taken mine if it hadn't been Wesley?

'We used to meet in the library before that night. I thought it were safest. And it weren't as cold as the shed.'

A sudden gust of wind rolled into us off the hill. Tousled some hair into Wesley's eyes which he swept away with a swish of the hand.

I started walking again and joined Wesley by his side.

'So it was Joseph I saw running away that night? Did he break the window too?' I asked.

Wesley nodded.

'But he didn't take anything?' I asked.

Wesley shook his head vigorously, as if riven by shivers.

'So was it you or Joseph who burned her diary that night, then?' I asked.

Wesley didn't quite shake his head. More shrugged it off.

'You're saying neither of you did?'

He nodded with haste and puffed his cheeks out on the exhale. His loyalty to Joseph was stopping him from committing much to speech. I could tell that revealing this much about himself, this quickly, had been unintentional. Even though I didn't have the whole story, I had no desire to drain my friend; slim as he was, eliciting further answers might turn him skeletal.

I colluded with his determination and resolved to find the other answers I needed without probing Wesley any more. He'd given me just about enough to satiate my curiosity for now. I rubbed his shoulder, and we walked the rest of the way in silence. He was protecting Joseph by keeping his lips sealed about anything else that had transpired that night. I could see how much love he had for the farmer.

As I walked up to the stables, I had questions on my mind: Did Joseph love the closest friend I had ever had, and what would this mean for all our futures?

'Good morning, Joseph,' I chirped cheerily at him, walking in. 'I'm so pleased you'll be doing all the mucking out today. I'm just in the mood to ride.'

The announcement was a violence-free assertion that there was nothing wrong with a bit of blackmail. We took Mabel out to the paddock and even though I could mount her on my own, Joseph put his hand out ready to boost me into the saddle.

'Will you be riding in the woods today, Miss Granger?'

Not to call me by my first name was surely a sign of humility and penitence.

'You've always called me Florence; there's no reason to stop now. And no, Joseph, I think I'd like to stay close to the farm today.'

With that I hauled myself up and forward, without using Joseph's proffered hand, and swung my leg over Mabel. To be in command of a horse with no one but me holding the reins was an immense feeling of power. To feel my thighs part further and rise with each of her breaths. To be that in tune with a body five times the size of mine and far more powerful. I felt like a conquistador with an ever-so-plunderable South America lying before me, and a firm belief that El Dorado would be mine for the taking.

'I'll start off with a canter.'

Off I went, with the breeze cooling my neck. I couldn't tell if it truly was colder up here or if it was just my imagination. I was elated, even though all I was doing was riding in a wide circle.

When I came back to where Joseph waited for me, he looked up at me with fear. 'I'm sorry I said I'd chop your head off,' he said.

'It's OK. I'm sure you didn't mean it,' I assured him.

'No. I really didn't. I just ... I've never done anything like that before I met her, you know,' he whispered.

'Annie,' I whispered back with a smile.

'Yeah, it's just 'cos she looks so much like a woman when

she's all dressed up and … I couldn't help myself.' Joseph shrugged and his cheeks got rosier with the pronouncement.

'I understand.'

'Do you?' he countered.

'Yes. I do.' And I wasn't lying. For the past few nights I had whisked *The Twelve Caesars* by Suetonius up to bed with me from Lord Belfield's library.

'You're just like Nero and Sporus in Ancient Rome.'

'You know I don't read like you do, Flossy. You'll have to explain yourself.'

Only Wesley had ever called me Flossy. It was weird to hear his nickname for me in the mouth of another.

'Well, Nero killed his first wife and had Sporus castrated to become a woman. Apparently, Sporus was very beautiful and Nero was able to marry her and she became an empress.'

'They were something else them Romans, weren't they?'

'Yes.'

'So you don't think I'm abnormal for liking her like that then, do ya?'

'No. I don't. There's precedent. If you were down in London you could find other girls like her down Piccadilly. You've heard of Boulton and Park? Or Fanny and Stella, rather?'

'No. Who were they?'

'They were born boys but they lived as girls and they got up to quite a lot of mischief with the gentlemen of London, if accounts are to be believed.'

Joseph's brow furrowed in disbelief. I think he had assumed he was the only man in the world with tastes like these. And why wouldn't he? So far away were we from the sins of the citadels.

'What you do in private is your business, Joseph. I shall not judge, and I shall not betray you. You've helped me learn to ride and I will help you, as long as you provide me with an answer to one question.'

'Go ahead. Ask me anything.' He puffed his chest out.

'Do you love Annie?' I asked, finally slipping down from Mabel's back.

He sighed and looked at the clouds which had just rolled in over the hill.

'In my own way. I suppose I do.'

Although I had more than a shadow of suspicion over the story Wesley had told me, an idea for the two lovebirds was sprouting in my mind. I understood why Cupid was always portrayed as a youth. I felt giddy at the prospect of watering the love of friends who were so fearful of being discovered. This would be our little secret and I was determined to keep it, even if they were not telling me everything about the night of the break-in.

Chapter Twenty-Two

I asked for prunes with my porridge because I was a bit bunged up. Baxter's eyes narrowed, but I couldn't very well tell her at the breakfast table, could I? It had been months of living together and four months since my last monthly came at the same time as hers. But I still couldn't trust her, really.

Wesley, being Wesley, was forever amiable and still plundered me with questions about Liverpool and what I'd seen last week. I wished I had gone to a department store just so I could tell him about the new products and things. Instead I fascinated him with a few lies about there being a big band at the station and the songs they played. I had to come up with something, as I couldn't very well tell them about the women's meeting I had gone to. It suggested my volatility. If I was willing to go to meetings with rabble rousers such as women fighting for a vote, then what else might I do to mark myself out as unnaturally mannish?

I had quite the thrall over Wesley still, but without fully conceiving it I had done a lot of work over the last few months to make myself seem smaller and less troublesome than I really was. Symptoms of my pregnancy had drizzled in, and the baby kick was just the first droplet on my nose to let me know that it truly was rain. With each mouthful of porridge I thought back to the signs that had spelled doom. I had been getting hot flushes, but now we were almost in July that was hardly surprising. A few headaches. Some dizziness. I was in shock from the assault, and the weather was heating up. All understandable occurrences for a woman without child. I was at a loss over what to do.

Three books left to restore, and my work on the library would be done. A woman of a higher class than me would be allowed to lie around and read the books I had bound. Yet, my thoughts were not of leisure, they were about work – and how little of it I had now ahead of me.

Knowing both Sibyl and Lady Persephone to be avid readers it felt quite the tragedy that neither of them would get to enjoy the spoils of the library being refreshed in this way. Not even the child inside me would get to enjoy the feel of these books in their hands. Rose Hall was so aesthetically pleasing, but surely the place had been cursed. No one could truly settle into life here. Even children ended up being whistled away. Lady Persephone's child had been away when she died. What would happen to mine?

I longed to ask for help from someone with the power and the intellect to find a barren couple to raise an unfortunately illegitimate child in relative opulence. That's what happened to other girls in trouble. But it was unthinkable for me to give the child to Lady Violet and Sir Chester. The thought chilled my toes. Lord Belfield was incapable of raising anyone besides himself, but wouldn't he be in a position to help me? However, nothing I had learned in the previous months had absolved anyone at Rose Hall, nor made me trust anyone who held power. With the photograph of Lady Persephone in my mind's eye, I continued to work, with my thoughts swirling around who might have pushed her into the river the night she died. I chose to reflect on my suspects, rather than the uncertain fate of my baby.

Lord Belfield was in love with her sister. The twin boys he sired with Sibyl were born less than nine months after her death. Had he tired of his wife to such an extent that he took her out for a walk that night and cleared a new future for himself by murdering her? This would mean that his performance of grief was intensely theatrical, and that someone else had seen fit to take Persephone's diary and try to destroy it. To protect him, perhaps?

If it were Sir Chester who had killed Persephone, I suspected jealousy. He was enough of a sadist to kill her for the mere crime of gifting his brother with a son, while his own wife resented him too much to allow him to impregnate her. He was clever enough to muddy the waters by travelling down to London, but not without time to commit the act first. If he were a soldier on a field, I could see him on the winning side walking among the corpses and spearing the dead with a bayonet, just to be sure.

Lady Violet wasn't as simpering a sort as I had first imagined her to be. There was most definitely a more calculating part of her character that had revealed itself after the library break-in, though I had not seen her since our conversation about deceiving Lord Belfield and was curious for her visit. Could she not have been jealous of Lady Persephone too, barren as she was? The cottage she shared with Sir Chester was too far to walk to Rose Hall from, even on the clearest or warmest of nights. But could she have secretly invited her sister-in-law to go for a canter at dusk? If Joseph knew her well enough to come and clean up the library window glass, perhaps he might have kept quiet about which horses were with whom and when?

Or did Joseph kill Lady Persephone because she had chanced upon him and Wesley, as I had?

Or maybe it was Wesley? Would he have murdered her to keep his cross-dressing a secret? I could not ignore that he wore her dress. Just because he was the closest person I had ever had to a best friend, and meek as a kitten mewing for milk most days, couldn't he have become a spiteful hissing tomcat if she'd found him rifling through her armoires, finding dresses to entice Joseph with?

Even Baxter could have done it, bitter battleaxe that she was. I could imagine Lady Persephone's deception tipping her over the edge. Passing herself off as white when she was really an albino. How did she feel about having to serve a woman whose ancestors were enslaved and thus came from a lower class of human than she considered herself to be? Even though she only left the house for church and the market shops, she must know the area well enough to creep up on Persephone in the night, from behind a shadowy tree by the water. To think of her doing so was difficult for me. I still believed she would have preferred the surreptitious act of poisoning Lady Persephone than the physical exertion of pushing her into a river.

I felt the most guilt for contemplating Sibyl's motives. The woman whose mind enticed me the most. In me she finally had someone to discuss literature and politics with – the first to come along since her sister had passed away. Why would she kill the person who knew her best in the world? Was she jealous enough of her sister's white skin affording her a life she would never be able to live? Resentful for years of servitude to her younger sister? What curdled feelings chugged around Sibyl, seeing her sister coupled with the man who she knew loved her more, but couldn't marry because his place in society and her dark skin colour made it impossible? Yet if Sibyl had killed Persephone, someone else must have destroyed the diary. I couldn't believe it of her, and it just didn't fit.

I felt like a beleaguered detective and almost everyone with a connection to the house was a suspect.

The diary indicated that Persephone was afraid of a man, and even though that didn't discount the women completely, it was something I held closely in my mind. I had pieced together page after page over the past months, but none of those had revealed anything more specific. There was just one section left.

I could see any of them doing it. I trusted some more than others, but no one implicitly. The one thing I felt sure of was that someone had killed Lady Persephone. There had been too much fear and jealousy and hate pulsing through Rose Hall over the years for the death of a young healthy mother of one son to be a mere accident. Lady Persephone was not done with life. She had too much to live for and had sacrificed so much to maintain the standard of life she had reached, born as she was to two black parents. I was as certain as the baby kicking inside me that her death was a punishment for her achievement.

As Violet arrived late that morning, I stood at a first-floor window and watched her descend from the carriage. She seemed quite fine now. A vision in white. Cotton or linen, I couldn't tell from this height, but she strode in ahead of Wesley carrying her bags and I heard her humming one of Mozart's symphonies in the hallway. I rubbed my belly and wondered when he would begin to notice me, and if he would be quelled by my soothing hands. I am not sexing the child in retrospect here. He was always a boy. Sir Chester wouldn't have had it any other way. Or perhaps I always wished he would be a boy, because if Sir Chester found out he'd sired a girl on his first successful impregnation, the consequences would have been even more dire to consider.

Wesley brought me a note from Lady Violet that night that read:

Meet you in the library at 10.30 tomorrow morning.
V.

He sat on the edge of my bed and looked towards me expectantly. I hadn't seen the comb and oil in his other hand. I settled back into the home between his legs with a great deal more labour. First a kneel, then a swivel and shift into a cross-legged position which at first wasn't quite close enough to him. I put both hands on the ground and hopped my bum back a scotch until his hands were comfortably on my shoulders. Instead of going straight for the ends of my hair as usual, he kneaded my neck and made me growl.

'You're very hot tonight.'

So, he could feel it too? My whole torso felt like a furnace. I longed to tell him why, but even though I didn't fear his judgement, I definitely didn't want the dramatics without any solution. I didn't think him worthy of being the first to know. I wanted to tell a woman first.

'You can start my hair now, darling. It's getting late. Thank you for that though.'

And so he did.

In the middle of the first plait I asked him, 'Did Lady Persephone and Sibyl behave the same?'

'What? Like sisters, you mean?' he asked.

'Yes,' I said. 'When you look back, does it seem obvious?'

'Well, with Lady P, not really. You wouldn't think she were any different than ... what she were.'

'You mean she behaved like a white lady,' I probed.

'Well, she was white, weren't she? I know her mum weren't but she were. Right pale she was. Paler than me. Hated the sun.' He whispered that last bit.

'Yes, but Sibyl, who is very much coloured, is her sister,' I countered.

'Yeah, all right, I know. I know ... We thought Sibyl were up herself, if I'm honest. It's not that she weren't nice. It was just the way she were always trying to better herself. If she weren't working, she were reading and if she weren't reading, she were riding. It was like she was the one behaved like a white lady, in a weird way. But Lady P just was one. I can't see her any different.'

'Did either of them know about you and Joseph?' I asked.

'Oh, no no no no no. I were right careful when they were around. It was safer to tek him into the library because all the night-time action was on the first floor anyway,' he said.

'What do you mean?' I asked.

'Well, Lord Belfield were with Sibyl most nights. Once Lady P were asleep and them two were together, me and Joseph had the whole ground floor to ourselves basically. But the library were best because you can't hear nowt from in there once the door's closed and I'd lock it from inside.' He whistled air out through his front teeth, content at the memory.

'So, it was you and Joseph downstairs, Sibyl and Lord Belfield in his room? It's hardly discreet.'

'It's hardly a leap for the lord of the house and the lady's maid to be at it though, is it? That's why they're always being got rid of. The pretty ones are always on the move. Once the lady of the house gets a whiff, she's off. Or if the worst happens,' he mused.

'But the worst did happen! Twice. Sibyl had twins,' I said.

'Yeah, but that were well after. And Lady P didn't mind,' he said, pushing my head to the left.

I was reassured of his innocence. To consider him culpable in the death of Lady Persephone made my stomach squeak. The thought had lingered because I imagined him being jealous of her femininity. Though this didn't really seem to be the case. His access to Joseph was not hampered by her presence.

Neither was his animus towards Sibyl based on anything that was particularly solid. If not for her colour, or if she had been born into a fairer society, Sibyl might have ascended. Although he recognised this, he hadn't said so outright. Sibyl behaved above her station, because she was trapped by the circumstance of her colouring. I was sure Wesley could appreciate the bind she found herself in, considering that he was trapped by the circumstance of his own sexual nature.

'So she was well aware?' I asked.

'That's what I just said. They were the best of friends, them two. They ate together every night by the window. In summer they'd watch the sunset. One night I walked past the room and Lady P were doing Sibyl's hair. It's where I learned how to do frizzy hair gently. I watched them comb from the ends up, smooth the edges with the oils. Right jealous I was. Always wanted a girl-friend to play with, didn't I?' He squeezed my shoulder. 'They had a pomade thing too though. Dunno what were in that one.'

'Their mother probably sent it to them. She might have got it down the docks from their own people.'

'What's her mother like?' Wesley asked.

'Oh Wesley, she's ever so sweet. She really looked after me.' And with that the floodgates opened and I gave him every last detail of my trip to Liverpool to meet Sibyl and Miss Arabella.

I woke up crying the next morning. On my back, not sobbing as such, but panting my way up from a nightmare of smashed faces with distorted, jagged-toothed mouths

251

snapping at me from brambles that threatened to ensnare me whole. I didn't know I was crying until I felt the tears trickle away from my temples and into the inner pools of my ear. I waited for the little puddles to evaporate, but when this took too long, I rose up, wiped my face and readied myself for the day.

The smells of the kitchen were newly nauseating. The thought of imbibing anything milky was too tummy-tumbling to consider, but thankfully the eggs Baxter served the kippers with were poached and not scrambled. The wholemeal bread had too much butter on it, because she had buttered it for me, and the coating of my throat was ineffectively washed away by my glass of water.

I felt horrifically ungrateful. A mere half a year ago, I had cooked mine and my father's every meal and scrabbled to try and make it interesting for myself to eat with whatever we could afford. My father ate everything without complaint, which I always found sad, because if the food I placed before him had elicited some comment, then I might have felt at least somewhat noticed.

But maybe now he had moved some woman in? Out of desperation, rather than longing. How was he faring? Did he still go and see that curly-haired, caramelised prostitute down in the brothel by the canal? Dare he ask her about me, thinking her trade was the only option available to me after he'd thrown me out? Where did he think I was? Not pregnant at the kitchen table in the country house of one of his most loyal customers, that was for sure.

As I scoffed the last bits of breakfast, musing on my father, I felt eyes on me. Baxter's eyes. She was glaring at me in flashes, and I might not have noticed if it weren't for my self-consciousness. But could she tell? Did she have any ideas of what I should do? I knew I wouldn't be able to go much longer without telling her.

Chapter Twenty-Three

Lady Violet bustled into the library at 10.30 with an annoyingly sprightly energy about herself.

'Ahhh, there you are, Miss Granger,' she said, peering her head round the door. Where else would I be? Given that this was my place of work, which she had invited herself into.

'I must say you do have the air of the governess about you already,' she smiled. 'Sombre-coloured clothing and a churlish facial expression notwithstanding. I have brought you some books which might be of use to you, my dear.'

She picked up the chair from the desk where Lord Belfield usually sat and brought it over to me.

'Lady Violet, I must apologise for my countenance. I did not sleep impeccably well last night.'

'Oh, you poor lamb,' she said, petting the skirts on top of my knee. Here she was consoling me in a way I had never predicted. To think this was the same woman who had bucked and brayed and waddled into this house only months before, racked with fear and wearing piss-soaked stockings.

She laid the first book before me and I gasped. *Advice to Young Mothers* by Margaret King Moore.

'Goodness, Miss Granger. Are you sure you're quite all right? Do you want me to come back later?'

'No, no. I'm fine, I promise. Someone just walked over my grave.'

'Oh yes. Happens to me all the time.' She blinked rapidly as if something were in her eye. 'Anyway, I brought this because it's been of immense benefit to me in knowing what to expect, and frankly you must be the lady of the house's greatest ally if you are to be a successful governess.' Then she whispered. 'If she sees you as a threat, then you'll be out on your ear. You must stay as you are. The plainer you are, the better.' She pursed her lips, and again I could not help but wonder if she knew what Sir Chester had done to me.

I nodded. What followed were the books of her own child-hood on simple arithmetic and language, with her exercise books filled with Latin and French sentences written out in a rote fashion with perfect handwriting. Instructions on how to conduct conjugations and such.

Amo, amas, amat . . .

Je veux, tu veux, il/elle veut, nous voulons, vous voulez, ils/elles veulent . . .

It was all quite militaristic. Being one of the smartest girls in my class, I had been called to the front to teach on many an occasion. Lady Violet prattled on and I resolved never to be anything like what was expected of me. If I could give birth to this baby in secret and find another existence to live after having the baby adopted, then I would definitely become a governess and use my funds to go to evening classes in London. I'd heard of Bloomsbury and Kensington. There might even be a university that would accept me as a student eventually. I just needed to untangle myself from the current traps of my predicament.

She sighed when she closed the last book and looked at me expectantly.

'This is all a lot to be going on with. Thank you, Lady Violet. I'm a fast reader, so it shouldn't take long.'

She was staring at me intently. 'Was there anything left legible in the diary at all?'

I stared back at her, but her gaze was clean.

'Yes. I managed to piece some fragments together, and some of the pages are not too badly burned,' I said.

'And?'

'And what?'

'Well, what did it say? Pray tell?' Her eyes bulged with the insistence.

'She was scared of a man. But . . . She hasn't yet said who. I still have work to do on the final pages, the ones she wrote right before she died. They took the full force of the flames, after the back cover burned away, but I think I can salvage enough from them to find a name at least.'

'And if you do find a name? Will you go to the police?'

The police? That had never been part of my thinking. Should it have been? I had envisaged telling Lord Belfield about the culprit, once I had worked out who it was – and assuming he was not himself the killer. I couldn't see him doing anything as dastardly as murder. I hadn't seriously suspected him of doing anything Jack the Ripper might tip his hat at. No, thus far, I had not seriously considered him a murderer. Though, he may have pushed her to commit suicide with his words. Perhaps urging her to jump off the riverbank or from a bridge. His frame was too slight. His fingers too elegant. Chester was the violent one. Lord Belfield's weapons were his words and his mind. He was a wily one, but not a homicidal one. Although Lord Belfield, like Chester and Joseph, was physically and logistically capable of having killed her, he was by far the less likely of the three. Baxter, Violet and Sibyl were more implausible suspects still, even though nobody's innocence was truly proven. I was spiritually sure it wasn't Wesley. I wouldn't be able to wrap my head around him doing it.

'Is there someone you suspect?' she prompted me.

I was wary of sharing too much. Half my suspicions might send Lady Violet into a rage, after all. 'Do you have someone in mind?' I asked instead.

Lady Violet looked away. 'If I were to disclose my suspicions to the police, without some solid proof, it would do me more harm than good.'

I realised that even her higher class than mine would lend her no credibility. 'Disclosure would soften the ground we now stand on,' Lady Violet said, picking some fluff off my shoulder.

She was right of course. The line of women cooped up in an asylum for making accusations against more powerful men was as long as the proposed train line from Cape Town to Cairo.

'I hope to God Persephone has left us with some clue. But only then can we go to the police,' Lady Violet continued.

'Yes, I understand.'

'Do you? Or do you judge me for not seeking justice for Lady Persephone before now?' Violet said, her mouth twisting. 'I can't just go to the police because I know she was frightened of someone before she died; I need more. There has to be more, in her diary. Otherwise, what if I were to point the finger at the wrong person? Someone might even suspect my husband. We both know his temper and – well, he also had a low opinion of her because of her origins and whatnot. But they both have a temper, really. Francis just does a better job at keeping a lid on his than Chester does.'

'It would be awful to accuse someone on no evidence,' I responded. 'I understand your reluctance. Considering everything you've been through.' She pursed her lips at me in pity and placed her hand on mine. It was cold.

'No woman is ever safe around the Belfield brothers. If I'd have known, I would have given my other suitors more of an airing.'

She had said this as if the acknowledgement of our shared lack of safety should make me cleave towards her.

'How'd you mean?' I asked, bile rising in my throat.

'Sir Chester was not my father's first choice for my husband. All my other potentials were richer than he was. And surely none would have been as mean as he can be. Chester hunts with little mercy for what he catches.'

I couldn't exhale. She knew. She *knew*, and she was sitting here counselling me on becoming a governess and having a chit chat about her potentially murderous brother-in-law, and as if her husband defiling me in the dead of night was just something to be alluded to in passing. I gulped down more mucus and pulled my hand away.

'Lady Violet, I must be getting on.'

'Oh, Miss Granger, of course,' she said, a bit too placidly. 'Please. I'm going to go and read one of the marvellous novels you recommended in the garden. Maybe Baxter might allow me another of her gorgeous apple juices. Though you must knock if you come across anything in the diary that would help us. I'm always here for you.' My shoulder jolted just before she reached to pat it.

'Someone walking over your grave again?' she asked.

I had never asked myself if I even liked Lady Violet. She had appeared as a frightened woman in need when I first met her. I'd cleaned her up and dispelled her shame from that abusive moment. I'd brought her books in her isolation in her bedroom. When she revealed herself as a bit of a busybody, bustling in with Joseph to fix the library window, I had found it encouraging. That she could be so filled with desire to clean up a situation that implicated all of us. But no, I was now certain that she disgusted me.

These people were sick. Moving those that worked beneath them like pawns on a chessboard, knowing they would be much more simply taken by life's vagaries than the kings, bishops and queens of the board. We were too easily sacrificed. I had thought Everett was far too impassioned by anarchism when he nestled into my bosom and spoke of what he would do to factory owners and landed gentry if given half the chance. I'd feared for him. But in truth, he should have feared for me.

I had spent close to seven months working in Rose Hall, and every green shoot of hope had been crushed under their heels. I had wanted to be a bookbinder, and had been dismissed as fanciful by Lord Belfield for thinking I could do so alone. I had dared believe in his dream of me becoming a governess to upper-class children, acting as a proxy mother but without the full responsibility I feared. Then along came Sir Chester, to assault such a hope away from me. Now, here came his wife to speak about everything that had happened to me in a way that was cool and detached.

They all deserved hell. And, I decided as I picked up the last book in Lord Belfield's collection, I was going to be the one to give it to them!

Chapter Twenty-Four

I had no doubt that I had to tell Baxter about the baby now. It felt gauche that she would be the first person I would tell, so instead I wrote to the women I felt closest to; Sibyl and Miss Arabella. After thanking them for their hospitality, I apologised for what I was about to tell them and then I poured my heart out about things I had only dared hint of in my previous letters. My father evicting me from our home, Lord Belfield convincing me to become a governess and then finally Sir Chester forcing himself on me and now leaving me 'in the family way'.

After describing the events, I then went on to write things I didn't know myself. That I was determined to have the baby adopted because not only would it be impossible to live a respectable life after giving birth to a bastard in these circumstances, but also because I didn't have the capacity to be a good mother. It was different for Sibyl, I wrote. I know she saw her colour as a bar to a decent life in a number of respects. Lord Belfield not feeling able to marry her as a negresse for one, and marrying her sister instead who, being the right kind of albino, could be easily mistaken for white. However, he was looking after her financially and it was definitely the done thing in the colonies to have a coloured mistress, was it not? I'd heard New Orleans was a positive hive of miscegenation.

Regardless, I wrote, I was just not a motherly kind of person. To know how to love children was not inherent in me. Not having had a mother, because I had killed her off with my own birth, I'd grown up a wastrel of a girl with no real instruction on how to conduct myself as a woman.

I didn't write this, but perhaps that was why I was so captivated by promiscuity. With my collection of trinkets from sexual favours for local boys in my area and finally succumbing to the most affectionate kind of lust with Everett, I had gone on to cause my own downfall. Without a mother to guide me, modesty felt like too high an ideal to reach for. And now look at me. Unmarried and with child. Without a mother, how could I learn to do what did not come naturally to me? I'd never even thought of becoming a mother, really. I'd always seen motherhood as something to avoid until a time when it was inescapable. When I had to get married to someone – or rather anyone – who was deemed appropriate by the exigencies of the allotted time. But now, because of Sir Chester, I was trapped. With the library of Lord Belfield fully restored, I was now merely his pregnant, sullied ward. When he found out, any solution he might offer was sure to leave me some shade of destitute.

So, I begged them. I had run to Rose Hall seeking refuge

and now I needed to make a plan to run away from Rose Hall and save the life of the one inside me. I begged them to find me a place that would take the baby. By the time it would be born it would be too cold to do something as charmed as leaving him on the church steps. No, I needed to give birth and have the baby whisked away from me. I had held Sibyl's baby and felt somewhat dispirited when he clamoured for my breast. I was sure it would be the same with my own. My sour, embittered milk wouldn't do him well in life. I wasn't competent in handling my own existence. I couldn't nurture the life of another. I just couldn't. It was unfathomable. So, I ended my pleading letter by thanking them in advance and hoping that whatever discussions they had among themselves and the women in their community would offer me a salvation that was more noble than it was convenient, at the very least.

I always imagined the baby kicking inside me. Never punching. I am sure if I had been able to be open about my pregnancy because I was a sensible married woman, elated at being with child for the first time, I could say all sorts of fun things like 'I am sure this one's going to be a footballer.' If I had imagined him punching my uterine walls, then I might have thought to say, 'He's definitely a boxer!' Maybe it's prejudicial of me, but I'd be disappointed at the idea of a child of mine being a brutish boxer entertaining people for grubby, gambled notes. The modern equivalent of finding out one's child is a gladiatorial slave. Boxers died younger, didn't they?

'Watch out,' Joseph said, just in time for me to duck my head. We were cantering up a hill and I hadn't seen the obstacle of a leaf-festooned branch for I was that distracted.

'You're off with the faeries, you are,' Joseph observed.

I sighed. Nothing I was feeling could be comfortably conveyed to him. So I spun the lighthouse torch out onto his sea instead.

'How's Annie?' I asked.

I knew they were still meeting in the shed when no one was visiting. I'd only caught him sidling into there once in the past weeks. I think Wesley only dressed as Annie in the shed, now. I didn't expect to see her in the corridors again. Although, in all fairness, my creeping around at night wasn't as frequent.

'She's all right, I suppose.' Joseph shrugged.

I knew he was still embarrassed that I'd caught him having relations.

'It's a shame you don't have anywhere to meet her that's a bit less rustic,' I offered.

'What's that mean?' he asked.

'Rustic?'

He cocked his head to the side.

'Spartan.'

He shook his head. I felt silly for using words that meant so little to him.

'Just a bit rough. It's damp in there still, isn't it?'

'It's all right.'

'I doubt she feels it's all right.' To which he smiled.

'I'm gonna make it nicer for you,' I added.

'There's no need. You don't have to,' he said, looking out at the green hill dotted with buttercups in front of us. A hawk swooped round it, following a current we'd never be able to see or feel.

'I want to.'

This was true. The lust between them intrigued me. It was our secret that was so sordid in the minds of others, but considering the vile minds of the Belfields, there was something cherubic about the meek way Joseph talked about Annie. It tickled me. I wanted to make the shed as boudoir-like as possible for them. Everett and I had had to be furtive about our goings on, but my bed was always warm and I sprinkled rose water on it before he came over. He always mentioned how nice I smelled and marvelled at my softness. I knew what men like Joseph and Everett liked.

But moreover, I'd begun to think of my legacy more in the past few days. Having lost my mother at birth, her figure in my mind had always been one of perfection. In my imagination she was ever so pretty and nice and generous. I was sure she did lovely things for people. What if I were to die in childbirth too? So many would cease to speak of me, for shame of actions that I shouldn't really be blamed for. I wanted people like Joseph, Annie, Wesley, Sibyl and Miss Arabella to remember me as a soft touch. Someone who did nice things just because.

As we cantered back onto Hurrel Farm, the birds in the trees tweeted in chorus and accompanied the sloshing sound of Mrs Hurrel washing something in the outside sink.

'Oh, now don't you look rosy!' she said to me. My heart was racing out of nowhere. I couldn't explain why. My toes tingled and I was feeling somewhat faint, but I knew I had to maintain a serious expression.

'Thank you,' I replied in a voice that I hoped offered her some assurance that nothing about me had changed.

*

Lord Belfield would return that week. This didn't leave me much time to execute my plans for the shed. On the Monday morning I awoke earlier than I knew Baxter would. It wasn't possible to do so soundlessly, but I had to hunt for the things I needed without disturbance. I found a wedding trousseau Miss Arabella had written about in one of her letters, quite close to the door but covered in a white sheet that was caked in dust. I tied a scarf around my mouth like a Wild West bandit and unearthed the required fabrics from the trunk. I then hustled away a few cushions from the morning room and headed down to the shed.

There were some crates with several bottles of last season's pear cider which had surely been forgotten about. The twenty or so sacks of grain were easily manoeuvrable, as long as I moved them one by one. Wedging them on top of each other in the corner, six long and two wide, gave me three layers, and two to use at the head as pillows. An eiderdown comfortably covered the top layers and most of the sides, but conveniently didn't reach the floor. Then the cotton bedsheets with Chantilly lace trim. I threw them out and lavender fragrance swirled from their folds. It really was quite beautiful. A white wedding bed that gleamed with sexual promise in a dark shed. I could imagine the things Joseph and Annie might want to get up to, now that they had a bed to lie on, from the depictions of certain sexual acts on the Pompeii frescoes that had been excavated.

The benefit of Lady Persephone being dead, I thought guiltily, was that no one would miss the things I had found. There was no daughter to pine for the things her grandmother had spent so much of her time preparing for her mother in

266

the months leading up to the wedding. Even if a new home had been found for them, they still had a whiff of tragedy. The veneer of fortune that all wedding gifts have had been dulled by their relegation to the attic.

I covered my creation in sheets of unused burlap, which were probably intended for gardening purposes but were as yet entirely untouched. Behind some bottles and cans on the shelves I hid the sari silks I had found in another corner of the attic that I assumed had been left behind by Lord Belfield's ayah. The only objects that might hint at the romance I was trying to induce from the space were the beeswax and sperma-ceti candles I was sure would be smelled even more strongly on a warm day, but still gave off a mellow honey and animal aroma.

I closed the door of the shed and felt so accomplished sitting down for breakfast, exhausted from the preparations I had made for future lovemaking. I had hoped doing so would be a distraction from the new movements inside me. But this was too optimistic.

While I knew I wanted to get as many things done as I could before I started becoming visible, I was also scared of there being some sort of accident. If I were earlier in the pregnancy then I might have been reckless riding horses and hoped for an accident. To fall off my horse or get kicked in the stomach would be a neat ending to a nightmarish scenario. But now, the nightmare was a stillbirth. After everything that had happened, I couldn't handle that. The baby had to live outside of me. I could never grow to love it, but I could definitely strive to give the baby away to someone loving. That was the beginnings of the plan anyway.

*

The following morning I woke up feeling aggrieved. I longed for Everett and had fallen asleep hugging a pillow I had stolen from the attic for myself; I sobbed into him, desperate for the darkness of his aroma. Mercifully, we had a decent goodbye. I got to touch the back of his neck and marvel at the wetness of his eyes as he told me how much I meant to him, and that he couldn't imagine a day or even a week without me in it. I imagined him in his final destination of Chicago, spattered in pig's blood and sprinkled with iron ore, bellowing at others in the evening square to alight the skyscrapers with their fatigue and indignation.

I don't know how true it is that I never felt soft before him. I definitely never felt pretty. I saw my hair as an unruly mass. He called it candy floss. My nose wasn't elegant. He said I looked Grecian and grazed his eyelashes over it en route to kissing my neck. I felt dumpy with a workaday frame marred by the slick fingering of boys who snickered at me after we were done. But beneath and on top of him, I became lithe and worthy of the affections he showed me. Cupping my belly, kissing the navel and rising to giggle into my bosom. Once, he had looked up at me from there, with moistened lashes and a sweaty forehead, and said so clearly:

'I love you.'

'I love you too.'

I yielded into him like I was the sun rising into his sky in the morning. I felt bright and alive, undulating beneath him. It was too dangerous to sing out, but a chorus rang out inside of my body and brought me into the world anew.

His face glistened wet in the candlelight. I was too ashamed to bring attention to it. So I brought him back up and thought he wouldn't want to kiss me. But he did. I'd lost sense of time a while before, but I was so comfortable and surely, the shape of his body being so easily accommodated was a sign. We were meant for this. Meant for each other.

It was more than I could have imagined. The excitement leading up to it. The amorphous length of time where he made me come thrice. The chit chat and talk afterwards where he told me what I should try reading next and I chastised him for not reading what I had last given him and he promised he would. He did read it. I rewarded him the next time he came round, but the fun was curtailed by the tragedy of my father walking in on me, in flagrante, on my knees in our kitchen.

The threat of destitution that sex visited upon me, willing or forced, was too expected to take my breath away. Was it not promised in sermons, and warnings from the women around me? Secrets on my street were only barely kept. I had felt the eyes of mothers on me. They didn't need the evidence my father had just encountered. I surely smelled too familiar as I passed by them in the market – but what I did was the opposite of sordid. Our minds met first, before our bodies did. Everett coming along had felt like a watering of my soil, but we both helped each other grow. Perhaps if he had been moneyed enough to go to a university and had peers his own age interested in his pluckiness, there'd have been less elation at finding someone in me who didn't think of him as silly, but rather an amusing kind of radical. I would have married him in a heartbeat, although we never got the chance to discuss it. I would have begrudgingly had his children too, even though I'd resent the interruption and the irrevocable changes that came from me being saddled with motherhood. An end to my life and a satisfying extension of his. But the cost of a life with him felt affordable. I wanted it.

If my father had not burst in on us, perhaps I could have played the situation better. Informed him that a young man wished to court me and make a neater display of our affection for each other. He could have come with posies and walked me around the park under the watchful eyes of our neighbours. Eventually, Everett and my father may have gone to the pub to discuss his intentions for me over two pints of stout. Then we would have been married and pretended the wedding night was the first time I had ever seen a man's private parts and I'd have made whimpering noises to convince any listeners that I was experiencing far more pain than pleasure, as was expected of me. Soon enough we would have left for Boston together. In Chicago I might have made friends with Lucy Parsons and Emma Goldman, writing pamphlets commemorating the Haymarket affair. I could have become a young mother in a new, steaming metropolis with immigrant families from all over – working and writing for the Labour movement Everett was so passionate about.

It was partially that passion that made his cowardice on being run off by my father so appalling. The Friday after my father burst in to find me on my knees in our kitchen, he located Everett in the square where we had met and brought him back to answer to him in our front workshop. When my father asked him when we were getting married and he answered that he was too scared to marry me just yet, that was a surprise to me too. I missed the person he had made himself out to be, more than the one who told my father I meant less to him than a good-time girl who had given herself over to him easily. Everett confirmed that he had spoiled me and didn't intend to redeem me.

He had told me that we would have a life together. That he believed in women working alongside men. Being paid the same as them. He had read almost everything I had read. We both liked Mary Wollstonecraft. I gave myself to him with more ardour than I'd given to the boys I used to play with, because it meant something to both of us. He made me believe that. He made me believe in him.

I imagined the baby was Everett's and I had allowed him to impregnate me that day after his tongue opened me up. Filled me up and bound us to a future of our own making. I touched myself to honour him and the love we felt. Bridging land and ocean, I brought him back to me. Imagined him with and in me for ever. Such a dependable memory that made me swell every time. I could come so easily thinking about him, and it obliterated thoughts of Sir Chester, at least for the moment. With Everett, my thinking came more easily. Every time I touched myself thinking about him, I reminded myself what it was to feel bigger. To be tended to and well fed. Full.

I was rising earlier, against my will, in those days. The clip clop of two horses that dawn was ominous. I knew who it was before I padded to the window, enshrouded by my blanket. Looking down at the gravel drive, I saw the brothers returning, together this time. Lord Belfield and Sir Chester were back in Rose Hall.

Chapter Twenty-Five

I wasn't scared of Sir Chester in the way that I used to be. The worst had already happened, I told myself, though I couldn't ignore that if he was Lady Persephone's murderer then perhaps there was something left for him to take away from me.

After lunch, we passed one another in the hallway and he smiled before he nodded at me and walked off, waggling his finger in his ear. His silence must have been a tactic to keep me in suspense. Nothing he could do now would stop me from my sleuthing, though. I resolved that after finishing work in the library that day I would again try to decipher whatever legible writing was left behind in the diary.

Lord Belfield didn't visit me in the library. I spent my time in there covered in a blanket for comfort at my desk, reading. I refused to tell him my work was done. I had no guilt that I would sup at his table and sleep in his home while performing no more labour. He had brought his brother back into the home where I had been defiled and expected me to be thankful that at least I wasn't alone with him. But I *was* alone. The fox roamed the halls with bloodied teeth, and I, soon to be the fattest hen in the hen house, had no one left to warn about him. I don't think Lord Belfield could even bring himself to look at me with his brother in the house and was probably just hiding out in his room like Lady Violet did. Both with their bottles and their books, with the rest of us meant to squirrel around furnishing their lives in the rooms below.

I was tentative with the burnt diary. The charring meant that every time I untied the cloth I had placed it within, flakes of coal-black paper fragmented away from the body of the book. Wearing gloves wouldn't have helped. There wasn't much to save. No chance of it being salvaged, really. I kept returning to it. Hoping more than knowing that there would be some trace of a sentence that would illuminate Lady Persephone's thoughts in the weeks before her passing. I read again the first few pages that I had read before. All lovely innocuous witterings about their trip to London, and how much she missed her son Daniel, and the like.

The pages that were stuck together required bravery of me. Once they were prised apart, they might crumble. I had a brass letter-opener and a damp cloth. I moistened the page edges and prised them apart. I held my breath while doing so, as if a petit souffle from me would disintegrate each page. I managed three of them, but the fourth ripped halfway up, and everything after that page was blackened together and fused. I had freed up as much as I could. Not quite full pages of text, but snatches of pages. All speaking of Rose Hall as a prison. And one name kept appearing. Chester.

Chester hates me with such ...   I was dazed bec ...
                              he punched me in the head

That must have been him. There was no way this was
some other violent man. I saw him as the threat in her life. A
man who unearthed her secrets. He could have done to her
what he did to me. Lord Belfield was not a protector. On the
night he came to my room to pull his brother off me, did he
not say, 'Not again'? I wasn't safe from Chester. Why would
Lady Persephone have been? He also held her albinism above
her as a bargaining chip. He could have blackmailed her into
anything. These were all suppositions, of course. But the last
mention of him on the fourth page was the arrow that hit
the bullseye.

Chester ... do me an injury ...   believe he will
kill m ...

This was all I needed. The relief breathed into me. I need
not suspect anyone else. It was him. It was Chester. When
he had attacked me, had I not seen myself dying during the
act? My despoilment hadn't been my first fear. I feared he
was there to kill me. All the way through I thought it would
end with him killing me. A final stabbing. A strangulation
if he'd had the chance. Lady Persephone would have been
caught unawares, or perhaps lured, out in the open air. Far
from any staff who might hear. Far from the husband who
could intervene and pull his brother off her.

The suspicions of those I longed to love more fully could
now be lifted. Sibyl was not spoken of as a potential murderer.

Wesley and Joseph hardly mentioned at all. And of the people Lady Persephone held dear: Violet spoken of kindly; Lord Belfield a jovial if cowardly sort in her descriptions.

It was Chester. The same assailant. I couldn't confront him. I couldn't even name him with my own words of accusation. Lady Violet might have encouraged me to go to her, but surely she would baulk at naming her husband to the police. But I could cause his downfall anonymously. I could find some sort of justice that would rob my rapist and Lady Persephone's murderer of his freedom. I held the scale and the sword with no blindfold to hamper my sentencing. *Justitia.*

That evening, honeysuckle enticed me into the garden. I knew Joseph and Annie were going to be in the shed. Perhaps I wanted to stand guard for them? I busied myself in the kitchen garden first. It was a good seventy yards away from them, so I truly was affording them privacy. I snapped off runner beans and tweaked off courgettes, laying them in a metal bucket that I'd rinsed out. I hummed along to the song I loved singing most in school assembly.

'*For the beauty of the eeeeeearth. For the beauty of the skiiiii-iies. For the loooove, which from our biiiiiirth, over and around us liiiiies . . .*'

I wandered over to the cherry tree and started plucking the fallen fruit from the grass below. After having stepped on a few, I became a bit more ginger in my steps, tip-toeing onto the clean patches of green. I lowered my humming, but now I was less than twenty yards away from the shed and could hear absolutely nothing. The evening was quiet and I was the loudest thing in it.

I gave up my charade of pretending I was in the garden doing anything besides lurking around listening for the sounds Everett and I used to make. I kept my basket in the crook of my elbow just in case one of them came out and I needed a good excuse. *'Oh, I was just cherry-picking and needed to relieve myself in that bush there.'* And I crept up on the shed from behind, where there was a fist-sized hole for me to look through.

There, on the bed I had made, festooned in candlelight, lay Annie and Joseph. She was at the top of the cot, a lock of hair covering her left eye, wearing a nightdress with a frill trim at the neck, cuffs and hemline, leaning against the back wall with her legs open. Between her legs lay a topless Joseph with his head in her lap and her soft elegant hand strumming the furry chest I'd only peeked at. The smell of Joseph was overpoweringly animal, but not unpleasant. I imagined she found it intoxicating. I could only catch snatches of their conversation.

'—You're definitely getting into heaven for how you look after her, and ...'

The voices were so faint. They were obviously used to speaking this quietly. I was no more than six feet away and I could only just decipher what they were saying.

'Oh, give over. It's her who looks after me. It's why I have to find a wife before she goes. I couldn't do all the—'

They were talking about Mrs Hurrel and the farm? So, Joseph could discuss his predicament with ease with Annie. Obviously, their relationship was impossible anywhere but in the shadows. I looked at her face. She wasn't embittered, but pleasant and placid. She was listening to him with such gentle feeling, though I thought she might look on him as keeping her in somewhat of a bind.

Then he told a joke and she bent forward, laughing soundlessly. Mouth agape and huffing out a laugh that made the candles flicker more. Joseph looked up at her face, pleased with himself. He liked to make her laugh. He tickled her belly and she swatted his hand away. But he kept looking at her, moved the hair out of her eye and caressed her lip with his forefinger before lying back down again. I didn't know he had this in him. The joker. The romantic. Annie just looked like a more comfortable and even prettier version of Wesley, but it was Joseph's transformation that fascinated me. This hulking mass of a man who was so barrel chested and unguarded, much more fair in his colouring in the candlelight. Annie made a joke and his shoulders heaved up and down and his eyes squinted with his mirth. He looked bear-like and child-like and snug in this shelter I had furnished for them. But things took a turn back to the sensual when his chortles subsided. He rubbed his underwear again and I saw him harden. I knew how big he was already, so that wasn't a surprise, but the look on his face as he reached for Annie was sheepish. She reached down and I held my breath and backed away from the hole in the wall. I'd seen enough. They deserved their privacy back now.

Back at the cherry tree, with my basket of cherries and bucket of courgettes and runner beans, I put my hand to my mouth to stifle the giggling fit that was besetting me. To see Joseph like that was a revelation. He was more than one person. It shocked me to see how little I knew of him. How protective he was of his humour and softness. How could someone so serious and taciturn in day-to-day life, be such a sweet man who wanted to be canoodled and given fellatio by someone as pretty and soft as Annie? I mean, it made sense that as the man of his house, who commanded a farm, he had too much on his plate to be anything but gruff-voiced and direct in his daily interactions. But to see him so animated was beguiling.

He reminded me of my father in certain ways. My own dad, whom I never heard anyone call 'Douglas'. It was always 'Mr Granger'. The only one to call him by his first name was my grandma, and it was only 'Douggy' if she was exceptionally pleased with him. But the transformation of my dad around her wasn't extreme. Merely more deferential and less acerbic, which although keenly perceptible to my child's eye, was nothing too disturbing. But seeing Joseph made me think of him for another reason. That sheepish look. It wasn't dissimilar to the way he had looked at the mulatto prostitute by the docks. To see a woman have sway over my father made me think differently about myself. That sexually, to have something they wanted, shifted the power balance temporarily. I felt lucky that my father beat me less often as I grew, unlike other girls on my street. But the absence of laughter in my house had depressed me terribly. I wished I had made more time to try to make him laugh. To know what it was that made him chuckle.

A chilling presence was at my right shoulder. I turned my head as I walked back towards the house and there, smoking an oily cigarillo, was Sir Chester.

He looked well. Smooth-faced and pomaded hair intact at this late hour of day. My heart constricted and I suddenly noticed the sweat cooling my shoulder blades. My right eye itched but I didn't have a hand free to scratch it. I froze mid-stride and locked eyes with his glare. He reached into my cherry basket and fingered its contents while he blew out a stream of smoke, and then popped a cherry into his mouth, pulling the stalk off as it was clenched between his teeth.

'Aren't you going to say anything?' He raised his eyebrow at me.

'There's nothing to say,' I whispered.

How long had he been following me? Had he seen me peering into the shed? Did he know they were in there now? Had I destroyed more lives than my own? Given what I now suspected him of, I had even more reason to fear Chester.

'I didn't know you were so green fingered.'

'Well, that's not a surprise, because you don't know me,' I spat.

'Oh, but Miss Granger, I do. My brother informed me that you were just a whore who he took in out of kindness.'

'You're disgusti—'

He spoke over me. 'Which explains why you were making eyes at me from the moment I arrived. You *wanted* me to come up that night.'

'I have never hated any person as much as I hate you.'

'If only you hadn't made so much noise, I would still be able to visit you.'

I just stared at him. He longed to shock me and I wouldn't give him the satisfaction of seeing me shiver at the thought.

'You do know that you're unnecessarily intelligent?'

'Excuse me?' I seethed.

'It's why you struggle and make such terrible choices.

Reaching above your nature. Striving to become a bookbinder when you should have just married one. Swishing around with the imperious nature of a future governess when you're clearly more suited to being the wife of someone more intelligent than you.'

His pity was all the more galling because of his sincerity. He even put his bottom lip out to show his concern.

'The only reason you are so obsessed with me is because I'm more intelligent than you and there's nothing you can do about it,' I shot back. 'There are no books you can read or places to travel to. You're a failed man. Nothing to speak of besides the pittance you inherited and some ideas you gathered up from the newspaper. That's why you live in Lord Belfield's shadow. It's the absence of any original thought. You're not on his level.'

He was smiling at the rage I was exhibiting, but not disturbed enough for my liking.

'And what's more, I didn't even feel you inside me that night.' And I spat this at him. 'You're nothing.'

Frightfully predictable, that it was my critique of his manhood that caused the physical eruption. His hand came up and I assumed it was going to be a slap to the face. But no, it was a punch to my head, directly above my ear. The cherries spilled everywhere, and my vision blurred as the punch's impact sang its way through my brain and down my spine. My nerves started to jangle from the heat. The cherries had gone everywhere and with that I started to cry. Gulping sobs at yet another scene of destruction he had caused. But I had to swallow my sobs. What if Joseph heard us and came running to investigate? Annie left shivering in the shed, with a wide-open door exposing her to the retribution of the outside world? If this was what he was doing to me, what would he do to them?

Where was Lord Belfield? Lady Violet, even? I had protected her from Sir Chester once. Where was she to protect me? She had ostensibly been so trustworthy and conspiratorial about the diary, but now that her husband was unleashed on me, she was nowhere to be seen.

I grabbed at the cherries and the fallen bucket of courgettes and runner beans. I couldn't feel the pads of my fingers. I couldn't bend them to scoop the cherries up. Chester grabbed a clump of my hair from behind and stood astride me, purring into my ear.

'You can't be that intelligent, otherwise you would have realised your predicament. The only option available to you was to become my mistress. This resistance you're putting up, pretending you don't long for my cock, hasn't made it go soft at all. I will have you again. And don't you fucking think I won't hunt you down. You can't run away. I'll hire investigators. Every bookbinder in the country will know what a whore you are. Try and become a governess and I'll be befriending them over Sunday lunch, telling them what a grave mistake they have made letting a woman like you care for their children. Not even Violet is stupid enough to think her barren womb will make me release her. I get everything I want, and I keep it. Accept your place and my power over you, or I promise I'll destroy you.'

He threw me down to the ground just after releasing his yank on my hair. To finish his point, he found the most concentrated patch of cherries and stomped them into the gravel.

I watched him walking away. I wouldn't and couldn't kill his baby inside me, but by God, I would most definitely burn his whole house down.

Chapter Twenty-Six

It pained me to do it, but I had to blackmail Joseph in order to wrestle some justice for myself out of the situation. An assault on Chester's assets was the only way to begin crushing him. And it had to be quick. Based on the activity in my womb, I would start showing soon. I was waiting for the day Baxter would tell me she could see me fattening.

Perhaps if I'd had the ability to go to the police, I would not have needed to place Joseph in such a position. The importance of Joseph's masculinity to him helped to make him my victim. I could force him into silence because of my knowledge of Annie and what it would do to him to be accused of sexual impropriety. I had decided that I could always beg Joseph's forgiveness once he understood why I couldn't handle passing the meting out of justice to an outside institution. I didn't trust the police to do what was right as much as I trusted myself.

It would be at least a few more days until I heard from Sibyl and Arabella. My head ached from the blow it had received yesterday, but my new plan had calmed me down.

There was so much to hide. The baby inside me. The fact that the books were all restored. But most of all, how calculated and vengeful I had become as a person. I'd arrived at Rose Hall feeling industrious, but at this point I looked back on myself with a soft compassion for how meek and optimistic I had been. I was glad Wesley and I had stopped going to church. It wasn't a place of solace for me anymore. Church wasn't for people like me. I was too far gone.

I slipped up to the farm at the end of the workday at 5 p.m. I needed to be back before 7 p.m. in order to not raise suspicion. I also needed to avoid being seen by Mrs Hurrel. So I climbed over the fence of their southern field and came up on the stables that way. I waited until I saw Joseph wander out of the cottage towards the field and hissed out at him.

'Psssst.'

Alarmed as a March hare who had been given a Christmas wreath to jump through, his eyes locked on me and he shook his head and shrugged. I beckoned him towards me hurriedly.

He arrived in the stable.

'I don't have time to explain, but I need you to let me take a horse a far way on Saturday. You can't come with me. You can't know what I'm up to. And if you find out in the future what I was up to, you are going to keep it to yourself because you owe me.'

His face was pained. I didn't want to do this to him, but

there was no other way. I wouldn't expose him, obviously. But I needed him to think I might.

'There's no need to threaten me. I always knew you couldn't be trusted.'

Now I was pained.

'You can trust me. I'm just ensuring I can trust you. Grow up.'

He sighed. Said nothing.

'I have a lot of respect for you as a man, you know. I do.'

'Yeah all right. You've got what you wanted. No need for the extra. I'll see you on Saturday. Same time.'

He walked off and left me. If he'd been my brother, I would have shouted at him and told him to come back and hold me.

My mind had been planning this arson underneath my daily thoughts for some time. At first, it was a mere flirtation with vengeance: *Oh, if I were of the right mind, I would burn his house down to cinders.* But now it was a matter of political retribution against their class. The callous way Sir Chester, Lady Violet and people of their class operated. One might have asked why wouldn't I raze Rose Hall to the ground instead? Well, firstly there was too much of value in the home. I'd spent six months restoring the library and I was not about to rid my work of all importance, and furthermore, Baxter and Wesley lived there too. I would not make them homeless. Sir Chester had no library to speak of, and without them at home, there were also no staff living in, so I wasn't putting anyone else in danger. Sir Chester was the one I was gunning to destroy.

I had imagined driving a kitchen knife into his chest and

pouring boiling water onto his face. In spite of his assault, it was me who would end up in jail then. Lady Violet was complicit and thus deserving of losing her home and possessions too. She had entered my life as a victim, but in the intervening months had transformed herself from someone snivelling to someone Machiavellian, although her motivations remained as murky to me as ever. She wasn't a woman I could be in solidarity with. She was someone who would comfortably hide out in her bedroom while her husband marauded the rooms above her, hunting for me, his prey.

Mabel was sweating beneath me. I hadn't thought of horses having reactions to temperature before I learned to ride. I knew them to occasionally be tempestuous, shaken by loud noises or bolting from explosions and violence, but not to be as sensitive to worldly conditions in the way we were. That Mabel would shiver and sneeze in the cold when I first met her was fascinating to me. I could greet her with a neck squeeze and gauge her mood.

She was fine today. A bit perky. A bit excited. And very pungent. An eye-watering mix of her hormonal animal smell with a base note of waxy lanolin and a top note of daisies or the like.

The day was marvellous. I had hugged Mrs Hurrel on arrival and gifted her some cinnamon and star anise I had got in a Liverpool market, and she had swaddled herself away in the kitchen while Joseph and I cantered off around the farm together. I had left him by the lake and told him not to move until I got back.

He wouldn't converse with me on that ride, which wasn't fine by me at all, but with my alibi tight, what could I do but go on and pursue my plan?

The hills, being so beautiful, were quite the invitation. On a day as glorious as that, what else could happen to me but good? Everything being so verdant and pulsing was confirmation that the world was in tune with me. After a one-hour ride, where I had conveniently seen no one, I turned into the valley leading towards the cottage where Sir Chester and Lady Violet lived.

Idyllic. A scene from a biscuit tin of perfect tranquillity. A cottage on top of a hill, with a thatched roof and white front door and bay windows. I rose onto the plateau and breathed in the smell of peonies by the front gate. When Joseph had brought me here on a ride only a month before, the bushes had been a cacophony of greens with tight balls of the lightest hues, only some of them with the pink stripes that promised they were fit to burst. Now, here they were in fulminations of explosive pink frills. Such an eruption, the flowers appeared violent in their prettiness.

I tied Mabel up to the gate and took out my bottle of water. In this heat I would be sure to lead her to a lake to drink on our return. Sweat dripped down her middle flank in droplets on the floor beneath her belly. Her breath was still steady, but had a rasp to it. Surely mine did too. The baby turned and, being alone, I could clutch my middle. I leaned on the gate and looked in on the dark windows. I felt no guilt and no fear.

It was my intention to drive Sir Chester and Lady Violet out of nature. Away from this scene of such serenity that they did not deserve. Their cottage gone, where else would they go but steaming, sooty, smoky London. The place where their restlessness and ambition would be channelled into the rivetingly dirty streets where they could labour away in the fashion and politics that would surely make their hearts beat. With no possessions they could be born anew and make their teeth as sharp as their words were. They would leave here with nothing. I could give birth in Liverpool and the offshoot of Sir Chester's misdeeds would be nurtured to become something opposite to him. Modest and good natured.

I thought of this as I walked around the house, wondering where the thatch of the roof was driest. It was too densely packed and almost wet on the underneath. At first, I thought my best bet was to chuck up my paraffin bottle onto the roof where the heat from the fire would work its way down. But on inspection, even if the thatch did catch alight in the way I hoped, it wouldn't penetrate the lower layers. All that would appear was a singed circular area of fire that was too evidently an act of arson. That would not do.

Walking around to the back of the house I saw the kitchen. On the dining table, a lamp. I gave my fire a narrative. The lamp hadn't been put out properly and somehow had been overturned. Gas only a few feet away accelerated the explosion. The raging fire below being so intense, the thatched roof created a cauldron of domestic fire. Everything inside, incinerated. The hay of the roof being the last to give out. The last orange flames enveloped by blackness pouring out in billows from the windows below.

I smashed the kitchen window with the broom from outside and I hurled through my paraffin bottle. The cinder-sounding smash was delightful. I could smell the fumes as I flicked in a lit match. It didn't hit the wet patch on the table and fizzled out on the stone-tiled floor. The second match was too quick. The speed of it blew the flame out before it landed where I had wanted it to. My third was the one that struck. I tossed insouciantly. As if I were Marie Antoinette compelled to lay flame to Le Petit Trianon by the revolutionaries who wanted to see her cry at the frivolities of her life being destroyed – but with all the performed calm she could muster, she wouldn't give the crowds what they wanted. A tossed match by the woman who had hoped they'd have cake to calm themselves out of hunger. But of course, in thinking that, I was aligning myself with the wrong side. No, let me be Boadicea laying flame to Colchester in the name of justice. Riding away from the dwelling Rome had sullied with its machinations. Her one mistake being that she was too brazen as a warrior, wanting everyone to know she was victorious. I would quite happily settle for knowing what I had done. No one else knowing I was courageous enough to commit arson did not make me any less brave.

I walked away from the licking flames of the kitchen, not indulging my fascination with the fiery destruction I had just caused. Back with Mabel at the front gate, the windows smashing let me know the fire had caught. Only a few wisps of grey smoke swindled their way around the corner, the front of the house placid as ever. But not for much longer. I untwined her reins from the gate and wiped my hands in the white lather by her neck. So slick was it that I had to wipe it on my bosom, where it made my blouse translucent. Hopefully that would dry by the time I was back with Joseph. Cantering off down the hill, we came to the fork and I looked back on the house. The fire had now reached the front. It was a glorious roar. The house was gasping, almost. A hoarse guttural giving out of itself with cackling crackles.

I had done it. I'd destroyed their lives. I took the pin out of my hair and let it fly free. My soft herby curls bounced on my shoulders and I felt so tall.

Joseph was carving a figure out of wood when I returned and thanked him. He gave it to me – a peace-offering. I took it as an award for brave commendation in guerrilla warfare and we chatted amiably as we cantered back onto the farm.

Mrs Hurrel had made us a sweet pea and leek tart. The mustard in it made it all the more interesting to savour.

'You're looking so flushed and rosy you are, aren't ya?'

She knew.

'It's the heat,' I mewled.

'Oh, I know. He's up at all hours in the summer.'

'I don't like it when it's hot,' Joseph said.

'You could have fooled me. He's gallivanting all over the place these days, Florence. He's probably got some girl in the village he's courting and not telling me.' She winked at me and chuckled to let me know the entertainment was on my account.

'Oh, give over, Mother.' He blushed.

'I'm sure it's sunset walks on the moors and all sorts,' she teased.

'I thought I noticed some flowers missing from the bushes on the way here,' I offered her.

'Oh, don't you bloody start as well,' Joseph grumbled.

'Well I'll be needing to get a fancy-man myself, won't I? He'll be well rid of me soon!'

She got up at this and went to the range to spoon out some of the stewed gooseberries and cream.

Jokes continued and Joseph was so easy with me, even though he'd been somewhat churlish when I bid him good-bye earlier before heading off to set the fire. He wouldn't put two and two together until way after the fact. Considering what I knew about him, he wouldn't tell anyone because he couldn't. Even though by now, my sin was greater than his by a long shot.

I hugged Mrs Hurrel goodbye and promised to reveal my secret for looking so healthy next week. I'd have to stop coming to see her soon, but by playing innocent, I felt innocent. I'd miss her.

I had added a layer to my existence. I was both a bookbinding woman en route to becoming an elegant governess, and a pregnant harlot who sought vengeance and justice. Why this felt so good, only God knows. With no news of the fire the following morning, I went to church.

Chapter Twenty-Seven

It was before lunch on Monday when I heard Lady Violet howl. I stayed where I was in the library until Wesley came and told me.

'Their house has only gone and burned down,' Wesley whispered into my ear. They had been planning to go back that afternoon.

With no work to do I was entertaining myself looking over books I would never be able to read, from Abyssinia and the Gold Coast. Musing over what they might say was almost as interesting as truly knowing. They looked religious. My leisurely perusal of the books I had been working on for months was fascinating, but this was the satisfying interruption I had been dying for. I threw my hand against my mouth and gasped loudly. Wesley had no reason to think this wasn't a surprise to me.

The howling turned into screaming. The adolescent boy

who had come to tell them stood there, aghast. Sir Chester ran out of the front door, jumped on his horse and galloped off with such fury, I expected the ground beneath him to give way. Wesley and I watched from the library window as he came into view. Wesley shook his head, open mouthed, guiltily gleeful I could tell, because his eyes twinkled and his mouth wanted to form into a smile. I stayed rigid. No one had seen me go to their cottage two days before and Joseph could be trusted to keep his mouth shut, but still ... My blood pumped afresh. Retribution gave me new life.

'It's such a shame,' I said to Wesley.

Lady Violet's howling had descended to whimpering that ascended the stairs and disappeared into her guest room.

'It were probably the heat though, weren't it? It were probably just a small thing, but with the sun on it ... Must have been raging.'

With Lord Belfield comforting Lady Violet in her room, we were free to go and tell Baxter.

The kitchen was struck through with the highly sweet and green aroma of cherries. A sprinkling of the little flowers covered Baxter's apron and her feet by the range as she stirred the pot in which she was steeping them in warm but not boiling water. Tender came her hand around the bend of the pot. She listened to Wesley pour out the only details we knew and shook her head.

'That's a right shame, that is. A beautiful cottage, even though he never appreciated it.'

'Who never appreciated it?' I asked.

'Sir Chester. Hated the place. You wouldn't think that from the way he was galloping off just now though, eh?'

Wesley said. She watched Wesley explain and then her glance came on me, looked me up and down. Her scan of me cooled the sweat on the back of my knees and made my neck twitch. She turned back to the stove.

'He's never been one for gratitude,' Baxter said.

Wesley shook his head and tutted.

I longed to tell someone that it was me that had visited destruction on them.

'Shall we polish? Keep our mind off things,' I offered Wesley. With such a crisis, Lord Belfield wouldn't know I wasn't squirrelled away in the library.

As we clinked and clanked our way through the special cutlery with cloths and polish, Wesley and Baxter took turns telling me stories about the local calamities over the years and the upsets that had been visited upon the Belfields. Our convivial nattering had increased over the months as they had both come to trust that I never passed information we discussed onto Lord Belfield. Sir Chester's attack had confirmed that I was definitely not 'one of them' upstairs. No matter how much I had read, I didn't belong to their class.

Wesley took up their lunch of tea and sandwiches and came back down to our lunch of pork pie, cheddar cheese and pickled onions. The cherry cordial that smelled so tantalising wouldn't be ready for a few days yet, apparently. Our sweet-smelling gossipy idyll was broken into by Lord Belfield's voice at the top of the stairs.

'Miss Granger,' he shouted.

It cut right through us all. I rose, sure that I was stuck to my crime like treacle on an apple, and that it would lead me

294

to a prison cell. Were there police waiting for me at the top of the stairs? Would I ever see Wesley and Baxter again?

An exhausted and red-eyed Lord Belfield waited for me, leaning against the front door, wearing his waistcoat. He was rubbing his forehead with his right hand.

'I suppose you've heard?' he asked me.

I nodded simply. 'I'm sorry for their loss.'

He looked at me quizzically. Was that even an appropriate thing to say if no one had died? Was my behaviour suspicious to him?

'Yes, well. Who knows if anything can be salvaged? Thank goodness we're still insured.'

I hadn't considered this. I hadn't considered much of the aftermath and what provisions might be in place for things like the disaster I had visited upon them.

'I just wanted to ask if you might sit with Lady Violet when she wakes. I had to give her a sedative to calm the poor lamb's nerves.' He leaned in. 'She was already in a bad way, and now this . . . It just—'

'Yes, yes. Of course. I'll just clean up after lunch and wait by her door?'

'Oh no, go straight in. I left her door open.'

'Right.' I nodded.

'Right.' Lord Belfield gritted his teeth and scratched his eyebrow. His nails were pinkened from nibbling. He was on the edge of saying something else indelicate, I could tell.

'And are you going to be all right, now that this has happened?' Lord Belfield said.

'How do you mean?' I asked, almost afraid that he could smell the smoke on me.

'Well – I've tried not to leave you alone with him.'

'Ah. I see.'

This was a moment I could have told Lord Belfield that Chester had murdered his wife. Instead of Chester receiving compassion, he could be summarily dealt with.

Yet I couldn't trust Lord Belfield's actions. He had no reason to believe me, and I would have to explain the diary. Our conversations had made me certain his brother was not just a man who lashed out on those weaker than he, but a truly homicidal monster. If I couldn't convince Lord Belfield and he realised that my rage had made me burn his brother's house down, it would be me behind bars and not Chester.

'I don't know what effect this will have on him. He's ... I mean, you well know!' He shrugged and shook his head while biting his lip like an adolescent. It was frightful that someone as frequently clueless as he was had all of our fates and livelihoods in his control. He looked like a shepherd who had accidentally driven his sheep off a cliff.

'It's just that they have nowhere else to go now, you see.'

So they'd be staying here for a short while before going down to London like Sir Chester had always wanted, surely.

'Is that what Sir Chester will want?' I asked.

'Broke as he is now, what choice does he have?'

'Won't the insurance money be enough to ...' I trailed off.

'That won't be handled for a good while yet. And these days they investigate. Intentional arson for a pay-out. It's become more common, so they'll be looking for that. Signs that they might have done it themselves out of desperation. I mean ... it's unthinkable. But they'll be looking to determine that's definitely not the case,' he said. 'And in the meantime, with Chester here. And you here . . .'

'I see.'

'I'll do what I can to protect you from him of course,' he blustered. 'But it's very important that you're careful too, you see. Keep out of his way, my dear. It's . . . I don't want to promise anything I can't do effectively.'

I swallowed down a globule of mucus at the back of my throat. It was now possible my vengeance had worsened my circumstances in a way I could have easily foreseen, if I had not been so determined. I longed for Liverpool and the bed of Miss Arabella. An escape from this place of permanent endangerment. I was now the mouse of Rose Hall who had invited the viper to stay.

If Wesley had been a woman, I would have told him I was pregnant by now. Our routines of intimacy were such that we had all sorts of little details that communicated ourselves to each other. His visits before bed to do my hair were loved and wanted by me, but if for some reason I needed to be alone because I was sullen and needed solitude, or amorous and wanted to touch myself, I would push the door completely closed and latch it shut. This didn't happen that often. Only every once in a while. He never punished me for it the following day, like he had when I'd been annoyed with him recounting the question he had savaged Sibyl with. Surely he touched himself in the way I did? I thought of Everett. He thought of Joseph. Regardless, the agreement was that if my door could not be opened with only a gentle push, he must not turn the knob to unlatch it. I had given up locking my door soon after Sir Chester's assault. A lock hadn't stopped him and there was no one else to keep out who was dangerous, really. Lord Belfield, Lady Violet and Baxter had no reason to come to my room. It was with Wesley that I had communication of no words. A pursing or a jooking of the lips in a particular direction, imperceptible to anybody but ourselves.

Most nights I read him yet another story. Never the same one. He was voracious for new ones. Mysteries that took place in London were more desired than any other these days. But that night, I didn't want to read. Too much had happened, and to swattle our way through page after page of violence and intrigue was far from appealing. So I asked him a leading question.

'If you had a choice, would you rather be a boy or a girl?'

Wesley's fingers, twirling down my first plait, paused. His knees softened as I felt and heard the sigh escape his gullet.

'A girl, obviously.'

Should it have been obvious? I didn't think it was. He had more freedom than I did. All he knew were dresses and wigs and kisses. The toil and pain and labour of womanhood didn't concern him. He only played at being a girl, so why would he choose that? I thought he was smart because he got to enjoy all the fun, frippery parts at night and still had the freedom of manhood during the day. He could not choose to shackle himself to the pain of monthly periods and what was sure to be a painful childbirth. And even if he could, why would he? We'd spoken of hearing the shrieks and smells of childbirth before. Surely he didn't mean that. He didn't want that?

'Why?' I asked.

'I don't know. I'd just prefer it. I know I would,' he said.

'Oh.'

'Are you surprised?' he asked.

'A little. But . . . I guess it's understandable.'

Was it for me to tell him this was understandable, when it really wasn't something I understood?

'I'm pregnant,' I said.

His fingers stopped. I turned around to look at his face, aghast, supping at the air like a fish in a pond. He couldn't form the words. He sighed and looked down at his hands, bereft of the plaiting I had shocked him out of.

'Is it Sir Chester's?' he asked, looking back up at me with concern.

I punched his shoulder. 'Of course it is, silly. Who else's is it gonna be? Joseph's?'

'Well, I didn't want to presume, did I?'

'So instead you infer that I'm the Whore of Babylon?' I laughed.

'What does infer mean?' he asked.

'Never mind.' I shrugged.

He formed his lips to say something, paused, swallowed and then asked, 'So what are we gonna do?'

I walked over to my desk and picked up the letter that had arrived that morning, but I did not desire to open it yet. My unavoidable fate would be outlined inside. I did not feel ready. Frankly, I was quite frightened.

'I wrote to Sibyl. I want to give the baby away in Liverpool. If I give birth there, it will be easier, I think. I asked if I could. At theirs, I mean.'

'Oh right. So you think she's written you back to start planning that, do ya?'

'I don't know. I'm hoping so,' I said.

'Why haven't you opened it yet?'

I felt crazy looking at him. I must have looked it too, with five and a half plaits in my head and my as-yet-untamed but combed-out hair bursting from my crown.

'Because it's the only plan I have. If they can't help me . . .'

'They will. Open it.'

I breathed deeply, took the nail of my little finger, which I always kept a bit longer, and slit the letter open. I read it out loud. I could give birth in their home. Miss Arabella insisted. They had a nunnery willing to take the baby. But the direction from Sibyl said that I wouldn't be able to get myself to Liverpool without Lord Belfield being informed as soon as possible.

'Let's do it tomorrow,' Wesley urged.

'All right.'

He got back to plaiting my hair and humming a tune I couldn't quite make out. On the last plait, he said:

'You know, I thought you were on the edge of saying we should have raised the baby together or something.'

'That wouldn't work.'

'Why?' He sounded hurt.

'Because you'd constantly be fighting to breastfeed him yourself!'

That made him giggle, that did.

'You're not wrong there, love. You're not wrong there.' We both laughed, then both sighed. I wasn't out of the woods yet, but I didn't feel alone.

Chapter Twenty-Eight

We told Baxter together the next morning over scrambled eggs on toasted bread. After I said the words 'I'm with child' we all sat there in the steam of the kitchen feeling a bit glum. There was no good to come of this, and we all knew it. The space we had created for ourselves was crumbling. I knew I had brought more mirth than sorrow, but the seriousness in Baxter's ice-blue eyes cut through me. The stairs at the back of the kitchen led to a second entrance that was open to the summer air outside today. A pigeon came to peck at the doormat where some crumbs had interested it. We all turned around and watched it pecking, hoping the distraction could lessen the foreboding in us.

'How long have you known?' Baxter asked.

'Two weeks,' I responded.

She crossed her arms and sat back in her chair, which made her chin round and soften. I squinted at her.

'How long have you known?' I asked.

'Two month,' she replied.

'Why didn't you—' I started.

'Anything could have happened. There were no need to worry yuh.'

This was why I hadn't told her first. She was so reticent to form a bond with me, it left me out in the cold with my ignorance. I wanted hugs and head cradles and whispered assurances that it was 'All gonna be all right.' I'd so wanted to be her baby when I first arrived. Her stern demeanour not being off-putting to me because of the house I grew up in. But here we sat, in our personal silos, where even Wesley and I had to hide our platonic affection for fear of her judgement. If she had taken me in as her proxy daughter, maybe this wouldn't have happened in the first place. She'd have warned me about Sir Chester being on the prowl. Taught me how to jam a chair underneath my doorknob. Helped me stay safe.

'When are you gonna tell him upstairs?' she asked.

'Today. Sibyl told me to tell him as soon as possible.'

She rolled her eyes at that. I had no idea why.

'Oh and she thinks that's wise does she?' Baxter muttered.

'Yes?' I waited for her to enlighten me as to why it wasn't a good idea. But Baxter just sat there, resolute and grumpy as ever. Why was she being this way? Also, why was she so suspicious of Sibyl's advice to me? There was nothing untoward coming from her and this was someone she herself used to feed. Was it because she knew that she had birthed Lord Belfield's twins illegitimately? Or was there some other reason Sibyl shouldn't be listened to?

'Well, that's that then, isn't it?' she said, getting up, and so moments later we did too.

I was fuming with Baxter as I rose to go to Lord Belfield. I'd hoped for a maternal bond from her, but again, on a day of further crisis, she had confirmed that we were mere colleagues.

I knocked on Lord Belfield's door and it cracked open. He was dressed in a different waistcoat today. A cerulean one with navy embroidery. Light cotton trousers and slippers. He smelled a bit frowzy and because of his scrumpled hair, he still seemed slightly undone.

'Would you come down to the library at your earliest convenience?'

'Today?'

'Yes, my lord.'

'Right, yes. Give me half an hour, will you?'

The door closed on me. I had no right to intrude on him, but I had no idea what he got up to all day, even though I'd been working at Rose Hall for half a year. There was no spark between him and Lady Violet, otherwise I might have suspected an affair between them – considering what a cad he had proved himself to be with Lady Persephone and Sibyl. I'm sure there were many bawdy jokes to be told about knocking up two sisters, in the taverns my father frequented.

He actually came down to the library an hour later. I had set out my tools to be in the middle of something when he came in, but because he was a little later I had become complacent and he found me sitting in the window reading *The Naturalist on the River Amazon* by Henry Walter Bates. I shot up and snapped it shut, eliciting a haze of dust which wafted its way into my nostrils. I sneezed almightily.

'Bless you.'

I tried to thank him, but another one was en route. This one, even more raucous, ripped my throat open and made it sore. I couldn't stop myself from spluttering onto my front.

'Bless you!' He laughed.

'Oh my goodness. I'm so sorry. It's all the dust and I suppose the pollen and . . .'

I did sound quite bunged up.

'It's quite all right.'

Having caught my breath, I sobered into what I needed to tell him.

'I think we might have to close the door, Lord Belfield.'

'Oh? Oh, all right.'

He did so and I sat in my desk chair. He came to sit in the window alcove I had just occupied. I'm sure he was sat in the warmth my rear had left.

'I've something quite awkward to tell you,' I said.

'Oh, Miss Granger, I always negotiate under what I can truly afford to pay anyone. It's natural that a human finagles what they can in order to provide some cushion for their own survival.'

My eyes widened quizzically.

'I know the library is finished.'

I stared at him.

'Oh yes. I mean that as well of course,' I said.

'As well?' He leaned towards me.

'Yes. As well,' I confirmed.

'Go on.'

'I'm with child,' I said clearly.

'Jesus Christ!'

He brought his hands up to cover his eyelids for a moment, before recovering himself and bringing them down to clasp them in front of his chest and whistle through his teeth.

'If only the conception was as immaculate as his was,' I replied drily.

He huffed into his hand and then freed his mouth to wag his finger at me.

'That's a bloody good point, Miss Granger.'

I started crying. The levity I had tried to inject was not going to save me. Now he knew I was hurtling towards a certain conclusion which would rip me away from the books that surrounded me and the future he had dangled.

'Dear me,' he said. 'So you didn't want to tell me about the library being finished because you were scared I'd throw you out onto the streets?'

This was only somewhere near the truth. I didn't tell him I had finished because I was happier not working and continuing being paid. I'd elongated my schedule as far as I could push it. Nevertheless, it was a lovely neat narrative to acquiesce to. I nodded and put my own head in my hands.

'Miss Granger. Who else knows about this?' he asked.

'Sibyl and Miss Arabella. I wrote to them. Sibyl told me to tell you,' I said.

'So you want to give birth there, do you? Not here.'

'Yes. I'd rather that.'

'And then what?'

'There's a nunnery in Merseyside. They'll find a family.'

'Over my dead body.'

The voice came from the other end of the room. Lord Belfield and I turned to see Sir Chester, flushed with anger, his hair flopping into his eye and Lady Violet tugging at his shirt cuff. She tried to keep him from stalking forwards and failed.

'That is my. Bloody. Child!' Sir Chester said, his voice rising with every word.

'Could you lower your voice, Chester, for crying out loud.'

'She's not getting rid of it,' Chester hissed.

'Well firstly, let's have some decorum about ourselves again, please. I can't believe the two of you. Snooping around my house like amateur detectives. It's out of order.'

'Just as well we did. It's underhand, what she's planning.'

'Yes, well I would have told you eventually.'

My head snapped back to Lord Belfield. Oh, would he now? I considered his loyalty to his brother, in spite of knowing his true nature, to be quite stomach-churning. What would it take to break that bond?

'You could at least have told me, Miss Granger,' Violet said coolly. 'I would have helped more than Sibyl.'

In my head I screamed. How dare she? I knew that she was aware of what Sir Chester had done to me, but this mild admonishment that I should have chosen her as my confidante instead of Sibyl was all too much. I wanted to shout at her. *You can shut up or I'll burn down your mother's house too!* Instead I ignored her and stood to face her husband.

'You sir. You . . . You have utterly destroyed my life. I would never release this baby into the care of someone as nefarious as you. How dare you think you will dictate what happens here? You will never lay a finger on me again!' I was shouting.

'Do you hear me? Never again. I could have done *anything* to this baby up till now.'

'Why haven't you?' Lady Violet asked.

Before I'd found out myself, I might have imagined asking Sibyl if she knew of a local woman I could visit. And I had mulled over it a little. But I'd been assailed by images of myself lying on someone's kitchen table, being invaded with whatever contraption, or flushed out with whatever poultice or potion they concocted. Giving birth wasn't without its dangers, but it felt a lot less dangerous than going some-where potentially unsanitary to have something unspeakable done to me.

I just shrugged.

'There can be some sort of arrangement made, obviously.' The way her eyes glinted suggested something. Lady Violet had known, or suspected, I was pregnant. She had considered a number of options. She had a plan to manipulate me. I would play along with her for now, but I was sure to think of a way to avoid having my fate decided by her.

'I will not have my progeny given over to some grubby orphanage,' Sir Chester emphasised. 'He will be fair enough and his hair won't be as bad as yours, so we can pass it off as our own. I'll have her sor—'

'Chester,' she said abruptly.

This shut him up. He took his tobacco out, but his pout-ing was too prominent to go unnoticed. There was no love between them, and he was far from a hen-pecked husband. She couldn't control him as such. But she could steer him when she wanted, evidently. Tell him which side the wind was coming from.

The silence between the four of us was thickened by the smoke coming from Lord Belfield's pipe and Sir Chester's cigars. My eyes were smarting from the acridity.

Lady Violet broke the stalemate.

'You may want to write to Sibyl in the morning,' she offered.

'What?' Lord Belfield crumpled his brow and blew out a smoke ring. 'Why?'

'If Miss Granger trusts her as a true friend, then perhaps we would be right to do the same, Francis. She's proved herself able to be rather discreet thus far, where you're concerned, after all.'

If Lady Violet's grand plan for me and the baby involved Sibyl, I would acquiesce to all her suggestions until her decisions swung out of my favour.

'I feel lightheaded. I'm going to bed,' I said.

'Oh my. You poor thing. I'll walk you up.' Lady Violet began to rise.

'Pray, stay seated. I'm fine.' I raised my palm to her. 'I'll be fine. Please.'

She nodded gently and repositioned herself on her seat. I was sure I could feel the three pairs of eyes on me as I left the room, but just when I reached the library door I looked back to see that it was only Chester. He looked set to blow, but was exercising restraint to contain himself. Was I safer, or more endangered, now that he knew I carried his child? It was impossible to know.

Chapter Twenty-Nine

I demanded Lord Belfield bring me to Liverpool ahead of time. To live with Sibyl and Miss Arabella from July to November was quite the liberty to take on their behalf, but I was truly terrified that if the baby were stillborn that Sir Chester would slit my throat in a rage at my failure to deliver him the son he longed for.

Lord Belfield and I travelled in the carriage to Liverpool together. I felt brazen enough to ask him what I had been pondering. 'Was Chester really very different when he was a boy?'

We were on a smooth part of road leading out of Oxenhope when I asked, which afforded Lord Belfield the opportunity to look pensively out of the window onto the green fields bordering us.

'There was perhaps a time when he wasn't so determined to be invulnerable. We had a frightfully calamitous journey from Delhi to Kashmir and he bawled the whole way, which

I found distasteful. It was a wonderful adventure, all things considered. But ... even then, he was just so darn wicked. Of course, I could be naughty on occasion, but unlike him I didn't like hurting things or people. He was always kicking the dogs. Maybe if one had bitten him back ...'

He turned to look at me. Expecting a reaction? He hadn't given me anything remarkable to comment upon.

'If I'd known you were in danger, I never would have—'

I put my hand up to halt him.

'It wasn't your fault,' I said with half belief.

'Well, the thing is I thought you'd be all right because you weren't a woman of ...' he leaned forward to whisper '... *ill repute*.'

I have no idea whose modesty he was protecting. The sound of the horses stopped the rider from hearing us. We had a bell for alerting him.

'He never pestered Percy. She was my wife, obviously, but I didn't have to even warn him off her. And Sibyl was safe from his advances. For obvious reasons.' He rolled his eyes and looked to laugh, but I just stared back at him, because the foundations for his jocularity were shaky.

'But I suppose it's all working out in a shockingly bizarre way now, isn't it?'

I didn't respond and instead took my turn to look out on the fields through the window. It was not the right time, but I did have money on my mind. With the library finished I had done my part. It felt ironic that I would be left in Liverpool with only enough to get by, and not the significant sum from the completed library restoration. As the train juddered along through the tauntingly pleasant verdant landscape, I ran my tongue back and forth over the new and sensitive chip on my left molar.

When we arrived in Liverpool's Georgian quarter I was steaming like a locomotive from the journey. We had only two tavern stops and being presumed to be Lord Belfield's pregnant wife was quite amusing. I felt cosseted from the world's judgements. People looked down and away from me as his wife.

He had dressed up for the journey in the same way as when I had first got to know him. A light brown and beige summer suit with chocolate-coloured shoes. A pistachio bow tie and a boater. I didn't wear mine because I didn't want us to match to that extent. The blazer of his suit had a tapering from the last button, fanning outwards elegantly like an upside-down tulip. His white shirt was ever so crisp. Most of Rose Hall's laundry was carted off for laundering once a week. But I had found out only a fortnight before that it was Baxter that ironed his necessaries.

'He trusts only me with his shirts,' she had said proudly. I thought this was a tragic thing to be proud about.

He carried our suitcases into the house. They weren't very heavy, but looking at him open his blazer so as not to stretch the buttons, I realised that it was the first time I had seen him lift anything besides a book, glass, cigar, fork or spoon. The brothers served themselves at breakfast, as was custom.

Neither Miss Arabella nor Sibyl were in the hallway as I expected. Obviously, they couldn't greet us on the doorstep, because for Lord Belfield to kiss his negresse in the open air would be a scandal. Also, with my pregnancy showing, it might have seemed as if I were a white wife being humiliated by his embrace of his coloured mistress.

I followed him in and heard the boys snoring in the back room. My breath was taken away by the vision of Sibyl at the top of the stairs. The skirt was a light blue, with layers that tapered into each other, similar to the tulip-like elegance of Lord Belfield's suit, but with more delicacy because of the frills of cream lace at the hem. Her blouse was ivory and pulled in her waist beautifully. I wasn't sure if she had lost weight or was just wearing her corset as tightly as permissible. She had an impish smile and twinkling eyes that I suspected had a touch of kohl in the corners. The rays of light behind her made her look angelic. She was so undeniably pretty. But no one ever said that about her. It felt like it was only Lord Belfield and me who saw that, but only I that felt a burning need to proclaim it publicly.

'I'm coming up there,' he said.

'I'm sure you are,' she replied.

He began to climb the stairs and she angled her head to bring me into her gaze. 'Hello, you.'

'It's good to see you,' I said.

I closed the front door behind me and left them to their recoupling procedures on the upstairs landing. Their giggles were eventually cut off by the bedroom door.

Miss Arabella was sitting by the back-yard window, fanning herself.

'Ah,' she said, rising. 'Now look at you,' she whispered. The boys were entwined in their rocking cot between us. She hugged me and I think I held on for too long, but she didn't wriggle her way out of it. We didn't talk because I was too tired. I sat on their settee and she brought me a moistened cloth to wipe my hands and a glass of water which had a hint of lemon to it. I drank that down and fell into a slumber just like the twins, so happy to finally be away from the cloying energy of Rose Hall.

Our sleeping arrangements were practically the same as before. The boys slept with Sibyl and Lord Belfield, which I found highly unusual. I slept with Miss Arabella, and she plaited up my hair before bedtime instead of Wesley. I read her stories while she did it, too, though they were of a more romantic variety than the ones Wesley enjoyed.

Lord Belfield would head out around midday and return around supper time. The boys adored him. They were still small enough to fit one on each knee. Lord Belfield was much more playful than I had imagined he would be. He was also less scruffily kept than he let himself get at Rose Hall. Although, for what he would have said were 'obvious reasons', he and Sibyl never went out together. A fine shame for sure, because they were well matched as a couple, being of similar height. The thought of them walking through a park in stride together aroused me. Him picking her a flower. Her picking lint off his collar. A new shade of rage came into me, watching him play the family man at home and then stroll out into the world unencumbered by the reality of his coloured partner. That Miss Arabella accepted her dead daughter's husband in her home as the secret lover of her other daughter baffled me. I wanted her to be cool with him. Instead, she laughed at his jokes and gave him the largest portions of the food she cooked. It pained me that 'everything working out in the end' always left the Belfield brothers wholly unscarred.

Lord Belfield stayed for a whole week, and I was desperate to get shot of him by the end. He took my friend away from me and I was unfathomably jealous of him. On the Monday he left I was desperate to get Sibyl out of the house and back to discussing books and women's suffrage and names for tribes in Africa that I had never before heard of.

I suggested a walk in the park with the boys. We strolled towards the lake with our pockets filled with bread crusts, carrying one twin each. The pram was so cumbersome; it was only appropriate for certain journeys.

There were a few more lines under Sibyl's eyes than usual. She twisted her neck from left to right to alleviate tension, and a shock of guilt ran through me. I knew that the labour of having Lord Belfield stay was significant, but I thought I was easier than him. Maybe asking them to look after me was more egregious a demand than I had thought. I resolved to try and engage her in discussion about him, to show how not resentful of him I was.

'Where did you meet Lord Belfield in Paris, again?'

'We can call him Francis when he's not here, goodness.'

I laughed at that. 'OK, sorry. Francis.'

'He came to see me perform; I told you. I didn't notice him from the rest. You know they all look the same when they're in a crowd. The fact that they all dress the same doesn't help.'

I had considered this. Swarms of men walking towards me always looked like they might envelop me in their uniformity.

'Anyway, he came into a bookshop I was in the following

day. Started telling me what I should read, to cover up his surprise that I could read at all. He was ever so flustered. And I liked that he liked me. That was it.'

A negro family was walking towards us. We nodded first, and they nodded back. It was fascinating. The recognition. It wasn't so much a 'How do you do?' It was more like an 'Aren't we doing well in spite of all *this*? So far from home.'

Of course, this *was* my home, but . . .

'Do you think women will ever get into Parliament then?' I asked.

'Not women like me or you. But yes, some day. It's inevitable,' she said, wiping the dribble off one of the boys' chins. 'Well actually, you probably could be one of the first under the right circumstances. But then someone would do an investigation, find out that you're not completely white and expose you as a Creole seductress trying to infiltrate British government with savage Voodoo spells or some such.' She chuckled.

Now, this really did thrill me.

'I think you'd make ever such a good politician.'

'Well, that's never going to happen. I'll leave that to the Fawcetts and Pankhursts.' She scoffed.

We were by the lake now. She wasn't sour, even though she was dismissive. The silence that descended between us was comfortable. We gave the boys little clumps of bread to throw, but they couldn't project them, so we had to throw the crumbs ourselves. It was such fun. I still knew I didn't want to keep the baby, but I did like these children. But raising a child on my own wasn't really an option. I had read a novel or two where a woman of the aristocracy had to be whisked off to the continent to give birth somewhere rural, returning from her Grand Tour unencumbered except for some vases and paintings to prove that the visit had been a cultural undertaking rather than a sin-washing endeavour. But such an ordeal wouldn't be fitting for me, as a lowly bookbinding governess in training.

A couple came towards us who electrified me entirely. He was a tall African, barrel chested in a bowler hat with a moustache that broke above the gap in his teeth. I would have thrown all my money on him if he were in a boxing ring. But conversely, I would also have placed the twins on his shoulders for a run-a-round the park with no hesitation if he invited them to, so affable was his countenance. If he sang, I'd be a puddle from the cleansing boom of the baritone that surely lay within him. And next to him was a woman who reminded me of myself, in spite of our many slight differences. She was light skinned, though not as light as me. Much shorter. More squat than petite, with doll-like cheeks and clear brown eyes. But her hair. Her hair was the same colour as mine. The darkest possible blonde, that glowed gold at the edges where the light could illuminate it.

'Y'all right, you two?' he said. Deep and sonorous as I had presumed. Not African-accented. He was from here, and I presumed so was she.

'Yes, afternoon to ya,' Sibyl responded for the both of us. The woman smiled at me with her eyes as well as her lips. I was that shocked, I couldn't speak for a while.

'Why is it that coloured people can see I'm not all white?' I asked Sibyl when they were out of earshot.

'Well, we know what to look for, don't we? We know our own,' she said, rubbing my shoulder.

'So you knew when you first saw me?' I asked.

'Yes. It's clear as day, dear.' She chuckled. 'I mean, it's even clearer now that your nose is spreading a bit.'

I had thought my mind was playing tricks on me. I lifted a hand up to touch my nose.

'Oh, don't worry. It happened to me too. It goes back once you've had the baby. Percy was dead scared of it happening to her, but she was all right,' she said.

It saddened me that she didn't speak of Persephone more often. I hadn't probed because I didn't want to stoke her grief.

'So she didn't want people finding out about her?'

'She wasn't that bothered. I was the one that told her to do it. Made all our lives better in most ways. But she struggled with the stress of it all.'

'Why?' I asked. I had thought being seen as white was all to make things easier.

'The denial went against her nature. There was no dignity in it, you see. My mother and father felt we should be proud of where we're from. To uplift the race and all that.'

'You speak like you're not from here. You were born here.'

'But I'm not *from* here though, am I?'

I stared at her unblinkingly. It felt dangerous, what she was saying. 'This is their country. Not ours.'

'What about the boys?'

'Yeah, them too. We'll never belong here. They'd kill us in a heartbeat if they could.'

I saw her as positively seditious. I didn't even know I agreed with her until the words had come out of her mouth. To say it out loud felt illegal. Now that I wasn't seeing myself as all white, it felt more solid underneath me. All the stories I read and the shaking of heads and jokes about jiggerboos and sambos and the like had convinced me. They wanted us there, and them here. A pure nation with a rich empire and only a few visiting dignitaries.

The only thing was that until I'd met Sibyl, I had thought I was one of *them*. But I wasn't really. I'd never belonged in that way. I'd just been lied to. I had no ill feeling towards my grandmother, because I'd been foisted on her and she was only doing what she thought best. But my father? He could rot in hell for duping me so. I hated him. I had a family some-where. A multi-hued family was out there, and they knew nothing about me. I was broken off from them, and look at me now. Alone and pregnant, with no home to call my own and someone else's mother sleeping next to me at night, who I was scared of hugging in my sleep again, because I couldn't be sure I'd ever let go.

On the way home, I made Sibyl tell me about the tribes of the Gold Coast and what Africa was like before the white man came. I really wanted to know. I needed to know.

That night before bed, I looked in the mirror and decided I actually liked my nose a bit broader than usual. I looked healthier, somehow. I felt more comfortable with myself. I rubbed my belly and because the future was still so uncertain, I decided to just focus on how I felt at that moment. Cosy.

Chapter Thirty

'How long were you in labour for?' I asked Sibyl.

From being mortified by his every movement, I now pinged with anxiety if I hadn't felt the baby in a while.

We were in her bedroom. She was feeding Artemis and I was rocking an only-just-about-asleep Apollo in my cradled arms. I hadn't been looking at her when I asked. I was looking at him, so I didn't notice the chasm that question had opened up between us. After some seconds, I looked up at her, to find her eyes were searching my face with trepidation. She was assessing my mettle. Not knowing how much I could take knowing.

'My mother died giving birth to me, Sibyl. I know it's dangerous.'

'The pain is all consuming. I cursed Eve a thousand times a minute, I promise you.'

Curious that she chose to refer to the Bible now. It occurred to me that with all her political principles, she was possibly the most ungodly woman I had ever met. A huge reason why I liked her.

'Where does the pain come from?' I asked.

'Where you would expect it. It starts there, but then it radiates out. Every extremity of you will be engaged in the pain of it.'

'Hmmmmm.' Of course, I was scared witless, but I was too proud to show that.

'It would be just my luck if this baby killed me, to be honest. Sir Chester would piss on my grave every day.' A macabre joke felt more fitting. Sibyl looked away from me, her expression unreadable. Had she not been able to escape his clutches too? Was that something we shared? I dare not bring a memory back if so.

'Was Persephone's pregnancy difficult? Does Daniel know you're his aunt?'

'Which question do you want me to answer first?' She laughed.

'Sorry.'

'No, it's OK. Daniel came very quickly. A few hours at most. He was a very colicky baby, actually. We didn't know if he'd make it. But apparently he's fine now. Persephone was devastated when he was sent away. And we were scared his features would reveal themselves . . . but he looks like Francis. Very much like Francis.'

'And he's never been here. Doesn't know anything about you?'

'What purpose would that serve? It was impossible for him to come here. Not even Percy could come more than twice a year.'

'So, Miss Arabella has never met him?'

She shook her head. Artemis was asleep now too. The guzzling sounds of their snores brought a hush over us. Miss Arabella poked her head round the door, saw us gently nuzzling the boys, smiled at us warmly and then slowly closed the door, with not even the slightest clicking sound from the latch. Sibyl motioned for me to bring Apollo to their cot and we laid them down together, side by side. Covered them with a white sheet. Artemis brought his arm over his brother for an embrace. They looked like Romulus and Remus, toasted from the Roman sun and filled with wolf's milk; both their heads haloed by bounteous black curls.

We sat in the bay window seats and looked down on the street below.

'Did you ever consider running away before you started showing?' Sibyl asked me calmly. She had bided her time to ask, and I was grateful, because I did wish to talk about the decisions I had made.

'I needed to tell Francis in order to have the means to get to Liverpool. And if Chester hadn't overheard me, perhaps Francis would have sent me away without his brother knowing – but it doesn't matter. The baby needs to go to a safe home, not to Rose Hall, and I don't plan to go back there.'

She patted my knee and let me know I didn't need to go on. Emboldened by her questioning of me, I felt more comfortable to ask the question I had kept in my mind's waiting room.

'Are you and Francis in love?' I dared.

She looked at me smartingly. 'That's a silly question.'

There was residue on the back of my hands from the shea butter we'd used to massage the boys after their baths. I rubbed my cuticles and caught sight of some steam in the far distance. That way lay the Mersey. Perhaps a chug boat? Or just the chimney of a house closer to the water?

'I love you more than I do Francis.' She patted my knee again.

My shoulders gave way. I'd not noted them being hunched, but with Sibyl's words, some nervousness seeped out of me. Did she understand the effect this was having on me? Did I? The longing I had for such affection. I'd only ever known it fleetingly. Seen it on occasion. Read about it and mused on it constantly.

'Francis is a coward,' Sibyl said with no bile. It was just how she felt. 'He's barely qualified for the life that was chosen for him. It was Percy and I who alerted him to the worth of his library, you know?'

I didn't know. How could I have? He'd never told me otherwise.

I looked at her, aglow from the street lights.

'We were ecstatic when we got to Rose Hall. She had more time to read than I did. But we would squirrel ourselves away in her room. Reading and writing. We were enraptured.'

She was only just about with me in the room as she descended back into memory.

'There was so much to be done. We wrote to women all over the country. Cathy in Leeds. Pearl in Birmingham. Mary and Grace in London. It was such an exciting network. Just reams and reams of words. We'd read their letters together and respond separately. And then we'd read until dinner time. Francis barely went into the library. That was our lair. It gets too chilly in there though, unless it's summer.'

I nodded.

'Don't know how you put up with it.'

'Blankets. Hot water bottles . . .' I told her. 'Why is Francis so protective of the library, if he never used to go inside it?' I asked. He'd done well to give the impression of a scholar as we'd worked side by side.

Sibyl gave a half-smile. 'Chester was agitating for money, and Francis had the collection valued. It's astonishingly valuable. Francis isn't protective because he loves the books, but because he plans to make a lot of money selling them. And, no doubt, pull the wool over Chester's eyes about how much he has sold and how much he has made.' She paused. 'Did you clean up the African books, too?'

'Only a little. They're not fragile but I was too nervous. They're bound differently. I couldn't believe that they even wrote in Abyssinia to be honest.'

'Ethiopia,' Sibyl said firmly.

'Sorry.'

'It's all right. I didn't know either, until we went to Leeds.'

'Who went to Leeds?'

'Me and Percy. To see Ida B. Wells talk. Cathy told us to come.'

'And Lord Belf— Sorry, Francis. He didn't come?'

'Thank goodness, no. He wouldn't elect to hear about that sort of thing.'

'Why?' I thought back to his pretentions of supporting the suffragette movement.

She sighed, scratched at her neck and squinted.

'He doesn't like to think about what his grandfather got up to in Jamaica. Where the money came from, and all that.'

'Was it really all that bad? Across the board I mean?'

She looked at me pityingly. 'It was worse.'

'How much worse?'

'The Caribbean was a factory of death. More of us went there than anywhere else. It was and is frightful in America, don't get me wrong. But a slave only lasted three years in the West Indies. It's in his grandfather's diaries. The ethical wrangling of it all. They knew what they were doing. Francis knows where the wealth came from. Even though it's not polite to talk about it, and never has been, they all know what they did to us,' Sibyl said.

'The lynchings?' I asked.

'The everything. The lynching is just a modern phenomenon. Trying to stem our ambition by terrorising us. They're scared of us reading and being their equals, you know.'

'But we're safer here. I mean, now we are,' I said.

'They'd kill us all if there weren't so many of us,' Sibyl said.

'You can't think that.' I balked.

'Why can't I?' she asked, staring at me coolly.

'Because we can change things with education, Sibyl. We get the vote. We fight for fair wages. We build the schools, the hospitals,' I pleaded.

'They'll still own everything. I want my own and they won't let me have my own here, will they? This house isn't even my own,' she stated.

Well, why would it be? I knew Lord Belfield had paid for it. That's why he was always complaining about his financial constraints. I couldn't help but see the link between Everett's desire to tear down the system, and Sibyl's belief that she needed to leave it behind. Was I the only one who wanted to believe it was in our power to change things? Why were they so willing to leave behind this place we had all called home at some point? Why was it so easy for them to abandon the idea of this being our mother country?

'I thought you'd at least be happy he is taking care of you. You looked happy with him,' I said.

'Did I?' She smiled.

'Yes. Very happy,' I sneered.

'Well, I've always prided myself on being good at my job. Circus performer, lady's maid and now mistress of my sister's widower.' Her throat cackled, but there was no gleam in her eye. She'd smoothed the edges of her rage. Kept her grief concealed. She ran her hands over her skirts.

'I was just being nice because he finally agreed to put the house in my mother's name.'

'Miss Arabella will own this house?'

'She does now. That's what I have been fighting for,' she told me.

'Well, that's some security at least.'

'Not quite. We'll never be safe here. We'd be safer if we all went home.'

Her look drank me in. A soft appraising of me that made me flush. My earnestness had never felt more futile.

'I'm happy for you Florence, for the safety you enjoy. It will just never be mine.'

That hurt me. I wanted to understand her. I wanted to assuage her pain. Was she this embittered because of her colour? Was this how being treated so differently made one feel? I saw how people stared at her in the street. Barely a nice word was said about her in Rose Hall, even though I was certain she was as poised and mannerly as I saw her being in public day to day here. It felt more like she had been hated into this position, though there wasn't anything too acidic about her. She didn't sound bitter in fact. Just resolute.

'I thought writing to all these women came from some hope of our vindication,' I offered.

'It does. But I'm not white. I don't want to spend the rest of my life fighting for crumbs.'

Neither did I.

'Do you see me as white still?' I enquired.

'No. I never did really.'

'Why?'

'Well, I suppose the rebellious troublemaker in you made me think of you as apart from them. It's just that because you look white to others, you feel you can fight from the inside. I'll never be let inside like you. I just want to sail away. You want to be the one to light the match. I admire that about you.'

With that, she stood up and walked out to go to the loo. I shifted into the position she had been sitting in and looked out on the night sky, the warmth where her rear had been now warming mine.

Chapter Thirty-One

The last months of my pregnancy flew by. We read a lot. We wrote a lot. I was fascinated by the network of women Sibyl and Persephone had written to. They were all so energetic and incendiary. Day to day, we appeared like calm dilettantes, but in our letters we were campaigners and leaflet distributors and meeting organisers and readers and writers and everything we had been told not to be.

At the end of a hard day's writing, I was sitting up on the bed, carefully holding Lady Persephone's diary. I felt that I couldn't tell Sibyl about it. It would kill her to think of me and Lady Violet rifling through it, I feared. To know that it had been partially burned. And the suggestion that Persephone had been killed by Chester. The guilt clawed at my gullet with scraping nails. I couldn't think of how to make that better, beyond the vengeance I had already taken. I didn't know if it was a good idea to have even brought the diary with me. It had been through hands that were not Lady Persephone's own. The thief had to have read it to know that it was worth breaking into the library to burn, I realised.

I had fallen asleep and woke up to Sibyl sitting next to me. Shaking my shoulder to come down for dinner.

'Why are you reading a burnt book?'

I was speechless. She became suspicious.

'I'm so sorry.'

'What? Why?'

She reached for it. Took it from my lap and looked it over.

'It's Persephone's diary,' I said.

She handled it gently, seeming to know that it could crumble to ashes. She delicately turned to the first pages, where more of Persephone's writing was intact.

'I wanted to tell you. I'm sorry. I found it in the fireplace after there was a break-in.' I bowed my head.

'Here?' she asked, baffled.

'Oh no. At Rose Hall's library,' I said.

'And you found this in the fire?'

'Yes. We don't think the thief took anything from the library. We think they wanted to burn her diary, to hide something.'

'It's not Percy's.'

'What? What do you mean?' I asked, taken aback.

'That is not my sister's diary. The handwriting is kind of similar to hers,' Sibyl said, pointing. 'But it's too ... dainty. Hers was more robust. More swirling. The notebook is the same kind, though.'

'Oh ...' Confusion flooded into me.

'Wait, why do you have this?' Sibyl asked before I could collect my thoughts.

'Lady Violet told me to look after it.'

Sibyl scrunched her eyebrows. 'She would have known Percy's handwriting, though.'

'Oh no, she didn't ever read it. Just left it with me, on the night of the break-in. She thought if Lord Belfield found out about the break-in I would lose my position, and to see the diary incinerated would break his heart. So I kept the evidence, as it were ...'

She looked at me with pity.

'You've done far more than your job for that man.'

A tear seeped out. Deep into the well of me, I had poured buckets of fear and gratitude so that the water inside was sour with a film of green. I had felt like trouble. I had believed bad fortune spread out from my actions like cholera. But here was the sister of the woman whose death I had spent almost the past year investigating, looking on me with pity and compassion. It was all too much. My tears became sobs. I heaved up the pain and the longing. That I was now a twenty-year-old woman with a baby inside of me, the baby of a man who had defiled me.

Even though I held him responsible, and had burned his house down, there was a part of me that still believed it was my fault. That I had caused this. That if I had not been so titillated by the prospect of sex, then none of this would have happened. I had spent every moment since my father threw me out combing through the days of my early childhood, looking for the moment I could have turned course. Was it when I had hurtled towards Everett and got aroused by him talking of anarchy and revolution? Was it when I had begun to enjoy the feeling of the boys in the local area taking their cocks out for pleasuring? Was it when I had first begun to enjoy stories of swooning princesses and imagined myself being kissed and coveted? Was I doomed once my grandmother died? Was I imperilled for having killed my own mother in childbirth? If I'd had a mother, would it have been easier to follow Christian instruction? If my mother hadn't died, I might have been a good girl.

I had no room to wonder about the diary in that moment. The sorrow hurled up in a bellow through my throat. I howled into the pillows, soaking them with my tears. It was a purging of sorts. Sibyl's hand rubbed my back. Eventually, there was nothing left and the silence she held for me drew me back into life.

'Come,' she said.

I waddled down the stairs, walking sideways, her in front of me holding my left hand as my right hand glided down the banister. We came into the kitchen. I knew I looked wild. I was in a long white nightie, thick blue socks and a purple argyle cardigan. My unbraided hair all out and asunder. Surely my eyes were as red-raw as my throat now was, and my cheeks splotchy too.

'Yes. You see!' Miss Arabella said. 'That's how you know the baby is getting ready to come out now. When you want to cry, cry, cry. That is the time. He wants to come out.'

'That's not true. I didn't cry much,' Sibyl mewed.

'Oh, now you want to lie?' Miss Arabella threw the wooden spoon from the stew pot down and the red tomatoey oil splattered the tiles. 'God will punish you. Yes.'

Sibyl went to the corner where the boys were lying on their backs, playing with their toys on a blanket. They had grown so big during my stay. More complex beings, too. Apollo was the jollier of the two. Artemis gave you unflinching eye contact that made you feel like he had been here before. He would smack Apollo for toys he wanted, which could elicit a scrawling cry from Apollo. It was becoming easier to tell them apart. Apollo liked to use Artemis to lie on, massaging his brother's scalp mindlessly, while Artemis looked directly up at you like he was doing now.

Sibyl heaved up Apollo and plonked him with me. To have his chubbiness and heat was so comforting. He rubbed my belly and the turns and somersaults and punches were not scary to him. He just pushed back on the baby sometimes. My detachment from the children fascinated me. I loved the twins immensely, but it didn't increase my affection for the baby in me whatsoever. And I did feel guilt for this. That I loved children, and these babies specifically, but I didn't want my own. It made me feel even more broken, like a telegraph line that used to communicate messages of such warmth and import, but now lay redundant with frayed electrical wires grotesquely spooling out into dead air.

'I cried for all my babies,' Miss Arabella said. 'You should not be scared. You are young. Your body can take it!' She placed a plate of tomato stew and fufu in front of me. I had insisted on using a spoon when I first arrived, but it was actually easier to use my fingers like they had taught me. I fed Apollo from my plate. He pulled my hand towards him every time.

'Look at this one now. Hey! You are something else, eh?'

Miss Arabella loved them and their antics. She studied them like an anthropologist charting each expression for the sweetness of the novelty.

She never spoke of Lady Persephone. When Sibyl did, a dead glaze came over Arabella's eyes until the anecdote was over. She didn't add anything or counter anything. She just waited until her grave had been walked across.

After dinner, we washed the boys, rubbed them down in shea butter and rocked them to sleep. With them in their cot, and the bedroom door left open, we sat huddled in the kitchen, wrapped in blankets with hot cocoa. Miss Arabella told me about all her childbirths. Three in total. Sibyl, then Persephone, and finally Orion. How different they had all been. Sibyl came quickly but caused the most pain in the final stretch. Orion had been the most straining throughout. Persephone brought her the closest to the brink, because with her birth she had lost the most blood. Something that surprised me at first was how we never spoke of Orion or Persephone being albinos. That I had found this out in the most scandalous way, with Sir Chester tossing the news like a grenade in my crowded bedroom, I hadn't told either of them.

Sibyl spoke of her childbirth with more gravitas. Apollo came first. Artemis soon after, but he was blue-lipped and silent. Miss Arabella had smacked him into existence.

'This is why he is so miserable.' We all laughed.

Once the laughter subsided, Sibyl made an admission.

'I was scared I was going to die too,' she said.

'Why?'

'My placenta didn't come out fully. It was—'

'But I knew what to do,' Miss Arabella interrupted. 'You

see, if we'd had one of these doctors, they don't always know. I was with my mother for all the births in the village. So there was no chance I would not have done the right thing quick enough. I was calm. I was not going to lose another child.' She sipped from her cup.

Orion had disappeared into passing whiteness, which was a sort of death – I thought back to Arabella's letter to Persephone, with its language that had so puzzled me at the time. Persephone had literally drowned in a river on a spring night in the Lake District. Yet the house was not cloaked in grief in the way I might have expected. Maybe it was the boys and their giggles and farts and crying? But it was also the feeling that I sat sipping cocoa with two survivors in sorrow's kitchen, where they had licked out all the pots and could warn me what they tasted like. The songs they were teaching me to sing let me know that as long as I did my best to survive I would one day learn to laugh at what had once made me cry.

I didn't feel bold enough to ask Miss Arabella how she felt about having two black children who had white skin and flaxen hair. Now that I had lived with them for a few months and seen two photographs and a painting of Persephone, I was further fascinated by how it was possible to fool white people so easily. My own features, as well as hers, made it glaringly obvious that we were merely rather light-skinned negroes. I didn't look white in the way my father or grandmother did. Knowing that for certain meant I could also now admit that I didn't *feel* white anymore. I had once, of course. I felt so slighted by the bullying children who called me everything black under the sun. I had then felt like an aggrieved white child whose only crime was to have parents who had gone to

Jamaica, where there were obviously so many negroes. I could be bullied merely because we had once been so closely associated with them, even though I never grew up knowing anyone coloured at all. Perhaps that was the reason I hadn't even begun to suspect. It wasn't until Sibyl practically laughed in my face about it that it seemed rather obvious and silly for me to not have thought about it for so many years.

We still went shopping together, even though my pregnant belly was obtrusive. I didn't need a story round here, because no one knew me. There were a few times on the tram when enquiring women asked a few questions. I had my story prepared about having a husband in the Navy. But I never had to use it. Walking back from the George Henry Lee department store with new bonnets and some gloves from Miss Arabella, I wasn't so concerned about treading on any hurt. 'Why didn't Persephone enjoy being white?' I asked.

There were a whole host of connecting questions I wanted to ask under that. Was it all worth it for the financial rewards and security of now being tethered to Lord Belfield? Was Sibyl ever jealous of Persephone for being allowed to marry him when she could not? Did it hurt Persephone to deny herself? They all felt too mawkish to ask, so instead I settled on why she didn't 'enjoy being white'.

'You know what she would tell me? She would constantly say how bored she was. For all the niceties and access we gained through it, it didn't half leave her feeling empty. You know, she always said the same thing: "They don't like us, Sib. They really just don't like us."

'Because she got to hear all the things they say when we're not around. It wounded her, that did.'

I put my arm through hers. There was no mention of this in the diary, and although I wondered if Sibyl had taken a careful enough look to be sure it wasn't Persephone's, perhaps this absence was another sign that she was right. Perhaps the words I'd been pouring over for months were not Persephone's own, but someone else's. Someone with a motive I could not begin to understand.

We wandered towards an arcade because the clouds had started spitting. Under the black arches with gold filigree and gilded lettering were small stores with gaudy displays.

'The diary made out that Percy was frightened for her life,' I said. 'That she was frightened of Chester. Scared witless, it felt like.' I felt Sibyl's bicep twitch, though she didn't withdraw her arm. I had jolted her.

'The diary may have been falsified, but it's true that we've always been frightened. Taut as banjo strings. Children chasing us into our homes. The threat of being discovered and exposed when I helped her pass—'

'Chester stalking the corridors of Rose Hall,' I interjected.

'I suppose. I mean, we were scared of him. But he wasn't around that much. Shunting off to London as much as possible. It's all just a little too convenient that diary though. I wish I had taken the real one when I had the chance. It was right there.'

That someone had gone through the effort of falsifying and then burning a diary felt preposterous to hear but impossible not to accept. Sibyl knew Persephone better than anyone. But why would someone fake a diary, then try to get rid of it? Did they mean for someone to find it? A seagull's droppings fell twelve feet ahead of us and we swerved as if it were inches from our noses. We both laughed but it did nothing to lift the heaviness of the moment.

'Something is obviously heinous here. My sister was not suicidal. She wanted out for sure – but not ...' Sibyl sighed. 'The person who forged the diary surely had something to do with her death, or knows something about it. It's just all so ...'

I felt her shoulder slacken next to mine, and I reflected that even though Chester surely could not be suspected of creating a substitute diary for Persephone, one that accused him, I still felt he was the most likely killer. How it fitted together, I had no idea.

'You don't want to know?' I asked.

'I'm tired. I have to leave this place,' she said under her breath.

Even though she had spoken quietly because of where we were, it wasn't a throwaway comment.

'Are you sure?' I said.

'Not just for me. The boys. They'd kill them in a heartbeat,' she said, catching sight of herself in a shop window and smoothing some hair that had sprung free from her chignon.

She wasn't being paranoid. I knew that seeing Ida B. Wells talk had changed her. There weren't the same lynching practices here, but that same hatred lay just underneath a sneering veneer. A riot could happen right here under certain conditions. We weren't different enough from America to be indifferent to her. We weren't far enough away from enslavement to think that they didn't long to have us more completely back under control. What I read only convinced me all the more. We were not silly to be this scared of retribution. Through disclosure of my own racial origins, I could open a gate onto violence and discrimination I had only had brief tastes of so far. But I knew that all too easily it could become my every day.

'Knowing what happened to Percy won't bring her back and it most definitely wouldn't make me want to remain here,' Sibyl asserted. 'I hate the familiarity of this place. I don't want to keep making a home in the place that took my sister from me. That took my brother and father from me. I want to know what it's like to live in a place where people look like me. I want to look into faces that might love me back, instead of my smiles doing nothing to change their hostility. We've done nothing to them ...'

She shook her head and pursed her lips.

'I just want to go home.'

I had never thought of anywhere besides England as home. Jamaica was not even spoken of in my home, but I had presumed it wouldn't be safe for me to go there. And Africa? Darkest Africa? Wild jungles and lions and pygmies? I couldn't quite bring myself to see there as a potential home for me, either. I knew it wasn't as uncivilised as I had been told. I knew that was a lie. But now, to think of it as a place that offered more of the warmth, comfort and conviviality that Sibyl and Miss Arabella had given me ... Had I not seen their home as the only place I wanted to be to give birth to my baby in peace?

I had wanted to tell her that I believed Chester was the one who had killed her Percy. But she didn't want to know. It wouldn't have helped her to know. I was the one fuelled by revenge. I saw her as more noble for choosing respite. An escape to safety for the family that remained.

'You're free to come with us if you like,' she offered. 'Now that my mother has the house as an asset ... We'll find our way soon enough.'

'What would I do if I came with you?' I asked.

'Teach, silly. You'd make ever such a good teacher.'

Chapter Thirty-Two

It was a full moon on the night my labour pains started, which did not bode well. It felt like a simple cramping at first. It woke me up. My moaning awoke Miss Arabella beside me, and she snapped upright. An assortment of devices lay on the cabinet near the window. I felt groggy and wasn't sure it really was time, because there was no moistening. My waters hadn't broken, and there had been some twingeing for the past month or so. This just felt like the most intense twinge yet. But Miss Arabella was certain.

She marched me downstairs and sent me to the outhouse while she filled up a rubber bulb with warm oily water. She ran between the kitchen and the frosted outhouse with the bulb, and compelled me to give myself an enema. The process in itself wouldn't have been so bad if it weren't so bloody cold. I was shivering after five minutes. After the third or fourth flushing, the whole thing seemed redundant to me. Why was an enema important now, of all times? But then I thought of how awkward I might find it to have a bowel movement in the bedroom, during the pushing that was to come, and was grateful for the last clear eviction.

Washing my hands in the kitchen sink, it came. A different pain. Sonorous. A promise. I felt like a tuning fork that had been struck against the wheels of a steam train. It struck up and through me. From my groin, emanating outwards, along the nerves in my chest and nape of my neck. I was scared. I had never felt anything like this before. My breathing became locked and loaded. Each exhalation was now studied. A hope that I might push down and into the pain to shorten it.

I climbed the stairs back to Miss Arabella's room and swatted her assisting hand away. I couldn't take it just yet. I felt so singular in my fear. It was as if my baby had planned it. The baby was not due until next month at least, so Lady Violet and Sir Chester would still be lying in wait at Rose Hall for his arrival.

We didn't raise Sibyl from her slumber. I wanted to, but Miss Arabella was more conscious of the long haul and refused. I tried to read. Impossible. Miss Arabella could, though. She drank her tea and sat in a chair by the window. I decided to dream of elsewhere. This was effective. To dream of myself as a hawk flying around the world. Trying to find the shortest routes over oceans. Cape Town to Cairo to Rajasthan to Vladivostok to Vancouver and so on. Every city and territory I had ever read about. I visited them all and when a contraction distracted me, I imagined coming down to the ground and feasting assiduously. Then when the pain subsided, I would fly again. This trance-like avian astral projection was a delight. I could swallow down the pain and whimper all through the night. Miss Arabella dozed off because I could keep myself that quiet. I decided it was simply a matter of fortitude. No need to rouse any neighbours, or Sibyl and the boys next door. I could just soldier through.

The sunrise was as late in its arrival as we had become accustomed to. Sibyl knocked before entering and she and Miss Arabella whispered to each other, thinking I was dozing. The boys woke up and I was left alone as they got them ready for the day. A neighbour had been paid to tend to them.

Midday came and I was starving, but Miss Arabella refused me food. Another level of pain arrived. These contractions were contorting. My belly was rolling into itself. The pain was a kneading one. Deeper and more pernicious. A howling, laughing, vile pain. I screamed. It felt like evil was inside me. How it burned into a dull cracking in my lower back. I didn't think I would be whole at the end of this. What was inside me was determined to rip me open. Surely now was the time. I begged Miss Arabella to look at my downstairs. She had shaken her head when I asked, but she looked anyway.

'It is not time. Nowhere near.'

Oh, but how? How?! We had had so many phases of pain already. I couldn't even form words anymore. Sibyl watched me and was crying. Miss Arabella smacked the back of her head and she wiped the tears away. What was going on? The church bells told me it was six o'clock. I couldn't hallucinate myself into the sky anymore. I was starving and tired. Miss Arabella just kept telling me to move around. I hugged the walls. I leaned on the banister in the hallway. I punched the pillows off the bed next door. I was soaked through with sweat. My ribcage hurt from the caterwauling and yelping I couldn't hold myself back from. I hated it. I hated him and him and him and him. I couldn't imagine loving a thing that caused me this much pain. I wanted him out of me and in the arms of Violet, even, if that meant it would be over. If I got through this pain, I promised myself I would never put myself through this disgusting act of female existence again. How did women do this time and again? I would never join them in this as a serial-birthing mother. No! I couldn't.

The pain made me lucid enough to rant and rave at Sibyl. I cursed Chester in a tirade of expletives. Named every tribe of Africa she had told me about, in alphabetical order. Told her all the dirty jokes I knew. The boys were at home but they were downstairs so it was fine, I told myself. They cried and I competed with them. On all fours, I cried into the rug and I hauled everything I had ever felt and smelled from the memory stores in my diaphragm, no matter whether it was fetid or fresh. After everything had been expelled, I lay back on the bed with no idea how I could be expected to have any energy left to use to push on with, let alone push this child down and out.

At some point, Miss Arabella brought in a friend of hers. A dark-skinned, buxom woman who told me her name was Miss Beatrice. I could barely greet her. Until that was, I received the gift she had brought. Laudanum. Blessed laudanum. My grandmother had warned me of women who had lost their lives to it in their loneliness. But for me, it made sense that this would be my first taste. It was bitter and brown-reddish as the drip-off from a plant-pot. It soothed its way through me. Miss Beatrice and Miss Arabella looked at me down there.

'She has small hips. That is why?' Miss Beatrice said in her lilting accent. She wasn't from here. But she didn't sound like Miss Arabella.

'Come. Drink di' Cerasee, my love. Come.'

I spluttered out the first sip. I wasn't expecting a taste that could exceed the laudanum's acridity. It was quite honestly abominable. The honey in it just added a layer of complexity, not strong enough to contradict the bitterness of this concoction.

'Drink it,' she said firmly. She wasn't playing around.

'All in one. Come on.'

The belch that came out of me must have been horrendously foul smelling, but no one recoiled.

Time passed and the contractions came back twofold. I could feel them. They weren't painless. But as the drug took hold, I separated from the pain. I could ride the waves more manageably. Instead of flying above the world as I had done the night before, I just sat in the top corner of the ceiling looking down on myself below. Me, paled but with reddened cheeks and forehead, my nightgown translucent, sodden with my own sweat. Sibyl and Miss Arabella and Miss Beatrice. Three black women encircling me who had been through this before. I had asked for this. A space of safety. I knew I wanted to be among them for the birth. I wondered if Miss Beatrice was from Jamaica. I thought she sounded like she was.

'Did you know my mummy?'

In my laudanum haze, I kept calling for my mother.

'My mother's name was Emily. My mother's name was Emily.'

I was whispering it over and over. I felt she must have given birth to me in a similar scene. Did she die surrounded by black women? Did they all cry when she died?

The following morning I looked out of the window and saw that the moon was aflame. She was ochre dusted from the sun that was just about to come. I wasn't going to die. I knew it. I wasn't going to die. This baby would not be the end of me. I would give birth to him, hand him over to the nunnery and never see him again. I would be free for the rest of my life with my faculties intact and sure of the blessing of my body and what I was capable of. Wherever I ended up, I would survive. The shame of my former sins couldn't hold me down. I just wanted to live free from everything that had been done to me.

I was ready to push before they told me it was time. I stood up and leaned forward. Sibyl held me up by my left shoulder and Miss Arabella by my right. Miss Beatrice in front of me. I was so scared I would splatter her and told her so.

'Nuh bodda 'bout dat. Yuh haffi come on now. It time!'

It burned. I felt like I was set to be ripped open. Searing acidic flames around my lips and vagina and everywhere there. Just a screaming acidic fire of nasty burning pain. My back ached something chronic. I was a yawning whale, roaring into the glorious light of morning. The push push push of it sent me into panic. Couldn't I be stuck here? Stuck with a baby only half out of me? What then?

'Push den! Push nah! Unnu come on!'

Miss Arabella and Sibyl were breathing in tandem with me. So, I gave it more. Because the impossible increase of pain made me feel the end was near. I needed to be on the other side of the swelling. What sweet relief for this all to be over! That's what kept me going for those last three or five pushes. I would have no strength left, but I would be done. A big riptide of a push got that infernal baby out of me, and a pealing cry let me know he was alive, after a little rasping rattle. The cord was clear of his neck. They laid me back on the damp bed.

'It's a boy,' Miss Beatrice said.

'Yes, I know,' I panted, sounding and feeling annoyed.

They put him on me and I pushed something slippery out of me. It didn't hurt at all. The afterbirth. I was done.

I was taught how to breastfeed. I didn't really want to, but the milk in my breasts was bursting to get out. I cared very little for the boy. I didn't hate him, because it wasn't his fault he was here, but no feelings came over me to convince me that running off into the night with a baby made sense. I was gasping to hand him over to the nuns. If I were a barren woman, maybe I would be desperate to know what it was like to give birth to my own baby, and willing to take in the baby of another. Having been through it, I felt newly sensible. I knew the process both emotionally and intellectually. Now I could leave the tasks of motherhood to others, and return to my passions. Books and the written word.

But this was not to be. For that very evening, Lady Violet swanned into my bedroom with the pigeon-shaped woman from the church suffragette meeting. No words were uttered in explanation, for none were needed. We had been spied upon. So connected were the ladies of the echelons above us, that my howling had incited Mrs Slocombe to inform Lady Violet of the early birth of my baby. My hope that the baby would get a fresh start away from the corruption of the Belfield family was snatched away from me.

I would not speak with them. Mrs Slocombe plonked herself at the end of my bed and spoke at a volume that underscored how obnoxious she was. My feet were bound into the twist of the sheets she was clamping down with her weighted position. Lady Violet sat in the window. Smirking.

I left Liverpool a week later with Lady Violet and the baby. We looked like a family. The baby boy was no longer a grey-coloured, squawking creature. He was a baby. A brown-eyed, brown-haired, lick-curled baby. I felt less than I knew a mother of a newborn baby was meant to, and that felt appropriate to the circumstances.

I had promised Sibyl that as soon as I got word that they'd sold the house from under Lord Belfield's nose, which they had been hard at work on for weeks now that it was in Miss Arabella's name, I would return and we could steal off to the Gold Coast together.

Chester had obviously heard the carriage coming from across the way, and as I alighted his eyes bore into me with such concentration, I feared he might slice me in two. He snatched the baby off me. Cuddled him to his chest and cried onto him.

'He's not dark,' he rejoiced.

Lord Belfield appeared from behind Chester, putting a hand on his shoulder as he leaned over to see the baby. 'Wesley is preparing your room,' he told me, 'until arrangements can be made.'

Behind me I heard the crunch of gravel as Lady Violet stepped out of the carriage. Perhaps she had wanted to delay the sight of her husband fawning over another woman's baby.

'Arrangements?' I questioned.

'For a wet nurse,' Lady Violet said, at the same moment as Lord Belfield said, 'For your future.'

It would be as I had suspected. I would be kept while I was useful, and then tossed out. Whatever future Lord Belfield had in mind, I would have no say in it.

Lord Belfield motioned for me to enter the house. 'In the meantime, there's someone to see you in the library.'

I raised an eyebrow at him, but he gave nothing away. Some appraisals man from an auction house who had come to tell me I had destroyed his collection with my binding work? Reduced the value of it or some such? Feeling puffed up and indignant, I walked through the library's open door.

I got the shock of my life to find the man sitting at the desk by the window was the man I knew best in the world. There he sat, drinking a whisky and smoking a pipe.

My father.

Chapter Thirty-Three

If I could have run from him I would have done. He made no
move to strike me. It had been years since he'd laid his hands
on me in that way, but the memory of his belt licks being
thrashed into me still made my back tingle. He wouldn't in
front of people, anyway. That was always behind closed doors.
But still ... Seeing him sat in Rose Hall made me want to
bolt. I couldn't even dash up the stairs, because my body had
changed. My core had changed. It felt like my organs were
still migrating back towards their normal positions after
having been squeezed out of their natural homes. I focused
on maintaining my breath. I pulled my shawl tighter too, not
because of the chill but to keep the dampness of my blouse
from view. My areolae were swollen and leaking. I would be
mortified for my father's eyes to nestle on the wet patches.
I made my way to sit on the couch opposite him. I couldn't
greet him first.

'How do?' He nodded at me as if I were the lady at the post office.

'Good morning, Father.' Resting into our new formality.

Lady Violet had the baby, and she had retreated up the stairs with Sir Chester trailing behind her. Rose Hall felt like quicksand. All my wrestling and strategising and letter-writing had nevertheless drawn me towards the inevitability of this moment. My baby boy raised by a wolf and his wily wife. The sins of my sex splashed onto my person. All avenues into the future blocked off, because I had brazenly given in to my own pleasure and not successfully prevented men from taking theirs from me. I was defeated.

'I suppose you're somewhat surprised,' Lord Belfield started. He strained his neck muscles and brandished his bottom teeth into the awkward grimace reserved for Englishmen to use in moments of social discomfort.

'One might say that.' I scowled openly.

'Well, your father couldn't be kept away any longer. None of us are promised tomorrow, Miss Granger, so the fact a chance for reconciliation is now here must be viewed as fortune.' He cuffed his palms together and made his lips even thinner. His empty shibboleths would continue to pour out of him if I did not change course.

'How did you know where I was?' I asked my father.

'I've always known where you were.' He puffed out a stream of smoke. The tobacco was not his own. He was smoking Lord Belfield's and I could tell because he was being so chuffingly liberal with it. The smell of the smoke in our own home was far more meagre, the way he would ration his tobacco out. He'd gone from a troll under a bridge to a bloated dragon in an opium den. His moustache was thicker. And greyer.

I turned my gaze on Lord Belfield, the man who had furnished my father with both tobacco and information. I had never known loyalty was in such short supply from men like him. My father had always known where I was, because my father had been informed soon after my arrival. It was idiotic of me to think that I was operating with any degree of autonomy. I had never been free. Not truly.

'Your initial proposal of working for me without your father knowing was improper,' Lord Belfield muttered.

I ignored him.

'So what is to become of me now?'

My father's eyes were blue. Not the enlivening crystal blue that elicits swooning compliments. They were cold pools that no longer swirled. To feel him look at me now was frustrating. His eyes pleaded with the words he couldn't bring himself to say. A more passionate man would take this opportunity for an outburst that conveyed emotion too long held in. Instead, I got a sense of his chilling desperation. It felt like he had missed me.

'I'm too tired for this right now. Lord Belfield, might my father and I have some time alone in the library tomorrow morning?'

Lord Belfield looked towards my father for approval.

'She talks like she's the lady of the house now does she?' my father said.

Lord Belfield chuckled and shrugged. 'Well, Douglas, it has been her home. And she is now more of a lady than any of us might have imagined.'

I could barely conceal my exasperation. 'I'm tired,' I repeated.

'Yes, yes. My goodness, after all you've gone through. I dare say.'

I rose.

'Mind how you go now,' my father said as I neared the door.

There was some pathos still lingering in me for him. There was so little training for a man in how to raise a daughter alone. It took a lot for him to speak softly to me. When other people were present it more often forced him to do so.

The violence of my ejection from our home together still smarted, but he was here. I could fashion some sort of future for us, whether together or apart. Still, it was bizarre to see him, slightly shrunken and notably older, in a place that was now so familiar to me and alien to him.

Wesley was at the bottom of the stairs. Of course. I was glad he had heard everything and I wouldn't have to repeat myself. He put his arm around my waist and the other at my shoulder, and we rose up together. Of Lady Violet, the baby and Sir Chester, there was no sign.

The new frilled sheets on my bed felt friendly. I recognised the satin softness from the shed boudoir I had set up in the summer. They'd been washed, thankfully, because to have my baby in cleanliness was of such importance. I knew that dirt would endanger the baby. I always noted the howls of mothers who had lost their child in the night came from the most squalid parts of town. Nevertheless, the tenderness Joseph had shown Annie and vice versa was an unusual preparation for the maternal scene I now found myself in, I thought.

Wesley brought the baby up to me not long later. He was hungry, and that was the reason they had sent him to me. After I had fed him I handed him back to Wesley, who coddled him in a way that I approved of. The baby reached for his chest and we both looked at each other and laughed. He'd not had enough, and I'd thought he had. I clamped him back onto my breast. There was so much to tell Wesley. Our tones were dulcet, yet it felt wrong to pelt him with too much. I asked him to read to me – a first. We went back to the beginning of *One Thousand and One Nights* and I fell asleep with the baby in my arms and Wesley, glowing in the candlelit night, became my Scheherazade.

To eat my breakfast in bed like I really was the lady of the house was such a luxury. Wesley brought it up on a tray, risking Baxter's ire to give me some comfort on a day that had a pall over it. Apparently my father and Baxter were having silent meals together in the kitchen. I wondered what I could tell my father about my time at Rose Hall. To become a horse-riding governess would be a step up, much as it wasn't the bookbinding craft I'd honed for all my life. A young mother on the run from Chester was the worst possible outcome, but I would have to become such if I ever wanted to sleep without fits again. If only Sibyl were closer. She thought so much quicker than I did. It was as if she could see several leagues ahead at sea. Whether the shape of the clouds promised calm waters, or a brewing storm. My conversation with my father would throw light onto what the actual move forward would have to be.

He was standing at the shelves when I entered the library.

Lord Belfield must have let him in. The sides of his mouth turned downwards, scanning the collection in appraisal.

'Good morning, Father,' I greeted him.

'There's no need for the airs. He's not about now.' He didn't turn to look at me.

I made my way to my desk. Everything neatly arranged. The last of the books I had worked on were stacked on the right-hand edge.

'So, I take it you weren't worried about me.'

'I was. He telegrammed me after Christmas,' my father said.

'So why are you here now?' I asked.

'To ensure your bastard child is dealt with appropriately.' He finally turned around.

So he knew. Was there anything Lord Belfield had not told him?

'I have hardly had a say in that matter. And certainly not in the child's conception,' I told him.

'That's right,' he sneered. 'Pretend it's someone else's fault. You couldn't keep your drawers up barely five minutes in this house before the lord's brother's carrying on with yuh under his own wife's nose.'

'That's not how it happened.'

'Oh, is it not?' He scoffed.

He was by my desk now. Thick fingers, nails freshly scrubbed, picking up my stack of books one by one for inspection. His grey waistcoat over a green tartan shirt. I used to lay his clothes out some mornings when he was hungover. He didn't know what went with what half the time, and I made him look more sensible.

'Rippling here. On a wonky line. You're not up to my standards, lass. Not by a long shot!'

He held up my red leather-bound book. I was in the docks for a bookbinding trial I had no time to prepare for. He was picking at strings that no one else could see. There was no rippling. And if the line had been wonky, I would have restarted. Achieving perfection was more of a money maker. I'd had the time to achieve it. He wanted my spirits cut down.

'So, you're struggling at home are yuh? No one to make your meals. No one to darn your socks,' I spat back.

'You're not too old for an 'iding, my girl. I promise you that.'

I had the heat in me. 'But you are soon to be too old for anyone to remember to even call on you.'

'I am warning yuh,' he said.

'When I left, you looked in the mirror and saw a lonely old man. You lost my mother. You lost your mother and then you lost me. So who's gonna look after you now, eh?'

I'd shot him. For some seconds I had him blown. His jaw set to swallow the pain of what I had said.

'I'll never let you back in my house.' His finger pointed at me.

'I'd never step a foot back in that house.' I stared back at him. 'I'm glad you got shot of me. I may not be perfect, but I'm more alive than you are. I've got more people who care about me than you do. I'm going to be all right.'

He lowered his finger and shook his head, staring at the desk leather.

'And to think ... You know everyone ...' he started.

I leaned forward. He was about to say something that would shift us into somewhere different. I was about to learn something about him. The air was charged.

354

'Forget it,' he muttered. Marched off.

Did he have a limp now? He was rocking into his right side.

'You're really on your own now.' And with that, he slammed the library door behind him.

I lay back in the chair and let all air leave me.

It surprised me to learn that day that I liked breastfeeding. I had always been curious. How it felt to have a being mewl for you, and to provide the suckling his mouth was perfectly formed for. But what I hadn't expected was the cyclical nature of it. The baby fed me in turn with sensations of goodness. I was glad for the experience, even though what had caused it had been so traumatic. I had thought I would explain Chester's assault on me when my father and I spoke, but had wanted to see him emitting some softness. He saw me as a harlot still. Would he even believe me? But also, what good would it do? Now I was sure he would never be soft with me, disclosure made even less sense.

Mounting the stairs after our conversation in the library, my tears dried up of their own volition. I couldn't impart sadness into the baby. That wasn't right. Against my will, I cared for him. His wellbeing. He was more mine than Chester's, I was becoming sure. That he had been inside me for so many months had absolved him. The whole ordeal had convinced me that there was no evil seed for me to be afraid of from the child I had birthed. My child was born *tabula rasa*, as we all are. The sins of his father did not live on through him and if I could keep the baby from Chester, all would be well. For Chester would surely shape him into a boy of his own imagining, and throttle him if there was any resistance.

I cooled down with him at my teat. My determination wasn't quiet, although it did not disturb the still pond of my face. I would just play along until I saw a chink of space for his freedom. Now I knew my father would not have me home under any circumstances, I was very much released. No way back – only forward. My brain whirred as I napped.

Wesley woke me.

'Lady Violet's outside.'

The fog of slumber wouldn't lift. I squeezed my shoulder blades into each other, woozy from sleep. I'd been dribbling while the baby nestled into me. Wesley took him from me and I smoothed my hair down as best I could and wiped the side of my mouth.

'Bring her in,' I whispered.

Wesley went over to the door with the baby held to his chest and leaned back so his head wouldn't drop as Wesley's other hand turned the doorknob. I wondered where Wesley had learned to move with a child like that, and remembered his saying that his own mother was giving birth deep into her forties. As one of the eldest, Wesley had raised children and held knowledge I might never get to know.

Lady Violet entered and came to sit on my bed without asking. The air between us wasn't convivial. She decided where she sat and what the tone of conversation would be. Her audacity.

'We've found a wet nurse,' she said. 'She'll be here tomorrow, and Chester wants to see the baby this evening, too.'

I had been preparing myself. But it still felt too soon.

'For how long?' I asked, sitting up straighter in the bed.

'Just a short while. They'll be drinking and celebrating in

the way men do. We're lucky it was a son really. Very lucky indeed.' She thinned her lips and shook her head.

'I won't have him raised by him,' I spat.

Lady Violet chuckled ominously.

'You needn't be that worried. People of our class hardly raise our own children.' She smoothed her skirts. 'You've never met my nephew Daniel, have you? Up in Scotland since well before his mother's passing. Imagine . . .'

This was true. I had been here a year and not yet met the son of Lady Persephone and Lord Belfield. As far as I knew, Lord Belfield had last seen him in the summer on a business trip to Edinburgh. He'd visited the school, had tea with his son and left. It didn't warm me to think of the child being raised in some damp stone school where any affection would be battered out of him in preparation for his tyranny in the colonies.

'All sorts of things can be arranged.' She shook my ankle, and I felt the tenderness of my joints and cringed.

Violet was at least partly to blame for all of this. If only she had not disturbed us so soon after the birth, along with her accomplice who smelled like dairy and wet coins.

'Let me take him now and you can come and get him from the drawing room after dinner.'

I gritted my teeth as the only answer and looked away from her. With that she stood and took the baby from Wesley's cradled arms. She took all the warmth from the room along with my baby. I shivered from the injustice of it all. Wesley grabbed the bowl of oil with the big comb and sat where she had been and patted the blanket between his thighs. I heaved myself out of bed and sat between his legs, trying to calm my anxiety. With a wet nurse arriving tomorrow, I would soon be thrown out, never to see my child again. Why was this fear so choking to me, when I had been planning to give him away on my own terms? The only thing that made my ribs feel less taut was the melodic humming of Wesley as he parted my hair for plaits yet again. It is only in retrospect that I remember the ditty he hummed was unnerving because, considering the circumstances, it was suspiciously cheerful.

Baxter said nothing to us at dinner. She seemed smaller, somehow. Her hands shook slightly as she ladled soup into our bowls. Was this a new development? I couldn't be sure because I had been so concerned with myself throughout the pregnancy, I had stopped paying attention to her. I had no idea of how she felt about my father, even though I knew they had eaten together on the night I arrived. He was eating with Lord Belfield, and I assumed Sir Chester, that night. I assumed he had embarrassed Lord Belfield into extending the invitation, motivated by a desire to avoid me. We were of the same household, and yet his status at Rose Hall was higher than mine by virtue of his sex.

They rang the bell for us after dinner, and Wesley walked me up to the drawing room. We could hear the crackle and spit of the fire from outside the room. He hugged me and then squeezed my shoulders, as if I were a lover going off to war. I kissed his cheek and turned to twist the knob and retrieve my baby.

The men were arranged around the fire. Lord Belfield was sitting in an armchair. My father and Sir Chester were standing by the hearth. As I walked in, Lord Belfield bellowed his greeting.

'Ahhhh, Miss Granger!'

Lady Violet sat on a chesterfield by the window, holding the baby. I was glad the baby wasn't too hot and near the fumes of the smoking men. But perhaps next to the window was too chilly. As soon as I entered she beckoned me over and pressed him into my arms.

My father had a cigar primed for lighting. Sir Chester stepped forward with a long match aflame. My father concentrated on the end of the cigar, rolling it in the licking fire, puffing like a fish. Sir Chester, with an air of accomplishment, looked at me. He believed he had won. At that moment in time, so did I.

'So I'm sure you'll be happy to hear, Miss Granger, that Lady Violet has found a position for you,' Lord Belfield said.

'A position?' I asked.

'As a governess,' he confirmed. 'You'll start in the new year.'

I steadied my lip, which longed to tremble, but I couldn't stop the chill spitting its way both down to my toes and out through my temples.

'The family were mightily impressed with your references.'

Lord Belfield chuffed his palms together and rubbed. I could hear their dryness from where I sat.

'And what about the baby?' I asked.

'He'll be very well taken care of, obviously,' Sir Chester said.

He was not gloating, for there was no need. My defeat was total.

'Who decided all of this?' I asked.

Lord Belfield looked at me innocently. I turned to look

at Lady Violet. She was completely captivated by the fire. The blaze danced in her eyes. Although she remained straight-backed, I could see my defeat was also her own. I had no choice in the matter. Neither had she, really. Even the fleeting moments of agency we had enjoyed were essentially winds that blew us onto the course determined by the larger-lunged men by the fire.

'You'll be glad for a chance at a decent life, lass, which is more than most get after what you've done.' My father belched. 'You'd make a terrible mother.'

Brutus. Such a callous assessment coming from him, of all people. To be condemned as inadequate by my own father, in front of others. Ejected from his affections from birth. Evicted from his home on discovery of my relationship with Everett. Now, rejected from respectable womanhood with my rapist as a witness. The gases of a noxious invective swirled within me. If it were not for the fact that I was holding my baby, I would have risen up like the apprentice of Medusa to curse him into stone that I could smash to smithereens.

'You're an embarrassment to the memory of my mother,' I hissed.

The jolt that ran through me seemed to spark into Lady Violet next to me. Her neck snapped towards me.

'Careful . . .' she whispered.

She meant it as a warning, but I took it on as encouragement.

'What man sups brandy with the man who raped his own daughter? She'd be right ashamed of you.'

The silence that followed my words was thickened by the potential for violence. It felt like the baby I held was the prince who had forced a ceasefire. But all sides' arsenals were steaming, screaming for continued use.

'You led him on, I am sure! I probably don't know huuulf of what you got up to.'

My betrayal was complete: hailed as a whore, while I held his grandson, and he signed my life away. He was tipsy, I could tell by the slurring. This didn't explain the acid of his resentments, though. If he didn't have the mantelpiece to lean on, I guessed he'd have started swaying.

'This is all getting rather h—' Lord Belfield started, seemingly trying to temper things.

'Her own mother didn't even want her.' My father slumped his way to the armchair opposite Lord Belfield and crumpled into it.

The pathetic sight of him galled me. This was the man I had longed for. Begged to love me in a million different unsaid ways. Now here he was, spilling things he had never even deigned to tell me privately. That my mother hadn't wanted me in pregnancy. He wanted to cut me to the dark meat.

'Left us by the docks. Didn't even stay to wave,' he grumbled.

My head got tight and new pain arrived sharply behind my left eye. I handed the baby to Lady Violet and got up, walking over to his chair. I wanted to grab him by the chin, but I couldn't bring myself to touch him. I would kill him if I had such close proximity to his throat.

'What are you saying?' I asked, with my chest heaving.

His look to me was one of revulsion. He had always hated me, but there was also something about me that made him feel ashamed. His expression was both condemning and pained.

361

'She found her mother and she didn't want to leave her.'

His pupils had widened.

'She were selfish, is what it is. She was stolen from her mother by the lord and lady because she looked white enough. Didn't grow up knowing her. So she went back to Jamaica to find her. That's where I met her,' he said, shattering lie after lie. 'I even helped her look. But when the time came she wouldn't leave.' He was sputtering.

Lord Belfield, Lady Violet and Sir Chester couldn't make sense of it. They looked on at us quizzically. But upon this explanation, a new rage coursed into my fingers. I now knew that I did indeed have the power to kill.

The words screeched out of me before I knew I had consciously formed the accusation.

'You lied to me!' My hands shook with the ambition to clench his throat. 'My mother's not dead.'

'Well, she could be, now.' My father looked away from me, back into the fire.

I backed away from him. I ran to Lady Violet's seat and took the baby back.

'You're all liars and rapists and murderers.' I shook my head. The baby wasn't sleeping anymore. The beginning chords of his cries rippled up to me along with the smell of something repugnant.

'Miss Granger, forgive me, for perhaps it's not the right time for a superfluous defence, but your father not telling you the whole truth about your mother doesn't make *me* a liar,' Lord Belfield protested. 'I have – always – told you the truth.'

It astounded me that Lord Belfield was hurt by my

362

assertion. He shook his pipe out into the ashtray in harried disappointment.

'And no one here is a murderer,' Sir Chester piped up. 'Obviously.'

With nothing left to protect, I went for his jugular.

'You killed Lady Persephone,' I stabbed.

It was as if I had just brought a chandelier down on my head, to crush me and slice up my flesh. Every stare in the room slashed into me further. Lady Violet's surprise was the real performance. I suppose me destroying my chance at any sort of life need not drag her down, too.

'Why would I kill my brother's wife, you silly girl?' Sir Chester said, baffled.

I had been convinced of his guilt for so long that his confusion, but moreover his sincerity, made my mouth taste like hay. His motive had been so clear, that not even the suspicion the diary was faked had truly dissuaded me.

'I mean, not only the ingratitude. But now this sheer lunacy.'

He smoothed his still-neat hair back into its coif.

'The fact I wasn't here on the night she died should have thrown you off, detective. All this snooping and all you've been left with are empty accusations. And now other people's children will be instructed by someone who's as mad as a hatter. Good lord.'

He relit his cigar and marvelled at me. Shook his head and smirked.

'It's all the excitement. I mean the baby is freshly here and her humours are all out of sorts. Percy was the same – took her a while to come back down to earth.' Lord Belfield immediately concurred on his brother's innocence, although he knew of all his other crimes.

'Don't worry, Miss Granger, tomorrow you get to say your goodbyes. You can go back to Sibyl until the new year, when you'll start your new position. It's all just been rather stressful for you.'

We were being dismissed. Lady Violet grabbed me by the elbow. Here I was, being steered away from the men who decided upon my life after a tumultuous hearing.

'Come, come,' she whispered.

Yet another madwoman, being led back up to the attic.

Chapter Thirty-Four

One might have suspected that the lifting of the veil on such revelations would have made sleep nigh on impossible. This was not so. The exhaustion of knowing things I had never suspected drew me into a whirlpool of confusion. I was too tired of lifting myself out of impending doom. Had I not done enough? The letters written and the continual investigations I had conducted – even the fire I had lit – all led me to a conclusion that the drunken men in the drawing room had engineered. Lady Violet at the last was silent. For what could we do? She had dragged me back here, after all. Was she too not just an agent of her husband's will, when all truth was told?

I surrendered to sleep. The baby took only a short while to calm down as I fed him and rocked him gently. I wanted to protect him. Keeping him would be an end to my life in any meaningful way. But why was it that I could not find a home for him away from the corruption of the cursed Rose Hall? The lives of everyone that came here were blighted.

'You're a very good baby, you are,' I said over and over again. If things were different, I might have made promises to him at this moment before bedtime. That I would always protect him. That I would make sure he was always safe, even though I knew what was coming the next day. I was too tired to cry. So, I just rocked him and said the only thing that I knew for sure and was worthy of repeating.

'You're a very good baby, you are.'

There was a hand on my mouth in the dark. I was sure I had fallen asleep with the baby in my arms, but now they were empty. Now I was fully supine and alone. Where was my baby? I fought against the verbena-scented hand and took a sharp intake of air in through my nostrils. The moonlight meant it only took a second or two for my eyes to acclimatise and see that my bedroom door was open.

In the doorway stood Annie. Why was Wesley all dressed up? Was Joseph nearby? Annie was holding the baby. I exhaled and some of my panic abated. There were no words. The hand on my mouth belonged to Lady Violet, who was calmly sitting on my bed, staring at me. Her eyes were serious. I looked around the room to see that nothing had been left. My belongings were gone, apart from my winter coat, which lay at the end of my bed, with an outfit laid on top of it. I doubted I would be able to button it up from all the weight I had gained. My mind had caught up to the situation. We were making a run for it.

My limbs jolted with newfound energy. I swung my feet

out of bed and allowed Lady Violet to help dress me. I had no idea how they had managed to pack all my things without me being roused from my slumber. How tired had I been?

'Where?' I whispered into Lady Violet's ear. I was surprised that she was one of my rescuers – but perhaps, under Chester's thumb, she had done things she was not proud of.

'Liverpool?' she whispered back.

My heart skipped. Of course. Once dressed, we filed out. I would never see this bedroom again, I knew that much. We slinked past Baxter's door. Her light was on. She wasn't coming, obviously. Did she know we were leaving?

No lights were lit on the first floor. The men had been drinking so heavily, were they quite conveniently conked out? Our movements through Rose Hall were soundless. We knew the place so well: every creaking floorboard, every loose banister. The only danger was the baby Annie was carrying. He really was a good baby, to be this quiet even with all this movement.

We headed towards the kitchen, but at the library door I paused. Annie and Lady Violet turned towards me. My face must have been pleading. I wanted to fetch things.

'We packed it,' Annie said, still at the level of a whisper but clearer now we were away from the bedrooms.

I went to protest 'Bu—'

'We got everything,' they whispered, both visibly annoyed.

I was delighted at their foresight. Down to the kitchen we went, avoiding the creaking front door to Rose Hall, and then up and out into the garden.

The iced grass crunched under our feet as we scuttled towards the bridge over the river. I was worried for the baby's temperature, but Annie had him bundled up in an extra tartan blanket. It would have been safe to talk now we were gaining distance from Rose Hall, but the spell cast on us was yet to break. It didn't lift until we saw the steam of horses breathing across the bridge. There, on a moonlit country road, atop a carriage, sat Joseph.

'Are you sure you got all my tools?' I asked.

'We got more than that besides. Look!' Annie said.

She swung a carpet bag up onto the seat where I had space to the left of me. Lady Violet and Annie were sat opposite.

Besides my box of tools were a selection of books. Some of which I had worked on, others not. Annie handed them to me one by one. All Lady Persephone's Greeks that had once belonged to her father, the ivory bound lectionary, the Abyssinian Bibles, the Arabics from Mali and quite a few more. As well as the letters I had read, now bound up in fresh string.

I was more than stunned. How had she known what to grab? Everything else I had worked on I could find some way to see, read and touch at some other time in the future. What lay beside me were the priceless ones. The pillaged ones. The core of Lord Belfield's collection, that he had been hoping would lead to his financial redemption.

Lady Violet placed a blue velvet drawstring pouch into my lap.

'I got the key to his safe. Those are your earnings.'

I placed the pouch on top of the books and used my left hand to draw it open. Inside was a bundle of notes and around twenty brass coins. It looked to be near double what I was owed from Lord Belfield.

My mouth formed an O and I started to gasp heavily and rock back and forth in my seat. All the worry of the past year suddenly had shape to it. The cloud that had plagued my thoughts and kept me up into teeth-grinding nights. The fear of being left destitute robbing me of all forms of solace.

Such a moment of succour would have elicited eloquence from many, but the early morning mists surrounding the carriage conspired to constrict my vocal cords. My eyes darted between them both.

'Thank you. Thank you,' was all I could say, as the three of us escaped in the thick of the winter's night.

Annie patted my knee. 'There you are, pet. I'm going to get some shut-eye.' She leaned back against the jostling carriage.

The quiet that arose between Lady Violet and me was cumbersome. I had always felt marked by the sins of my duplicity. Yet here we were, racing towards whatever freedom we could find, and the only way it had been possible was through night raids of Rose Hall. Secretly reading letters and pilfering priceless books out of a lord's library, and grabbing monies from a safe not even I was aware of. All of the values that were beaten into us throughout our childhoods had been completely shaken off in order to become the feminine version of sleuths who moved in the shadows of the novels that I devoured so readily. Perhaps it was the relief of a full purse which gave me the confidence to ask her the question that would denude Lady Violet's morality once and for all.

'Was it you?' I asked finally.

She said nothing for quite some time. With Annie asleep and Joseph out of earshot, we were practically alone. Yet her fear was still palpable, and she looked on me with trepidation.

I tried to keep my face free of judgement. Thankfully, the baby roused, his lips forming like a fish feeding at a pond's surface. I took my breast out and gave it to him. The purity of the moment was enough to beckon out her confession. I wasn't going to run to the police after what she had done for me, and I think she knew it.

'It isn't what you think,' she started.

I think my eyes might have widened looking at her. I hadn't always known, but I was now sure of her innocence, whatever the explanation. But her guilt still won out, and it was as if she found that she couldn't speak when looking at me. Lady Violet wiped a handkerchief over the window's condensation and looked out into the dark.

'Percy was the love of my life.'

She wrung the handkerchief into a long twist between her fingers. 'No, that's not right . . . She *is*.'

Lady Violet had often struck me as bloodless, but now I thought back to her hysteria on having to re-enter Rose Hall. She had not been mourning a sister-in-law, but a lover. Fascinated, but desperate for more than an admission of yet more sexual inversion at Rose Hall, I decided to prod as gently as I could.

'What happened the night she died?' I said softly.

Lady Violet looked at me and shame contorted her features. But she had started so she realised she would have to tell me the rest. She looked back out into the night.

'Well, I loved her first,' she said with a low, pained laugh. 'Let's start there. You know we all met in Paris? Francis's interest in Sibyl just gave us the excuse necessary to remain, and then I sowed the seeds of his marriage to Percy by subtle

370

suggestion that she would be the perfect wife for him, so that we could all return to England together ...' Lady Violet looked at her hands, clasped in her lap. 'Chester was clueless, thankfully. And in the beginning, Francis was too, of course. We were just two sisters-in-law who got along swimmingly. Chester was away a lot of the time, so I could come to Rose Hall as much as I pleased. Then Daniel came along, not long after they married. And I was ... jealous doesn't quite cover it,' she said. 'I knew it was fortunate as a cover for – Well, anyway, Chester assumed my mood was because I wasn't pregnant yet, and so his campaigning got more ... violent.'

I could only imagine.

'I'm sorry,' I told her. She ignored me.

'But Daniel was a delight. And I started coming even more regularly, to see them and to get away from Chester. Daily, really. We became our own little unit. Percy, Sibyl, Daniel and me. Francis was quite shut out. I think he started to realise then. He suspected before but then he saw ... well, he didn't quite catch us ... But he knew.'

'I understand.' Or at least, I thought I did. Lord Belfield had seemed to observe far more than I'd been comfortable with, and I could imagine him rooting Lady Violet and Persephone out.

'And for many years, he was fine with it. Quite a bohemian set-up, really. But we were all fine, as long as Chester was away. But then came the Wilde thing.'

'Oscar?' I asked.

She nodded.

'Yes. The whole trial. Months of it. The whole thing

371

spooked Francis. The thought of it all ... coming out ... as it were.'

'Oh, I see.'

'He called us into the library. Newspapers splayed out before him. Said we had to stop seeing each other. I mean, that was impossible.' Lady Violet shook her head. 'We'd just be more careful, I offered. But he wouldn't hear of it. Then he started up about Daniel. That we had to send him up to Scotland to boarding school, before he could become confused by my presence. When in fact it was all he had ever known. It got quite heated. I countered that he'd be more confused about his father sidling into Sibyl's bed night after night.'

'So Lady Persephone really did know about that?' I asked.

'Knew? It was how we all met. We all went to see Sibyl ride in the circus. I spotted her in the bookshop the next day. I introduced her to Francis, for goodness' sake. And of course, then she introduced me to Percy. It was love at first sight for both of us. All of us. It should have been such fortune.'

'And Chester was—' I began.

'He's just not a thinker.' Lady Violet sighed. 'Percy and Francis were at least good friends. They were decently matched in that way. And Sibyl is so ... amenable.'

The tone having lightened, and her generosity of confidences flowing more freely, meant I could ask what was needed to seal things up.

'How did she die?' I asked.

The cart rocked into a pothole. Annie stirred and we both looked at her to see if she would rise. Her zephyr-like snoring stayed steady.

Lady Violet looked back at me resignedly. The lines by her eyes scrunched up and then smoothed out, along with her long exhale.

'We were celebrating on the bridge. She had found the key to Francis's safe. Daniel going had sent her into such a depression, and it was the first happy moment she'd had since he'd left. We knew we could get away to Paris. Then when he was old enough, we could get back in touch. Know him again when he was an adult. And in the meantime, we would live as libertines. It's quite possible for women of means in Paris to do that,' she added. 'Under certain conditions. So, we were dancing. Waltzing. I was leading. Spinning us. I wasn't holding her tight enough.'

She looked up at me in despair. I smiled gently at her to keep her talking.

'And then we were getting faster and faster. I mean, we were quite giddy. And I was squealing. Because I was just that happy. The end of Chester. Percy and I together. We were going to be free of them entirely. But then . . . she slipped.'

I coughed. She took this as a poke of disbelief and spooled out a further explanation.

'Well, all right,' she snapped, 'she stumbled, because of the way we were spinning. Her hand slipped out of mine and then . . .' Violet's face crumpled. 'It happened with such speed. One thing after another. Her hand slipped out of mine. Then she stumbled towards the side of the bridge, where the bricks were loose. One gave way, I think. And then she was gone. Her skirts opened like a pink peony in the breeze.' It was almost hard to look at Violet as tears began to stream down her face, recalling the worst moment of her life. 'She burst away from me and then she was gone. I heard her hit the water and I screamed. It was so hard to get down to the water, I didn't know how. And then I found it – the path. And I went down, but she wasn't there. So I got in, and nearly drowned myself trying to find her. But it was futile. She'd gone. I think it was the weight of her garments. I couldn't get to the middle where she had gone in, because of the force of the current, and I had to hold on to the bank or I'd be gone too. So I just stood there, waist deep, shouting her name.'

The gossips in the village may have been wrong about Persephone's murder, but her death was still a tragic one, and had destroyed Violet's life almost as much as her own. And Chester may not have been the culprit, but he was responsible, I felt, as I thought back to the conversation when he told me he'd thought Violet might be pregnant, because the pair both seemed so happy before Persephone's death. Their delight had been in the thought of escaping him.

The baby had stopped feeding and I put myself away. I hadn't realised I was crying onto him. My tear glinted on his cheek from where it had slid off my chin. Seeing me busy myself with him, and not looking at her, seemed to make Violet shaky.

'You don't believe me,' she accused.

'Why would I not believe you?' I replied.

I was scared that we would reach Oxenhope before she had finished. I knew now how Persephone died, but not what happened after.

'That's not everything though, is it?' I said. It did not explain the faked diary, nor the night the library window was broken and my key lying on my desk, when I was so sure I hadn't mislaid it.

'Is it necessary for you to know every detail?' she defended herself.

'You've come this far.'

She stretched her neck up and stared at the roof, then back at me. Then back out of the window.

'I couldn't go back to Rose Hall as I was,' she explained. 'The Hurrel farm was closest. I thought I could just hide in the barn until the morning came and I was drier. I don't know, I just needed to hide. But Paddy and Langston got agitated and Joseph came out. I don't remember what I said to him. I was hysterical. He calmed me down, helped me get ready to return to Rose Hall before dawn. He went and found Mabel and Bilitis, back by the river. I don't know why he sheltered me but ... it is the only reason I was not hanged,' she said.

'But it was an accident.'

'No one would believe that. Above all, Francis wouldn't. He wouldn't be able to stop himself from persecuting me. And it's not just his temper. Punishing me for her death would really be punishment for loving her in the first place. And if Chester were to find out about Percy and I ...' she said.

'So you wanted to frame him?' I asked.

'Chester shouldn't be alive,' she retorted. 'Let alone free. Look what he did to you! And you only had one night of it. Imagine what I endured. His downfall has been a long time coming.'

I did agree. 'So that's why you forged the diary?'

'And was I not successful? Did you not think him capable?'

she asked. I wondered if she felt any shame at all over her machinations.

'More than capable.' Violet's was such a desperate act, although I could well believe Chester had driven her to it. But I had no idea how it had all been executed, and I was still puzzled.

'How did you get my key?' I asked.

'I cut a hole in your skirt pocket,' she admitted. 'A small enough one for you not to notice, but a big enough one that with the loosening of a stitch or two it would eventually fall through. Of course, I had to stalk you in the corridors. All day, it took. It fell through your pocket onto the stair carpet.'

'So if you had access to the library, why did you break the window?' I asked.

'I didn't,' she said, rolling her eyes.

'So who did?'

She looked over at Annie's sleeping form.

'What? Why?' I asked.

'They burst in on me. I was burning the diary in the grate. Skilfully, I might add,' she said with a touch of pride that astonished me. 'I'd used resin to accelerate the flames over certain parts. Dampened the pages with Chester's name on it, so they remained more intact. I wanted you to be the one to find it; I thought you would be upright enough to go to the police if you thought you'd found the smoking gun ... And I doubted you'd feel any protectiveness over Chester. Then came a key in the lock. I had just about enough time to jump behind the curtain. And then they were ... you know.'

'You listened to the whole thing?' I tittered.

'I had no choice. It was all very ... I mean, they weren't loud, obviously, but certain sounds were ... unmistakeable.'

'I caught them at it once too,' I said.

'Yes. I heard. She told me.' Violet gestured in Annie's direction. 'But you weren't angered like I was. I took a peek. Saw her in Percy's dress and stormed out of my hiding place. Pulled her off him. Joseph was practically paralysed, poor thing. I mean, it did balance the scales somewhat. I had his secret. He had mine.'

'That you were all inverts.'

'Not quite,' she disagreed. 'I mean, Annie and I are against our natures, you could say. Joseph is just ... Joseph.' Lady Violet shrugged. 'He sees her as a girl. And the way she explains it, she should have been born a girl. Joseph isn't like me and her. We're inverts, but he's normal – in the way he sees himself, at least. Annie is just one of the many girls he will no doubt be aroused by over the course of his life. But Annie and I are subjected to judgement in ways he will never be. Others would find it confusing, but it does make sense to me. We became quite friendly when you were away. She's really such an innocent thing.'

We both looked at her. It did hurt a little – not just to discover that Annie had hidden so much from me about the break-in, but also to be shut out from Violet's understanding of Annie, whom I still saw as Wesley when out of women's clothes. I saw two people, where she and Joseph saw only one. I had thought the dressing was the thing. A perversion. Violet saw her as she wanted to be seen. Annie on the inside.

'There are more like her in London,' Violet added. 'We

would see them when we went to the theatre. Foppish boys and suspiciously large women around Piccadilly and Covent Garden. Pansies and princesses, the lot of them. She'll be fine among them.' Violet smiled over at our companion. 'I secured a job for her at the frightfully fashionable hotel on the Strand where Sarah Bernhardt stays – the Savoy. What she does at night will be her own affair.'

'I see.' Although I couldn't. Not really.

'I've wished I was a boy sometimes. Because my nature inside of a man would have ... Well, if I were a boy, things would just be ... easier.' If Violet had been a man, I reflected, she would have been truly terrifying. Unstoppable.

The philosophising of their sexes couldn't dissuade me from knowing how things had played out.

'So who broke the window?' I asked.

'Joseph did,' she said. 'I told him to, once we'd given Annie a moment to rush upstairs and change out of Percy's dress. I wanted to make sure the diary wouldn't be traced back to me. I suppose I blackmailed them into things, really. It all became far more dramatic than I intended. I just hoped you'd find the diary the next day.'

So it *was* Joseph I had seen running into the forest. All of my surmising had been anticipating the dripping dagger being revealed. Yet here we were, and no one really needed to be brought into a court of law. Punishments had been liberally dealt out on us all along the way.

'All's well that ends well, I suppose.'

'Yes,' Lady Violet said decisively, 'but it ends with us. I wouldn't have told you if I didn't believe your precociousness would threaten us all. You mustn't confess this to anyone. No one can ever know. Not even Sibyl. She wouldn't forgive me. Promise me.'

The look she gave me was slicing. It was almost as if to say that although she may not have killed Lady Persephone, she most definitely would kill me. So in that way, I would never be fully unburdened.

'I shall take it to my grave,' I said.

It was a promise I had no intention of keeping.

When we got to Oxenhope, Violet shook Annie awake. She was sniffly already.

'Go and say goodbye then,' I said.

She joined Joseph and it took a few minutes for her to come back to us with reddened eyes. Had there been a final kiss between Annie and Joseph? The station was deserted, so it would have been possible.

The movement out of the cart and onto the platform with our luggage was all quite swift, as we were not too lumbered. Lady Violet was definitely the one who had left the most behind. For Annie and me to have only a suitcase each was not remarkable. But for a lady of Violet's class to be travelling this lightly was rather unusual.

Joseph wouldn't wait with us for the train to Crewe. He needed to be ensconced back at home before our disappearance was noticed, so he would not be suspected of aiding and abetting our getaway. Lady Violet shook his hand and I hugged him, inhaling his wholesome and wheaty smell. A trustworthy aroma. I was choked up with it, but I couldn't allow my sadness to override the moment.

He merely tipped his hat towards Annie before retreating

down the platform. She cried soundlessly as we watched him slowly walk away from her down the platform and I held her hand. I was savaged by the abruptness of their departure. The only thing that made us realise he was too was that as he turned the corner, we saw Joseph's shoulders heaving up and down.

Morning came and we arrived in the Georgian quarter of Liverpool again. It was chilly and the windows were frosted shut. Sibyl opened the door all buttoned up. What greeted me in the entryway to Miss Arabella's home was breathtaking. An emptied-out house. In the short few days that I had been gone, it had been completely packed up. There was nowhere to sit in the living room, so I went into the kitchen. The table and chairs remained, as did the pots hanging on the walls.

Sibyl wore a dark green skirt and black jacket. She giggled upon seeing Annie. Not viciously – it was merely amusement. I assumed she thought we had disguised her in order to get away as three women, rather than two women and a man, or something.

Miss Arabella followed her in and greeted everyone cordially, including Annie. She couldn't tell.

'And so, we are going home,' Miss Arabella announced, looking at me expectantly.

Annie and Lady Violet were headed to London. Had I agreed to go to the Gold Coast by staying quiet? Did it not make sense?

'I can't come with you,' I said to them. 'Maybe one day. But . . .'

I looked down at the baby in my arms.

'We could take him,' Sibyl suggested, very, very gently.

I did not allow myself to hesitate. I handed the baby into Miss Arabella's arms.

'Ah! No no no no no,' she said, shaking her head and looking from my face to Sibyl's grave expression.

'Yes,' I said. A sob forced its way out of me. 'Yes, you must,' I said through my fingers over my mouth. I would never have asked, but it was what I had been longing for all along, if I were honest with myself. I was fuddled by what I was feeling. I had felt my attachment to the baby was purely a physiological matter. Yet, the gravity of the separation was soul-wrenching.

'Please,' I squeaked.

They looked at me pityingly, but they seemed as if they understood. We had planned for him to go into the nunnery, but this was far better. That my child would not have his heritage bleached out of him in the way I had done. They would raise him speaking well of me. I trusted them to help him understand. There was no one in the world I trusted more than Sibyl and Miss Arabella. The shock of it all was galling, but the solution was now obvious. Where better for my pale son to be raised, than with a black family with a history of albinism? No one would question it. Two lighter-skinned twins and a child that was practically white, if not quite, if a census-taker ever mounted an investigation. Sibyl's Irish triplets.

The boys were sleeping in their pram. I kissed my fingers and rubbed them on all three of their lips.

I turned to Miss Arabella and Sibyl.

'You can call him Orion – if you like.'

*

Out in the street, Annie passed Sibyl the carpet bag. Lady Persephone's letters and original diaries, along with African books that were now headed back to the continent from whence they came.

'What's in here?' Sibyl asked.

'Don't look inside it yet,' I said. 'Violet has something she wants to tell you.'

I was exposing her, despite my promise. They deserved to know. Or at least, I felt they did.

Lady Violet was surprised at my temerity, but I would soon never see her again. I was now free of child, with an ample amount of money. What could she do to me?

'It's not anything I wanted to happen,' she spluttered. 'We were just . . . Percy was my friend.'

Miss Arabella's palm came up to stop her.

'No. Stop. Please, please. We know, and we do not want to know,' she said.

'But maybe Florence is right. I should—'

'No. NO! Please. You will shut up now. We do not want to know.'

I could see that for a moment, Lady Violet had hoped unburdening her secret to Persephone's family would alleviate some of her guilt. Arabella patted her on the shoulder.

'Please. You know Miss Julienne of Norwich yes? *All shall be well, and all shall be well, and all manner of thing shall be well.* So that is that. Please.'

Lady Violet hung her head and stifled her sobbing as I had done inside. I was glad to see her humbled by someone that was not me. Miss Arabella's mercy was the salve we were all quite thankful for.

Sibyl and I hugged deeply. We had said everything already. I couldn't tell her anything further, knowing we would never stop talking if I did. She gave me a locket with a picture of herself in it. The same face from the first picture I had ever seen of her.

Miss Arabella hugged me last. 'You will always be my daughter,' she said. 'Always.'

And with that, they headed off to the port. To the golden coast of Africa they called home.

We hobbled off their street, spent with our emotion. Worn out from the goodbyes, but sure of where we were now headed. The three of us would travel to London from Liverpool Lime Street. Annie into a fresh life of newfound womanhood in the Big Smoke, one that would conceal the bulk of her past. Lady Violet would be subsumed by the smog that greeted us at Euston station, where she could swindle off to Paris with her forever grieving heart. And I would go back to the only place I felt I might one day belong.

Epilogue

The irony that I felt I must go to Jamaica in search of the mother who had been compelled to give me up in search of her own mother, when I had just done the very same thing, has never been lost on me.

The boat was a gleamer. I had never seen one as sparkling, the wood smelling of both salt and pine. My room was pleasant, if small. It was too cold to spend long on the deck as we left the grey docks of Southampton in the ice winds January is known for.

It was a full week before I ventured out and was social with the other passengers. My time at Rose Hall had taught me how to pass as belonging to the class of people I travelled with. I assumed my mother's maiden name – Miss Goodwin.

I gathered it meant more to be a teacher in the Caribbean than it did where I hailed from. I was moving up in the world. But back then, I knew nothing of the geography, and a map means very little to you until you've visited a place. Chantilly School in Big Woods, Hanover, was at that time practically nothing more than a dot on a drawing on a piece of paper.

I met my colleague at dinner with the captain. We were headed to the same Jamaican parish. A Miss Caroline Campbell. She seemed nice enough. She read as much as I did – more, even. So there we sat on the deck, talking about novels for most of the trip, as the waters got warmer with each passing day.

Eventually, on the day the clouds broke, we stood at the ship's fore. The sun glinted on the water that had shifted from teal to azure. There was a sea moss webbing the water. Miss Campbell told me that it was *sargassum*. It's what gave the name to the waters we were entering: the Sargasso Sea. The captain confirmed it when he was strolling past us and said that Bermuda lay not too far off to our left. Apparently the *sargassum* blooms on top of the water. It drifts back and forth between Africa and Europe and the Americas. For the rest of my life, I must admit that my heart did the same.

Author's Note

As she offered her little finger into the baby's mouth she sensed July staring upon her. Without turning to July, nor taking her gaze from the baby, the missus said,

'She looks just like him. She's so fair. Not like a n***er's child at all.'

Then looking up to find July's eyes upon her she added,

'But she's adorable.'

Before returning to her cooing.

'What did you say she was called?' the missus then asked.

The Long Song, Andrea Levy

As soon as I read the passage above, I knew it was my purpose to ask the questions that sparked my mind as a Black Briton who always wondered about the lives we led on this island before the arrival of the Windrush generation. That we lived noteworthy lives was without question. But what of the offspring of Dido Elizabeth Belle, Francis Barber, Ignatius Sancho, et al? Whatever happened to those babies who got lighter with each passing generation? This novel is intended to be an antidote to the intentional erasure of the Victorian colonial project.

The women writers who align with some or all of my identity and experiences have gifted me with literature that spurred me into the confidence to write my own stories. I would not have thought myself eligible to even pick up a pen if not for the work of Andrea Levy, Brit Bennett and Tsitsi Dangarembga. It is an honour to be able to pick up the mantle laid down by those who have done the arduous work of expanding the canon. I am only here because of the space you afforded me to write into.

Acknowledgements

Some women are made. But me? Myself? I like to believe that I was created – for the special purpose of writing. My mother made me into a reader, and our home library of black women's writing, which spanned the diaspora, helped me find myself when I thought all was lost.

To my first real girlfriends Elena Georgiou, Namrata Das and Charlene Springfield; I didn't know how much I depended on you until I couldn't any more. One day I will be compelled to tell the story of my shoeless dash to freedom. There was a reason why I chose Joel Samuels' door to knock on first. At the gates of Camden School for Girls, you saw me in a way I had always longed for, and you have never stopped seeing me. I'm so glad it was you and your mother Rosie Parker. Our talk in the garden, which clarified a shared mission passed down through the ages. The restoration of the divine feminine. Becoming a woman was hard, but becoming a feminist – with bell hooks as a guide – was actually comfortable. Doing creative writing at the Open University, my stories being written at that red table in Tufnell Park, was the final subversive stitch.

I always say I blossomed in Camden. There, I gained shelter and a launching pad. My dreams became believable. Whole families are deserving of my praise and gratitude. The Doorns. The Dabells. The Goulds. The Abels. The Hewitts. Generosity of such magnitude won't ever be repaid. My deepest thanks are reserved for Adrienne and Kyro Brooks, who gave me the most when having the least. It's always the way.

The loves of my life? My sister Shupikai Shenje. The grandest and most humble intellect I know. The only one who really knows the miracle that is our survival. We were meant for each other, and I would be your sibling in every lifetime. Loving axmed maxamed has changed everything. My muse. My big-brother-in-arms who expands my consciousness. The world is new because of you, and I know we will reach our promised land. Most importantly, for introducing me to the superbly inspirational work of Destiny O. Birdsong without whom I would never have dared to have a black woman with albinism feature in my story. I can only hope I have achieved the respect and sensitivity I told you I wanted her to feel when reading my story. My forever bestie, Frankie Decaiza Hutchinson. May we always tell the same stories and find new reasons to laugh at them so raucously. To Jamie McDade, who drove so many miles to be with me the weekend after my mother died. Some acts of kindness grow more in significance with each passing year. This is one of them. Nobody's son is your rival. To David Hemus. Loving you made me supple. You opened me up for the ones that followed and helped me see how abundant relationships should be.

There is not enough space to thank everyone who I call a friend. To the women of Risley Avenue Primary School who gave me the most nurturing working environment I've yet known. Yvette, Paula, Keeley and so many others who made me feel beyond welcome and invited me to 'bingo' on Fridays. You've no idea how much it meant to me. That last Christmas party where I sang *'Ain't Nothing Going On But The Rent'* by Gwen Guthrie. I hope you know I never let you down on that score! My sponsor Beryl Pothin. My therapist Kris Black. My mentor Nikesh Shukla. Tinuke Craig. Dzifa Afonu. Winnie Akadjo. Christina Fonthes. Asia James. Chloé Filani. Eleyna Dervis Salih. Rebekah Ubuntu. Natalie Scott. Lady Phyll. Kamari Romeo. Kevin Morosky. Topher Campbell. Ajamu X. Josh Rivers. Alexis Caught. Meg Amber Lightheart. Tarik Elmoutawakil. David Sheppeard. Duncan Jarvies. Hanna Keil. Björgvin Friðgeirsson. Dan Breed. Lukas Southard. James Field. Vanessa Kusah. Xavier. Brendan. Koos. Patrick. You've all made life worth living. I'm grateful to you all.

To the writers alongside me. Travis Alabanza and Shon Faye. The dolls are writing! I've said it before, and I'll say it again: to be writing at the same time as you feels prophetic. I really really see it for you both. To my first readers. My good renaissance sis Jhnell Persijn and *'Little Miss Béké'* Lauren Sims. I wasn't quite convinced in what I'd achieved until I got your feedback. You mean the world to me!

My editor Tilda Key is a keen collaborator and in the best way helped me exceed my own expectations. Thank you for the most thrilling ride. But also of course, thank you to Brionee, Stephie and the whole team at Little, Brown.

To my agent Silé Edwards. You took a chance on me, but from the time we met, there was only ever one choice. You. This has been the best professional relationship of my life, but the love is so real. Thank you for giving me such a promising career as a novelist. We rep our ends in the most literary way!

But most of all to Mummy. I feel you with me all the time now. I love you so much. Unconditionally.

Miss you x